Elements of Educational Psychology

BY THE SAME AUTHOR

Elements of Social Psychology
A Textbook of Educational Psychology
A New Deal in Secondary Education
The Teaching of English Spelling

What Basic Education Means

Craft in Education
General Psychology
Abnormal Psychology

Making the Most of Your Mind
Saral Shiksha Manovigyan

Vyavaharik Manovigyan
Samanya Manovigyan
Samaj Manovigyan
Asamanya Manovigyan
Shiksha Manovigyan
Saral Manovigyan

ELEMENTS OF EDUCATIONAL PSYCHOLOGY

HANS RAJ BHATIA

FIFTH EDITION

Orient BlackSwan

ELEMENTS OF EDUCATIONAL PSYCHOLOGY

ORIENT BLACKSWAN PRIVATE LIMITED

Registered Office
3-6-752, Himayatnagar, Hyderabad 500 029, Telangana, India.
e-mail : centraloffice@orientblack.com

Other Offices
Bengaluru, Bhopal, Chennai, Ernakulam,
Guwahati, Hyderabad, Jaipur, Kolkata,
Lucknow, Mumbai, New Delhi, Noida, Patna

First Published 1949
Fifth Revised Edition 1973
Sixteenth Inpression 1999
Twentieth Impression 2004
Reprinted 2009, 2010, 2014, 2016

ISBN : 978 81 250 0029 7

Printed by
Commercial Press Service
Kolkata - 700 012

Published by
Orient Blackswan Private Limited
17, Chittaranjan Avenue,
Kolkata - 700 072
e-mail : kolkata@orientblackswan.com

Preface

In preparing this volume the main purpose of the author has been to place in the hands of Indian students a simple and brief textbook on educational psychology. Most of them take to the study of the subject without an adequate understanding of the common mental activities or of the terms used to describe them. This has been found true not only in the case of undergraduates at Indian universities but also in the case of graduates who join a training college for teachers. It is to meet the needs of both types of students that *Elements of Educational Psychology* has been written.

The book attempts to explain the broad facts and principles of educational psychology shorn of speculative theories on the one hand and detailed statistical data on the other. It is not meant for advanced students but seeks to help only those who are preparing for the teaching profession.

In dealing with the several mental activities and functions and their growth and development, the educational situation as presented in Indian schools has been kept in view and illustrations have been selected mostly from Indian life.

The book contains a minimum number of quotations and references. They may give a scholarly appearance to a book but they are apt to be confusing to students who take to the study of a subject for the first time. However, a brief list of books is given at the close of each chapter to help such students as are interested in pursuing the study of topics in greater detail. Questions have also been added not to help students to pass examinations but to enable them to test what they have studied as well as to suggest to them practical implications of facts of educational psychology.

The author has been teaching educational psychology to Indian students for several years and has profited much by doubts and difficulties presented by his pupils, past and present. He also acknowledges his deep indebtedness to authors whose books he has listed at the end of each chapter.

PREFACE TO THE SECOND EDITION

In this edition the text has been revised and some corrections have been made. Some diagrams have been added to the chapter on the Nervous System, a section on Mental Hygiene has been added to the chapter on Conflict and Repression, the chapter on Intelligence and its Measurement has been mostly re-written and a section on Cumulative Records has been added, and a new chapter on Attainment Tests has been added. These changes and additions are due to rapid advances in educational thought and practice and will, it is hoped, add to the usefulness and popularity of the book.

PREFACE TO THE THIRD EDITION

In this edition quite a number of changes and additions have been made. Some sections have been entirely re-written and some new sections have been added. The important sections of Mental Hygiene, and Judging and Testing Personality have been entirely re-written in the light of recent advances in psychology. The different methods of personality assessment have been briefly described and examined and the treatment of mental hygiene has been made fuller. The notable additions are : Instinct Theory, Drives, Needs and Motives, Gestalt View of Perception, Thalamic Theory of Emotions, Attitudes, Security and Achievement, Lewin's View of Group Behaviour, Intelligence Testing in India, Vocational Selection and Tests of Special Aptitudes, Educational and Vocational Guidance, Child Guidance Clinics and the Education of Retarded Children. This may seem a formidable list but the book is being widely used in Indian universities and the needs of the syllabi obtaining in different universities have made these additions and revisions absolutely imperative. Further, it is hoped they will add to the usefulness and popularity of the book. The author is grateful to all those professors of training colleges who from time to time have been sending suggestions both to him and the publishers. He ventures to hope that they will kindly continue to do so.

PREFACE TO THE FOURTH EDITION

In this edition a number of sections have been re-drafted, some sections like Homeostasis, Affection, Anger, Emotional Stability, The Problem of the Day-Dreamer, The Problem of the Bad Memoriser and Measurement of Interests and Values have been added and two chapters on Growth and Development, and Guiding the Individual Child have been added. It is hoped that these revisions and additions will bring the text up-to-date, dealing with some new concepts and topics in educational psychology and add to the usefulness of the book which has had wide acceptance during fifteen years or so.

PREFACE TO THE FIFTH EDITION

ADDITIONS and alterations made in this edition are quite important and are sure to make the treatment of the subject fuller and more up-to-date. New sections added are on Homeostasis, Social Behaviour, Abnormal Behaviour, Culture, Some Studies of Environmental Influence, Affection, Security, Need for New Experience, Self-actualisation Dramatic Play, How Interests Expand, Sources of Interest, Jealousy, Dreams, Why Do We Forget, Creative Thinking, The Self-Concept, The Nature of Learning, Motivation in Learning, Need of Guidance in Learning, Wechsler-Bellevue Intelligence Tests, Social Nature of Behaviour, Socialisation, Basic Processes of Socialisation, Kinds of Groups, Social Facilitation and Inhibition, Competition and Co-operation. And sections expanded and revised are Branches of Psychology, Autonomic Nervous System, Educational Psychology, Methods in Educational Psychology, Age Differences in Play, Conditions of Attention, Recall Association of Ideas, Types of Learning, Development and Education, Transfer of Training, Breaking Bad Habits, Self-control and Character, Adolescence, Educating the Adolescent, Imitation and Attitudes.

286 Adarsh Nagar, HANS RAJ BHATIA
Jaipur 4
1 November, 1972

Contents

CHAPTER ONE

The Nature and Scope of Psychology

1. WHAT IS PSYCHOLOGY ?

IT is a matter of common experience that our friends and neighbours differ from us in many ways. They have different likes and dislikes, different tastes and temperaments, different habits and hobbies, different abilities and ideals. Some of them like society, others prefer to be alone, some are habitually punctual, others are always late, some are quick in doing things, others fumble for a time before they are able to accomplish any task ; some are easily provoked, others lead a life of peace and poise. What makes them so different ? How do such differences arise ? What are the causes of such differences ? Answers to such questions are given by the science of psychology. Psychology helps us to understand the behaviour of people around us, to find out how and why they behave differently and what forces have worked to make them so different from us, and to study human nature and the manifold ways in which it expresses itself in the life of different individuals.

Psychology has been defined in many different ways. It has been called the science of mental life, the science of mental processes, states, activities or functions, the study of behaviour in its mental and bodily aspects, a systematic inquiry into man's relations with his environment and the like. In short there are as many definitions of psychology as there are textbooks and a beginner is often confused as to the nature and scope of this science. But in spite of these differences psychologists are agreed that the chief purpose of the study of psychology is to know more about human nature and human activity.

There are many fields of knowledge which deal with human nature. History tells us of the changing thoughts and habits of nations and of the individual men and women who helped to bring about these changes. Economics tells us of the ways in which people work, earn, sell or buy. Politics rests upon our understanding of human nature. Biology tells us how the body is made, how it works and performs several acts of seeing, moving and holding things and how the body varies from one person to another. But the science of psychology is concerned with human nature as no other science is. It studies the several activities of man directly and for their own sake, not to understand the course of history or of social changes nor, like biology, to learn the functions of the several parts of the bodily organism but to obtain general laws about the activities and behaviour of human beings. Men and women live in a world and respond to its influences. The world is composed of things and persons, and they interact with this world, accepting some influences and resisting others. This interaction between the individual and the world calls for scientific study, and psychology is the science which seeks to study all human activities with a view to obtaining general laws about them.

Thus psychology may be defined as the science of behaviour, a systematic study of all that man does in response to a world of things and persons. In this definition there are two terms which need explanation, *science* and *behaviour*.

2. Science

The term *science* describes any systematically arranged body of verified knowledge. It deals with a particular type of subject, or with certain kinds of facts or events. For example, physics deals with energy, with facts about heat, light, sound, electricity; chemistry deals with matter, with how material things are composed and decomposed ; biology deals with living things, plants and animals, with how they grow and develop; and psychology deals with human behaviour, with the thoughts, feelings and actions of men and women. Thus each science deals with a group of related facts and principles. Secondly, the subject-matter or the body of facts dealt with by each science is obtained by means of carefully controlled observations made by specially trained observers, whom we call scientists. Thirdly, each science tries to formulate general principles governing facts included in its field of study. These general principles are very necessary for without them it is not possible to understand new facts, to explain them by relating them to already known facts, to foresee their occurrence and to control their recurrence. These laws are not axioms like those laid down in geometry, they are verified statements regarding the relations which exist among observed events. Fourthly, all knowledge called scientific must be definite, accurate, reliable and verifiable.

Psychology as a science concerns itself with facts of behaviour. Its specific subject-matter consists of facts about an individual organism's activities in relation to environment. These facts it obtains, like other sciences, through carefully planned observations. Among these facts it tries to discover relations so that some general statement about their occurrence and recurrence can safely be made. These are the laws of psychology which tell us in broad outline the nature and course of human activity, and they help us not only to understand human behaviour but also to predict and control it.

Human activity may be studied in two ways. Commonly we study it in terms of goodness and badness and describe it as right or wrong. This is an appreciative approach in which we try to judge behaviour in the light of some standard of worth or value and the sciences which follow this method of study are called *normative* sciences. For example, ethics is a normative science of behaviour, logic is a normative science of thought. Another method of studying human activity is what may be called descriptive and all that we do is to describe human activity as it is observed in different stages, aspects or phases without any regard to its moral worth. Right or commendable behaviour is as interesting and important as unworthy or bad conduct. False thinking is as important as true thinking. Sciences which follow this method of study are called positive sciences. Psychology is a positive science. It is concerned not with how we ought to behave but with how we actually do, not with facts as they *ought to be* but with facts as they *are*. It does not seek to influence or improve behaviour but only to describe it as it is observed in the life of an adult, a child, a lunatic or a genius. Behaviour in all its aspects is interesting to the psychologist and questions of worth do not enter into his methods of observation and study.

3. Behaviour

The word *behaviour* is used in a very broad sense. It includes not only motor activities like walking, playing, digging or building but also such activities as give us knowledge, for example, perceiving, imagining, remembering, thinking or reasoning, and emotional activities like feeling happy, sad, angry or frightened. They are all activities of the individual, his life depends on them and it is difficult to think what the individual would be without them. They all are included in the term behaviour. 'Any manifestation of life is activity' says Woodworth and behaviour is a collective name for all such manifestations. Whatever an individual does from the most passive state of sitting still and looking at the wall to the most active striving after a goal like chasing a thief or writing an article, is included in behaviour. Movements of limbs and acts of hearing, seeing and smelling are as much behaviour as thoughts, emotions and memories. Behaviour expresses the entire life of an individual.

The individual is both a body and a mind. It is a psychophysical organism whose life is an integral unity of mental and bodily activity. Though for purposes of study and description we distinguish between mental processes and bodily changes, between thoughts, memories and emotions on the one hand and movements and actions on the other, in actual experience there is no mental activity separate and isolated from physical activity. Life is one single continuous flow of activity and its mental and bodily aspects though distinguishable are not really separable. They are two ways of looking at the same object. Behaviour is both mental and bodily.

Now the individual cannot be studied apart from the environment in which he lives, moves and has his being. He does not exist in isolation and his activity does not take place in vacuum. What we have called behaviour is the activity of the individual organism in relation to its environment and when we say that psychology helps in understanding and predicting behaviour, we mean that an individual's activities are to be studied as responses to definite situations or environment. Walking on the road a child sees a big dog rushing towards him, is frightened and thinks of running away and hiding himself. His behaviour cannot be understood apart from the situation in which it has been aroused. Now the influence which the environment exercises on the organism and rouses it to activity is called the *stimulus* and the activity that is so aroused is called the *response*. A pin-prick makes us jump. The pin-prick is the stimulus and jumping is the response. A noise makes us turn our heads. The noise is the stimulus and the act of turning our heads is the response. All forms of behaviour are responses or reactions to stimuli.

The environment in which behaviour takes place need not necessarily be material or physical. It may consist of other organisms and their behaviour. The stimulus may not be a pin-prick or a noise but a question, a frown or a sneer from a friend. The reply to that question or the behaviour aroused by that frown or sneer will be the response. Man not only walks, puts on clothes, takes tea or shaves his beard in response to physical stimuli but he does them in a manner approved and commended by other individuals who are members of his group or society. Many of our activities are responses to physical environment, such as breathing, keeping our balance against a strong wind, eating food to sustain ourselves or closing our eyes to avoid dust, and they fulfil individual needs. But there are other activities which are essentially social, though on that account the individual does not need them the less. They take place in a group. We love some people and hate others. Our likes and dislikes are influenced by those of our group. The stimuli of such responses are social and are derived from our interactions with other members of our group. Fashions, etiquette and customs are forces which we cannot ignore in our conduct and they form a part of our social environment. Thus each act of behaviour is a response to a stimulus which is a force or action affecting the organism.

But the individual does not come into his behaviour all at once. It has been a matter of slow growth and development from the early years of infancy to maturity and old age. What a grown-up man is able to do, think and feel today is the result of a number of changes that have come about in his physical and mental life. His limbs have grown, his sense organs have matured and his abilities have become more definite and perfect. In fact, life is growth, maturity and decline, and its span is marked by certain stages such as infancy, childhood, adolescence, youth, maturity and old age, at each of which behaviour is marked by certain characteristic features. Psychology studies this growth and its several stages. It compares child and adult, youth and old age so as to obtain a full view of behaviour in all its stages of growth and development.

We began by saying that the science of psychology tries to explain how behaviour of one individual differs from that of another. But while it is interested in differences between one individual and another, it seeks to formulate, as far as possible, the general laws of behaviour holding good even of very different individuals. To that end it compares not only child and adult or youth and age but also man and animal. The behaviour of man under different diseases and defects like insanity and hysteria is also studied to obtain a complete picture of the subject-matter.

Thus whether we define psychology as the science of mental life, the study of interactions of the individual with his environment or the science of the activities of an individual, we are not far from the common objective of understanding, explaining, predicting and controlling behaviour in a systematic and scientific way.

4. Other Definitions

It would be interesting to know some definitions of psychology which have been given up for one reason or the other. The earliest psychologist defined it as the science of soul. By soul was meant a being existing inside the body and directing it as a sailor directs a boat. Recently it has been described as a vital principle animating each human body and giving its activities a unity which it otherwise would lack. But the term soul is theological in its bearings and psychology did not make any progress so long as it was given that definition. The soul is beyond experience and knowledge.

Later, psychology was defined as the science of mind but the attempt to describe mind intelligibly did not succeed. Some said it was an immaterial substance, others described it as the sum-total of our mental states and processes or a bundle of sensations, perceptions and ideas. But how this bundle or sum-total was made up, how its units of ideas and perceptions were related and under what principle of organisation they followed each other, was not explained.

Others defined psychology as the science of consciousness. Conscious life is likened to a stream and its activities like pain, grief, seeing, can be known only directly by the individual to whom they belong. But this definition does not work. In the first place there are other sciences which study a number of conscious activities like speech and sensations. Secondly, there are a number of activities of which we are conscious in the beginning and which on being performed a number of times become automatic and do not require attention. Riding a bicycle, for example, required concentrated attention in the beginning but later could be done with ease and without attention. Such habitual acts though outside the field of consciousness are still within the scope of psychology. Recently we have come to believe that some unpleasant experiences are *repressed*, forgotten and banished from conscious life. But they continue to influence conscious life without our being conscious of them. They lie in the field of the unconscious, and are certainly a part of our study in psychology. Therefore the definition of psychology as the science of consciousness is too narrow.

The definition of psychology as the science of human behaviour set forth in this book is more recent and popular. It is broad and covers all the relevant facts. It helps psychology to achieve the position of an exact objective science employing methods of observation and experiment. Both mental and bodily facts receive their due consideration and the knowledge obtained can be fruitfully applied in other fields for the simple reason that it relates to the entire life and behaviour of individuals.

One school of psychologists headed by J. B. Watson, in their anxiety to establish psychology as a natural science, define it as the science of behaviour but use the term behaviour in a very restricted sense. The facts of science must be capable of objective observation and since bodily behaviour, muscular and glandular activity, alone can be observed from outside, behaviourism regards that to be the sole subject of psychological study. It refuses to consider mental states and processes as in any way causing or forming a part of behaviour. If such states and processes exist behaviourists are unable to find exact methods of studying them. The view taken in this book should not be confused with behaviourism for we have clearly recognised that behaviour has both mental and bodily aspects and the one cannot be separated from the other. The mental side is as important as the physical side. Running is an activity which, no doubt, can be observed from outside and studied objectively. But certainly it would be better understood if we know that the individual is running to reach an object or to escape a danger, that is, towards a thing or away from it.

5. Methods of Psychology

The main method of psychological study, as of all science, is observation. Without careful observation it is difficult to make any progress in science and psychologists in the anxiety and effort to advance their knowledge of human nature rely mostly on observation and experimentation. To observe is to find a fact and to experiment is to make one. Experiment is observation under conditions which we ourselves have set so as to control fully what we have to observe. Observation is not an easy task, one has not merely to look on but to be a trained observer who reports strictly what he observes and guards against the tendency to see what he likes to see.

The psychologist has a special opportunity for observation. He can observe and study activities from within as well as from without. He can observe such mental states and processes as fearing, wishing, feeling pleased, as well as such outside activities as walking, smiling, frowning, playing. In studying the behaviour of an individual we can observe ourselves his overt acts as involve the activity of limbs, the changes in sense organs or the expression on his face and also ask him to observe his inner life of thoughts and feelings, fear and anxiety. This advantage is unique with psychology. In studying plants or insects, chemical elements or energy we can only observe from without. We cannot expect the things observed to speak for themselves and report what is going on inside them. But our understanding of behaviour depends on two types of observation, observation from within by the subject himself and observation from without by himself and others. The former is called *subjective* observation, the latter, *objective* observation.

Subjective observation or self-observation is called *Introspection* in psychology. It is to look into the working of our own minds and report what we find there. It is to attend to one's own experience, to turn inwards in self-contemplation and observe the states and processes of one's own mind. It is not an easy task and many psychologists think it is an unreliable method of study. In the first place, they say that introspection is self-destructive. It destroys the very object it has to observe. It records experiences going on in our minds but the more successfully we introspect, the more readily the thing we want to observe is missed. We are angry and wish to observe our anger. But the moment we take up this attitude : 'I am a student of psychology and want to study my anger,' the anger disappears. By attending to the mental activity, we withdraw our attention from the object of that activity and so arrest the activity itself. In defence it is suggested that we can avoid this drawback by recalling our mental activities later and observing them.

Secondly, it is said that introspection is purely a subjective method and can reveal to us the mental processes of a single individual only. It will not help us to arrive at universal knowledge which is the object of all science. But although introspection gives us knowledge about individual minds, we can compare knowledge thus obtained and arrive at general laws which would be true of all minds.

These difficulties of introspection are stressed mostly by behaviourists who deny there is any mental life at all. They can be overcome by practice and training, by remaining alert during introspection and by comparing results obtained by several experts. Besides, there is one great advantage of introspection. The subject-matter which we have to observe is constantly with us, and we can introspect at all times and at all places.

For older psychologists who defined psychology as the science of consciousness alone, introspection was the only method of inquiry. But now that the scope of the science has become wider to include the whole of behaviour or mental life, it is necessary to supplement introspection with other methods. Certainly introspection cannot be used in the study of animal behaviour or of the behaviour of children and insane persons. Thoy cannot report the result of their introspection if they introspect at all. There we have to rely on *objective observation*. It is observing the behaviour of other individuals. Their bodily behaviour, the movements of their limbs, their facial expression, their heart beats, their breathing and the like are observed and analysed. They are further interpreted as conditions and expressions of various mental processes, so that we may be able to know general laws as to what kind of behaviour follows in a particular situation.

This method is specially useful in studying the mental life and behaviour of savages, children, animals, people whose language we do not understand and illiterate people who, even if they can introspect, do not find suitable words to convey an adequate idea of their mental processes.

But many of our observations, subjective and objective, turn out to be inaccurate and need to be tested, confirmed and amplified by *experiment*. Experiment is simply observation under carefully controlled conditions so that the process to be observed is not mixed up with others and leads to the same result however different conditions are. Everyday life frequently presents such problems and laboratories offer solutions after making experiments. For example, we return from the market and feel tired. We attribute fatigue to the great noise which accompanied our activity in the market. But it is suggested that it may be due not to noise but to the amount of walking, talking, standing we did, to the strain of shopping, calling for things, comparing, selecting, and making payments for them and the like, to unusual things we did and several other conditions. Is our fatigue due to noise alone or to all these conditions combined? The only way to answer this question is to keep all conditions constant or absent except one and to find out the result of this one factor. If we want to find out the effect of noise, we study it under changing conditions or we stay and live in a place where other conditions are absent but noise is present or other conditions are present and noise absent. This analysis and isolation of objects and processes to be observed are of the essence of experiment. Experimental methods use a variety of apparatus and cover a wide range of investigation. We may study the different ways of memorising, the effect of different factors on learning, how quickly people respond to certain stimuli and the like. The tremendous growth of psychology during the last fifty years is due mostly to experimental methods.

We have seen that behaviour grows and develops and one important task of psychology is to study the growth and development of behaviour of individuals from birth to maturity. This is called the *genetic* or *developmental* method of study. Behaviour is largely determined by such factors as heredity, environment, diet, home conditions, attitudes of parents, experiences and many other things. Certainly it is the responsibility of psychology to trace the influence of such factors on development, to analyse condi tions favourable to healthy normal development and to in vestigate those which produce such abnormalities as delinquency, crime and insanity. We may trace the growth and development of particular individuals from infancy to maturity or we may describe how processes of behaviour or activities like perception, thinking, feeling and the like grow from simple forms into more complex ones. It is difficult to subject children to experiements for that would be playing with their lives and may be risky. Nobody would like to expose children to harmful influences just for the sake of seeing what harm they do them. All that we can do is to observe children from outside as to how they react to different types of influences, diet or environment. The psychologist is on the spot and watches the behaviour of individual children.

But he cannot be present at all times and is, therefore, obliged to employ the *case history* method in which a number of investigators join to prepare with the help of the individual, to reconstruct his entire history from what records are available. The psychologist, the teacher, parents, associates, doctors and all those who came in his contact are called upon to contribute to that record. The individual too recalls incidents of his early life and the influences which worked most in moulding his life. But case histories have to be prepared with great care, ruling out such factors as prejudice, vague impressions or hearsay. Memory is fallible and allowance should be made for that. *Anecdotes* of early life are important but unless they are reliable and are reported without trying to make out a spicy story they cannot give us real knowledge about the early behaviour of the individual.

The case history method has been used mostly with individuals whose behaviour deviates from the normal. When a person develops abnormal depression giving up all striving, abnormal intense fear of animals, excessive shyness, stealing or back-biting we try to obtain information about his heredity, home environment and the like, and to discover what undesirable influences were responsible for his abnormal behaviour. The co-operation of parents, social workers, doctors and others is sought to obtain as complete a picture as possible and the object is to help the individual to get rid of the abnormality.

But the case history method may also be used with great advantage with eminently successful people to find out what great influences helped them to achieve success. Such a study will be of great benefit to young growing people who may follow in the foot-steps of such people and make the most of their opportunities and lives.

The genetic method is very useful in educational and abnormal psychology.

6. Branches of Psychology

Psychology has been defined as the science of behaviour. It deals with general conditions under which normal adult human beings act, think and feel. It is interested in the universal characteristics of behaviour and seeks not only to describe them but also to relate and explain them by reference to some general laws. This is the scope of what may be called *general psychology*. But the scope is so wide and the recent growth of psychological knowledge has been so tremendous that for purposes of detailed and accurate study, the subject-matter has been marked out into special fields or branches. Some of them are simply different approaches to the subject, taking a slightly different point of view in studying behaviour and others are special applications of general psychology to special departments of life. General psychology draws from, and in turn contributes to, these special branches and sub-divisions.

Genetic psychology studies growth and development. Its cardinal principle is that no item of behaviour springs full-blown into mature stage and in order to understand how human adults come to behave as they do, we must know something about their early growth. Thus it inquires into what we inherit and what we acquire, and the several ways in which our inheritance is modified in childhood, youth and manhood. How do we become what we are, what is growth and development, what changes take place in thought and behaviour at different stages of life, are questions which form the genetic point of view in psychology. It attempts to study not only growth and development of individual minds and behaviour but also of individual activities, habits and abilities. Teachers and others who deal with children are specially interested in it, for it reveals to them why some children develop irrational fears and anxieties, acquire habits of stealing or telling lies or brag and bully. Genetic psychology, revealing what factors determine personality, character and intelligence in children, helps their right education.

Comparative or *animal psychology* is a study of the behaviour of animals, involving a comparison of the developed mind of man with the lower manifestations of animal behaviour, and also of these with one another.

Physiological psychology studies the physiological processes accompanying behaviour either as a cause or as an effect. This branch is very useful as it explains how we behave, that is, act, see, hear or smell. By revealing differences in the physical constitution of persons it helps to explain differences among individuals. Recently it has thrown a flood of light on how gland activity determines behaviour, particularly emotions.

Abnormal psychology deals with the behaviour of individuals who are unusual, that is, different from the normal. Such people think, feel and behave in an abnormal way due to some maladjustment, defect, disorder or disease in their mind and personality. For example, some people say 'no' to every proposal, they are negative in their approach ; some are too shy to come forward and meet their fellow-men ; others think that the whole world is against them and is trying to injure them; still others are unreasonably afraid of frogs, dogs or darkness. Some people have more serious trouble, they hear strange noises, think that they are going to die very shortly, feel they are flying in the air or imagine themselves to be some great men. Others have changing moods, lose memory or have no practical sense. These disorders are a problem for society and abnormal psychology investigates the causes, nature, symptoms and prevention of such disorders. Abnormal behaviour is exaggeration of normal activity and their study gives us great insight into our own thoughts, feelings, fears, anxieties and actions. Some of these disorders are due to physiological defects or diseases, and some of them are purely mental, due to upheavals and tragedies in life and experience. Psychologists have devised a method known as *psychoanalysis* to cure such disorders and relieve the sufferer.

Applied psychology is the use we make of general psychology in the several areas of life and work. Thus we have *social psychology* dealing with the behaviour of people in groups, how they react to social situations, how customs, traditions and fashions, propaganda, war and revolutions, considerations of prestige, social conformity and status, affect and mould their behaviour and personality. *Industrial psychology* deals with methods of selecting, training, counselling, and supervising people employed in business and industry. How to increase efficiency and production, how to keep workers happy and contented that they do their best in work, what relations should obtain between different sections of people employed in business or industry and the like are some of the major problems of study in industrial psychology. *Child psychology* deals with growth, development and behaviour of children, it studies children at various ages and stages of growth and the several influences which affect such growth. This branch of psychology has greatly changed our attitude to children and improved our ways of upbringing and educating the young people. We also have psychology of advertising, psychology of salesmanship, psychology of religion, in fact of every field of human activity. Of these a very important field deals with the applications of psychology in the solution of educational problems, how young people should be taught knowledge and skills, how they should be helped to acquire habits, develop healthy attitudes, sound thinking, emotions and sentiments, what is the nature of their intelligence and how their personality develops. How our knowledge of the laws of human behaviour is proving helpful in the various activities called education is the story which this book tells in the pages that follow. *Educational psychology* is concerned with the psychological aspects of teaching and of formal learning processes in schools.

Psychology is a young but growing science. From a science that began less than a hundred years ago with the study of 'mental states', psychology has grown to a science which today is concerned with virtually all aspects of human behaviour.

QUESTIONS

1. Give a definition of psychology and explain your definition.
2. Psychology is defined as the science of behaviour. What do you understand by the terms *science* and *behaviour* ?
3. Discuss and criticise the following definitions :
   a) Psychology is the science of consciousness.
   b) Psychology is the science of mind.
   c) Psychology is the science of mental states.
   d) Psychology is the study of responses to stimuli.
4. What do you understand by behaviourism ? How does your definition of psychology as the science of behaviour differ from it ?
5. What are the methods of psychology and how do they differ from those of other sciences ?
6. Distinguish between objective and subjective observation. What is the value of Introspection ?

7. What are the drawbacks of Introspection and how can they be remedied?
8. What is an experiment? Describe an experiment in psychology.
9. What are the several branches of psychology?
10. Explain the following :—
Behaviourism, genetic psychology, psycho-analysis, positive science, stimulus, response.
11. What is environment? Discuss psychology as the study of an individual in relation to his environment.

REFERENCES FOR FURTHER STUDY

1. Angell : *Psychology* (Macmillan).
2. Boring, Langfeld and Weld : *Foundations of Psychology* (John Wiley).
3. Dexter and Omwake : *An Introduction to the Fields of Psychology* (Prentice-Hall).
4. Gilliland, Morgan and Stevens : *General Psychology for Professional Students* (D. C. Heath & Co.).
5. Gray : *Psychology in Human Affairs* (McGraw-Hill).
6. Heidbreder : *Seven Psychologies* (The Century Co.).
7. Hollingworth : *Psychology* (Appleton).
8. Hunter : *Human Behaviour* (Univ. of Chicago Press).
9. Husband : *General Psychology* (Farrar & Rinehart).
10. Keller : *The Definition of Psychology* (Appleton).
11. Munn : *Psychology* (Harrap).
12. Murphy : *General Psychology* (Harper & Bros.).
13. Murphy : *An Historical Introduction to Modern Psychology* (Harcourt Brace).
14. Powers, McConnel and others : *Psychology on Everyday Living* (D. C. Heath & Co.).
15. Ross : *Groundwork of Educational Psychology* (Harrap).
16. Stout : *A Manual of Psychology* (Univ. Tut. Press).

17. Townsend : *Introduction to Experimental Method* (McGraw-Hill).
18. Warren and Carmichael : *Elements of Human Psychology* (Houghton & Miflin).
19. Watson : *Behaviourism* (Norton & Co.).
20. Woodworth : *Psychology* (Methuen).
21. Woodworth : *Contemporary Schools of Psychology* (Ronald).

CHAPTER TWO

Psychology and Education

How is the science of Psychology related to the theory and practice of education ? What use and value has the study of psychology for the teacher ? Why should every teacher study psychology and apply it in his daily work ? These questions are no longer difficult to answer. For during the past few decades psychology has made large and rapid advances in knowledge and its influence on education has been more profound than that of any other science. As a result, the entire character of education has undergone a radical change and psychology has been accepted as a useful guide to the teacher.

1. THE MEANING OF EDUCATION

The meaning of education like the meaning of life, culture, religion, is clear enough to most of us until we are called upon to define or express it in a phrase. And then our difficulties begin. The term 'education' means so much, covers so wide a range of activities and has been given such varied and numerous definitions that we cannot do better than quote some of them to begin with :

Education is a preparation for life. It is an acquisition of such knowledge and skill as will help the individual to earn his livelihood and find a place in adult society.

Education is character-building. Through precept and example teachers should cultivate among young people good habits and healthy sentiments.

Education is a harmonious and all-round growth and development of human power or faculties, mental and physical. Young people have several faculties and they should be given a balanced growth.

Through education young people should become good citizens and learn to perform those duties which a country expects of every son and daughter.

Education should teach us the right use of leisure. Life is a struggle full of fatigue, worry and boredom, and education should teach us how best to relax during leisure hours.

Education is a process of self-expression through free spontaneous activity. Young people are free to follow their instinctive impulse and live their own life.

Education is adjustment to environment. It is a process by which young people are brought into proper relationship with influences from the world and society.

From these and other definitions it is not difficult to understand that education means change, growth and development. 'It is a process in which, and by which, the knowledge, character and behaviour of the young are shaped and moulded.'[1] The uneducated person changes, grows and develops into the educated. At birth the child is weak, helpless and ignorant. He depends on others for all his primary needs, he understands nothing and does nothing except to grow physically. He is uneducated. Gradually, he acquires knowledge and skill, he is able to accomplish things and supply his needs without help from others. As he grows there is a change in his knowledge, character and behaviour, his powers of understanding, appreciation and achievement develop and mature. He has become educated. This growth, development and maturity, that is, the changes that take place in his knowledge, character and

[1] Drever : *An Introduction to the Psychology of Education*, p. 1.

behaviour during his life, are termed education. This meaning is implicit in all the definitions given above.

Now this change or growth takes place whether we will it or not and may be for the better or the worse. In the interest of progress society wants that this change and growth should have a purpose and a direction, and that the changes that come about in a child's life should be those which are needed and desirable. Society, therefore, exercises control over all those forces and influences which bear on this growth. This control is exercised through two agencies, firstly, institutions like the home, the church, the community, the market, the playground and more specifically the educational institutions like the school and the college, and secondly, persons like parents, relatives, priests, authors and more specifically teachers and professors. The educational institution is specially designed and teachers are specially trained to help young people to grow along definite lines, in a specific direction, towards a chosen goal and therefore exercise control by selecting influences which will mould and shape the knowledge, character and behaviour of young people. Now knowledge and character in another person can be revealed to us only in and through his behaviour ; education may be defined as a ' process of controlling and modifying the behaviour of the young so as to produce a recognised type of behaviour in the adult '.[1] Or as Dumville puts it, ' Education in its widest sense, includes all the influences which act upon an individual during his passage from the cradle to the grave '.[2]

2. Education and Instruction

For too long education meant only instruction and even

[1] Drever : *An Introduction to the Psychology of Education*, p. 1.

[2] *Child Mind*, p. 1.

today in many schools it is believed that imparting knowledge is all that education means ; knowledge is virtue and knowledge is power, and therefore the more learned a person is the more he is educated. The ignorant mind of the child is an empty mind and the main task of the school and the teacher is to fill this empty vessel with grains of wisdom. With growth of science, knowledge has grown from more to more, and the school has entered into a race with science adding new subjects of study to the curricula and condensing knowledge into compact and logical forms which can be easily stored in the head of the pupil. Education has come to mean a passive reception of knowledge by pupils and teachers help them to store by rote memory all kinds of facts and information. In examinations pupils try to prove that they have kept the store of facts undisturbed and unchanged.

Now knowledge is the food of mind and facts when rightly understood and assimilated become faculties, as Adams puts it, but often young people who score very high marks in examinations do not succeed in life. And many a learned man has been ridiculed for knowing much and accomplishing little. The reason is that knowledge is a means of education, of acquiring good behaviour, and when the means is taken for the end and knowledge and information are sought for their own sake, the object of education is defeated. Instruction is only a part, and not the whole, of education. That is why in most modern schools great stress is laid on games, dramatics, hobbies, craftwork and the like so that young people may develop a practical sense, a social spirit and a good taste along with knowledge.

If knowledge is to have an educational value, it should be acquired in a living manner, through verification and application to the relations of life. Only then can it function as a food for the mind, broaden and enrich the intellect and mould and shape behaviour. Knowledge has an important place in education but to be of real value it must be developed by pupils themselves from their own experience. They must compare facts of experience, recognise relations among them and draw their own general inferences from them. Only such knowledge will lead to a real understanding and control of physical and social environment, and function as education.

3. Education as Science, Art and Philosophy

Education is also understood as a body of knowledge about principles and methods of education. It concerns the working of educational institutions, the conduct of pupils, methods of teaching and problems arising out of pupil-teacher relationship. This body of knowledge had grown fairly systematic and is based on the accumulated experience of teachers, past and present. Teachers under training have to acquire it before taking up actual teaching in schools. It is the *science* of education and its aim is to organise our experience of education into a body of general laws and principles. But a teacher has to do more with the actual work of teaching in the class-room. He is a practical educationist concerned more with the art of education or the craft of teaching. Long experience of handling his material, pupils and curricula, has built in him more or less permanent attitudes towards his work, and on these his success rests whether he is aware of it or not. Many successful teachers cannot explain the secret of their success. The art of education is the skill and tact which one diligently acquires through sustained practice in teaching.

But this is only a distinction, not a difference. Art and science, practice and theory, bear on each other. A knowledge of principles and methods influences practice, and practical experience yields new and verifies old principles.

But why should we educate? What is the end and goal of education? A discussion of the aims and ideals of education, of the purposes and values educational effort should try to realise, is a philosophic quest. Philosophy deals with ultimate ends and can prescribe better the true and final aim of education. Although a few are conscious of it, every system of education must have an aim, a direction in which teachers should educate young people. Some of the definitions of education given in the first section of this chapter deal with the aims of education and fall within the study of what is called the *philosophy* of education.

4. Psychology and Education

The relation between psychology and education is very intimate. Psychology has been defined as the science of behaviour. It seeks to understand and explain behaviour in terms of mental and bodily activities. Its chief problem is how and why we behave, how we think, know, feel and act and why we think, know, feel and act in the way in which we do. It tries to understand the conditions from which acts of behaviour arise and to arrive at general principles which govern behaviour so as to interpret, control and predict it. Education, as we have seen above, is an attempt to mould and shape behaviour. It tries to help young people to grow and develop along certain lines, to acquire knowledge and skill and to learn certain ways of thought and feeling so that they may be absorbed in adult social life. The science of psychology must be basic to such an attempt, for any influence on behaviour, to be effective, must be planned and worked according to the principles of psychology. Education, therefore, must be based on psychology and from the very first step which he takes to educate the child, the educator must depend upon psychological knowledge.

Education deals with young people and the conditions that promote or retard their growth and development; it selects and strengthens those influences which promote healthy growth and tries to eliminate and weaken those which retard it. As a result of this study it formulates certain principles on which organisation and administration in schools should be based; it has to study the needs and interests of children and provide for their healthy satisfaction and expression; it has to devise effective methods of teaching so that children may learn more quickly and better. All this is not possible without a knowledge of psychology which explains how young people grow, what dominant interests mark the several stages of their growth, how they differ from one another and grow at different rates, how they learn new skills or acquire new knowledge, how they react to the influence of teachers and class-mates. Psychology is expanding rapidly and our growing knowledge of the minds and behaviour of young people promises to be an effective guide in the solution of our educattional problems.

The Swiss schoolmaster, Pestalozzi, was the first to see that the educator can draw great advantage from a study of the minds of pupils and that the art of education must be based on an accurate knowledge of mental life. He wanted to ' psychologise ' education and instruction. But people did not appreciate the value of this advice mostly because the type of psychology available for study was not of much help to the teacher. Psychology in those days was understood as the science of mind. It aimed at an analysis of mental states and processes like thinking, feeling and remembering and its only method of study was introspection. Since this method can be used effectively only by a mature adult, the body of knowledge it yielded concerned only mature adult human beings and their ways of thought and feeling. It could not help us to understand the life and behaviour of young children. Many thought that the child was just a little man and our knowledge could be obtained 'by reducing the scale of adult psychology'. They could see no reason for studying the mind of the child as distinguished from the mind of the adult; if they could find out what the adult mind was and how it worked, they could find out what the child mind was and how it worked, because the latter was simply a miniature copy of the former. Such teachers had very wrong ideas about children and it is not surprising that they did not see any good in psychology.

Happily in recent times many excellent practical teachers depended on their own experience of children. They consulted parents and each other, compared notes of their experiences, and putting them together found that the child is not a little man, and that in physical, mental and normal characteristics he is essentially different from adults. They began to say that in the development of the human mind from birth to maturity important changes occur not only in the strength or range of mental activities but also in other respects so that the infant, the child or the youth is different from the adult. The new psychology as the science of behaviour began to use objective methods of study and when they were applied to the study of children it was found that the important thing about children was not analysis of their mental states but of their growth and development. Thus was laid the foundation of reliable child psychology giving intelligent attention to a study of the physical, intellectual, social and normal development and well-being of childhood and youth. This is proving of great help to the teacher and the dream and hope of Pestalozzi is coming to be realised.

Even today many teachers are indifferent to the study of psychology and believe that it is at best a training college subject. For success in the teaching profession the earlier it is forgotten the better. A knowledge of psychology does not help one to become a good teacher. He is a craftsman who must have considerable skill in his craft and this skill is acquired only through insight, experience and practice. Such an attitude of indifference is due partly to the fact that in most training schools and colleges the type of psychology taught is of the old-fashioned introspective type and teachers under training see no good in it, and partly to the fact that they find a number of old experienced teachers make very good teachers without a knowledge of psychology and a number of good students of psychology make very indifferent teachers. This is quite true. Though much depends upon the way psychology is taught it should not be overlooked that psychology does not make its students good teachers. The art of teaching does not depend entirely on the information which psychology supplies but the ability to teach can be used to better advantage if it is helped by a knowledge of what factors will favour learning and what retard it. Psychology will help the teacher to avoid many mistakes which he otherwise may be able to correct only after long experience. Many experienced teachers have to offer tips to new teachers, such rules of thumb as have been drawn from their long experience in the school work, but is it not more desirable that when scientific studies have made available sound psychological principles for the help and guidance of teachers, the rough-and-ready mode of doing things should be replaced by knowledge, understanding and discrimination such as the science of psychology offers?

Others believe that psychology is a study of man in his several activities and states; it analyses him into thoughts and feelings, ideas and memories, fears and hopes, joys and sorrows, and looks upon him as a collection of them. Education, on the other hand, deals with man as a living, thinking, feeling being who acts and feels as one. It treats him as a living whole rather than as an aggregate of parts. The teacher's attitude towards the child is creative, ethical, living and concrete ; he is interested in making a better person of him. The psychologist's attitude to the child is abstract, analytic, scientific and matter-of-fact. The latter seeks to describe the child as he is, the former tries to think out what he can, and ought to, become and what are the best methods of helping him to do that. Therefore, it is urged that study of psychology can only do harm to the teacher by destroying his living, sympathetic and creative attitude to the child. But this is overdoing the difference. To find out what children ought to become will be considerably easier if we know what they are. Psychology, instead of being a danger to the creative and living attitude of the teacher, may be of real help to him in planning his work of educating the child. Many eminent teachers like Pestalozzi and Froebel have been keen students of psychology.

The American psychologist William James who did much to lay the foundations for our present day empirical systematic psychology emphasised the limitations of the applications of psychology to education in his book : *Talks to Teachers.* 'I say moreover that you make a great, a very great mistake, if you think that psychology, being the science of mind's laws, is something from which you can deduce definite programme and schemes and methods of instruction for immediate school room use. Psychology is a science and teaching is an art : and sciences never generate art directly out of themselves. An intermediary inventive mind must make the application, by using its originality. To know psychology, therefore, is absolutely no guarantee that we shall be good teachers. To advance to that result, we must have an additional endowment altogether, a happy tact and ingenuity to tell us what definite things to say and do when the pupil is before us. That ingenuity in meeting and pursuing the pupil, that tact for the concrete situation, though they are the alpha and omega of the teacher's art, are things to which psychology cannot help us in the least.' (Pages 7-9). There is an element of truth in what the famous psychologist says, a knowledge of psychology may not be a guarantee that we shall be good teachers, yet it may be argued with justification hat without a knowledge of psychology the teacher is likely to be less competent in his task. Today psychology has grown into a vast science and has provided a very useful framework for the educator in which to view the learner and the learning process, and to examine his educational methods.

For the past few decades the theory of education and the science of psychology have made rapid advances in knowledge. Besides, they have been and are advancing hand in hand. Not only does the teacher turn to psychology for help in the solution of his practical problems, but in the course of his work, comes upon problems which he himself cannot solve and which he passes on for detailed investigation by psychology. Thus the teacher is helping to advance psychology. Carrying on surveys, tests or classifications the teacher may have to face problems to verify half-truth, or confirm his conclusions. The psychologist takes them up for scientific inquiry and thus is led to advance his science. Many have been so impressed by this close relation as to think that education is nothing more than applied psychology and that the entire theory of education can be drawn from the science of psychology. While this is making too large a claim for psychology, it cannot be denied that the two are depending on each other for further growth and advancement.

But obviously there is one thing which psychology cannot do for education. It cannot provide education with aims and objects. Why do we educate at all? What is the purpose and goal of education? For what ends and ideals is the whole programme of education being undertaken? Psychology cannot help to answer these and related questions. It is a positive and descriptive science, dealing with things as they are. It is not concerned with aims. It seeks to understand and interpret behaviour as it finds: it does not distinguish between good and bad behaviour and it is interested in the one as in the other. It cannot enter into the question of the worth or value of behaviour. For education, on the other hand, aims, ends, purposes or goals are of fundamental importance. It has to mould and shape the lives of young people and it cannot do so blindly without any ideals. If their growth and developments are to be helped, it must be done with a definite end in view. Education must have a direction. Now this direction cannot be pointed out by psychology. It is the task of philosophy to help to choose between ideals.

But is that aspect of education which deals with aims and ideals independent of psychology? Not altogether so. Education has not only to aim at certain ideals but also to find out ways and means for their realisation. If psychology cannot give ideals to education, it can certainly suggest the best means of achieving them so that maximum results may be acquired with a minimum of trial and error. If the end of education is beyond the scope of psychology, its methods and devices, its means, efforts and programmes, are determined entirely by psychology. Such changes as the teacher would wish to make in the behaviour of his pupils for the achievement of any aim will have to be made according to the principles of psychology. How far the teacher's methods and efforts have succeeded in obtaining the desired result, how far they should be modified to improve the achievement, are questions in whose solution psychology can be of very great help. Even in the determination of aims and ideals psychology can tell whether an aim is hopelessly in the clouds or whether it can be achieved. In India where most of our ideals are conceived from a religious standpoint, teachers often begin to expect impossible virtues from young pupils. Some prescribe humility to such an extent as to kill all self-assertion, others want very young children to learn lessons of selfless generosity. Psychology will tell them that they are attempting the impossible.

In the previous section a distinction was drawn between the art, the science and the philosophy of education. The art and the science of education, the practical steps, means, devices or methods through which educational effort works and a systematic knowledge of the general principles on which they are based and from which they are derived, depend on psychology. The philosophy of education, dealing with aims and ideals, may be said to be independent of psychology, but in the determination and achievement of aims, psychology can be of great value in helping us to choose between possible and impossible aims and in adjusting suitable means and methods to aims.

To sum up: the claim made by Drever that 'we can settle hardly any essential and vital question in education except in a merely academic way, and without reference to practical problems, independently of the science of psychology ',[1] is not a wide claim.

5. Psychology and the Teacher

Of what use is the study of psychology to the teacher? What psychology should he study? And how should he study it? These questions are sure to disturb the mind of a beginner and answers to them will determine his attitude to this science.

There are three ways in which the study of psychology can help the teacher. In the first place, it will enable him to know and understand just the people for whom he is employed and for whom the whole school organisation is intended, the pupils. Secondly, as a result of this knowledge the teacher will feel in himself greater power over the pupils to mould and shape them in a definite direction, the goal of education. Thirdly, psychology will help the teacher to know himself and accordingly to adjust himself better to the school environment.

There was a time when a knowledge of the subject to be taught was all that was expected of a teacher. He must be a scholar, able to divide his subject into parts and topics in which each lesson proceeds from the simple to the complex, from the concrete to the abstract and from the familiar to the unfamiliar. But today the most important qualification of a teacher is that he should know his pupils. This has been very strikingly expressed by the remark, too often repeated, of Sir John Adams. The verb to teach has two accusatives, one of the person, another of the thing as *the master taught John Latin.* He should not only know Latin but also John and the knowledge of John is psychology which the teacher must study. The old teacher laid

[1] Drever: *An Introduction to the Psychology of Education.*

most of the stress on Latin, the new lays it on John. *Teach the child rather than the subject* is the essential principle of new education. Work in and outside the classroom, the school programme, the curricula, the selection and grading of lessons, should be determined and arranged in the light of dominant interests and urgent needs of children at different stages of mental development. A child grows, develops and prospers, and if the teacher in his work takes stock of the possibilities of his growth and development, of his instinctive nature and inherent urges, his growing needs and interests, that is draws upon his knowledge of child psychology, his effort and programme will be more successful. The school exists for the pupil, not the pupil for the school. The whole organisation of the school work is maintained for the welfare and benefit of the child and this the teacher cannot try to secure unless he knows what the child himself is, how he grows, what are the needs of his growth, what different interests are inborn and what interests he has acquired, how to secure his interest and attention in the school work. All this is psychology and the teacher needs a close study of it.

Now there are two ways of studying pupils. They may be studied as individuals, unlike all others, and they may be studied as a class, like all others. No two pupils are exactly alike ; each child is a unique individual ; this is his individuality. And any two pupils, even altogether unrelated by blood or race, are very much alike; not only have they the same type of sense organs and limbs but they also grow and develop according to certain psychological laws. The teacher must know the individual pupil. Though he is called upon to deal with large classes, his attention should be directed to each pupil as a unique person. He should not know them as belonging to mechanical groups, but as members of an organic whole. Each of them is one of a kind and differs from every other pupil of a class. The teacher should know these individual variations and respect such variations when treating his class individually. He can know his pupils individually on the playground, in the hostel, on trips and at the desk in the classroom. Secondly, the teacher should know the pupil in general, that is, the laws of development common to all young people. For this, he will draw upon the science of psychology and study books like the one he is now reading.

This knowledge of pupils will give the teacher a peculiar influence over them. Remembering them and knowing them by their names, he will approach them with self-confidence, enthusiasm and personal relationship and will be in a position of advantage to mould and shape them better. Knowledge is power, and a knowledge of minds gives power over them which the teacher can use for the achievement of educational ends. Again, psychology describes how the mind learns; it is for the teacher to help minds to learn. Psychology describes how habits and sentiments are formed ; it is for the teacher to assist children in forming good habits and healthy sentiments. Psychology describes how powers of observation and constructive imagination grow; it is the task of the teacher to help the growth of these powers. Psychology describes how children learn, grow and develop; it is the responsibility of the teacher to understand the processes of learning, growth and development and to help children under his care to learn, grow and develop better. Psychology describes intelligent behaviour and methods by which intelligence can be tested; it is for the teacher to use tests of intelligence to find out how intelligent his pupils are and if they are making maximum use of their intelligence in acquiring knowledge and understanding their problems in both life and study. Psychology describes the processes of adjustment and maladjustment; it is for the teacher to make sure that his pupils are well-adjusted to school work and their companions and to guide them to avoid errors of adjustment. A knowledge of psychology will give the teacher power over pupils and control over his teaching methods, pupils' learning activities and their growth and development, and the teaching material and school procedures and programmes. Thus psychology is the science which underlies the art of teaching.

Thirdly, the teacher will be helped to know himself, and estimate his achievement better. Psychology will give him a knowledge of the range of human capacities and ability to compare his own capacity with those of his fellow teachers. It will help him to estimate his worth more justly and live in peace with his colleagues. Many teachers go through life uncertain about their abilities. They expect high praise for their work and, not getting any, they feel depressed. It is really desirable for peace of mind and efficiency to know one's good points and one's weak points, and to act accordingly. Such knowledge helps one to use one's strong points to the greatest advantage and to reduce one's shortcomings. 'Know thyself' is a good motto for the teacher and a study of psychology will help him to that end.

How should the teacher obtain his knowledge of psychology? The best way is to read widely but critically in the various branches of psychology. This will give him only abstract and general knowledge which he must supplement by analysing his own behaviour and mental processes, by trying to remember the thoughts, feelings and actions of his own childhood, by carefully observing children in his own home and class. It has already been stressed that he should know each individual pupil. Such objective observations and study will help him to obtain a true picture of himself and his pupils and to verify and correct some of the opinions he has formed about them and about his own capacity.

6. Educational Psychology

We have defined psychology as the science of behaviour, of an individual's responses to environment. This is general psychology : educational psychology is very often described as an attempt to apply this knowledge to the field of education. Educational psychology is regarded as a branch of applied psychology and most textbooks describe facts and principles of general psychology and then show how they can be used by the school. But this is too vague. Educational psychology is a science in its own right and though draws most of its material from general psychology, it has its own standpoint and scope.

If general psychology deals with facts and principles about individuals, educational psychology chooses one type of individual, the pupil, and concentrates on him. It deals with individuals undergoing education in or outside the School. If general psychology deals with responses to environment, educational psychology deals with responses to a special kind of environment, the educational environment. Hence we may define educational psychology as a study of the behaviour of pupils or of individuals in response to educational environment. Its scope is narrower and more specialised and it employs all the methods of general psychology with special reference to its narrow scope.

Our main concern is the individual pupil. It is him that we want to shape and educate. We must know him and we must know how to mould him. This gives us two divisions of the subject, one dealing with the nature of the pupil and the other with the changes to be made in his nature. Our first problem is to know what he is capable of, what abilities he inherits, the nature of his intelligence, what forms of behaviour are natural and inborn, what is his original nature, what needs are innate and how they motivate his life and activity. Our second problem is to find out what changes can be made in this original nature and how best these changes can be made, how and what he learns, how habits, attitudes and sentiments are formed, how new needs are acquired and how personality develops. In the chapters that follow an attempt will be made to solve both these problems.

Four general areas of psychology are of special interest to the teacher and form the major planks of educational psychology: the psychology of development, the psychology of learning, the psychology of motivation and the psychology of group behaviour.

From the psychology of development the teacher learns about human growth from infancy to maturity. This growth is physical, intellectual, emotional and social, and the teacher must know the conditions which promote this growth and the conditions which block it. This growth can be distinguished into definite stages and each stage has its own characteristics. Obviously the teacher must have a working knowledge of these characteristics so that he adjust his teaching and school programmes according to the abilities and interests of pupils at each stage of growth. The content and methods of teaching will vary with different classes of the school because pupils of different classes are not equally developed and are at different stages of growth and development. The psychology of development is making rapid progress and the teacher must draw upon its findings to make his teaching more effective.

The psychology of learning is the heart of educational psychology and is concerned with how we acquire and change our patterns of behaviour. We are for ever acquiring and changing habits and attitudes, likes and dislikes, thoughts and sentiments, knowledge and skills. All this is learning and how this process takes place most efficiently, how teaching should be made more effective for efficient learning, how to measure different kinds of learning, what conditions help us to retain what we learn and to use effectively what we learn, and how learning varies with different levels of ability are questions of prime importance to the teacher and are studied by this branch of educational psychology. In the school many types of learning are taking place every day from muscular skills to complex intellectual attainments and the teacher must study the psychology of such learning.

The psychology of motivation is concerned with why we do what we do, with primary sources of activity, from the instinctive urges and desires to fears, ambitions, needs, goals and purposes, with major interests of pupils. No amount of skilful teaching will have any effect if the pupils in a class do not *want* to learn or have no *interest* in learning. How to arouse interest will depend largely on the teacher's knowledge of children's needs, wants, enthusiasms, goals and ambitions, their feelings and emotions which determine the direction of children's effort and activity.

Very often children's emotions are ignored or suppressed and then they develop maladjustments which block all learning. The teacher must know about the various types of maladjustments so that he guards against them or helps children to overcome them. This branch of educational psychology is called *mental hygiene* and every teacher must be familiar with its general principles.

Group psychology is very important because the school is a community in which every child lives, works and plays in a large number of groups and his behaviour and learning is very largely affected by other members of his groups. His class-mates, his team-mates, the boys with whom he goes to school, his friends—all are infleuncing his outlook, learning and personality. The climate and tone of the school expresses the pattern of group behaviour in that school and the teacher must know the various factors which contribute to this tone and climate. And he must realise that he himself is a part of this community and his influence on his class is very decisive. The group psychology will help him to understand his own role and in improving the social climate of the school.

Evidently therefore modern psychology of education, that is, educational psychology, offers a great deal of help to a teacher in his attempts to understand children and how they learn.

7. Methods of Educational Psychology

How does educational psychology gather facts about the nature of children and how they grow, learn and develop? It employs all those methods and techniques which general psychology employs and which have been described in detail in the first chapter such as observation and experiment, genetic method, case histories. In addition it employs two important techniques which every student of educational psychology must know.

Our main subject is growth, development and learning. We may study how any aspect of human personality like learning speech, social adjustment or skill grows from the elementary stage to a complex one. Or we may study how a group of children pass through the several stages of growth and development. This is called the *longitudinal* method. Another approach is to study a number of children at different chronological ages and study the patterns of growth at different ages. This is called the *cross-sectional* approach. It may not yield reliable conclusions if the children are drawn from different strata of society.

To understand an individual pupil it is helpful to determine his status in the group. Two procedures are commonly used to obtain the reactions of a group of pupils to one another. The first is called the '*Guess Who*' technique which may be described as follows.

The teacher announces : 'Here are some descriptions of children you might know. See if you can guess one or more child in the class who fits each description'. Then some such descriptions are given.

> This person is always eager to do things for others.
>
> This person is very good in games and sports.
>
> This person is very good at study but he does not wish to work with others.
>
> This person is always finding an excuse to fight with others.

The information obtained from questions like these can help the teacher to understand the group. The pupils should be assured that their answers will be kept confidential. Various schemes have been worked out to give each child a score for each trait based on the number of times he was mentioned or to determine the role each child plays within the group.

Another simple and commonly used method of securing intra-group ratings is called *sociometry*. It is used to study inter-personal relations among students of the same class. The teacher tells the class that they are going to form committees to work on a project and that each student should note down on a piece of paper the names of three of his class-mates with whom he would like to work. Thus each student indicates his preferences from among his class. Collecting this information the teacher tabulates it into a *sociogram* and finds out names of students who have been mentioned most and those who have been mentioned least or not at all. The most voted names are 'stars' or 'central figures' and the least voted are 'isolates'. Stars usually have a strong influence in determining the nature of the group and isolates are children with personal problems. They may lack a sense of social poise, may be unable to make friends though they badly need them and seek in a variety of ways to overcome their aloofness or to compensate for it. Thus the teacher is able to understand the group structure of his class, who are the most popular students, if there are any cliques in the class and why some of them are so unpopular. In such a study the social adjustment difficulties of some children are pushed to the fore-front. The teacher can use sociogram to improve interpersonal relations in the class.

SOCIOGRAM

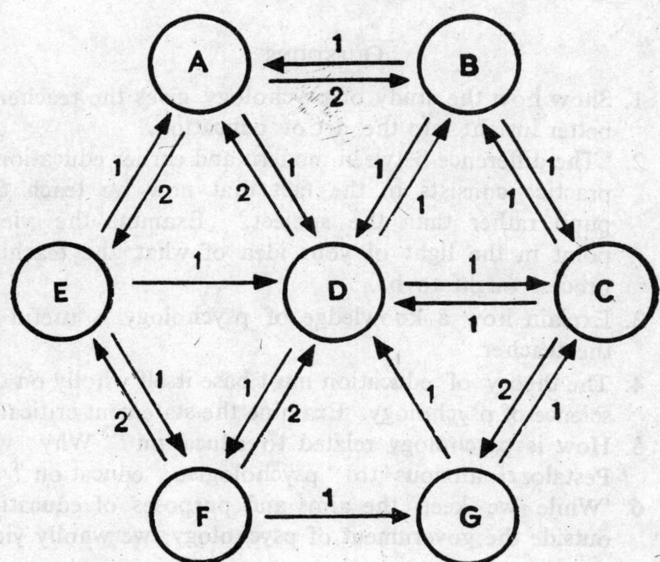

The seven circles represent boys and the numbers by the line indicate first or second choices. Number D is the most chosen boy and number G is the least chosen. In the same way in a class there may be boys whom nobody chooses, they are isolates. A majority are mutual choices. These sociograms can be used to advantage with children of the age of 8 and above.

Measuring devices like intelligence tests, tests of attainments, personality, aptitude, interest and the like are also widely used in understanding the mental and intellectual status of the individual pupil and these will be described in the chapters that follow.

Besides we have questionnaires, interviews, rating scales, biographical and autobiographical records. Cumulative records are also very widely used and these have been described in their proper contexts.

QUESTIONS

1. Show how the study of psychology gives the teacher a better insight into the art of education.
2. 'The difference between modern and earlier educational practice consists in the fact that now we teach the pupil rather than the subject.' Examine the viewpoint in the light of your idea of what the teaching process ought to be.
3. Explain how a knowledge of psychology is useful to the teacher.
4. The theory of education must base itself wholly on the science of psychology. Examine the statement critically.
5. How is psychology related to education? Why was Pestalozzi anxious to 'psychologise' education?
6. 'While we keep the aims and purposes of education outside the government of psychology, we wholly yield

the methods to it.' Explain this statement, and discuss the bearing of different branches of psychology on education.

7. 'A good schoolmaster studieth his scholars' nature as carefully as their books.' Examine this statement.
8. What is the place of knowledge in education? How best should knowledge be acquired? Distinguish between education and instruction.
9. What is the aim of education? In what way does psychology help us to formulate and select ideals in education?
10. Is education merely applied psychology? Discuss the scope and methods of educational psychology.

References for Further Study

1. Cruze: *Educational Psychology* (Ronald Ross).
2. Douglass and Holland: *Fundamentals of Educational Psychology* (Macmillan).
3. Drever: *An Introduction to the Psychology of Education* (Arnold).
4. Dumville: *Child Mind* (Univ. Tut. Press).
5. Gates, Jersild, McConnel and Chaliman: *Educational Psychology* (Macmillan).
6. Griffith: *An Introduction to Educational Psychology* (Rinehart).
7. Griffith: *Psychology Applied to Teaching and Learning* (Rinehart).
8. Hartmann: *Educational Psychology* (American Book Co.)
9. Huxley, Aldous: *Ends and Means* (Allen & Unwin).
10. James: *Talks to Teachers on Psychology* (Longmans).
11. Jordan: *Educational Psychology* (Henry Holt).
12. La Rue: *Educational Psychology* (Thomas Nelson).
13. Leary: *Educational Psychology* (Thomas Nelson).

14. Mursell : *Educational Psychology* (Norton & Co.).
15. Nunn : *Education, Its Data and First Principles* (Arnold).
16. Pintner : *Educational Psychology* (Henry Holt).
17. Pressey and Robinson : *Psychology and the New Education* (Harper & Bros.).
18. Raymont : *Modern Education : Its Aims and Methods* (Longmans).
19. Rivlin and Schulet : *Encyclopaedia of Modern Education* (Philosophical Library).
20. Ross : *Groundwork of Educational Theory* (Harrap).
21. Ross : *Groundwork of Educational Psychology* (Harrap).
22. Sandiford : *Foundations of Educational Psychology* (Longmans).
23. Skinner : *Educational Psychology* (Prentice-Hall).
24. Sorenson : *Psychology in Education* (McGraw-Hill).
25. Stroud : *Psychology in Education* (Longmans).
26. Sturt and Oakden : *Modern Psychology and Education* (Kegan Paul).
27. Thomas and Lang : *Principles of Modern Education* (Harrap).
28. Tilton : *An Educational Psychology of Learning* (Macmillan).
29. Trow : *Introduction to Educational Psychology* (Houghton Mifflin).
30. Watson and Spence : *Educational Problems for Psychological Study* (Macmillan).
31. Woodruff : *Psychology of Teaching* (Longmans).

CHAPTER
THREE

The Nervous System

1. MIND AND BODY

OLDER psychologists believed that a knowledge of the body is not essential to the study of psychology. Certainly if psychology is defined as the science of consciousness or mind, a knowledge of how the body works is not necessary. But if its scope is behaviour and activity, as pointed out in the first two chapters, the bodily structure that makes behaviour possible ought to be closely understood. Behaviour is conditioned both mentally and bodily, and answers to questions like what the body is made of, how it is put together and how its several parts function will tell us about the bodily conditions of behaviour.

Our subject is the child or the pupil and he or she is both body and mind. He or she is a psycho-physical organism and his or her behaviour has both bodily and mental aspects. These two aspects change together and influence each other. It is a matter of common experience that it is difficult to do any mental work, even to concentrate attention, when we are physically exhausted; and bodily activity appears irksome when we are mentally tired. Again, good digestion, brighter psysical environment, fresh air make us more hopeful and friendly and help us to think and learn better, and worry, fear, depression, anxious thoughts tell on our bodily health, weaken digestion and disturb sleep. Mental processes like thoughts and feelings start bodily activities, as a desire to play leads to taking off the coat and running into the playground or a memory persuades us to write to a friend ; in fact most of our daily activities are started and accomplished by hand through thoughts, memories, expectations, joys, sorrows and the like. On the other hand, bodily activities lead to mental processes and almost everything that we do during the day makes us think, imagine, remember, accept, wonder, doubt, feel pleased or displeased, plan and choose. Thus mental states determine the changes and activities of the body and changes and activities of the body influence the mind. Mind is one aspect of the life-process. It has its place, its function, its part to play in relation to, and not apart from, the body.

But how are body and mind related? Some believe that mental changes form one series and bodily changes form another. The two series do not influence, but run parallel to each other, so that every change in the one is matched by a corresponding change in the other. Mental processes and bodily activities are like two rails running parallel to each other. At no point do they meet or intersect. Changes in mental life are caused by mental processes and changes in bodily activity are caused by bodily processes. This view is known as *Parallelism*. Others believe that mind and body are causally related. The two influence and determine each other. My desire to read is the cause of my walking across the room to the table on which a book is lying, and injury to any part of my body sets me thinking, gives me pain and leads me to plan for its treatment. Mind and body act on each other. This is known as the theory of *interaction*.

The new school of psychology, *Behavioursim*, undertakes to explain all the activities of mind and behaviour in physical and chemical terms. It does not take into account conscious states and processes. All that man does, thinks, and feels is traced to internal bodily changes, to activities of muscles and glands. And these are studied by the objective methods of observation. Mental processes which can be studied only through introspection are no longer to be studied for they are of no moment to behaviour. But, as has already been pointed out, the same bodily behaviour can be differently conditioned on the mental side. Throwing a stone may be due to our fear of a dog, simple playfulness, our desire to frighten a crow or to hit an object. While we cannot accept all that the behaviourists say, we must admit that they have contributed largely to the rapid advance of the study of psychology. They have stressed that behaviour should be objectively studied and that without a knowledge of physiology and the nervous system behaviour cannot be fully understood. Education deals with growing pupils. They grow in both body and mind and growth in body is determined and accompanied by growth in mind. To be able to influence this growth as education claims to do, the teacher should understand not only the mind of the child but also his body, the fine complex nervous mechanism without which mental life or behaviour would not be possible.

2. The Human Nervous System

The human body has been aptly described as a 'living machine'. Like all other machines it is made up of a great many parts which work together for a common end. Like them it requires a constant supply of power or energy, and its energy is derived from food. Like them it must be kept in good order, used carefully and protected from injury. When it works well it is said to be in good health.

But the human body is far more complex in its structure and function than ordinary lifeless machines. It is capable of a large variety of functions and movements through a highly complex mechanism called the nervous system. Not only has it to maintain the life process by continuing to breathe, digest, assimilate, to regulate the circulation of blood in such a manner that an exact amount must be delivered to each part day and night, but also to adjust itself to numerous details of environment, first by understanding and then by adaptive movements. Considering its complexity and effectiveness, the human organism is a marvellous structure and it is a pity that most of us are quite ignorant of how it works.

This complex human organism is not perfect at birth. It gradually grows and develops, that is, changes in structure, functions and activities. This is an important difference between the child and the lower living organisms like the moth and wasp. Growth is a very important characteristic of human children. Of all living creatures man has the longest period of immaturity and growth extending over infancy, childhood, adolescence and youth, because his growth requirements are the greatest. We usually speak of this growth as ending in the middle twenties.

Man's nervous system is so complex that it is capable of infinite modifications and during this long period of growth, responses to environment have to be so numerous and various that there takes place a delicate differentiation of function among the various parts. The greater and finer the differences in the nature of the external stimulus, the greater and finer the differences in the function of the responding organism. During this long period of growth the various parts of the organism grow delicately discriminative and develop distinctive functions.

Obviously the range and complexity of human responses to environment is immeasurably large. It is because the human nervous system is very much more complex than that of other organisms, and what is more remarkable, is capable of modification in an immense variety of ways.

Often the whole system is likened to a telegraphic or telephonic system. Messages come from all parts of the body. They may start from the skin or any sense-organ. If the situation which those messages reveal is simple and needs a simple adjustment, no reference is made to the headquarters, the brain, and the situation is managed by lower parts. If the situation is complex, it has to be referred to the central part, the brain, whose function is to coordinate the functions of the various parts of the organism.

It is not possible to describe here the working of the human nervous system in detail, but a bare outline of the system together with a simple description of the various parts will help readers to understand the physiological background of behaviour.

For purposes of study it is convenient to divide the nervous system into three parts :

a) The Peripheral Nervous System ;
b) The Central Nervous System ;
c) The Autonomic Nervous System.

Let us describe the structure and function of each part in outline.

3. The Peripheral Nervous System

All behaviour means activity in response to impressions received from outside and the peripheral part of the nervous system consists of nerves which receives stimuli and make responses. These nerves which receives impressions of the outside world and carry them to the brain are called sensory nerves. Since they carry a message or impulse inward, they are also known as ingoing or *afferent* nerves. The nerves which bring from the brain a message or impulse for movement are called motor nerves. Since these impulses travel outward they are known as outgoing or *efferent* nerves. Sensory nerves are nerves of knowledge; motor nerves are nerves of movement and action. They are so specialized that they can do only one kind of work.

Sensory nerves cannot bring back the reply nor motor nerves carry the impulse to the brain. So there is only one-way traffic and the impulse goes only one way.

A man who does nothing, is not active, in any manner, unless in some way he is being influenced by changes taking place inside or outside him, by impressions received from the outside world or inside the body. The bodily structures specialised for receiving such stimuli are the sense-organs. They are also called *receptors*. The eye, ear, nose, tongue, and skin have different and exclusive functions. The eye sees but does not hear or smell, the ear hears but does not taste or feel cold. Some receptors are specialised for receiving changes from inside the body such as, pain, hunger thirst. Most of these receptors or sense-organs are located at the surface of the body and sensory nerves are closely connected with them.

Movement or activity such as holding a pencil or pushing a chair takes place through our limbs or hands. But limbs or hands are powerless unless they are moved by their *muscles*. The muscles are moved by motor nerves which receive impulses or messages from the brain. Although we are not aware of changes in muscles, motor nerves or brain, yet when we act or move it is entirely due to such changes. These muscles are known as *effectors* because they effect or bring about changes in the environment.

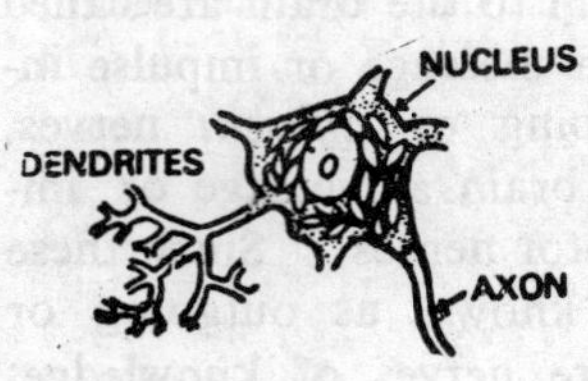

Diagram 1 : A NEURONE

The structural and functional unit of the nervous system is the *neurone*. It is an individual nerve cell of microscopic diameter and of great variation in length. Each neurone comprises a *cell body*, an *axon* and *dendrites*. It has a single *axon* and many *dendrites*. The axon is smooth and slender and may be several feet in length. The dendrites are short and look like the branches of a tree. They are thin and hair-like. The nervous system is made up of numerous such neurones, and impulses or messages are carried from one neurone to another.

The dendrites are the receiving stations that pick up impulses or messages and the axons pass them on to other neurones through dendrites. Their work is their own and they do not change function. The point at which the dendrites of one neurone come in functional contact with the axon of another neurone and receive impulses is called the *synapse*. The synapse has only one-way traffic and the impulses are carried only in one direction. The impulse comes to the synapse over the axon of one neurone and is taken up by the dendrites of another.

The nervous impulses travel only one way and the connections formed between sensory neurones on the one hand and the muscular neurones on the other endure so that the nervous impulses tend to travel the way they did in the past. The synapse resists their going any other way. Thus actions are easier the way they were done before, and breaking new ground is difficult.

Nature has provided each organism with a number of useful ways of behaving which help adjustment to environment and the struggle for existence. When a specific stimulus is presented, a certain fixed and predictable response in made. When anything irritates the nostrils, sneezing occurs; when bright light suddenly appears, we blink. They are reflex actions, and they occur in a fixed mechanical way because certain connections between the sensory and the muscular neurones or fixed from birth. The whole path covered by the impulse from the sensory neurone to the muscular neurone is called the *reflex arc*. In simple reflex actions such as sneezing, breathing, blinking, coughing, the reflex arc is a short one and only a few neurones take part. But in some complex actions many

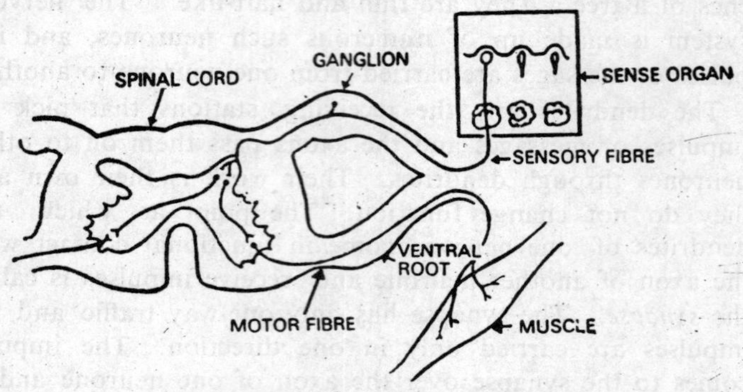

Diagram 2 : THE REFLEX ARC

more cells work together, their function is coordinated by the brain and the impulse travels a much longer path.

4. The Central Nervous System

The central nervous system consists of two parts, the spinal cord and the brain. Both of them are designed to coordinate the several activities of the body.

The spinal cord is that part of the nervous system which lies within the backbone, and consists of a bundle of nerves. Its function is twofold. In the first place, it directly converts impulses received from the sensory areas into motor impulses. It contains spinal nerves, thirty-one pairs of sensory and motor nerves combining afferent and efferent fibres. Secondly, through it, nervous impulses travel to and from the higher brain centres. When a message is sent to the brain, it sends back impulses to the cells in the spinal cord, and they, in turn, transmit motor impulses to muscles. Thus the spinal cord works as the relaying centre for all behaviour involving reference to the brain. It connects the brain with the peripheral part of the nervous system.

It also controls activity connected with organic sensations and with sensations arising from the skin. Reflex actions which involve a direct connection between sensory and motor areas are also controlled by the spinal cord. Mechanical, automatic activity like walking, running, sitting, spinning, riding a bycycle, is also to a large extent controlled by the spinal cord. This means that it directs most of our daily routine which consists of mechanical movements.

The brain is the highly developed and enlarged portion of the central nervous system contained within the skull. It is the chief centre for interconnecting the outgoing and incoming impulses, for coordinating the receptive and the reactive, the sensory and the motor, activities of the organism. It includes the central part or the *cerebrum*, the *mid-brain*, the *cerebellum*, or the hind-brain, the *thalamus* and the *medulla oblongata*.

The cerebrum is the upper part of the brain structure. It consists of two hemispheres with a layer or rind of grey matter. This layer is called the *cerebral cortex* and in function is an important part of the cerebrum. In this cortex are the nerve centres controlling by far the greater part of behaviour. It is the seat of all higher mental control. It is believed that the two hemispheres are mapped out into areas, each area dealing with a special mental function. These areas are called lobes. Thus the occipital lobe is connected with vision and other lobes are connected with hearing, smell, speech and the like. Thus

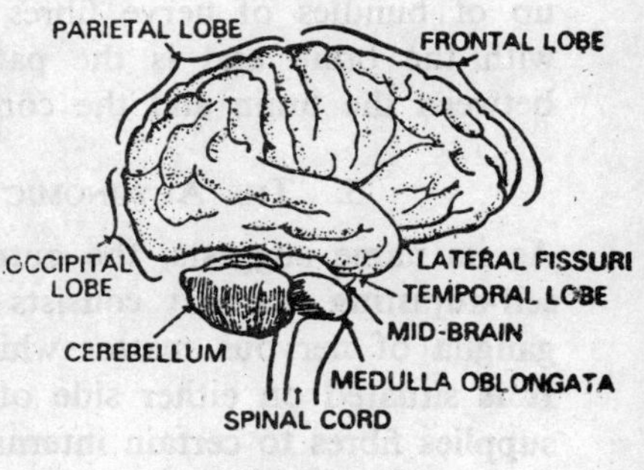

Diagram 3

THE HUMAN BRAIN

localisation of brain function has been arrived at after long study in which it was observed that injury done to any part of the brain resulted in an injury or loss in the corresponding mental function. Later researches of psychologists like Lashely have proved that in spite of this localisation the cerebrum acts as one whole and is the directive agency of behaviour. The several parts cooperate and the entire system works as a unit. Just as no behaviour is merely seeing, hearing or smelling—we may do all these things together—so no change in the cerebrum is isolated. The several parts and lobes work together.

The mid-brain regulates complex movements such as are involved in locomotion and which do not require any reference to the higher powers of the cerebral cortex. The cerebellum or the hind brain is situated behind and beneath the cerebrum. It helps to maintain the equilibrium of the body and keeps it erect. When it is removed the organism is unable to maintain its balance. The *thalamus* is a large mass of special connecting centres located in the centre of the brain. All sensory impulses pass through it to the higher centres. Some believe that it controls emotional and instinctive reactions. The *medulla oblongata* is made up of bundles of nerve fibres connecting the spinal cord with the brain and is the pathway for impulses passing between the brain and the cord.

5. The Autonomic Nervous System

As its name suggests, the autonomic nervous system is a self-adjusting one. It consists of a number of centres or ganglia of nervous matter which send out nervous fibres. It is situated on either side of the vertebral column and supplies fibres to certain internal organs. Its function is to regulate involuntary processes, circulation of blood, digestion, and action of the glands.

The glands of the body are cell structures which secrete different substances. They are of two kinds. In the first place, there are duct glands which secrete their fluids through ducts or channels to the body surface or into the alimentary canal such as the tear glands, sweat glands, salivary glands. Secondly, there are ductless glands which do not have such channels and pour their secretion known as *hormones* into the blood stream. They are also known as endocrine glands and are active in emotional behaviour. In fear and anxiety, the salivary glands fail to secrete and the frightened or excited person has dry lips. Worry, fear and anger have a very harmful effect on digestive functions as they upset working of the stomatch glands, and good company, cheerfulness, hope and zest help the digestive process.

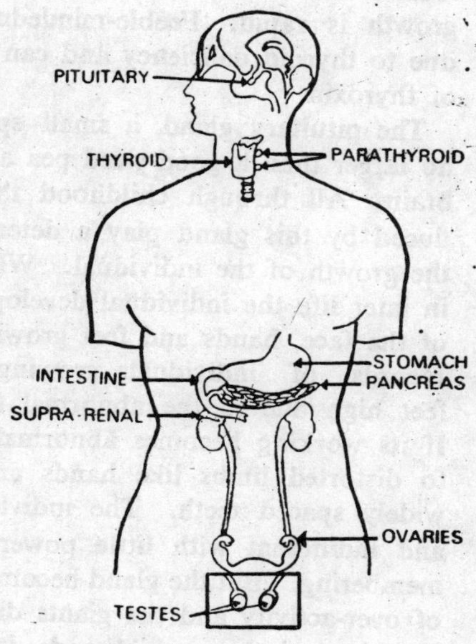

Endocrine glands, that is, glands that secrete within, have much greater influence over behaviour and deserve closer study. The most important of them are the *thyroid*, the *pituitary*, the *suprarenal* and the *gonads*. If these glands are over-active or under-active, it makes a difference not only to the growth and development of the individual but also to his temperament and outlook on life.

The thyroid gland lies at the base of the neck in front

of the wind-pipe. It secretes a chemical known as thyroxin in which the principal ingredient is iodine. When the gland is destroyed by disease, the person becomes less smart and alert and more sluggish and dull. He is slow, stupid and forgetful, and cannot concentrate effectively on any task. This is known as myxoedema. If the gland is lost in childhood, physical and intellectual growth is stunted. In the worst case the person is very small in size and ugly. He is a cretin. These defects are partially cured by supplying extract taken from the sheep's thyroid. Thyroid deficiency is also made up by adding iodine to table salt or the water supply. When this gland is over-active the individual is easily aroused to joy, anger or fear. He is restless and irritable. If he is still in the growing stage, his growth is rapid. Feeble-mindedness in children is often due to thyroid deficiency and can be treated by the supply of thyroxin.

The pituitary gland, a small spherical mass of cells, is no larger than a good-sized pea and lies at the base of the brain. All through childhood the several hormones produced by this gland play a determining role in regulating the growth of the individual. When it becomes over-active in later life the individual develops into a giant, the bones of the face, hands and feet growing very large. There are records of individuals growing into giants eight to nine feet high due to the abnormal functioning of this gland. If its working becomes abnormal in mature years it leads to distorted limbs like hands and feet, curved spine or widely spaced teeth. The individual is irritable, sluggish and indifferent with little power of concentration or remembering. But the gland becomes exhausted after a period of over-activity and the giants die young. When the gland is under-active in childhood, it produces midgets who are different from cretins in being more sociable and intelligent. If the midgets are given pituitary extracts when they are still young, their growth is increased.

The suprarenal gland is placed above the kidneys and secretes a hormone known as *adrenalin*. Its activity is closely associated with emotional behaviour. Its removal leads to death in about three days during which the body grows very weak, temperature drops and the heart beat becomes low. Over-activity of this gland makes a man pugnacious and virile, and the same over-activity in women leads them to develop masculine characters such as the growth of moustaches and deepening of the voice.

The gonads are sex glands and determine human sex development both physically and psychologically. They lie in sex organs and their activity leads to secondary characters. For about ten years or so the gonads remain relatively inactive. Then suddenly they appear to awaken and grow to adult size and start working normally in a comparatively short time. It is a matter of common experience that young people grow suddenly and quickly during adolescence and physiological investigations have established that during this period the maturing of gonads or reproductive glands plays a direct part in it.

The male gonads are the *testes* which are lined with cells which produce spermatozoa. They also produce the cells which develop the hormone that is absorbed into the blood stream. This hormone is *androgens* and is in constant supply. It the gonads are removed before puberty, the so-called secondary characters like the change in voice, development of hair and the like do not appear, there is an unusual increase in height but the individual lacks sex desire and aggressiveness. If the gonads are removed after puberty growth is not affected but there is loss of sex feeling.

The female gonads are the *ovaries*. They secrete two hormones, the *estrogens* which affect sex desire and *progestin*, which plays an important part in pregnancy. The estrogens enter the blood stream during the time of ovulation when the mature egg cell breaks out of the ovary and starts its passage to the uterus.

Glands do not function in isolation, they interact. Recent biochemical research has revealed that the pituitary, the gonads and the hypothalamus are closely related. The hypothalamus plays an important role in emotional behaviour. The pituitary is a sensitive regulator of the reproductive life of the individual and of the mammary glands in a nursing mother. The pituitary and the other glands are interconnected mainly by way of the blood vessels which carry the secretions of each gland to all the cells of the body ; and a rich vascular network around each gland guarantees a supply of blood. Since both glands and their blood supply are under the control of the autonomic nervous system, their joint action is guaranteed by the close integration of the various parts of that system.

To sum up : the endocrine glands by pouring their chemical secretions into the blood stream not only regulate the pace for much of the physical growth but also the delicate changes in the different types of tissues in the entire nervous system. They control changes in the reproductive organs, in voice changes, in the breasts and body lines, in behaviour during adolescence. Most of the students of human behaviour today are convinced that they are an important key to the understanding of sexual and other forms of emotional behaviour.

Thus the body is the foundation and seat of behaviour; it is built of cells and their products; these cells are woven into tissues. Larger structures of these tissues are of three kinds: the sensory apparatus consisting of sense-organs, the reacting apparatus consisting of muscles and glands, and the connecting apparatus.

6. HOMEOSTASIS

In the previous section we have stressed the need of several glands to work in harmony and balance as personality and behaviour depends on it. W. B. Cannon in his book : *The Wisdom of the Body* introduced the term *homeostasis* to describe the principle of self-regulation or self-balance in the organism, the capacity in the organism to maintain a balanced state of physiological equilibrium, assimilating and repairing its resources even as they are depleted in the process of living in and adjusting to its environment. Working and resting, eating and eliminating, seeking and avoiding, adjusting to extremes of hot and cold weather, in the midst of these changes, in the rise and fall of external conditions and inner activity, the organism is usually able to maintain a fairly constant middle course, a balance between extremes without which growth is not possible. In fact life is a recurring swing of the pendulum between extremes and the organism is striving to maintain balance.

To maintain a constant state of physiological and chemical condition is very necessary both for survival and growth. Blood temperature and pressure must remain within certain limits, as must the balance of its chemical composition, such as its carbon dioxide or its sugar content. If there is any disturbance in these bodily activities chemical changes take place to remove this disturbance.

The individual at any stage has a number of physiological needs which must be fulfilled. These bodily or tissue needs create a state of restlessness or tension if any of these needs is left unfulfilled. The child needs food, air, water. The hungry child is restless, irritable and inattentive, but to make up the want of several chemical substances like protein, sugar, calcium the child craves for those things which contain these substances. When the child wants calcium badly the child takes to eating clay or lime. The body also maintains a proper temperature and becomes ill or dies if the temperature rises above 98.4 degrees fahrenheit. In very cold water blood rushes to the skin to keep the body warm and in hot water it moves away from the skin to keep it cool. Sweating and the dilation of blood vessels in the skin are other reactions to heat and are examples of the effort of the organism to regain balance. All the energies of the organism are mobilised and directed towards the recovery of homeostasis. It is only when the environment is conducive to the maintenance of homeostasis that energies are released for growth, for self-assertion and other activities outside the organism.

Teachers should thus understand that young people whose homeostatic needs are not satisfied, who are in the grip of tension due to hunger, thirst or want of fresh air or who are suffering from deprivation of one chemical substance or the other cannot undertake or maintain directed activities of learning. They will lose all interest in what is being taught, will have no curiosity and will not learn.

But this state of complex physiological equilibrium that the organism seeks to maintain and which we have called homeostasis is not a crucial determinant of behaviour. Rather the human organism is always seeking situations which will disturb this balance in order to have the satisfaction of producing his own new point of balance at a higher level.

Questions

1. How is the mind related to the body? Discuss the several views.

2. Discuss the physical basis of mental life and show how it determines the life and behaviour of children.
3. Give a short description of the nervous system and the brain.
4. What are the chief endocrine glands? How do they determine behaviour?
5. Write explanatory notes on the following:—a neurone, localisation of brain functions, spinal cord, reflex arc, homeostasis.

References for Further Study

1. Clandenning : *The Human Body* (Knopf).
2. Corner : *The Hormones in Human Reproduction* (Prin. Univ. Press).
3. Gates : *Elementary Psychology* (Macmillan)
4. Harrow : *Glands in Health and Disease* (Dutton).
5. Howell : *A Textbook in Physiology* (Saunders).
6. Marquis : *Comparative Psychology* (Prentice-Hall).
7. Morgan : *Physiological Psychology* (McGraw-Hill).
8. Parker : *The Elementary Nervous System* (Lippincott).
9. Thomson : *Instinct, Intelligence and Character* (Allen & Unwin).
10. Warren : *Human Psychology* (Houghton Mifflin).
11. Watson : *Behavioursim* (Kegan Paul).
12. Woodworth : *Psychology* (Methuen).
13. Young : *Motivation of Behaviour* (Wiley).

CHAPTER FOUR

Human Behaviour

PSYCHOLOGY has been defined as the study of human behavour and education as a planned effort to mould and shape it. But the term behaviour is not as simple as it seems. The mere fact that Behaviourism interprets it in a narrow sense shows that the term must be defined with care and in detail. An attempt has been made in the first chapter to indicate what is understood by behaviour and a detailed discussion of what behaviour means and implies will be taken up in the present chapter.

Educational psychology, for the very simple reason that it occupies a midway position between education and psychology and has to consider the individual in relation to an environment with a view to influencing his behaviour, is compelled to deal more fully with all that behaviour implies. There are certain facts and principles which are fundamental to behaviour and determine our standpoint and treatment of the psychology of education. They may not find a place in the common run of books on general psychology; some of them are hardly mentioned, but for a better understanding of the behaviour of the young people who take education in schools as well as for a better determination of the influences which are going to mould and shape that behaviour in education, it is essential that they should be treated here in detail.

1. LIVING ORGANISM

The human being capable of behaviour is a living organism. This is a simple fact but its significance is usually lost sight of in education and the teacher in his attempt to influence young people's behaviour, is apt to forget it. What are the characteristics of a living organism? What features or qualities distinguish a living organism from a machine? An answer to these questions is useful for the teacher.

In the first place, a living organism is a unity; it works as one. No doubt it is made up of distinguishable parts of organs but the parts work together as a whole. 'Each part behaves as if it knew what all the other parts are doing.' Often an organism is likened to a living machine composed of a large number of cells, 'built in nature's factory' and fitted like other machines for doing certain things. But it is such a machine that even simple forms of its activity are affected by the whole organism, the parts never act in isolation and they are in the service of the whole organism. Even when we analyse the function of parts or organs for a closer study we cannot deal with them adequately till we know the whole organism. Bodily organs take individual shape but always in relation to each other, and even during the earliest stages of development unity of responses shows itself. The organism is one and works as one whole.

From this follows an important educational principle. From the very beginning of the life cycle the activities of the child should not be studied in isolation from the rest of his behaviour.

Secondly, the living organism is self-maintaining, self-moving, self-repairing, self-feeding, self-changing, self-regulating and self-reproducing. No machine, however elaborate, is capable of doing any of these things. A living organism moves from within; all its activity is directed by its own laws. Not that its behaviour is arbitrary and haphazard but that it follows its own laws. A machine, however complex and perfect, cannot move unless somebody moves or starts it. A living organism maintains itself with food; if any part is injured or cut off it has a wonderful capacity for recovering from the wound, and in some cases, for growing that part again. It guards itself against danger, it is free to change its responses to environment, and it continues its kind by reproduction. In brief, a living organism is autonomous.

Thirdly, every living organism is unique. No two are exactly alike. All through the organic world there are great differences among individuals of the same species. In the plant world, for example, it would be impossible to find two leaves, two blades of grass, or two plants exactly alike. Some slight differences serve to make each one of them unique. Modern psychology teaches that no two human beings are alike. They differ in size, health, knowledge, ability, colour of the hair, gait, tastes, temperament, intelligence and innumerable other characteristics. These differences are due to heredity, environment, training or individual effort. But whatever the causes of differences, the fact of individual variations forms one of the most pressing and constant problems of the teacher. However thorough his knowledge of childhood may be and however learned he may be in the science of child psychology, he must learn to know the particular child that concerns him. He must exercise a check against the very common tendency of drawing hasty conclusions concerning an individual from the general laws about the class or group. Fourthly, living organism is a growing organism. Growth is found in all organic life, plants, animals and human beings, and has been studied with respect to structure and function. The psychology of the child cannot be accurately or sympathetically understood except in terms of growth. He is not a finished product like the adult or a machine. His responses to environment are constantly changing, he is always starting something for which we are not prepared. The teacher, instead of feeling upset or annoyed, should mark such changes and adapt his treatment of the child in the light of these changes. He should approach the child with patience, for often growth is slow.

Lastly, a living organism changes and grows not entirely because of something inherent, something happening within, but also because of what happens to him from without. Organisms do not grow in vacuum. Recent research has emphasised the individual so much that the influence of environment on growth is apt to be overlooked. Growth takes place not only because of something which is in the organism, but because that which is inside is released by that which is outside. Every experience may make a more or less important difference to its growth and development. The child is like other living organisms in having qualities and impulses and a direction of his own; but these are subject to encouragement, guidance or education, as well as discouragement, obstruction and perversion. He responds to environment and himself changes as a result of these responses. This interaction between the organism and the environment is what makes education possible and fruitful.

2. Behaviour and Environment

The individual is in active relations with his environment. He acts and makes changes in his environment and his environment influences and changes him. His behaviour consists of his dealings with the environment. All behaviour is a function of the individual as well as of the environment, both of which undergo changes as a result of the interaction. This interaction goes on continually. As has been pointed out in the last section, the relation between the individual and the environment is not a fixed but a growing one.

What is environment ? And what concrete forms do the individual activities take in relation to it ?

The individual is subject not to *an* environment but to many environments. In the first place, there is the physical environment in which he lives, moves and has his being. It consists of material objects and things. The individual needs air to breathe, food to eat, clothes and shelter to protect his body. He resists harmful physical influences such as too cold or too hot wind and weather. His heart leaps up when he beholds charming scenes of nature. Secondly, there is the cultural environment consisting of customs, traditions, ways of the people among whom he is born, their beliefs and ways of thinking. He accepts some, suspects and rejects others; some help him, others obstruct him; he moves to strengthen some of them and to weaken others. Thirdly, the environment is mental, consisting of ideas, opinions, attitudes, prejudices. He is always reflecting on his thoughts and feelings, and acting or not acting according to them. Each individual lives in a world of ideas all his own and his behaviour is very much influenced by it. Fourthly, his environment is social, consisting of combinations of human inter-relationships and institutions. He has his own family, neighbours, friends, rivals, colleagues, playfellows, leaders and followers. He not only talks but talks to people. He is a social being, depends on his group for help and co-operation, resists those individuals or groups who oppose or thwart him and shares group life with them for common joy and happiness. He helps to build institutions and profits by those built by others.

The environment is a general term for all those internal and external forces, conditions and influences which affect

behaviour. The individual is affected by almost everything that surrounds him and in turn changes and influences those things that affect him. His growth is determined by his environment. But everything in the environment does not help growth. Some influences are stimulating and inspiring; they provide for healthy expression and exercise of children's abilities and interests. Others discourage and suppress them and the child grows in a wrong direction.

3. Characteristics of Behaviour

Behaviour is fundamentally different in kind from the action of any machine however elaborate. The contrast is indicated in the first section where the distinctive features of a living organism are described, and it will be more fully developed in the present. Let us take an example. A dog is lying on the road. It smells food in the neighbourhood. It walks up to one of the houses. It pushes open its gate-window and enters. It finds the inmates of the house taking their meal. It stops. A morsel is thrown at it. The dog picks it up and moves out. The gate-window has got to be pulled. The dog cannot do it with his mouth full. It puts down the morsel on the ground, pulls the window with its mouth, picks up the food and jumps out. We understand that the dog wanted food. When I want something to eat, I go to the kitchen, open the cupboard and get some sweets. I interpret the dog's behaviour in terms of my own experience.

On the other hand, the movements of a bicycle are mechanical. It cannot move unless I push it ; it moves in the direction in which its handle is set, it moves as its pedals work, it cannot of itself avoid obstacles, increase its speed or come to a standstill till the rider wills it. Its movements can be predicted and are automatic. It has no wish, will or purpose. It does not think or learn. Its movements are mechanical, that is, follow automatically as a result of certain conditions.

No machine can act as the dog did. The dog's activity is termed behaviour and differs from the movements of the bicycle in several ways.

Firstly, behaviour is spontaneous. It is the outcome of an inner drive or urge, it is not the result of an outer compulsion. A table moves only when it is pushed, a pen writes only when it is handled and moved, a car runs when it is started and driven but the dog behaves because it wants to. It may be said that a feeling of hunger or an idea of food compelled it to act, but in the first place, the feeling or the idea belongs to the dog and in the second place, in the course of its behaviour it could have at any stage changed its mind and acted differently. Its behaviour is its very own.

Secondly, behaviour bears no proportion to the duration or strength of what causes it. The car moves only so long as it is driven, the lamp burns so long as there is electric current, but the dog continues to behave long after the momentary thought of food or hunger. Its behaviour in which activity is varied, obstacles are overcome, and effort is continued, is out of all proportion to the thought or feeling that started it.

Thirdly, behaviour varies. Mechanical action simply repeats itself. The car runs in very much the same manner, the lamp burns as it did before. But every time the dog moves to satisfy its hunger it may follow a different course. It may snatch bread from a child, kill a mouse. pick up a bone or prefer to be hungry. If one method fails. it may try another. If there are obstacles it changes its behaviour. Behaviour thus varies and adapts itself to changing conditions.

Fourthly, behaviour improves and shows progressive adaptability. The car does not run better because it has done so in the past nor does the lamp burn brighter on that account. The dog knows as a result of past experience that certain ways of obtaining food are easier and more satisfactory. It has learnt that the gate-window opens to a push from outside and a pull from inside. Its behaviour improves with practice, unsuccessful ways are given up and successful ones are repeated and perfected. A machine does not thus improve itself.

Fifthly, behaviour is directed to an end. It is purposive or teleological. The dog acts to satisfy hunger and continues its activity till its hunger is satisfied. The activity has purpose which sets it going and stops when the aim is realised. Mechanical action has no such aim or purpose. This is another way of saying that behaviour cannot be interpreted except in terms of mind and life.

Lastly, behaviour is continuous. Every single act has some definite meaning and place in the total course, with reference either to acts which precede or those that follow. We do something in order to do something else or to complete what was done before. The dog pushes the gate-window to get in, it wants to get in to obtain food, and so on. In behaviour one act grows out of another. The continuity of behaviour follows from its purposiveness.

Some behaviour is mechanical, such as the contraction of the pupil of the eye as a protection against bright light, or the jerking of the leg in response to a painful stimulus to the foot, or the flow of tears when a particle of dust gets into the eye or sneezing when anything irritates the nose. These are reflex movements. They occur automatically and mechanically on the presentation of a stimulus. Many people argue on his basis that man is just a highly complicated machine. Now it seems difficult to accept such a view in the light of what we have studied about behaviour. These characteristics are found not only in the behaviour of men but also in that of lower animals. The latter may not be as conscious of a purpose in their behaviour, or in some cases the consciousness may be altogether absent, but still their behaviour serves a purpose. Experiments have been made with some of the smallest unicellular creatures like the stentor or the amoeba and it has been found that their behaviour shows some of the broad features described above. The stentor is too small to be observed by the naked eye and yet it responds to stimuli in a way which is not that of a machine. It modifies its behaviour to suit changing conditions and adjusts itself to them.

4. Behaviour, Experience and Consciousness

Earlier we defined behaviour as being both bodily and mental and our detailed study of its main characteristics has revealed that behaviour cannot be interpreted or understood without reference to mind and purpose. We have also seen that behaviourism cannot give an adequate account of behaviour because it ignores mind and conscious life. We may not define psychology as the science of mind but in defining it as the study of behaviour it is difficult to escape dealing with mind which expresses itself in behaviour and experience.

What is this mind? There are two aspects of it which deserve careful treatment. The first is the function of mind or experience and the second is the structure of mind, the dispositions and the unconscious. Our knowledge about the latter is not complete and all that we can know about it is by interpreting the former, that is, experience.

Our experience is what we know most intimately. We are quite certain that we know, feel, desire, see, remember, imagine and act; and this knowing, feeling, desiring, seeing, remembering, imagining and acting is what constitutes our experience. Experience is what happens to us, what goes on in our mind. It is a characteristic of experience that it is not shared in common by different individuals. Two friends may have the same object of grief, for example, the death of a common friend. But each feels his own grief. Experience is private and personal, and can be studied and directly known only by the individual who has it.

Now it is our own experience that helps us to understand the behaviour of others. I am able to understand the behaviour of the dog, to interpret its purpose and desire because I have myself behaved in a similar manner in a similar situation. When I see a child trembling, excited and trying to turn away or hide himself, I conclude that he is afraid. I am able to interpret his behaviour in terms of my own experience. I remember that I behave in a similar manner when I am frightened. This experience is studied through introspection.

We not only *have* experience, feel joy and sorrow, remember and act, but also *are conscious* of our experience of feeling joy and sorrow, of remembering and acting. We are conscious or aware of what is going on in our mind and our behaviour and experience is influenced by this awareness. But consciousness is not identical with experience. It implies awareness and it is not true that we are conscious of every experience. We may have an experience without being aware of it. We may have wishes and act according to them without being conscious of them. We certainly have experience of which we are more intensely conscious than others. Although it is easy to know experience of which we are not conscious for there is no other means of knowing them except through consciousness, yet it is advisable to treat consciousness and experience as two distinct terms.

The second aspect of mind relates to its structure. If experience is its function, there are mind-sets or attitudes which constitute its structure and which determine experience. 'Our actual experience at any moment is determined by conditions which are not themselves actual experience, but the abiding after-effects left by prior experience.'[1]

The abiding after-effects of the previous experience are called dispositions. All experience leaves behind traces or after-effects which influence later experience; when I am introduced to a person, my second or third meeting with him is influenced by the first. The first experience had left a trace which though not present to my consciousness persisted as an unconscious factor to determine subsequent experience. I know that two and two make four but I am not all the time conscious of it. I am capable of recalling it when I need it. It is owned by me not as a conscious state but as an unconscious disposition. All knowledge we acquire, our past history and experience, persist as unconscious dispositions and bear on all conscious life as occasion arises. These dispositions should be understood as constituting a sort of mental structure which is being constantly formed and modified by conscious experience and is in its turn constantly determining and modifying later unconscious experience. They are sometimes described as unconscious but as will be explained later, it is better to call them sub-conscious factors, as they can be recalled when needed.

Some behaviour is unconscious, the individual is not aware of what he is doing. He mops his head, bites his nails, sucks his thumb and the like, and is surprised when others draw his attention to it. Such behaviour is due to hidden desires which have not been fulfilled and which are

[1] Stout: *Groundwork of Psychology*, p. 7.

still disturbing the individual. For lack of expression they were forced into the unconscious from where they continue to influence behaviour though the individual is no longer aware of them.

To sum up : behaviour is a general term including experience, experience is what each one of us knows directly and on whose basis he interprets other people' behaviour, some experience is conscious and some experience persists as sub-conscious dispositions to determine later experience.

5. Aspects of Experience

Conscious experience must be carefully analysed before it can be adequately understood. Let us analyse a concrete experience, for example, of a student attending to the teacher. The student in the first place is receiving certain sounds which make him recall certain ideas and images. He may imagine the pages of the book being taught, or the coming examination. He may be thinking of several things in connection with the lesson and may be trying to remember parts of it. That is, he is having sensations, perceptions, ideas, images, and memories. He is having knowledge and all these processes constitute *cognition* or the *cognitive* aspect of experience. Again, the student may be feeling interested or bored with the lesson. He may be liking or disliking it, feeling pleased or displeased with it. This feeling attitude of like and dislike, pleasure and pain, is the *affective* attitude and constitutes *affection*. Again, if he is pleased with the lesson he may be performing certain movements to attend to it. For example, he may be craning his neck, bending forward, sitting still, trying to get rid of all disturbing thoughts and making an effort to concentrate his attention on the subject. On the other hand, if he is feeling bored, he may look aside, try to scribble idly or make some mischief. All these acts in which he is trying to do something constitute *conation*. So every experience has three modes, knowledge, feeling and action, or as they are termed in psychology, cognition, affection, and conation.

They are three ultimate modes of experience and are present wherever conscious experience is present. They cannot be reduced to one another but none of them can be experienced independently of each other. We can distinguish them in our thought. Pure, unmixed knowledge, feeling or action is a fiction, though it is possible that any particular experience may have more of one or the other. They are always related to each other and are found in every experience. Experience is one continuous thing and they are only aspects or phases of it. This analysis is not a division but only a distinction. They are not faculties or powers of the mind.

Knowledge is present in all experience for some sort of awareness or apprehension of the objects of experience or of ourselves having experience is always there. A feeling of pleasure or displeasure is also present, for how else do we want an experience to continue or cease? No doubt sometimes the feeling is so weak that we are not aware of it but it is present all the same. And when we are pleased we strive to maintain or continue it and when we are displeased we strive to change or stop it. Thus conation is also always there.

6. Educational Applications

These facts and principles about human behaviour bear closely on educational practice. If the child is an autonomous creature and if his behaviour is spontaneous, his growth and development, physical, intellectual and moral, must take place through activities which are spontaneous and free. An organism is the source of its own growth and as a seed blossoms through self-activity, a mind grows through the exercise of its own effort. The principle of self-activity is essential to all organic growth and education should be a process of arousing this self-activity. It means that no influence from environment, no stimuli of any sort, no amount of educational material, not even the inherited tendencies, can have the slightest effect in promoting mental development except as these things are responded to by the individual to be educated. Teachers may provide materials and means for education but they cannot create the motive power nor can they perform the educative activities for a child. What the child himself does, not what the teacher does for him, or in his presence, develops and educates him. Modern education lays great stress on freedom, spontaneity and initiative, this is a simple recognition of the fundamental principle of self-activity. Children's education rests on what they do to themselves and by themselves and less on what is done to them or for them by the teacher. They grow and learn through their own activity, through self-expression, through their own responses of life's experience. The truth is emphasised by the popular slogans: 'All education is self-education', 'learning by doing.' It is embodied in a very concrete and living form in the Wardha Scheme of education.

If purpose is an essential mark of living behaviour, it should not be neglected in education. A child works and learns far better if he knows the goal or purposes to which his activity is leading. In all teaching it is really worthwhile to help children to understand the value and purpose of what they are going to learn. The most abstract and difficult tasks become meaningful when their purpose is brought out. Purpose is not fatal to spontaneity as purposes can be freely chosen by children. To this many teachers may object that it is not always possible to allow children real freedom of choice. But if it is not possible, the teacher can at least lead them to sympathise so with his purpose that they accept it as if it were their own. In many progressive schools such freedom is not only made possible but encouraged in class-room work.

The individual functions as a whole. His experience is a unity of knowledge, feeling and action. His education should mean not merely instruction and imparting of knowledge and information, but also cultivating of healthy feelings and emotions and development of rational will. An educated person is not merely one who has gathered knowledge but one who combines with knowledge a kindliness of feeling and charity, and a determination to strive after truth he knows and loves. The school should not be a mere knowledge shop selling facts but also a place where young people acquire skills of various sorts and enjoy doing so. Learning is a great adventure for young people and while it gives them knowledge and skill, it should take place in such a manner that the joy of adventure should not be lost to them.

7. Social Behaviour

The social aspect of behaviour has already been stressed. All human behaviour is social inasmuch as it is being guided and influenced from the moment each one of us is born by the behaviour of people around us. In the family the primary needs of the child are satisfied, he learns the basic skills whose pattern is the same as that obtaining in the family. For example he learns to eat, drink, wash, eliminate and dress in the manner other members of the family do. What parents say, do and expect and how brothers and sisters behave and work moulds the behaviour of the child. When later he goes out to play with children of the neighbourhood his behaviour is influenced by his playmates. When he joins school children of his class and play group as also the teachers who teach him influence his behaviour. Later he moves into several kinds of groups and each group pushes, guides, advises and forces him into correct and appropriate ways of living and behaving.

To begin with the child is selfish and self-centred but through these influences he becomes 'socialised', converted into a social being with patterns of behaviour similar to those obtaining in his society. He not only eats, drinks and dresses to meet his primary needs but does so in a manner and style approved by the society in which he lives and moves. This socialisation takes place through mutual interaction and inter-communication: one person affects the behaviour of another person, a person's behaviour is affected by the behaviour of a group and the behaviour of one group is affected by the behaviour of another group. Customs, traditions, norms, fashions, leaders, newspapers, radio, films, books, rumours, schools, colleges, temples, market places, mobs, audiences and the like are for ever influencing the behaviour of an individual and affect his learning. Even when other people are not physically present the individual is affected by the thoughts and opinions of his friends and members of his group, even though they are not present at the moment. Preparing to go to school the child will not put on any item of his dress which is likely to be made fun of by his friends in the school.

Some of the important processes through which society or group helps learning are imitation, social facilitation, competition and co-operation. Children in a family about the ages of two and four when closely observed will show that the child of two imitates everything his elder brother or sister does. When the older child starts going out the younger child does the same, if one wants candy the other too wants it, and so on. Imitation is particularly striking at this age when a child has not yet learned to do many things for himself and learns a short-cut to getting what he wants by imitating older children or persons. How we all imitate others in almost everything is not so obvious because we seldom pause to think about it. Imitation is a very striking feature of the behaviour of people in groups.

Social facilitation is the improvement of any aspect of a person's performance by virtue of the presence of other persons also engaged at the same time in similar activities. People eat and drink more in company than when alone, children learn more and better when they do so in a group. The presence of others acts as a stimulus and increases the strength of our motives. But the presence of others may also *inhibit* performance. Young people who are shy and sensitive may not be able to do their best because they are afraid of what others might say. This is *social inhibition.*

If there are inter-personal relations in a group the behaviour of members is somehow or other marked by both competition and co-operation. When children are working with others in a group a spirit of rivalry and competition is sure to enter into their behaviour and effort, and every teacher will bear testimony to the fact that children work better and more when they are competing with others in the class. Psychologists have carried out detailed experiments with groups of young people working in both competition and co-operation and their studies show that for better performance a co-operative spirit among members of a group working in a team is far more effective in the long run.

It is through social behaviour that people acquire beliefs and attitudes, social norms and ideals.

Teachers must study not only the structure of the class, how children take to each other, what children are more popular, what children are rejected, what cliques and fac-

tions are working in the class, and what climate of mutual adjustments obtains in it. He must try to create a healthy social atmosphere so that young people work in harmony. In this study he will be helped by sociometry already described in the second chapter. He should be particularly keen to spot boys who are bullies and a nuisance to others as also those who are too shy to mix with their classmates and stay away from games and the like. Normal social activity and development of each child should be ensured.

But the teacher should never forget that he himself is an important part of the social environment of the child. Not only should he present a worthy model in speech, dress, manners and behaviour for children to emulate but in group activity should keep himself in the background so that young people instead of being overawed and inhibited by his presence feel encouraged and stimulated to do better.

8. Abnormal Behaviour

Some behaviour is unusual, different from the normal and is a source of both unhappiness and inefficiency. Not all of children's wishes, needs and goals are fulfilled. May be that they are too weak, may be that the environment is not favourable or that the goals are too high, and they feel frustrated for not getting what they so very eagerly desire. They are unable to get on the swing, play football or climb a tree like older boys; they cannot get toys, candy or joy rides on which they had set their heart, their mother does not let them play with boys they would like most to play. Such frustrations produce anxiety and misery.

Often children have aspirations out of all proportion to their capacity. A child may very ardently desire to win praise for recitation, for running fast in a race, or for scoring high marks in an examination, and feels frustrated when he is unable to achieve his goal.

Or there may be conflict in his desires and motives. A child is both hungry and sleepy and does not know what need to satisfy first. Or it may be a difficult choice between doing sums in arithmetic and getting spanking and he runs away from home to avoid both. Perhaps the worst type of conflict among children occurs when they have both a positive and a negative attitude toward the same person, say father. They like him for his affectionate ways and gifts but they dislike him for his harshness and temper, and do not know what to think or do about the situation.

Thus frustration and conflict lead to anxiety and misery. Anxiety is vague fear that is acquired in experiences with many frustrating situations. The child feels great discomfort and is very unhappy. Most often the child is not aware of the cause of his anxiety and misery. If this anxiety and misery is very severe he may develop disturbances of bodily function and fall ill.

The normal way of getting rid of this anxiety would be to accept the difficult situation, resolve the conflict by following one course of action and try to do better in that direction. But often young people resort to such behaviour as would put a cover on their frustration, save their face and esteem and relieve them of anxiety and misery though only temporarily and often with worse consequences. Some children just run away from home to avoid conflict, others withdraw from the scene of frustration and conflict, seek solitude, sit in a corner and indulge in daydreaming, others avoid society and start believing that the world is against them. Some children would throw a temper tantrum, just lie on the ground, spoil their dress, kick their arms and legs in anger and start crying. Some children failing to do well in study try to compensate bydoing better in games or mischief. Others start weeping and striking their heads. Some defeated in school take it out on their younger brother or sister by scolding or beating him or her. Some of them may believe that the teacher is against them and favours other children. Still others may coin excuses to defend their defeat or failure and pass them on to others to gain self-respect. Boys failing in the examination may say that they are not book-worms, that examinations are not a real test of one's ability and that there is much favouritism in examinations.

These are not healthy responses and lead to maladjustments in behaviour. They only help to put off the problem, to disguise the conflict and allow it to produce anxiety again and again. The child who blames the teacher for his failure not only does not see the real cause but may also come into clash with the teacher thus aggravating his problem. Such abnormal ways of behaving land children in greater trouble with people outside and with themselves. Some of them may develop severe mental disorders like psychoneuroses and even psychoses which we shall describe in a later chapter.

To guard against such faults of adjustment and minor mental disorders there is a large body of knowledge called *mental hygiene* whose object is to maintain satisfying personal adjustments and promote mental health. The teacher should be familiar with its main principles. A very important thing he can do is to guard against bullying, ragging, ridiculing or severe scolding. He should know each individual child of his class and take care about unduly hurting sensitive children. There are children whom even a slap does not matter and there are children whom even a mild expression of displeasure is enough warning. He should be on the look out for any sign of faulty adjustments on the part of children and help them with encouragement, sympathy and understanding. Giving equal opportunities to all he should try to understand the personal difficulties and problems of each student in his class and help them to get over them. Problems of adjustments are best overcome by children themselves but the helping and understanding approach of the teacher will go a long way to resolve them.

QUESTIONS

1. Distinguish between living behaviour and mechanical action. Is man a mere machine?
2. All behaviour is reaction to environment. Can you educate young people merely by controlling their environment? Discuss the place of environment in education.
3. Distinguish between consciousness and experience. What are the ultimate modes of conscious experience? What significance have they for education?
4. What do you understand by self-activity? How far is it a distinctive feature of living organisms and living behaviour? Discuss its value as an educational principle.
5. 'No two individuals are alike.' Explain this maxim and bring out its bearing on the school work.
6. Explain the principle of 'learning by doing', and show how it is basic to the Wardha Scheme.

REFERENCES FOR FURTHER STUDY

1. Allport : *Social Psychology* (Harper).
2. Carmichael : *Manual of Child Psychology* (Wiley).
3. Dashiell : *Fundamentals of General Psychology* (Houghton Mifflin).
4. Drever : *An Introduction to the Psychology of Education* (Arnold).
5. Gessel : *Infancy and Human Growth* (Harper).

6. Gessel and Thompson : *Infant Behaviour* (McGraw Hill).
7. Jackson : *Guiding Your Life* (Appleton).
8. Jennings: *The Bioligical Basis of Human Nature* (Norton & Co.).
9. Jennings, Watson and others : *Suggestions of Modern Science Concerning Education* (Norton & Co.).
10. Kirkpatric : *Genetic Psychology* (Macmillan).
11. McDougall : *An Outline of Psychology* (Methuen).
12. Nunn : *The Evolution and Growth of Human Behaviour* (Houghton Mifflin).
13. Munn : *Education, Its Data and First Principles* (Arnold).
14. Ross : *Groundwork of Educational Psychology* (Harrap).
15. Starch : *Controlling Human Behaviour* (Macmillan).
16. Stout : *Manual of Psychology* (Univ. Tut. Press).
17. Stuart and Oakden : *Modern Psychology and Education* (Kegan Paul).
18. Taba : *The Dynamics of Educational Psychology* (Harrap).
19. Thorndike : *Educational Psychology : Briefer Course* (Col. Univ. Press).

Chapter Five — Heredity and Environment

ONE of the moot questions in the study and education of children is the role played by heredity in comparison with environment. There are two schools of opinion, one holds that the character and conduct of children is unalterably fixed by what they inherit from their ancestors and the other maintains that it all depends on what opportunities are provided by their environment. The controversy is between heredity and environment, nature and nurture.

1. Argument for Heredity

Heredity means that like tends to beget like and the fact of being a member of the human race bears with it a certain capital in terms of original nature. The child is what he is because he is a member of a certain family, race and sex. He resembles his parents not only in bodily form but also in likes and dislikes, abilities and intelligence, habits and character. Now it is held that this inborn nature is the chief factor in development and solely determines the possibilities to which the child can be educated. All education is limited by certain capacities and interests which the child inherits from his parents and which unfold themselves in a manner and order which is not influenced by the environment in which they live. The emphasis on heredity discredits all thoughts, effort and painstaking control of the environment in child education. Instances of personages like Babar, Shivaji, Ranjit Singh and others are cited to show how strenuously these people fought against hostile circumstances in life, how bravely they set at nought the discouraging forces in their environment and how they rose to power and distinction in spite of the serious obstacles and handicaps that blocked their way. 'Circumstances of life are to man what rocks and winds and currents are to a ship; merely accidents that make their qualities manifest but have nothing whatever to do with producing them.'[1] Thousands of young men are placed in similar surroundings; their spirit, far from being roused, is irretrievably damped and they die fighting a losing battle. If only a few reach the heights of achievement and distinction, it must mainly be due to their inborn nature and genius which shines in spite of obstacles. Therefore it is argued that inherited traits, original nature or native endowment finally determine character, conduct and personality.

Rousseau, Pearson and Galton are the chief exponents of the 'heredity' school and offer two main lines of argument in their support. In the first place, they work out a close relation between the child's physical and moral qualities. Children physically healthy and fit are morally good and commendable. Statistics, it is claimed, show such a high degree of correlation between the two kinds of qualities that it seems impossible that they can be derived from different sources. Since the physical qualities are without doubt inherited, the moral qualities must be so. It would mean that given a certain person to be tall, long-armed and dark-eyed, certain moral qualities can be safely predicted. Secondly, researches which Galton and others have made into the ancestral history of twins, scientists, judges, artists and kings seem to demonstrate fully the fact that distinctive mental ability is the result of inheritance rather than of education. The depressing history of the Jukes family emphatically silences all argument against

[1] Nunn: *Education: Its Data and First Principles*, p. 105.

original inheritance. Of 1667 members in five generations 300 died in infancy, 310 spent 2300 years in poor houses, 440 were destroyed by disease, 400 were wrecked by their own wickedness, 7 were murderers, 60 habitual thieves who spent on an average 12 years each in prison, 130 were convicted criminals and only 20 learned a trade. Such investigations as these seem to prove once for all that education is all paint; it does not alter the nature of the wood that is under it, only improves its appearance a little.

2. Argument for Environment

On the other hand, it is thought that a child is born with a great variety of possibilities and is capable of any sort of development within the range of human capacity. What a man has done a man can do if he gets favourable opportunities. The genius is as much a product of his environment and education as the idiot is. The mind of the child is a mass of clay, passive and plastic, to which environment may give any shape it likes, or it is a clean slate, a *tabula rasa* of Locke on which experience impresses its forms. The exponents of this view turn to the same Babar, Shivaji and Ranjit Singh and ask why their ancestors and descendants did not show the same degree of talent and achievement. These individuals were the product of the social, economic and political influences of the age in which they lived and could not have reached those heights of their career if their career had a different setting. Man grows into what his environment, training and education make him.

Education, therefore, is the be-all of a person's mental and moral make-up. This history of civilization bears testimony to the fact that man, a wild animal, has built a glorious edifice of culture, art, science, philosophy, religion, society through experience, learning, education and training. If heredity had been the sole arbiter of his fortune, he would have remained the same old primitive that he was twenty centuries back. Again, instances of reclamation and re-education are not lacking in which hopeless wrecks of life, through sympathetic and right guidance, have turned over a new leaf and started life afresh on a definitely sounder and better plane. Environment alone makes or mars a man and heredity is its insignificant shadow.

3. Their Bearing on Education

These two extremes of opinion have a strong hold on popular thought and since they bear on the attitude of teachers towards education it is very important that they should have a very clear perspective of the relative importance of heredity and environment. Those who emphasise the role of heredity despair of education and neglect it altogether. Whenever children fall short of their expectations and whenever efforts to cultivate better habits among them misfire, they drift into a mood of easy fatalism that heredity has predestined their characters, learning and behaviour and it is futile to try to avert the full force of the coming tragedy. They lose all hope in their pupils' improvement and let them pick up such crumbs of knowledge as they may from class teaching. Some teachers blame them for lowering the standard of the class and neglect them, saying that mangoes cannot grow out of cotton seeds. No doubt heredity sets limits which cannot be overstepped and certainly mangoes cannot grow out of cotton seeds, but if one works with knowledge and understanding one can improve the quality of mangoes by a careful regulation of the environment as one can make cotton grow into productive plants and yield a larger harvest. Pupils' natures are originally different and their growth is determined along certain definite lines, but it certainly rests with us to improve those lines along which they *can* develop and make the most of their inherited capital. Careful manuring, preparation of the soil, irrigation and such other aids as scientific cultivation will enable the seeds to grow into larger and richer plants. It is futile to expect the child to overstep the limits set by his inheritance, but the educator can always help him within those limits by providing favourable opportunities in the environment for the best development of his inherited capacities and powers. The tremendous influence of environment as a stimulating and selecting force on races becomes evident if we consider the astonishing regeneration of Japan in the recent past.

Others who neglect heredity and presume that education, training and environment can achieve all that is within human capacity are guilty of overweening optimism and incur considerable waste of effort, time and money in trying to realise the impossible. The best type of education, training and environment cannot create interest, capacities or talents which are denied to an individual by virtue of his inheritance. Even the most capable art teacher cannot make ordinary gifted pupils into good artists and his influence on some of them is not even appreciable because they have not inherited a talent or even an inclination for art and he cannot create artistic talent. Education can at the most select, stimulate and encourage any talent that is already there. It can eliminate those influences and circumstances which inhibit and stunt the full growth and development of inherited traits and capacities, and encourage and provide for those that favour it. There is a place in the world for almost every type and every degree of ability, and wise education requires that inherited inclinations, capacities and interests of every child should be studied early and every facility should be provided in his environment to develop all that is best in him as an individual.

4. Heredity and Environment

Both these extremes of thought wrongly assume that heredity and environment are two forces directly opposed to each other. They are neither forces nor are they opposed to each other. The question is not whether heredity or environment, nature or nurture, is the more potent or important force. The two aspects of life embraced under these two terms are not separable; neither of them has any meaning apart from the other. The first thing to understand about the issue so often raised is to recognise that there is no such issue. Every growing organism, whether a plant, animal or man, is not exclusively either heredity *or* environment but heredity *and* environment. It is a centre of free, creative activity, it is self-determined and autonomous, and what it grows to be is the result of both its inherited capacity and environment, which not only cooperate but interact. So the problems for education and society is not to decide a choice between these two aspects of life, but to know how the best possible environment can be provided for every child so that he or she gets from his or her entire inherited endowment all the value that is in it.

The true relation of heredity and environment will become clear if we study the part played by seed and soil in the growth of a plant. The seed has the power to grow into a certain kind of plant but how ill or well it will grow depends on what soil it gets. If it falls on a stone, in the sun or is crushed, it will not germinate; if it is sown in a poor soil with too much of heat or water, it may germinate but will not thrive long or bear fruit; and if it falls on good soil and has favourable influences like manure, water and sun, it will grow into a very good plant. The plant cannot grow without either the seed or the soil. It needs both,

The seed and the soil do not work independently of each other but are mutually dependent. Sir B. N. Mitra started life as a clerk on Rs. 60 per month in the Military Accounts Department and had evidently inborn talent for understanding and solving the most intricate of financial problems. His genius spurred him on and he rose to the highest position in the department. Could he have done so without either native talent or favourable opportunities provided by environment? Could he have done so if he had neither interest nor ability in his work; or if he had accepted employment in a school? Sir C. V. Raman could not be fitted into the same hole. The scientific curiosity in him could thrive only in the stimulating atmosphere of his physics laboratory. The uniform environment of the accounts department encouraged the one and would have discouraged the other because their inherited aptitudes were different and did not let them grow in the same direction. We cannot make every clerk employed in the accounts department do as well as Mitra did, nor can we make every clerk that leaves it a Raman. With all our most painstaking efforts at improvement we cannot add a jot or title to the native capacity of children; they will start approximately at the same level as we did and like us will struggle their way up. This, however, should not make us lose courage and look on heredity as the hand of fate which irrevocably stands in the way of progress. There is another side of the medal, too. Heredity is a great conservative factor which, though it cannot be altered, maintains the excellence of standard types of plants and animals and maintains man to preserve his level of accomplishment. Man's misfortunes, mistakes and follies do not have an irretrievable effect on his advancement and his inherited traits protect him a great deal from the dangers of a harmful environment.

5. What is Heredity?

What is it that children inherit? Do brothers and sisters have the same heredity? Do mental qualities run in certain families? Why do children take after one parent or ancestor more than another? Are defects also inherited? These and a score of other questions torment many a parent and teacher and the answers which they manufacture on the basis of folklore or with the help of their uncritical imagination often educate them to a very wrong attitude towards children.

The child grows from the union of germ cells from the father and mother and starts life as a little speck of jelly. In nine months time it grows into a fully developed baby but during this period of development it has received nothing from outside except food and water. What it grows into was potentially present in the little speck of jelly conception. The baby has no direct connection by nerves or even by blood vessels with his mother and nothing that she thinks or does can affect the quality of the food supplied to him by soaking from her arteries through the placenta.

Each of these germ cells has a nucleus containing twenty-three pairs of little strings of beads called chromosomes. The father provides a germ cell with twenty-three pairs of chromosomes and the mother provides another germ cell with twenty-three pairs of chromosomes. The two sets of chromosomes join together in pairs after having thrown away one member from each pair so that they enter into union with only twenty-three single chromosomes. Their union restores the normal number of twenty-three pairs and with this the baby starts life. This cell division and reduction of chromosomes explains why children in the same family differ from each other so widely. At each conception cells unite which have thrown away different chromosomes. The number of possible combinations, no two alike, which can be made by taking two sets of twenty-three chromosomes each and shaking them out runs into millions. The variation among children, therefore, is to a large extent simply a reflection of the fact that though legally they have the same ancestry, biologically they represent different selections from the ancestral assortment of chromosomes.

Thus each child inherits from the father and the mother alike. But it must be remembered that each parent was also the inheritor in equal parts from both his or her parents who in their turn inherited equally from their parents. Thus each child owes half of his original equipment to his parents, one-fourth to his grand-parents, one-eighth to his great grand-parents and so on into the shadows of long ago, in geometric ratio. The stream of life flows on and the child inherits his capital not *from* his parents but *through* his parents. This should explain why a child has the chin of his mother, the forehead of his father, the blue colour of eyes from his grandfather, the hair from his uncle, the nose from his aunt. Perhaps it would be more appropriate to say that children have drawn these traits from the same stock and represent different assortment of the same. Many children do not resemble any near ancestor at all and draw from some remote member of the line while many represent mixtures of traits.

Again, it must have been quite clear by now why children of the same family vary and why each member of the race is a unique individual. The fact of individual variation is a commonplace in modern psychology and educational thought, and in its light no manipulation of environment, no education or training will make all children come up to a uniform preconceived standard of achievement. Rather, education should provide the fullest possible expression and expansion of each individual child's mental and moral aptitude. His best development does not consist in making him reach an ideal of perfection set up by his parents and teachers but only that set up by his own inheritance.

6. Do Children Inherit Specific Traits?

A question is often asked whether children inherit from their ancestors specific traits or simply a general ability to develop along certain lines. The investigations referred to above incline us to the view that inheritance is very highly specialised and that certain types of talents and traits run in families; but this conclusion is obscured by three considerations. In the first place, what we attribute to heredity may be due only to the social heritage and traditional atmosphere in which children of a family are born and educated. In a family every child may be inclined to music, not because musical talent runs in the line, but because the example of adult members holds out a strong inducement to the younger people and the home is saturated with a musical atmosphere. Secondly, children are never an exact replica of any of their parents. They differ from them and often these differences make them directly the opposite of each other. It is not uncommon for tall parents to have short children or for short parents to have tall children, for stupid parents to have gifted sons and for artistic parents to have inartistic children. Such variations clinch the proof that specific traits *always* run in families. Thirdly, it is a well-known fact that a genius son of a genius father is an exception rather than the rule. Nature seems to pull the progeny of a genius to the average.

But by specialised inheritance it does not mean that if the mother can cook and sew well, the daughter will be born with such an ability. No child is ever born with ability to cook, sew or perform any other kind of skilful act. When we call a child a born writer, painter or musician, all what we mean is that he has a natural aptitude or bent of mind for the acquisition of that skill. He has a native disposition or tendency towards it and given an opportunity will acquire it more readily than others less gifted. Sometimes such a gifted child may see or search for such opportunities while others are indifferent but, without them his potential gifts may not find any expression and development.

But if it is depressing to learn that skills and traits assiduously acquired by parents cannot be transmitted to the next generation, it is encouraging to know that they will take their defects acquired through misadventure or disease with them to the grave. A lame parent will not beget lame children nor does a blind mother beget a blind daughter. 'The removal of rats' tails generation after generation will not yield rats without tails or with measurably shorter tails.' No doubt certain diseases are transmitted but that is because the poisonous taint has spread to the germ plasm. Such defects as do not reach the germ cells are not passed on to children.

7. Social Heredity

But though we cannot add to or improve the heredity of the next generation we can always pass on to it a better social heritage. Biological heredity should not be confused with social heredity. 'Children are born *with* a biological heritage; they are born *into* a social one.' If the doctrine that acquired characters are not passed on to the next generation is accepted, the only possible means of improving the race is adding to or improving social heredity. The only thing left to us is to help to build a better and healthier world for the next generation to live in.

The vast network of highly organised, exceedingly complex and rapidly growing and progressing human institutions and traditions, manners and customs, legal and moral codes, knowledge, technique and skill, art, literature and religion, ideals and values, constitutes a child's social heritage by which he becomes the heir to all the ages and which makes available to him the fruits of accomplishments of the race. This social heredity may provide the child with a more wholesome and stimulating attitude towards life and ideals and more rational and altruistic faith in common well-being. Our knowledge of the laws of health and our technique in applying that knowledge may repair some of the defects of physical inheritance and the right kind of social and educational atmosphere may reduce the handicap of a weak intellect. Children are born with physical and mental capacities and we can create for them a healthy and stimulating atmosphere in which their inherited capacities, interests and talents will not only have a freer play but also develop more effectively to the best advantage of humanity. Every latent talent will find scope for expansion and advancement in an environment saturated with wholesome influences.

8. Culture

The term social heredity may give a false impression that it is inherited unchanged from generation to generation. Some use the term social inheritance to indicate differences in behaviour due to specific ways of doing, thinking and feeling which are the traditions of a society, due to folkways, mores, codes of decency and respect, taboos and prejudices, due to social habits peculiar to any community. Modern thought gives it the name of *culture* to denote the complex whole of knowledge, thought, belief, art, craft, morals, law, tradition, custom, and any other capabilities and habits acquired by man as a member of society. Every child through processes of socialisation is initiated into the cultural heritage of his society and the family is the most important factor in transmitting that cultural heritage. How children are brought up, what affection they are given or denied by their parents, what parents expect from their children by way of regard or respect and the like affect a child's behaviour and personality. The differences between an Indian and an American child are not only differences of colour and physique but those of cultural background, their style and way of life. An American child, for example, may be far more aggressive and independent than an Indian child who is expected to carry out the wishes of his parents in everything.

In a study of Bali children made by Bateson and Mead it is shown how different practices followed by mothers in child upbringing affect personality development. After the usual motherly care and caressing in the first few months the mother suddenly changes her approach. She begins to tease her baby quite violently by refusing to pay any heed to his demands for affection and goes to the length of arousing his jealousy by showering affection on another baby in the presence of her own. Her own child screams and is frantically jealous but the mother goes on smiling and teasing. In a couple of years the child learns that his wailing will have no effect and he does not get the response he expects, and therefore he must withdraw and find fulfilment within himself rather any warm affection from his mother. He daydreams and withdraws from the social give-and-take. He is calm, quiet and serene. This is the result of the influence of culture on his behaviour and personality.

But cultures change, sometimes slowly and sometimes rapidly. Through conquest, trade and communication cultures are dominated, they mix and take on some patterns of the other. Modern technology is speeding up the process of cultural change and even most remote and rigid societies are forced to change. With modern means of communication distances are being conquered and different communities and countries are coming closer and learning a lot from each other. But in the midst of radical change in culture there are some ways and patterns which continue. Modern times have seen radical changes in the cultural pattern of Indians and yet there is a hard core which still persists.

9. What Education Can Do

The most important thing for the educator is to try to study children in his care and to know what their native traits are. Children should have larger opportunities to engage themselves in as many types of activities as they possibly can, both in the home and the school, and the parent or the teacher should be on the watch as to what types of activity interest a child most so that he may select such environment as will stimulate natural interest and inclination.

But what can environment and education really accomplish? The fact that heredity has set certain definite limits to the scope and effectiveness of educational effort should not be overlooked, nor should it cause us to give up all hope and responsibility. Heredity endows each individual with capacities, aptitudes and interests and it is for education to provide scope for their expression and expansion through favourable environment and lead them to the highest level of development. In the realm of human values it is not capacity or ability that counts for accomplishment, success and efficiency, and to that end education and training are just as, if not more, important; for capacity without training is blind and may misfire. We are all born with a number of bodily and intellectual tools but it is not their possession or presence that matters but their use, and considering that there can be a right and a wrong use of tools, it is clearly the responsibility of education to teach and ensure the right use of our physical and intellectual powers.

The importance of environment becomes evident when we consider how largely our ideas and sentiments are modified by the people we meet, the society in which we move, the books we read, the trade we ply and the wife we wed. Happily selected environment has worked miracles with many a hopeless delinquent, reclaimed many a hardened criminal, and made many a sinner atone for his sins. Tests have revealed that a large number of delinquent children are normal and their fall was due in most cases to harmful influences, person, ideas, to environment and education. A change of environment has regenerated many of them and enabled them to develop into honest, self-supporting citizens.

But while the educator has to study children's native endowment and work within its limits, he has to realise that, placed as he is, he cannot have the best conceivable in the present world. The ideals of perfection he has invented in anticipation of his children's development have to be toned down to what is possible and available. He will have to study the little world in which he has his own being and see what opportunities and means can be brought within his children's reach and what knowledge, skill and art should be taught to them in the light of rapidly changing conditions of life on this globe in the present century. He has to work for those ideals, skills, tastes and acquisitions which will be prized most in the future society in which the child will later as an adult find himself a member. And finally he must see that he himself is a very vital part of the child's environment and should not only present a worthy example but should change with the changing child and the ever-changing world.

The teacher must know the cultural background of children of his class. Out of what neighbourhood, from what type of home, from what social class, race or community does he come ? This will give him insight into what kinds of mores the family is transmitting to the child—what are their standards and goals which they have for their child. What are their modes of discipline and expectations from the child ? This knowledge would be very useful in view of the fact that the teacher may have standards and goals different from those of the family. He may not only be pulling the child in a direction opposed to that laid down in the family but may also be judging the child wrongly and unfairly. Very important it is that the school and the family should reinforce each other's efforts and programmes of transmitting the cultural heritage to the child. To that end parents and teachers must come closer together and share each other's values and goals.

10. Some Studies of Environmental Influence

Numerous studies have been made of the influence of environment on a child's growth and development and while their conclusions will be discussed in the relevant chapters a brief mention is here made of the detailed studies of some important areas of development.

In several studies children born normal but made to live under conditions of extreme deprivation of nourishment,

movement, fresh air and affection developed serious handicaps and mental deficiency. Complete social isolation left them at the mental level at which they were born. They did not talk, walk, stand or chew and even with very careful and diligent training they could learn just a few things showing how important environment is.

One study revealed that preschool attendance in the nursery school is associated with substantial increase in intelligence quotient and the author pleaded that within certain limits and for children of somewhat superior native endowment, intelligence is modifiable by environmental conditions.

Another group of studies have shown that in these days of congestion in towns there are fewer cases of juvenile delinquency in the areas close to playing fields than in other parts of the town. And delinquency is more prevalent in areas that are declining and where family life is not stable. Poor families living in slum conditions with little space and no equipment breed delinquents on a larger scale than affluent homes.

Children's intellectual performance and behaviour have shown considerable improvement when they are transferred from conditions of poverty, filth and neglect to affluent homes with loving care and comfortable living conditions. They develop wholesome attitudes and emotional poise. Some studies of orphans before and after their removal to homes where they were provided with all comforts confirm that poor environments retard development and happy environments stimulate growth.

From these and similar studies modern educational psychology concludes that the extent and form of mental development are dependent in part upon conditions or facts in the individual's environments during his period of growth and development, and in particular during the years of infancy and childhood.

Questions

1. What is the place of heredity and environment in education ?
2. Discuss the evidence for and against the inheritance of mental characteristics.
3. Distinguish between biological and social heredity and show what is the contribution of each to the making of an individual.
4. If what is learnt by parents is not passed on to the child, is it wasteful to educate ?
5. 'What a man has done a man can do.' Is this true ? What exactly does environment do for us ?
6. How far can education make good the defects of inheritance ?

References for Further Study

1. Blatz : *The Five Sisters* (William Morrow).
2. Fisher and Gruenberg : *Our Children*, Chapter 4 (The Viking Press).
3. Gerard : *The Body Functions : Physiology* (Wiley).
4. Hollingworth : *Gifted Children, Their Nature and Nurture* (Macmillan).
5. Jennings : *Suggestions of Modern Science Concerning Education*, Chapter 1 (Macmillan).
6. Kugelmass : *Growing Superior Children* (Appleton).
7. Morgan : *Physiological Psychology* (McGraw-Hill).
8. Nunn : *Education, Its Data and First Principles*, Chapter 9 (Arnold).
9. Riddle : *The Right of Infants* (Col. Univ. Press).
10. Ross : *Groundwork of Educational Psychology*, Chapter 4 (Harrap).

11. Schaffer : *Psychology of Adjustment* (Houghton Mifflin).
12. Scheinfeld : *You and Heredity* (Frederick A. Stokes).
13. Shull : *Heredity* (McGraw-Hill).
14. Tolman : *Purposive Behaviour in Animals and Men* (Appleton).
15. Waddle : *Introduction to Child Psychology*, Chapter 4 (Harrap).
16. Winchester : *Genetics* (Houghton Mifflin).
17. Woodworth : *Heredity and Environment* (Social Science Research Council).

CHAPTER SIX

Growth and Development

1. THE NATURE OF GROWTH

THE behaviour of a human being grows and develops. A man or a woman is called a grown-up person, and the fact of growth is brought home to us every day when we compare a child with a boy, a youth or an adult. Psychology as the science of behaviour must study its growth and development and education is concerned with shaping and moulding of behaviour and must take note of the general characteristics of growth and development.

To begin with it would be helpful to distinguish between the terms *growth* and *development* though the two terms are often used for each other. Growth means increase in size, weight or height. The body and its several parts become larger, heavier and longer. When a child has grown into a body his body has become larger, his arms and legs have become longer and his head has grown larger and heavier. But it is possible in some cases that the working of his body, arms and legs may not have kept pace with their size and his movements may be as clumsy and disorganised as they were before. We, then, say that he has grown but not developed. Development refers to the working and functioning of the organism and the individual. Growth can be measured but development can only be observed by noting changes in activity.

Some growth takes place from within, that is, the organism is so constituted that changes take place by virtue of the inner organic processes. This is called *maturation*. Given certain conditions organic growth has to be completed. Parents usually say that the baby will be able to hold its head, sit or stand after so many weeks or months. These changes are due to maturation and they are not influenced by outside conditions. Development, on the other hand, is the result of environmental influences and experience as a result of which the individual is able to move and work more effectively. All learning is included in it. A child can learn to write only when his fingers have matured enough to make fine exact movements but he has to learn it through use and exercise.

Some conditions are essential for growth. One is *food*. Without nourishing food derived from the inside organic system or given from without the child does not grow. The second condition is the supply of *hormones* from the ductless glands. We have already seen how the several glands, particularly the pituitary, contribute to the growth of the individual by pouring their secretions known as hormones into the blood stream. The third condition is *heredity* which determines the race, the sex, the size, shape and function of the body and its several limbs and organs. And the fourth condition is the *use* or *exercise* of the body and its parts. It makes for circulation of blood, co-ordination of movements and learning of skills.

2. General Characteristics of Development

There are a number of principles regarding growth and development which should be clearly understood by teachers and others who work with children. The growth of behaviour in an infant is generally so regular, and its successive stages are so predictible, that it is possible to lay down some general characteristics of the process of development of a normal child.

In the first place, growth is the result of interaction between the organism and the environment. We have already seen in a previous chapter how heredity and environment, nature and nurture, work together to determine the course of human development. By environment we mean not only the things and people among which a person lives and moves but also the food he eats, the socio-economic status of the family, the attitudes of parents toward children and the opportunities provided to them for free expression and action.

Secondly, growth is not random but orderly, and the order in which different traits develop in different individuals of any one species is the same. Human children sit before they crawl, crawl before they walk, and walk before they run. Laid on the floor with face downward they raise their chin first, then they learn to raise their chest and later they can sit with support. This sequence in development remains the same in all individuals.

Thirdly, growth is more rapid in the early years of life. In the very first year the infant grows three times in weight. It is easier to distinguish between an infant of one year and another of eighteen months than to tell a boy of twelve from one of ten years. It is because growth in early years is very rapid. That is why educationists are stressing the urgent need of providing facilities for early childhood education like nursery, kindergarten or Montessori schools.

Fourth, growth is continuous and gradual, it does not take place by leaps and bounds. Whatever form of behaviour a child learns it does so very slowly, all development and learning takes time to mature and become perfect. The child does not start standing, walking or climbing stairs all at once though people around see them doing so suddenly. He has been preparing to do so for quite some time. Minor skills, habits, new ways of acting and behaving are only slowly learned. That is why it is stressed that there is no place for hurry in growth as also in education.

Fifthly, each individual has his own rate of growth and this rate of growth he maintains throughout his life. Too often parents and teachers fret that one child does not learn as quickly as others of his age or class are doing. They seem to forget that there are large differences among individuals in their rates of growth, development and learning. And what is more such differences continue throughout their lives. Thus bright children continue to be bright and slow children continue to be slow. Now if teachers and parents could understand and appreciate this early they would not make unduly excessive demands on children placed in their care and the task of educating them would be more happy and less wasteful.

Lastly, growth takes place through the twin processes of differentiation and integration. At birth the baby is assailed by a large number of impressions of some sort coming to him by way of sight, hearing, taste, and bodily contact, and he feels that the world is 'one great, blooming, buzzing confusion' as the famous American psychologist, William James, put it. He is unable to distinguish between things and persons around him and it is only very gradually that he gains to differentiate objects and persons. In the beginning his movements are not regulated, they are random and generalised. Gradually he begins to see what movements to perform under certain situations. Seeing a bright object he tries to move his whole body toward it, later only his arm to hold it but with little success still later he moves only his hand and still later only his fingers or fore-finger and thumb. He has gradually passed from confused generalised behaviour to specific localised behaviour through a process of differentiation and discrimination. In the beginning every woman was his 'mama' but he soon learns to distinguish between his aunts, sisters, maidservant and mother. Thus he learns and develops through making and seeing differences.

But he is also learning to combine and integrate simpler patterns of behaviour into more complex ones. Walking, drinking from a cup, playing football may appear to be simple movements but on analysis they will be found to be a co-ordination of several minor movements. In walking the whole body is internally adjusted, the arms have to keep balance and the legs have not only to be regulated in their movement but also adjusted to keep balance. And then the eyes and the head have also to keep balance and guide leg movements. The baby learning to walk soon falls down because he has not learned to co-ordinate the several responses. The cyclist, the football player, the typist and all adult patterns of behaviour show integration and combination of several simple processes of both mind and body.

Thus growth and development takes place from vague mass activity to definite localised movements and from simple patterns of behaviour to more complex ones through the processes of differentiation and integration which go on side by side.

With this general knowledge of the essential characteristics of growth and development or of principles governing it, let us discuss briefly the several aspects of growth, development and learning. In a broad sense all education is growth and our discussion of the physical, emotional, mental and social aspects of growth will help to bring out clearly the main problems and topics of study in educational psychology.

3. Physical Growth

Physical development means growth in height, weight and body proportions. Parents and teachers are aware that children grow taller, heavier and stronger every day but they fail to appreciate the full importance of this growth.

We have already said that growth in body is very rapid in early years particularly from birth to the age of two. Then growth slows down till it again becomes rapid with the coming on of puberty. Again it slows down to the age of eighteen or so. The average weight of an infant at birth regardless of sex and race is 7.13 pounds, female infants weighing 0.12 pound less. During the first six months the weight of an average child is doubled. At the time of birth the average height of an infant is about 20.5 inches, it increases to 42 inches in five years. An average of 68.? inches is reached at the age of eighteen or so. It must however be clearly understood that these are averages and cannot be applied to individual children because the range of individual differences in rates of growth is very large. Attempts have been made to relate weight to height and find out norms of such relation but they are of little practical value for while height increases up to the age of twenty or so and never decreases, weight may increase or decrease according to the physical condition of the body. A child reaches adult height much sooner than his adult weight. Arms and legs increase in length as the child grows up but his skull is relatively much larger and does not grow in the same proportion.

There also take place changes inside the body, changes in digestion. heart beat and breathing. At birth the baby has no teeth and can suck only milk and water. As teeth appear soft solid food can be chewed and swallowed till he can break and masticate and digest hard nuts too. Although his heart starts beating before birth he starts breathing only after he is born. With breathing circulation of blood increases and the feeble movements of the heart gather strength. At birth the infant's heart-beats per minute are 140, gradually they decrease to 100 and come to 72 for a normal adult. Changes also take place in nerves, muscles, bones, and joints which become larger, stronger and firmer. Glands too change in their size and function.

Sex differences in young people are widely known. The common belief that girls mature sooner than boys is confirmed by detailed studies made by scientists. Girls reach their period of adolescence a year and a half sooner than boys. Generally boys are taller and heavier than girls at maturity but at the age of seven or eight an average girl is heavier. At twelve to fourteen girls are taller than boys but later on they fall back. But it must again be clearly understood that these are only averages and there are large individual differences among both boys and girls.

But bodily growth does not necessarily mean health and efficiency. Diseases and defects, malnutrition and minor disabilities lower the physical efficiency and strength of numerous children. Defective vision and hearing, bad tonsils and teeth are commonly found among school children and every teacher knows that they prevent concentration of attention and effective learning on the part of young people in the school. Then on an average every school pupil has at least one long illness which prevents his attending the school for more than a week.

The physical growth and strength of young people affects their behaviour in several very significant ways. How large, tall and heavy, and strong they are determines their attitude toward their class-mates in work and play so also their expectations of themselves. It is commonplace that the big boy bosses over smaller boys, orders them about and seldom fails to bully them. A weak, lean and small boy is meek, stands back and submissively obeys others. In games and physical activities big boys steal the show and the smaller ones just look on. Big boys think highly of themselves, expect more consideration from others and set themselves bigger tasks and assume bigger roles. Small boys think less of themselves, shirk difficult tasks and are content to do minor parts in any collective enterprise. Thus physical development is good not only for physical efficiency but also for healthy mental well-being.

4. Motor Development

But it is not uncommon to meet boys who have grown muscles and look big enough but who are functionally immature and whose movements are slow, clumsy and inapt. Motor development means the development speed, accuracy and co-ordination in movement, in the use of arms, hands, legs and other parts of the body. Many smaller boys score over bigger ones in running, jumping, manipulation, hopping on one leg, climbing a tree or a rope and in doing hundred and one things better and quicker because of their ability and smartness.

Motor development is very important for mental development, because it is through motor activities that the child makes experiments, manipulates, explores and gratifies much of his intellectual curiosity. It is through movement that he is able to know and judge the size and distance of things and places, the shape and quality of things and the depth of streams. It is through movement that the child is able to mix with friends and work with them. Motor development is basic to social development. Progressive schools lay great stress on craft work and play activities because both are very helpful to motor development and lead to intense intellectual and social activity. Some psychologists and educationists maintain that man is man not for the use he makes of his rational thinking but because of his ability to use tools and construct and create things of daily use. Motor activities inolve and stimulate mental activity.

There are no wide sex differences in motor development except that on reaching puberty boys take to activities of vigorous kind like high jump, climbing trees or football while girls take to dancing and catching ball.

Practice seems to be very necessary for developing speed and accuracy in movement but in early years the ability to perform new movements may be due to maturation. Most parents know at what age they should expect children to sit, stand or walk. The first appearance of these activities may be due to maturation but practice helps to make them quicker, more accurate and automatic.

Some children use their left hand more than their right hand. They are called left-handed as in spite of constant guidance to use the right hand they prefer to use the left in all activities in which they are free to choose. Throwing is always done by the left hand. In education the question is what should be done to the left-handed children. Such children begin to feel odd when they see everybody around using the right hand in holding, writing, catching or throwing. It gives them a feeling of inferiority and makes them shy, sensitive and reserved, and teachers make things worse by making fun of them and forcing them to use the right hand. The best time to persuade left-handed children to make the change from left to right hand is between the age of two and three years. Thereafter they should not be interfered with and on the contrary should be provided with facilities like suitable desks, scissors, and should not be allowed to feel frustrated.

5. Mental Development

People continue to learn and develop as long as they live. Different abilities appear at different stages but mental improvement continues till it begins to decay in old age. Mental development means growth in the ability to attend, perceive, observe, remember, imagine, think, use language or solve problems. As young people grow up they develop in understanding their environment and its problems, in expressing correctly their thoughts and feelings, and in forming goals and purposes.

Mental development is often described as adding to the stock of knowledge and information but if it is not accompanied by understanding and wisdom such knowledge is barren. It is also described as growth in discrimination and analysis in thinking, or as problem-solving and reasoning. But it would be better to enumerate the areas of growth more definitely.

In the first place mental development implies intellectual growth, increase in intelligence. It is a commonplace to remark that children become more intelligent as they grow up in age. During the last fifty years numerous tests have been devised to measure intelligence of children of all ages, and there are tests for infants and adults. The results of these tests show that intellectual growth is rapid in infancy, moderate in childhood and slows down in youth. When a person is tested mentally every year from the age of five to sixteen it will show if his score remains constant. Superior children continue to be superior and dull children continue to be dull.

A large part of the knowledge and understanding of children comes through attention, perception and observation. At first they are unable to discriminate between things but gradually with experience their knowledge of the external world grows richer and they are able to perceive finer differences among things. Movement plays an important part in this intellectual growth.

Secondly, mental development consists of better and

greater use of language which is not only the medium of communication but also the tool of thinking. Words are pegs on which ideas hang and the facility to use language is considered a mark of great mental development. Through long usage words acquire meanings and their use in the home, the school and the market is a part of daily living. Teachers rightly emphasise the importance of ready and accurate expression of thoughts and feelings for better social understanding. One who has this command of language can define his difficulties and problems which is the first step to their solution. It is through language that people are able to influence and persuade others. That is why most tests of language really test the ability to use language. Numerous studies have been made of the language development of children from different sections of society and they have shown that children from higher socio-economic classes have better language equipment.

Thirdly, mental development means the discovery of the universal in experience and forming what we call 'concepts'. Concepts are general ideas we form about things after having experienced a great many of them. After seeing a number of men, horses, chairs and the like a child begins to understand what is common to all men, horses and chairs. This general idea of man, horse and chair standing for all men, horses and chairs is a concept. The formation of concepts means both analysis and generalisation.

Because reading is introduced early too many children use words which they are not able to connect with things. This means they have concepts which they have memorised without having any intimate knowledge of things for which they stand. This is what is meant by saying that our education is bookish and verbal, it emphasises words without referring to any experience of things which they denote.

Concepts of children change and grow with experience. To begin with a child sees only armed and armless chairs but later when he comes across easy chairs, deck chairs, revolving chairs and the like his concept of chair grows richer and more meaningful. Therefore for growth in the formation of meaningful concepts it is necessary to provide children with large opportunities for varied contact with things. That is why systems of education for younger children like the kindergarten and the Basic System emphasise experience with concrete things and visits to places.

A fourth area of intellectual development refers to growth in the ability to solve problems. All thinking and reasoning involves meeting difficulties, facing problems and reaching out for their solutions. Many people think that children have no problems to solve but closer study will show that they have many problems. Playing games, piling blocks of wood, accounting for the missing toy or failing to open the cupboard for sweets young people are facing difficulties which are quite formidable from their point of view, and in solving them they give evidence of reasoning, insight and problem-solving ability. There is no doubt that such problems are very small and concrete but young people do make an effort to tackle them. As they grow up they are able to define their problems and even though their attempts to solve them appear crude they do try to use their past experience. Parents and teachers should come forward to help young people with information and knowledge necessary to meet their needs and to provide opportunities for varied experiences. Young people should be taught to put their best foot forward and to meet the challenge of life than to shirk hardships.

6. Emotional Development

Emotions are powerful motive forces in life and behaviour,

and schools and colleges are so much taken up by the tasks and programmes of acquiring knowledge and examinations that they neglect the growth and development of the feelings and emotions of young people. For success, efficiency and happiness the healthy development of emotions is no less important than the acquisition of knowledge and skill.

It is common knowledge that certain emotional situations like worry and anxiety, annoyance and indifference stand in the way of our effort to concentrate attention and do our best while others like strong interest, desire and enthusiasm help attention and effort. Some situations in the home and the school produce fear among children, punishment and rebuke make them timid. And some arouse affection and friendliness and make them brave and forward.

Some children are quite bright intellectually but are quite raw and immature in their feelings and emotions. They get upset at the slightest provocation, have strong likes and dislikes and are unable to adjust to others. It is the responsibility of the school and the home to provide for healthy emotional adjustment and development of children.

Recent psychology has emphasised the powerful role feelings and emotions play in life and has shown that the success and happiness of people depend largely on what control they have learned to exercise on the expression of their emotions. If education is an all-round development of personality the development of emotions cannot be neglected.

At birth and for some time thereafter the infant is either calm and steady or excited, tense and crying. This mass excitement is the first expression of emotion. At this stage there is no differentiation of excitement into anger, fear or distress. In the excitement his skin becomes red, he flourishes his arms and legs and twitches his face. It is only much later with growth of experience and knowledge of the external world that his emotions take distinct forms of anger, fear, hatred, disgust or joy.

Some psychologists have laid great stress on the value and importance of early emotional experiences and hold that they affect subsequent development of personality. Infancy and childhood are the most formative periods of life and strong emotional experiences are likely to have lasting effects on habits and attitudes of children. That is why modern education in the home and the school insists that children be treated more kindly and tenderly, and outbursts of anger, intense fear and the like which disrupt mind should be avoided.

In the course of emotional development two types of changes occur. In the first place with increasing understanding of the environment the situations which arouse anger, fear or joy change from simple to complex. In the beginning loud noise, violent pushing etc. cause fear, later children are afraid of darkness, dogs or policemen ; and still later the prospect of failure, punishment or disgrace frightens them. In the beginning the sight of mother and the feed gives joy; later sweets, toys, ride in a car or the affectionate petting of father gives pleasure, and still later the prospect of winning a prize, getting the applause of teachers and friends or a cinema show is highly pleasant. Thus in the course of development objects and situations which will arouse emotional responses change and grow in complexity. Young people's emotions are centred round concrete objects and places but older people's emotions are aroused even by very abstract and symbolic notions like injustice, exploitation, goodwill.

Secondly, changes also occur in the expression of emotions. A baby in distress gets tense, red and excited, a small child may break and throw things in anger or he may shout and wail, an older child may curse or even abuse, a young man may just turn round and walk away or may protest by keeping silent or even benon-cooperative. One other sign of emotional development is the marked self-control people exercise and display in highly trying situations. A highly educated, cultured person is he or she who keeps his or her emotions under effective check or even conceals them to such an extent that other people are not able to find out what his or her inner feelings and emotions are. All religions extol emotional balance and maturity as a highly prized virtue.

But emotional control may mean just suppression of emotions leading to hypocrisy and maladjustments or the individual may burst out violently as a reaction to rigid suppression of feelings and emotions. Modern education does not advocate suppression but expression in constructive and socially acceptable ways. Emotions are good, they are the spice of life and their development along healthy lines so that the individual enjoys doing and making things, mixing with people and contributing to the general welfare and prosperity of society should be the objective of all those who are in one way or the other responsible for the education of young people.

7. Social Development

Social development means the growing ability of an individual to live, move and work as a member of society, to learn social forms of behaviour like good form, etiquette, manners, folkways, traditions and customs and to work and get along with others for the benefit and happiness of others as well as himself. But this does not mean that he learns to accept passively the social ways. If that were so there would be no progress in society. He also learns to examine critically the customs and institutions of his community and work for the reconstruction and reformation of his society. It is only through the efforts of such social reformers who were fired with social purpose, with ideals of social service that social progress has become possible.

The social responsibility of educational institutions is to prepare young people to live in society, to socialise them and to teach them social modes and manners. This preparation begins in the family where the child learns to eat, dress and talk in ways approved by the family. He learns the language of the family, to work, live and co-operate with others ; he acquires their beliefs and attitudes; and in the school he learns to obey the rules and regulations of the institution. He obeys some and orders others, and he works for the prestige and good of the school community. He is careful not to offend others and often sacrifices his own interests for the welfare and progress of the community in which he is placed. This process of getting assimilated in society is called *socialisation*.

To begin with the child is very selfish, all his interests are centred round himself. He wants others to watch him, to see him play and eat, and it is only gradually through play and work with children of his age that he learns to think of others, share his things with them and work for the welfare and happiness of the group.

Parental occupation, the social and economic status of the family, how educated parents are, what freedom they allow to their children, the religious background of the family and the like influence the process of socialization.

Let us trace the several stages through which a child passes in the course of his social growth. It is about the age of a few weeks that the infant becomes aware of other people in the home. Some psychologists hold that it is in the second month that the infant responds to adult calls and begins to distinguish his mother. In about six months he begins to ignore some adults and respond to others. But.

the most important relation is that between the infant and his mother. She is a means of satisfying some of his urgent needs like that of feeding and affection, and psychologists have shown that lasting damage is done to human personality by the loss of mother at this stage.

As has already been pointed out the pre-school child is very self-centred and plays alone. He wants to do everything in his own way, does not share his playthings with others and wants to grab everything. Joining the school the child begins to share things with his friends, to accept rules and to find his place in his group. He chooses his friends, with some he is more intimate.

As he grows up his social awareness increases and so does his social responsibility. His own behaviour is largely influenced by what he thinks others will say about it. His own group is uppermost in his mind and loyalty to his very close friends is his chief concern.

During adolescence he strongly feels that he has a right to be accepted as an adult, to join counsels at home and in the school. Wise parents and teachers let him share responsibility and manage his own affairs independently of them.

Imitation plays a very powerful role in social development. Young people follow the example set by parents and teachers and it behoves the latter to set worthy example. Children learn a great deal from their companions also and much of the imitation is unconscious.

Another important factor is their participation in group life and work. Sharing activities, serious or recreational, children widen their social contacts, learn to compete and co-operate with others. Often he takes one of his friends as a model and starts imitating all that he does.

Finally, the customs, traditions, beliefs, ways of living, behaving and thinking of the family and the community to which a child belongs have great influence on his behaviour and help to induct him into the culture of the community.

Lately psychologists have taken pains to stress the harmful effects which unhealthy home environment has on the social adjustments of children. Homes in which parents are always quarrelling with each other, where there is great poverty, where parents drink, commit crimes, beat their children or are at war with neighbours, turn out children with distorted views of society and its working. Similarly schools in which discipline is very strict, teachers are prudes, punishment is common and severe, children are cursed and hated, develop children in very wrong directions. Happily modern educators and psychologists are aware of the harmful effects of such factors on the social development of children.

8. Development and Education

All education is growth and development, and practices, programmes and procedures of the school which do not promote the growth and development of young people are not educational and have no educational value. Old schools are being severely criticised for continuing to do things which today are believed to be useless from the point of view of children's growth and development.

Some time back the main purpose and goal of education was believed to be the acquisition of knowledge, the mastery of books and the passing of examinations. Thanks to the popularity of psychology the new goal of education is wider and more comprehensive, the growth and development of all aspects of personality. This means that the responsibilities of the teacher and the school have multiplied manifold. They have not only to impart instruction and knowledge but also to look after the health and physical needs of children, to provide for the healthy development of their feelings and emotions, to train mind and intellect for observation, analytical study and investigation, and to cultivate among young people healthy social attitudes and adjustments. This new outlook stresses all-round development of human personality, physical, mental, emotional and social. Of course this will greatly add to the responsibilities of the school and what other institutions like the home and the temple were expected to do in the past will now be undertaken by the school. But it is a healthy trend and if it greatly adds to the responsibility and burden of the teacher and the school, it is hoped in course of time it will also add to their importance and value and enhance the prestige of the teacher.

The emphasis on children's development has made parents and teachers shed their old outworn ideas about what they should do to children placed in their charge. They are now anxious to provide for the developmental needs of children. This will correct the defects of one-sided development of children. Too many children in school have bad health and poor physique, some of them are good in studies but other aspects of their growth have been neglected, some are poor in studies not because for want of intelligence and diligence but because they are ready victims of their raw emotions and fly into rage at every small thing. others are healthy in body, steady in their work but too shy to mix with others. These are examples of one-sided and defective development, and such students are the responsibility of the school.

Some educational psychologists insist that aims of education can be valid only if they are consistent with sound development theory, and have tried to describe the processes in concrete terms and to relate them to educational aims.

J. E. Anderson contrasting the infant and the adult finds

that the process of development moves along five interrelated lines each of which suggests a developmental aim of education. As a result of development the individual becomes *more and more sensitive* to different kinds of stimuli, more and more fully aware of his world. Secondly with development there is an enormous *increase in the range, variety and character of his responses* to his world. Thirdly as the child grows older he becomes capable of *functioning at levels of greater and greater complexity* and is able to solve problems demanding more refined and complex performance in perception, thinking and expression. Fourthly with the help of *memory* and *imagination* he can expand his span of activity backward into the past and forward into the future. Lastly development must bring with it *control and freedom*. With greater control over himself and the environment the individual becomes free, independent and self-reliant. Now who can gainsay that these are very sound educational aims and good parents, good teachers and good communities should exert their best to create opportunities for children that development should proceed along these lines and these aims should be realized.

R. J. Havighurst sees development as a series of learning tasks which he defines as tasks which arise at or about a certain period in the life of an individual, successful achievement of which leads to his happiness and to success in later tasks, while failure leads to unhappiness, disapproval of society and difficulty with later tasks. A task is appropriate for an individual when he has matured for it physically, when society expects it and when he is mentally competent for it. Here is a list of the developmental tasks given by Havighurst for middle childhood :

1. Learning physical skills necessary for ordinary games

2. Building wholesome attitudes toward oneself as a growing organism
3. Learning to get along with age-mates
4. Learning an appropriate male or female role
5. Developing fundamental skills in reading, writing and calculating
6. Developing concepts necessary for everyday living
7. Developing conscience, morality and scale of values
8. Achieving personal independence
9. Developing attitudes toward social groups and institutions.

These tasks are for American children. They may be slightly different for Indian children. They help in discovering and stating the purposes of education in the schools, and in timing the educational efforts. Quite a few scholars have attempted the task of expressing in concrete details the development tasks which form the basis of the valid aims of education. They are E. H. Erikson, A. Gessel, A. T. Jersild and J. Piaget.

Questions

1. Distinguish between growth, development and maturation by giving examples.
2. What are the general characteristics of growth among human children? Illustrate your answer.
3. Show what principles govern the development of children. Explain them in detail.
4. What is the course of development in small children of five years? What physical movements, mental activities and social characteristics are found in them?
5. 'Education is growth.' Discuss this statement. What factors help growth?

6. What do you understand by motor development? How do maturation and practice help it?
7. Describe some of the main aspects of mental development. How do children grow in the formation of concepts?
8. What is the goal of emotional development? How do children grow emotionally?
9. Trace the broad outlines of the course of social development among children. What important factors help it?
10. Outline a broad programme of school activities which will promote physical, mental, emotional and social development. What is the task of the teacher in respect of an all-round growth of personality?

References for Further Study

1. Douglass and Holland : *Fundamentals of Educational Psychology* (Macmillan).
2. Gates, Jersild, McConnel and Chaliman : *Educational Psychology* (Macmillan).
3. Griffith : *An Introduction to Educational Psychology* (Rinehart).
4. Jordan : *Educational Psychology* (Henry Holt).
5. Pintner : *Educational Psychology* (Henry Holt).
6. Skinner : *Educational Psychology* (Prentice-Hall).
7. Sorenson : *Psychology in Education* (McGraw-Hill).
8. Anderson, J. E. : *The Psychology of Development and Personality Adjustment* (Holt, Rinehart and Winston).
9. Havighurst R. J. : *Human Development and Education* (Longmans).

CHAPTER SEVEN

Instinctive Behaviour

THE individual is a product of both heredity and environment ; his character and personality are the outcome of his native, inborn capacities, and the changes and developments which occur under the influence of environment, and his behaviour is partly natural, inherited and non-learnt and partly acquired and learnt. The teacher, if he is to provide for an all-round development of the individual child, must know what elements in human nature are original, and what are acquired and developed as a result of experience. In this chapter we are concerned wholly with the native, inherited types of behaviour particularly with instincts.

1. TYPES OF ORIGINAL BEHAVIOUR

Firstly, we have the *organic reflexes* such as breathing, circulation of blood, digestion, secretion. They are stimulated from within the organism itself and are useful for its health and welfare. They do not have to be learnt and once started go on throughout life. They are automatic and cannot be changed or modified without danger to health. Secondly, there are *reflexes* like blinking, coughing, sneezing. the knee-jerk, swallowing. They have already been mentioned in connection with the nervous system. They are also to a large degree fixed, automatic and uniform, and serve the welfare of the organism. But they follow regularly only when a given stimulus is presented and are limited to various parts of the body. Thirdly, there are such complex activities as shrinking or running away from injury or danger, seeking food and shelter, curiosity, fighting, collecting or constructing. They are more or less complex responses to a more or less complex group of stimuli of external and internal origin. They are inherited, not learnt, and like every type of innate behaviour, serve a biological end. They are termed *instincts*. Since they can be modified in a variety of ways, they offer a rich opportunity to the teacher to exercise his influence for the well-being of young people, and make possible the entire educational effort.

2. Reflex Action

A reflex action or reflex is a constant, uniform, definite and direct response to a given stimulus and is caused by an innate connection in the nervous system between the organ which receives the stimulus and the muscles or glands which make the response. If anything irritates our nostrils, sneezing at once occurs. If a sharp tap is given just below the knee-cap, the leg will be automatically extended. If a bright light faces us, the pupil of our eye contracts. These responses are quick and occur always and as soon as the stimulus is presented. They are involuntary and often we are not conscious of them. They are not learnt and they are always ready for action. They are local movements, limited to a particular part of the body.

Reflex actions do not call for much attention at the hand of the educator. They are hardly educable. Most of them are merely defence reactions of the organism to ward off injury ; of some we are not even conscious, e.g. the contraction of the pupil in bright light; and some cannot be controlled. Stand behind a window with glass panes and let somebody throw suddenly and violently a bucketful of water against the window. You may know full well that the glass stands between you and the water, but you cannot help wincing. Most of the activities of infants are of the reflex type and their training consists in helping them to acquire control over such reflex actions as excretion.

3. The Conditioned Reflex

Though reflex actions cannot be modified or educated to an appreciable extent, they can be 'conditioned', that is, aroused by a stimulus different from the original stimulus. Every reflex act is touched off by some special kind of stimulus. The contraction of the pupil is caused by bright light, the knee-jerk by a tap under the knee. Now if along with this special stimulus, some other stimulus is vigorously presented, it usually makes the response stronger. When the two stimuli are given together a number of times, the second stimulus by itself is enough to bring about a response similar to that which first appeared. Bright light makes the pupil of the eye contract. If a bell is sounded along with the presentation of bright light quite a number of times the bell alone will make the pupil contract. This is a *conditioned reflex*. Ivan Pavlov, a great Russian physiologist, studied the conditioned reflex very thoroughly. He found that if a bell is rung in the presence of a dog, the dog shows no definite response. If, however, each time the bell is rung the dog is given a piece of meat, the dog will soon excrete saliva on the ringing of the bell alone. A reflex aroused in this way by a substitute stimulus is called a conditioned reflex.

This connection between the response and the substitute stimulus dies out if the original stimulus is discontinued. The substitute stimulus has to be presented together with, or just before, the original stimulus. If the bell is rung after the food has been presented no conditioning will take place.

Such conditioning is common in human experience as well. Children's mouths water when they see pictures, or listen to or read descriptions, of delicious dishes. Vomiting is a reflex act but in many adults it is a conditioned reflex. The jerks and jolts together with the smell of petrol while travelling in lorry cause many people to vomit. But some start vomiting before starting the journey, for others a mere smell of petrol or even passing by a lorry-stand is enough to start vomiting. With others the mere sight of somebody else vomiting is enough to touch off the response.

Conditioning is now used as a general term for so modifying behaviour that a different stimulus can arouse an activity. It is 'associative shifting', shifting the burden of arousing response to a substitute stimulus. Detailed studies of conditioning involuntary process and emotions in men and animals have yielded valuable data for education and helped the educator to control and influence the behaviour of children. Such facts will be discussed later in connection with emotional behaviour and learning.

4. INSTINCTS

The individual grows and develops through self-activity and this self-activity manifests itself in various forms. Children have a strong desire to build and construct, and often break things in order to reconstruct. They show a natural eagerness to know more about their environment, have a deep interest in collecting all sorts of things, wish to excel their playmates, quarrel when they are obstructed, are frightened by danger. No child has been taught to do any of these things. They are inborn natural tendencies to action and underlie all thought and behaviour. We call them instincts. Curiosity, fear, constructing, collecting, fighting, emulation, are some of the common instincts and serve as the essential springs or motive powers of all human behaviour. They are the bases from which the character and will of individuals and of communities and nations are gradually developed under the guidance and control of intellect.

Because the life of animals below the human level is completely controlled by instincts, it is believed by some that they are absent in men. Instincts are thought to be the special provision that nature has made for the guidance of creatures lower than man. We know too well how the young ones of the buffalo, the horse, etc. begin to swim just a few days after their birth, when they have had no opportunity to learn. Birds build peculiar kinds of nests, seek their food, fear harmful objects, instinctively. They begin their migrations as seasons come and go, without any consciousness that they are doing so to preserve themselves and their species. Insect life affords the most striking examples of purely instinctive actions. There are many instances of insects that invariably lay their eggs in the only places where the grubs, when hatched, will find the food they need and can eat. Certain beetles lay their eggs in small masses of dung. The mason-wasp lays its eggs in a mud nest, fills up the space with caterpillars which it paralyses by means of well-directed stings, and seals the nest up. The caterpillars remain a supply of fresh animal food for the young which the parent will never see and of whose needs it can have no knowledge.

Instincts are not altogether absent in man. We do not readily recognise instincts in man because his are of a more complex type, modified and complicated by development. James tells us that man possesses at least as many instincts as lower animals do. Others claim that the number of instincts in man is far greater than that in animal life.

Instinct is native behaviour as contrasted with what is learnt or acquired through experience. The individual has no fore-knowledge of what he is going to do in instinctive behaviour. Instincts are inborn, innate, original tendencies which make up the physical and mental capital with which an individual starts the business of life. Instinctive behaviour is directed towards the attainment of ends useful to the individual and the race.

5. Instinctive and Reflex Actions

Perhaps the nature of instinct would become clear if we compare it with a reflex. In the first place both instincts and reflexes are natural and inborn. The swimming of the young horse and the curiosity of the children are as much inherited and original as sneezing or blinking. They are not learnt or acquired but every creature begins life with them. If 'instinctive' means only 'native', then a reflex action is as much 'instinctive' as any typical instinctive action. Secondly, attention to the directed end is absent in both. We have no fore-knowledge of how we are going to act. In a sense both are automatic and mechanical. Reflex acts always occur in a fixed and regular way in response to an external stimulus. They occur when the stimulus is present and when it is present they occur naturally and necessarily. Thus when a bit of dust flies into the eye, certain movements of the eyelids follow, which tend to get rid of the intrusive speck of dust. Instinctive action also shows itself to be fixed, regular and automatic in the beginning but later on gets modified. Thirdly, both are directed to the attainment of ends biologically useful to the individual. They are very essential to the welfare of the organism. Fourthly, both are universal and are found in all the members of any one species. More precisely they are not individual traits but racial characteristics.

But in spite of these resemblances there are certain differences which distinguish them from each other. Instinctive behaviour is capable of being modified and developed in numerous ways while reflex actions are thoroughly mechanical. We blink our eyes, sneeze or withdraw a leg in very much the same way as our ancestors did many centuries ago. Secondly, instinctive behaviour is accompanied by conscious processes while the reflex behaviour is purely biological and is determined solely by physiological stimuli. Thirdly, as must have been clear by now, reflex action is simpler than an instinct. This has led many to believe that an instinct is merely a compound of reflexes, that the difference between the two is one of degree and not of kind. Such a view is taken by behaviourists who deny the mental side of human behaviour.

6. Characteristics of an Instinct

All this original equipment of instinctive drives or urges constitutes the mainspring of behaviour in children, and later through modification and development, of adult behaviour as well. Instincts provide the motive forces of our life and behaviour and though they are modified by other instincts and experience, they are often too plainly revealed in human behaviour. Let us therefore study their chief characteristics.

In the first place, instinctive behaviour as has been stressed above, is clearly innate or native as distinguished from those modes of behaviour which are learnt in the course of experience. Some define them as ancestral habits but we have already seen that habits and skills acquired by parents are not passed on to children. A father may be good at cycling, typewriting, tennis and yet his child has to learn these things from the beginning. The use of language was made by our parents, forefathers and ancestors and it is the same language that we use today. But all the same we had to learn it—we did not get it by inheritance. Instincts are not inherited ancestral habits. All that is meant by describing them as innate is that they are there from the beginning and are not learnt by experience.

Secondly, though we speak of instinctive action or behaviour, an instinct is more a tendency or disposition to act or behave. In a reflex action a stimulus leads to a response but in an instinct what is aroused is a tendency which persists for a time and gives rise to certain preparatory reactions before issuing into activity. When a child is frightened by a dog, he does not run away simply and forthwith. He takes stock of the situation, his lips begin to tremble, he is excited, he thinks of picking up a stone and throwing it at the dog, he may drop this plan, and shout for help and run away. He is making preparations to respond in a particular manner. The stimulus only arouses these preparatory responses because instinct is not a particular action but a tendency to response of a particular kind.

Thirdly, instincts are universal. They are not peculiar to an individual but are characteristic of the entire species. All members of a species respond in the same way. At a given stage normal children are expected to show the same instinctive behaviour. An accurate knowledge of instinct is necessary for all teachers and parents. Knowing the instinctive behaviour of one child, they can with reasonable assurance expect similar behaviour from other children.

Fourthly, instincts tend towards the well-being of the species and its individual members. Nest-building, migration, feeding, mating, fighting and the like are quite essential for the survival of the species as well as of individuals. Fear helps to escape danger, feeding to sustain oneself, fighting to get rid of the enemy and so on.

Fifthly, instincts do not imply any foresight of a useful end. They serve us but there is no forethought of this service. Commonsense may revolt at this blindness of instincts, but are we not afraid of a number of objects which we know are quite harmless? Although instinctive behaviour involves such mental processes as attention, perception, persistence of effort, yet the individual is seldom if ever conscious of the biological purpose which an instinct serves.

Sixthly, instinctive responses are capable of modification, adaptation and development under the guidance of experience, intelligence and environment. An examination of the origin and growth of human institutions would reveal that they are traceable to some instinct or the other. Take the case of law courts and the elaborate structure of law and order. Are they not merely a highly developed expression of the instincts of fear and fighting? The primary simple fear and hand-to-hand fighting have developed into filing lawsuits. The fact that man is plastic and capable of education depends on his original, instinctive nature being modifiable. Curiosity may develop into an ardent desire for truth, research and study or into a vicious habit of probing into the secrets of neighbours. It is certainly the task of education to see that instincts are modified in useful and desirable ways.

Lastly, not all instincts are ready for use at birth. Every instinct has its period of appearance, maturity and weakening. It may not be equally powerful at every stage of an individual's life. Thus social play involving rivalry, teasing, teamwork appears much later than free play of sheer physical activity. Pugnacity and play seem to become weaker with age. Sex instinct certainly does not appear till puberty when a boy or girl becomes more self-conscious in the presence of the opposite sex. Many believe that instincts are 'transitory', meaning thereby that they appear at certain periods of life and then die away unless they have opportunity of expression. But the fact seems to be that instincts take time to appear and mature and though it is very difficult to fix any period when specific instincts will take birth and mature, the educator should be on the look-out for evidence of new and growing interests among young people and provide wholesome opportunities for their expression, exercise and development.

7. Principal Instincts of Man

Instincts have been defined and classified in a variety of ways but McDougall's treatment in his *Social Psychology* remains the most outstanding. He defines instinct as 'an innate disposition which determines an organism to perceive or pay attention to any object of a certain class, and to experience in its presence a certain emotional excitement and impulse to action, which finds expression in a specific mode of behaviour in relation to that object.' Thus according to him it has cognitive, affective and conative elements. When a child is frightened by a dog, he perceives a certain situation and understands the extent of danger, he has the emotion of fear and he tries to run away or throw stones at the dog. In this instinctive behaviour he knows, feels and acts with regard to a particular situation.

McDougall believes that every instinct is connected with a specific emotion and offers the following list :—

Instinct	*Emotion accompanying it*
Flight or escape	Fear
Pugnacity or combat	Anger
Repulsion or repugnance	Disgust
Curiosity	Wonder
Parental instinct	Tender emotion
Construction	Feeling of creativeness
Acquisition	Feeling of ownership
Gregariousness	Feeling of loneliness
Reproduction	Lust
Self-assertion	Elation

Instinct	*Emotion accompanying it*
Self-abasement	Negative self-feeling or subjection
Food-seeking	Craving for food
Appeal	Distress
Laughter	Amusement

These he calls specific tendencies as they are aroused in definite concrete situations. Besides them there are non-specific, innate tendencies like play, imitation, suggestion and sympathy, which are aroused in all sorts of situations.

Tansley classifies instincts into three heads : the individual instincts like food-seeking, curiosity, flight, pugnacity and others which are useful for the preservation of an individual ; the social instinct of gregariousness which helps him to live as a member of a group; and the sex instincts like mating and the parental instinct are concerned with reproduction and perpetuation of species.

8. Methods of Modifying Instincts

The native equipment of the child in the way of instincts must be the starting-point in the process of education. It is the original capital with which he starts life, and the scope of possible education is determined by the extent and way in which it is modified and adapted. In animals most of the instinctive urges to behaviour are more or less perfect and ready for action, but the human child with his uniquely long period of immaturity is born more helpless. His instincts are more incomplete and consequently more adaptable. In fact they can be modified, adapted and developed in a large variety of ways. Children have a vague but strong desire to collect and hoard things. They collect all sorts of things, labels, boxes, feathers, buttons and what not. It may lead them to stealing or working hard to earn such collections. It may prompt them to collect good, useful things, give them hobbies which may later prove economically helpful or make them misers hoarding every pie they can lay hold of. Instincts provide the driving power and whether that power will be used for the welfare of the individual and society or not will rest on how these tendencies are allowed to work and develop by environment. It is the duty of education to modify them into healthy forms so that they may lead to more socially desirable forms of behaviour. Let us discuss some of the ways in which it is done.

In the first place, instincts die through *disuse*. If opportunities for exercise and expression are denied to a tendency, it may gradually atrophy and become extinct. Environment may be so controlled that the impulse is thwarted and gradually dies away. Birds kept in a cage for a long time and denied all opportunity to fly, do not fly when released from bondage. Children given to thumb-sucking give up the habit if for some time their arms are placed in sleeves which they cannot bend. The same method can be used in education. To discipline and control child behaviour, the situations that lead to undesirable responses are kept away from him. Many parents do not let their children mix and play with those children who are considered wicked and spoilt. Not having a wrong example to follow they will not know wickedness and profanity. Poor children are inclined to steal things belonging to the school and a wise teacher is careful that valuable articles are not left unguarded. After a classroom test pupils are given to whispering to compare answers or opinions about questions. This can be avoided by letting them have some time for conversation and denying them an opportunity for stealthy whispering. But firstly, not using an instinct is no guarantee that it will die out. It may break out with greater vigour later. Merely imprisoning the criminal is not enough to make him behave better. Secondly, it is negative training to starve an instinct from expression. In education, what is more important is to cultivate right impulses rather than to kill wrong ones. Thirdly, it is very difficult to be sure about the time when any definite instinct appears so that its exercise may be guarded against. And any premature attempt to keep away from the child unworthy experiences may do more harm than good.

Secondly, the expression of an instinct may be associated with positive pain so that it is not expressed again. This method of *punishment* is very common and many parents and teachers use it. They have a code of fines and penalties to check undesirable behaviour on the part of children. Idleness is punished by making them stay after school hours. Teachers often ask them to write 500 times, 'I must not tell lies again.' The aim is to build a painful association between idleness and staying after school hours so that the former may not be repeated. The method often succeeds because there is a general desire among all of us to avoid pain and the fear of punishment prevents us from doing many wrong things. But usually there is no connection between the wrong and the punishment and children do not understand why they have been punished. Sometimes the punishment is too severe and out of all proportion to the offence and children rebel against it to such an extent that they develop a distaste for all work. Only when the punishment is a direct and natural consequence of the child's behaviour, the child may desist. Extensive laboratory studies have been made of the effect of punishment in correcting wrong response but it is forgotten that the classroom is a different situation from the laboratory. In the classroom a child is punished not because he has committed any offence but because he has been found out and he connects punishment not with offence but with detection. Hence most of the punishments are not effective. Finally, punishment is at best a negative method. It may be used in eliminating a wrong response; it has no value as an incentive for the development of the right one.

The third method is a protest against the first two. Too severe a control by denying opportunities for self-expression and by imposing heavy punishments kills initiative among the children and breaks their spirit. Therefore they should be allowed full *freedom* to do what they wish and as they please. It is hoped that free, unrestricted expression will ultimately lead to an understanding of the undesirability of behaviour. Such ideas are a revolt against the too strict discipline practised in old days and rightly emphasise that every child is best educated through free and creative self-expression and self-activity. A. S. Neill, the founder of Summerhill School, has, in his books *A Dominie Log* and *The Dreadful School*, made a strong plea for freedom in schools. Freedom is essential because only under freedom can the child grow in his natural way. All discipline, suggestion, guidance and direction should be given up and children should be encouraged to learn things for themselves and by themselves, unobstructed by fear and hate. This method of absolute freedom is not practicable, for the freedom of one child is sure to stand in the way of the freedom of others and when rights clash, some sort of government in which one has to desist from some types of behaviour unfavourable to others is found necessary. Neill has not been able to do without it. Secondly, all instincts cannot be given equal opportunity of expression at the same time. If they clash, as they often do, some have to be suppressed in favour of others. The instinct to acquire property has very often to yield to the parental instinct and children often land themselves in dangerous situations to satisfy their curiosity. Thirdly, if full freedom is allowed from the very beginning, the continued exercise of instincts may lead to the formation of strong habits which may later be very hard to break. Still, this method of free expression is not without value if it is used with caution and with full consideration of the circumstances in each case.

Fourthly, instincts may neither be suppressed nor given free play but may be guided or redirected into healthier channels. This is known as the method of *sublimation*, of substituting worthy for unworthy motives. When circumstances do not permit the obvious means of gratifying an instinctive urge, the child may satisfy it directly. If he wants to run away from home, he may satisfy his craving by reading travel books. If he wants to fight in self-defence or in personal rivalry, he may be asked to fight for a cause or to defend, protect or rescue the weak. Sublimation involves a change of ideas and attitudes, the underlying theory being that it is possible to transfer the urge or energy connected with an instinct to another activity different from that to which it usually leads. The sex instinct, for example, cannot be gratified directly as it appears but the urge or drive may be attracted to some other form of creative work. Thus the disappointed lover or the adolescent may work off the sex interest in poetry, art or music. Sublimation often means nothing more than replacing the fantastic and fanciful by the practicable motive. For many women the profession of nursing or teaching sublimates the sex instinct. Vigorous physical games like hockey and football or boxing and wrestling sublimate among adolescents a tendency towards fighting. Young boys have a tendency towards rowdyism, an expression of the gang instinct. Keep them under a stern discipline and deny them any chance to be rowdy, or punish them every time they behave in a rowdy way, and you have done practically nothing to train them along right lines. You have either made them resent you and your programme or have persuaded them to postpone their rowdyism till such time when your control will be no more. But give them something worthwhile to do with themselves, redirect their fund of energy into creative and constructive channels where something done and achieved really matters, and you have started them on the road to good and sane social living.

Sublimation is by far the most satisfactory way of dealing with instinctive drives and urges. It neither represses instincts nor gives them a free rein. It is a great reconstructive method harnessing the strong mainsprings of behaviour to worthwhile ends and pursuits. A progressive school rightly maintains a large number of extra-curricular activities like games, dramatics, a library, debating societies, music clubs, scouting, hobbies, a museum, a magazine, so that young people may have a large number and variety of healthy outlets for their growing and expanding interests. Some teachers are able to persuade pupils to help them in class-control, organising games, social functions, hostel programmes and the like. Such co-operation from pupils provides valuable opportunities to the abler, older and stronger boys to exercise leadership and express their instinct for self-assertion which otherwise is expressed by the superior attitude and ability of the teacher. Many schools have developed a very stimulating atmosphere in which young people not only cultivate intellectual interests but form professional, artistic or literary ambitions or imbibe ideals for social service. In most cases it is the noble example of the headmaster and his staff which provides the leaven but the educational values achieved are great and noteworthy.

9. The Theory of Instincts

Instinct theories were furthered by William McDougall and Edward L. Thorndike both listing important instincts motivating behaviour. McDougall emphasised that instincts help us to perceive certain stimuli, experience emotions and act in a certain way. Perception and action can be modified but emotions remain the core of instinct and do not change much. Thorndike simply defined instinct as unlearned behaviour and left out its emotional aspect.

Just before and during the First World War theories of instincts were very popular and all branches of thought used the term. The economists talked of the instinct of workmanship and the sociologist of the instincts of groups. Freud proposed two fundamental instincts of sex and self-preservation and Jung suggested three primary instincts of nutrition, sex and herd.

The theory of instincts was first seriously challenged by L. L. Bernard who in his book called *Instinct* pointed out that the term is too generalised on the one hand and too narrowly used on the other. We speak of the sex or social instinct as also of the instinct to wipe one's lips. Later psychologists like Bernard, Dunlap, Watson and Woodworth severely criticised the instinct doctrine. Most human behaviour called instinctive is greatly affected by learning and is not innate. Woodworth pointed out that the term 'instinct' was being used to denote both a kind of behaviour and an urge or impulse to behave. The latter he called 'drive'. The drive is the motivating power and habits too can supply it. Hence it is not true as McDougall believes that all motivating power comes from a few instincts. Many anthropologists urged that human urges change with culture patterns in which people live and thus these instincts are not as universal and innate as McDougall would have us believe.

10. Needs, Drives and Motives

The most obvious human needs are those of physical survival and bodily comfort. These include the needs for food, air and drink; for protection from extremes of temperature and physical injury; for physical satisfaction of the sex urge which arises with the onset of puberty. The sex urge is complicated by several psychological needs of self-expression such as the great desire to be considered a lovable person, an ideal friend or a handsome husband.

There are other needs which are less obvious but not less important. Human beings have certain capacities, some of them are common to all and some of them are peculiar to individuals. Every individual seeks to express, exercise and develop them. In a way he is seeking from his very birth to develop all that he is capable of, to become what he potentially is. This need may be described as one for self-expression, self-development or self-realisation but it is clear that every one of us has need to use his powers: to do and make things, to try and experiment, to sail into uncharted seas. He wants to use his powers or capacities. These capacities or abilities contain within themselves the motive power to start them or keep them going. These needs are too numerous to need detailed description.

All human behaviour arises from some urge whether that urge is instinctive or acquired. Woodworth calls it a 'drive' meaning the energy that sets it going. Animal psychologists use the term for energy or action arising out of physiological needs like hunger, thirst, sex fatigue, elimination, protection from danger and the like. These drives often influence each other. For example, thirst reduces hunger and thirst and hunger considerably weaken sex urge. Several experiments have been made to study the mutual effects of drives and to measure their relative strengths.

Some of these drives are obviously natural and primitive but they get complicated, modified and re-shaped.

Take for example the parental drive. Although it is not so well defined as hunger or thirst the maternal urge for the care and upbringing of children is very powerful and universal. It is also natural and instinctive but are we quite sure that the mother's attitude is not influenced by circumstances outside the maternal relationship? There are teachers and nurses who have done and felt all that a father or a mother does and feels. Although the biological link is absent the psychological relation is very much similar. The parental drive, therefore, may have much that is due to developmental factors.

Then there are activity drives which lead to the use and exercise of capacities of various kinds. There is a drive to the use of muscles or the exercise of sense-organs or of intellect in exploring and discovering new things or for social life in which there is an urge to give and accept things, to and from the group in which we live, the need to love and be loved, to share the joys and sorrows of others, to co-operate with them in projects that will be for general well-being. Then there is the drive to seek self-esteem.

These drives are also connected with endocrine gland secretions. The removal of the pituitary or adrenal glands in rats as well as in other animals has been shown to lead to a reduction in general activity. Thirst and hunger drives have distinct bodily conditions. But the environmental situations in which primary drives work may later on lead to behaviour similar to that aroused by primary stimulus. Hunger in the beginning was caused by the contractions of the stomach but later may be roused by good food and company.

But soon psychologists began to realise that the term 'drive' is inadequate to describe all of human motivation. Human behaviour is far more complex than animal behaviour and physiological urges by themselves cannot account for all types of behaviour. For example, many individuals seem driven by a desire to collect books or works of art, others collect money or other forms of property, still others seem driven to acquire the good opinions of others. There are numerous social urges besides physiological drives and the term 'motives' is used to include both types.

Several psychologists have played at the game of listing human motives. Some classify motives into *primary* and *secondary*. Primary drives or motives are mainly physiological and satisfy tissue needs for nourishment, water, air and sex, secondary motives are acquired through learning and socialisation. One author speaks of biological and psychological needs like those of security, affection, social approval or self-esteem. The four fundamental wishes stressed by W. I. Thomas are security, sexual and social response, recognition and adventure or new experience. This list was very popular with social psychologists for a time and even now many hold that a wholesome and well-adjusted personality must realise more or less adequate satisfaction of these wishes. Some authors use the terms 'biogenic' or *primary* and 'psychogenic' or *secondary* needs, the latter meaning needs arising from social experience. A. H. Maslow's list is an hierarchy of five basic needs, one leading to the other in order of satisfaction and development. They are :

1. Physiological needs—hunger, thirst, sex and physical activity.
2. Safety needs—security from physical and mental deprivation.
3. Need for belongingness and affection.

4. Esteem needs—the needs for self-respect, recognition and prestige.
5. The need for self-actualisation—the need to realise all that one is capable of becoming, the need for self-expression and self-realisation.

Attempts have been made to measure the relative strength of human motives. The best known are those of Thorndike and Poffenberger who sought to collect objective data on the relative strength of human motives in any group. But motives are very difficult to define and measure and unfortunately psychologists' lists of motives do not agree. Though our drives and motives are there with us, they may be considerably affected by a number of temporary factors like rewards and punishments or praise and blame. Success leads to quicker and better activity and failure has a damping effect. These are *incentives* and the study of their effect has been made use of by industrialists quick to increase production and by teachers anxious to produce better results in public examinations.

Questions

1. What do you understand by instincts ? How do they differ from reflexes ? Discuss the possible ways of dealing with instincts in children.
2. What part do instincts play in the formation of character and how best can they be used for educational ends ?
3. Mention some of the chief instincts of children and show by citing one example how they can be used by the teacher.
4. Mention some of the main characteristics of instinctive behaviour and show what aspect of it makes education possible.

5. What is the place of repression and freedom in education?
6. What is 'a conditioned reflex'? Discuss its place in education.
7. What is the place of punishment in education? Should children be punished for every offence?
8. 'Let children alone and free to do what they like.' Do you approve of this principle in education?
9. What is sublimation? Discuss its place and value in education. What steps would you take in your school to sublimate the instinctive drives of young people?
10. Distinguish between drive and motive, between primary and secondary needs. Discuss the place and value of the desires for security and affection in education.

REFERENCES FOR FURTHER STUDY

1. Averill: *Elements of Educational Psychology* (Harrap).
2. Bode: *Modern Educational Theories* (Macmillan).
3. Dennis: *Readings in General Psychology* (Prentice-Hall).
4. *Elementary Educational Psychology*, ed. C. E. Skinner, (Prentice-Hall).
5. Fisher: *Mothers and Children* (Henry Holt).
6. Judd: *Psychology of Secondary Education* (Ginn).
7. Kilpatrick: *Foundation of Method* (Macmillan).
8. McDougall: *Introduction to Social Psychology* (Methuen).
9. McDougall: *An Outline of Psychology* (Methuen).
10. Menninger: *The Human Mind* (Knopf).
11. Munn: *The Evolution and Growth of Human Behavior* (Houghton Mifflin).
12. Norsworthy and Whitely: *Psychology of Childhood* (Macmillan).

13. Pressey and Robinson : *Psychology and the New Education* (Harper).
14. Rivlin : *Education for Adjustment* (Appleton).
15. Schaffer : *The Psychology of Adjustment* (Houghton Mifflin).
16. Symonds : *The Dynamics of Human Adjustment* (Appleton).
17. Thomson : *Instinct, Intelligence and Character* (Allen & Unwin).
18. Thorndike : *The Original Nature of Man* (Col. Univ. Press).
19. Thorndike : *Educational Psychology*, Vol. II, (Teachers College, Columbia University).
20. Watson : *Behaviourism* (Macmillan).
21. Woodruff : *Psychology of Teaching* (Longmans).
22. Young : *Motivation of Human Behaviour* (Wiley).

CHAPTER EIGHT

Some Prominent Instincts and Needs

INSTINCTS have been described as the great dynamic forces of human nature which determine the character, life and behaviour of the individual. If there can be no true education except through the activity of the child himself, the teacher should not only understand these mainsprings of activity, instincts, but should also appeal to them in as many ways as possible. Education is largely a co-operative enterprise in which the teacher and his pupils work together and help each other. To make them active partners in their own education, the teacher must work with his pupils' native instinctive tendencies, for that is the only way to arouse their best responses. Our whole educational effort and process must have its roots deep in the natural inborn tendencies of the child and no teacher can afford to work against them. In this chapter an attempt will be made to discuss in detail some of the prominent instincts and to show how best the teacher can make use of them.

1. CURIOSITY

The instinct of curiosity is aroused by strange, unfamiliar objects, and the accompanying emotion is wonder. The child approaches and examines objects in order to know more about them. This instinct is very powerful among children and helps them to understand their environment. Childhood is an age of exploration and children turn things over, break things, climb trees, wade in water and do scores of other things to satisfy their thirst for knowledge. Curiosity has been called the mother of knowledge and no doubt the vast body of knowledge which man has acquired in the field of science, art and philosophy, and the laboratories, libraries, research institutions he has built, are a living monument to the universal impulses to know and investigate. But curiosity may wrongly develop into idle inquisitiveness, a bad habit of asking questions just for the fun of it or of probing into other peoples' affairs. It is clearly the responsibility of education to guide and direct this impulse for knowledge into useful channels and transform it into habits of intelligent and constructive thinking.

Too often before the end of school life this instinct is completely suppressed by the over-emphasis on book knowledge and rote memory. The teacher should try to keep it alive and help its normal development. Curiosity is aroused by strange, unfamiliar objects but if the objects are too strange and unfamiliar, the child either fears and shuns them or is altogether indifferent to them. Therefore the teacher must present his material and lessons in such a manner that children consider them new enough to be known and understood and at the same time do not consider them too strange to be known and learnt. Experienced teachers base every new lesson on the knowledge already acquired and connect it with previous lessons so that children may not be upset by the newness of facts presented. But at the same time they are continually preparing their class for something wonderful coming ahead and keep alive their restless curiosity to know and learn more fully. Thus it is that the grading of lessons is one of the most difficult and one of the most important of the teacher's responsibilities.

Children's mental life is mostly sensory and they are interested in concrete things which they can see, touch, handle or manipulate. Instruction in primary classes for the most part should deal with the concrete and the sensory, and it is only much later that general and abstract ideas may be brought in. To arouse healthy and vigorous curiosity, the teacher should teach general ideas through concrete facts of experience which are familiar to children and which illustrate those ideas. He cannot always be presenting strange facts but he can excite genuine curiosity by posing questions about facts of daily life. Why does smoke rise upward instead of moving sideways? Why do we blow to extinguish a lamp, or to cool a very hot liquid? Why are days and nights not always equal? What is an eclipse? Children will be curious to know answers to such questions and through them a wise teacher will lead them to learn many useful things.

Often children themselves ask questions and though we admit that their curiosity is natural and their questions legitimate, most of us are annoyed by them. We wish either to evade answering them or to silence them with a rebuke. 'I don't know', 'It is natural', 'You are too young to understand it' and the like serve only to repress curiosity. The child begins to lose interest in his environment and the development of judgment and imagination which follows a healthy exercise of inquisitiveness, is stifled.

2. Construction

The instinct of construction is the hunger of the hand. The child wishes to handle, to push, to pull, to press, to throw and to manipulate almost everything that comes his way. In the early stage the tendency is vague and expresses itself in random movements in which there is no difference between making and breaking or constructing and destroying things. The child is not conscious of the adult values of things and turns them over without any purpose either of making or breaking them. His primary concern is free movement.

Gradually the child becomes aware of producing effects with his movements. He derives great satisfaction from making noises, tearing paper, biting bread or biscuit, piling blocks of wood and scattering them. Gradually, purposes and interests are formed, the need of tools and skill is felt and free play is directed into constructive channels. Doing, at first random and aimless, is transformed into creating and constructing. Long before they enter school, children learn to make and construct things. Sand, clay, paper, in fact any kind of plastic material, is used to make things. Birds, huts, shoes, caps, cups, animals are made from clay and paper ; broken pieces of wood, earthen pots, and cardboard are shaped into toys, and what skill fails to make, imagination readily supplies. A stick is a horse when placed between the legs, a towel placed on two chairs is believed to be a tent, a chip of wood is a spoon, and so on.

Our present system of education aims at mere instruction, at giving knowledge and information. It does not teach the use of hands or skill, and the constructive tendency among children is not given any opportunity for growth and development. Children should have a large variety of materials and tools to construct model ships, carts, houses, pen-stands, every school should have a museum stocked with things made by children and regular instruction should be given in handwork. Children learn better when they deal with concrete things, and learning becomes a game of adventure ; when making things they realsie purposes and ends which they themselves have conceived. Such learning is very effective as it is accompanied by strong interest in achievement.

The two great systems of child education, the kindergarten of Froebel and the 'Houses of Childhood' of Madame Montessori, are based on the principle that children should be surrounded by a large variety of objects and apparatus which they not only handle but also freely arrange and re-arrange to turn out new objects and patterns.

But the craft-centred scheme of Dr. Zakir Hussain, popularly known as the Wardha Scheme, provides the richest opportunities for the exercise and development of the instinct of construction. All subjects like language, arithmetic, geography, history, are to be taught in connection with and through the medium of craft. The craft chosen may be spinning and weaving, leatherwork, carpentry or metal-work but it is to be the main thing, the centre of the curriculum. The scheme is aptly described as a scheme of *basic education.* In providing for the great constructive tendencies of children and in harnessing their strong interests to creative work, the scheme provides for a sound foundation of further education.

3. Acquisition

At a very early stage children show eagerness not only to know and manipulate things but also to acquire and possess them. The baby refuses to share his toys with another and resents it if the neighbour's baby handles them. How children cry when their things are touched, how some of them sleep with their pet toy firmly grasped and how they display a sense of ownership by being petty and selfish about them shows what a great motive force this urge to acquire, collect and possess things is. Collection and ownership expand and express our personality as no other interest does. Searching for treasure we really search for ourselves and when this impulse is associated with those of manipulation and investigation, the invisible outlines of personality and character begin to be filled in.

The collective instinct shows itself in many ways. Children save and collect buttons, pins, leaves, feathers, cigarette boxes, labels, scraps of paper and what not. The urge to collect and acquire is basic to civilised life and is the foundation of all our notions of property and rights of ownership. But it may be developed into wrong forms. It may lead to miserliness, cheating, stealing, meanness, or it may lead to the acquisition of more and more knowledge, fame, honour and those prizes which civilised communities appreciate and respect. The capitalist who amasses limitless wealth only to found charitable institutions, the scientist who annexes degrees and titles for researches, the conqueror who wins province after province, the book-lover who buys every new book, all these are driven by the same urge to collect.

The school can make use of the instinct in several fruitful ways. Young people can be sent on excursions to collect specimens of leaves and plants, of soils and stones, of butterflies and insects, and this will be a very useful preparation for the study of natural science. They may be asked to keep albums of pictures, stamps, labels and present them in school exhibitions. This work is educationally valuable and the school should encourage the growth and development of such hobbies. Collecting is a hobby both interesting and easy, and each child can pursue one form or the other according to the means of his family. One school encouraged children to collect pictures of laughing and smiling faces, of sad and gloomy ones, of great men in several walks of life, and this gave children an interest to work for, which by itself is a great educational achievement.

The teacher should remember that mere collecting and acquisition is of little value. It must be the result of doing, of effort and activity, and it must lead to further effort to know and study, to inquire and investigate. It must be turned to some advantage even if it is pure amusement or entertainment.

4. Self-Assertion and Self-Abasement

In the presence of inferior fellow-creatures we all feel an instinctive desire to display our strength or superiority in some direction. This is *self-assertion* and is accompanied by the emotion of *elation*. And in the presence of superior fellow-beings our attitude is one of respect and submission, we crouch and cringe as if to acknowledge their superiority. This is *self-abasement* and is accompanied by the emotion of *subjection*.

These instincts are essentially social in character and can only arise in our relations with our fellows. They require spectators and are necessary for securing some sort of a social order within the group.

As soon as the child becomes conscious of his physical and mental abilities, the instinct of self-assertion manifests itself. Its earliest expression is to be found in repetition; the infant repeats those words and movements which it has learnt just for the pleasure of showing to others what it can do. He seeks the esteem and approbation of others. He wants to attract the notice of others and dominate those with whom he associates. His desire to occupy the limelight is revealed in every activity and he behaves in a manner which implies that he must be reckoned with. Often this tendency leads him to place his own interest above those of others. In its higher forms this instinct of self-assertion leads to self-consciousness and pride.

Dumville tells us 'This self-assertion is one of the most imperious demands of our nature, and it is a cause of much of our most persistent endeavour'.[1] The wish to be recognised leads us to undertake difficult tasks to prove abilities and demonstrate prowess, to differentiate ourselves from

[1] *Child Mind*, p. 38

other people in dress, deportment, pronunciation, taste or social status, and to seek titles, recommendations and honours. Self-assertion makes us aggressive, and failure in one sphere makes us seek opportunities to dominate members of our society in other spheres. A great deal of human emulation and rivalry is caused by this instinct of self-assertion and it gives rise to an enormous strength of ambition. How people sacrifice their domestic happiness and personal comfort, and work hard to be rich, eminent and powerful, to be looked up to, wield influence over others and to be considered unique and extraordinary, shows how powerful is the role of this instinct in life.

Education has a two-fold responsibility with regard to this instinct. In the first place, because individuals live together it is necessary for them to learn to control or submerge their self-interests and work for the common good. The child's desire to be in the limelight, to do what he wants, to do it without hindrance, must be sublimated or redirected into socially acceptable and useful conduct. In this redirection the child will first react violently and then more calmly. The task of education in the home and the school is to make this redirection less sudden and violent. Secondly, when children are thwarted, they often seek opportunities for self-display in wrong directions and develop anti-social traits. The naughty child, the bully and the tyrant are seeking occasion for self-display because the normal opportunities have been denied to them. The teacher should not do anything which will injure the self-respect of children. Confidence, encouragement, sympathy and affection will produce among children a healthy sense of self-respect and self-assurance and lead them to behave in socially useful ways. Children should not be compelled to feel small, insignificant, useless and unworthy by being rebuked too often, by being held up to ridicule in the class or by being ignored. They should be provided proper opportunities for self-display. They may be monitors, captains of teams, group leaders, secretaries of clubs and prefects. They may be invited to write on the black-board, to recite to the class, act in a drama or to manage a number of school activities. When they do commendable work they should be praised in public. Marks, distinctions, prizes and numerous extra-curricular activities will give a large scope to a majority of pupils to distinguish themselves in one sphere or the other and thus gratify their desire for self-display. If they do not distinguish themselves in studies they may do so in games or social activities. The object is to give them all occasions to develop a sense of happy importance by playing a respectable part in the life of the school. Self-government in schools and social service programmes give young people a growing sense of power and directs their self-assertive and aggressive desires into healthy social channels.

The instinct of self-abasement is the opposite of self-assertion and is accompanied by the emotion of subjection or submission. It is generally manifested in the presence of people who are superior to us. We crouch and cringe, our movements are slow and restricted, we avoid meeting their eyes and hang down our head. Often there is a feeling of reverence and humility. Children who are helpless, ignorant and dependent, usually manifest this tendency in the presence of parents and teachers who are stronger, wiser and bigger. They are unable to help themselves or to think for themselves and it is very necessary that they should be guided by their parents and teachers. They therefore submit to their authority and their attitude is marked by respect, humility and obedience.

If the instinct of self-assertion makes leaders in a community, the instinct of self-abasement makes followers.

Both are very necessary for social order. The teacher has very often to make use of the instinct of self-abasement to maintain order and develop discipline in the school. Discipline involves self-submission and obedience and the duty of obedience must be learnt before school work is possible. But obedience must be of the right kind. It should not be such as a slave gives to his master, a dog to a whip or a child to the birch. Such obedience and submission is undesirable as it leads to fear of punishment and kills initiative and intelligence. True obedience and discipline is based on both understanding and self-control. It also involves affection and the child obeys cheerfully because he sees in his teacher a well-wisher and friend. He recognises the moral, intellectual and physical superiority of the teacher and feels submission, humility and reverence towards him.

But every teacher is not able to evoke this attitude and spirit among his pupils. This shows that there must be certain qualities in teachers which go to make such teachers as are readily obeyed and respected. The teacher must have a good personality, good personal appearance, cheerful temper, ready expression, strong deep voice, determined look and strong physique. He should have graciousness of manner which indicates self-control and inner harmony. He should be really interested in his work and pupils, and should be well versed in the art of teaching. He should have a good knowledge of the subject and should take pains to prepare his lessons. His personal habits should be commendable. These and other such qualities will add to the prestige of the teacher and help him to evoke submission and obedience among pupils. To be respected he must be respectable. Such a teacher will have no difficulty in managing the class, bringing order and discipline among his pupils.

5. Sex

Sex is a powerful factor in life, and modern psychology has devoted considerable attention to its study. The sex instinct or need matures comparatively late in the development of the individual but since it is one of the most fundamental instincts of a living organism, its proper development and direction is one of the important and difficult responsibilities of education.

The psycho-analysts headed by Freud have made a special study of this instinct and attribute to it a very powerful role in all stages of human development. They believe that definite sexual interest appears in early infancy and what we call love is only a manifestation of the sex instinct. The first stage of its growth is narcissism which is marked by the child's love for his own body and all his pleasures and pains are experienced in connection with the functions of the body. This is succeeded by love of the parents to which they give the name oedipus complex. The boy tends to love his mother and hate his father. He considers the latter his rival. This complex, they say, is repressed, as it conflicts with the moral ideas of society This stage is followed by homo-sexuality in which young people fall in love with members of their own sex. This is an age of passionate friendships and there is a tendency in both sexes to stand away from each other. Adolescence is the name by which we distinguish this period and a detailed study of its mental and moral characters will be made in a later chapter. The final stage in the development of the sex instinct is the hetero-sexual in which young people direct their interest to members of the opposite sex. These stages do not always succeed each other in time, they may often shade into each other at the same age.

Popular thought invests sex interest among children rightly with great importance and wrongly with a mystery.

Parents and teachers are in open conspiracy to withhold knowledge and information about sex matters from young people and all reference to sex is tabooed in the home and in the school. But when young people begin to have experience of sex at the age of fourteen or so, they are sure to pick up what knowledge comes their way and develop some perverse habits too. Should not wise guidance and right knowledge help them to adjust themselves to this rising tide of the sex instinct ?

Modern psychologists are agreed that interest in sex life is normal in young children. In large schools it has been found that children at all stages discuss the sexual life of adults and in some cases imitate it. Many parents and teachers believe that this is not so and that some good boys and girls never indulge in any talk about sex. They think that a child who talks about sex is polluted and that a child who has any sexual practices is untouchable. This is silly and wrong. Sex interest is normal and most young people grow out of such habits if adults do not make an undue fuss about it. On the other hand, a frank and straightforward attitude towards sex in the home and the school will dispel exaggerated fears about masturbation, undressing and the like.

Many people believe that young boys and girls should be kept busy at hard games and studies during the period of adolescence so that they have no time to think about sex. Others plead that boys and girls at this stage should be segregated so that any opportunity to think of the opposite sex is removed. Both these steps are unhealthy. They only try to keep young people ignorant of sex and do more harm than good. In the first place, when children begin to experience sex they must obtain some knowledge of it, whether the knowledge is true or false. Should we not make sure that very sane and correct information is given to them? Secondly, segregation and a hush-hush policy will only put off information and not altogether withhold it.

Others believe that boys and girls should be induced to seek information from books on sex. But they little realise that such reading may only sharpen the interest in sex. The sex instinct works in a very subtle way and such reading as is supposed to give young people information about sex matters may have a very injurious effect on their character by developing in them an abnormal interest in the subject. Reading sex literature is one way of gratifying sex interest.

The sex urge should be neither prematurely awakened in the child by what passes for sex-enlightenment or sex education through sex books, nor greeted with outright criticism and condemnation on the part of parents and teachers when they see signs of its awakening. Curiosity and interest in sex are inevitable in boys and girls and the task of the educator is not to avoid the issue. Genuine questions should be answered through legitimate channels without any delicacy and embarrassment so as to avoid their seeking knowledge from crude and vulgar sources. But the great standby is the method of sublimation. Young people who have an abundance of physical activity, deep and wide interests, healthy hobbies, well selected reading matter and opportunities for normal social life, do not run any risk of being driven into morbid curiosity and secret sex habits. Poetry, dramatics, music, art clubs, games and other extra-curricular activities offer wholesome substitutes to sex interest.

6. Some Important Needs—Affection

We have already pointed out needs, drives, motives or desires as influencing human behaviour and described some of the attempts of psychologists to list and classify them. Some important motives have been mentioned. Even though some of these needs are entirely physiological to begin with they become psychological with experience and grow more and more complex as a result of the processes of socialisation. Let us study some important human needs.

The need for *affection* is very important in the normal development of a child. He longs to love and be loved, and if he loses his mother early in life and is deprived of her affection he does not feel safe and secure and is always seeking artificial aids to boost his morale and sense of security. She feeds, protects and fondles him, and the affection of the young child is influenced by the care she bestows upon him. The feelings of affection are mutual and parents need the affection of children as much as children need the affection of parents. It makes for the happiness of both.

Children are also attached to their playthings and fondle and care about them as if they were living things. Later when the child moves out of the home at first he feels insecure among unfamiliar persons and companions but gradually he develops affectionate relations with them. Bonds of friendship are as strong as family relations of affection, and throughout one's life the individual is for ever seeking affectionate and friendly bonds with others. Such companionship is good in its own right and is not sought for any ulterior object.

Those children who for one reason or the other have been deprived of affection always feel afraid of vague threats and uncertain hurts. They lack self-assurance and self-confidence and are afraid of being left alone and abandoned.

Children need the affection of their teachers, class leaders and their play companions and wish to be accepted and recognised by them. They seek in teachers those qualities which their parents possess such as kindliness, sympathy, genuine interest in their welfare and fairness. And every teacher who has had long and successful experience with young people will bear testimony to the fact that it is easier to influence them with love and affection than through fear and strictness. Therefore teachers should not merely take real interest in the children they teach but also develop feelings of affection and sympathy for them. It will make their task both pleasant and effective.

Love of parents, bonds of friendship born in the playground, and intimacies developed in group work are our valuable acquisitions, and money, power, popularity and the like cannot replace the need for love. The need for love is often described as the need for belongingness, and we all are eager to belong to groups, associations, towns, clubs and the like. Children want to love their school. Human history is full of examples of people who have made the highest sacrifices for love and affection.

7. Security

The need to feel secure is an important social need. Pain, want and discomfort make us feel unhappy, and so does the fear of these things or even the thought of them. More important than security is the *feeling* of security.

There is more than one type of security. *Physical security* means satisfaction of biological needs like food, protection from pain and disease and shelter from extremes of temperature. *Economic security* means freedom from want and is a means to physical security. *Psychological security* implies a feeling of well-being born of healthy and harmonious adjustments to social environments and leading to emotional stability and freedom from anxiety and worry.

Obviously psychological security involves, and depe[nds] upon, physical and economic security.

It would be better to speak of a sense of security which arises from a feeling that the individual belongs to some place and to someone, that he is wanted and needed, and that he has a definite function or role in the scheme of things. In the family parental affection is a very important source of security feelings. Children who are unwanted or rejected by parents are always handicapped in life and feel insecure. In homes where parents are quarrelling among themselves, where there is rivalry between them for the affection of the child or disagreement between them about the best way of bringing up children, or where children are forced to live with step-parents or step-brothers, children usually feel very insecure. Again children feel insecure if there are frequent changes in the locality of the home, neighbourhood, playmates and school. Frequent changes in school do not let children adjust happily to their changing environments.

In the class children feel insecure if the teacher neglects them, rebukes them too often or has a scornful attitude toward them.

But though the sense of security is very important for the child for his mental health and happiness, he should not be smothered with too much affection and protection. Many mothers having lost their husbands give too much affection to their children and do much more for them than they should. This too is not good. Children should be helped to look after themselves, to do things by themselves and for themselves. This self-reliance and self-help will give them much more confidence and freedom, independence and a strong sense of security. Both teachers and parents while giving their best attention and affection to children under their care must gradually teach them to do without their help, not to depend on them and stand on their own feet in dealing with their tasks and problems. The world is changing very fast, nobody can foresee the type of world in which young people will have to live as adults and the best security we can give children is to teach them self-reliance and self-help.

8. Recognition

We all are hungry for recognition. We wish to be accepted by others, to win their esteem and to be commended and praised. It does give us pleasure if our name appears in print, if our work is recognised by learned people. Teachers and parents know how eager young people are to get praise and how strongly rewards induce them to work hard at books and games. An analysis of the daydreams of young people reveals how strong and widespread is the desire for recognition.

The teacher's approach and classroom practices should be such that whenever any child does anything worthwhile it should be duly recognised and appreciated. It is not necessary that every time anything worthwhile is done the child should be rewarded but often mere mention of it in the classroom boosts the morale of the child and stimulates him to do better.

9. Need for New Experience

The desire for new experience is the desire for variety and novelty. The desire to get out of the rut is strong. We all feel bored by the repetition of experiences and situations and are always on the look-out for new ways of behaving and new ways of doing things. Happy is the home and the school where parents and teachers are for ever looking out for some new enterprise for their children, bringing in new material for work, study and play. It inspires young people with new zest and enthusiasm and their learning is quicker and more effective.

10. Self-Actualisation

Every individual has a desire for self-actualisation, a desire to develop all that is best in him and to make the maximum use of his talents and abilities. Grown-up people come to form certain notions about their abilities and seek opportunities for their use and employment. But if young people are provided a large variety of activities and experiences in the school like games, art, music, reading, dramatics, debates, magazine and the like they will in course of time discover themselves and find a field or area of work for which they are more gifted and in which they can do better.

This need is very difficult to assess because it is somewhat speculative, but it helps to explain why some people go beyond the primary and secondary needs and engage in activity that appars to have nothing to do with maintaining physical comfort and psychological security. Rather the need for self-actualisation may add to discomfort and insecurity. The first four needs in the list given by I. H. Maslow as mentioned in the last chapter are largely homeostatic and help to maintain physical, psychological and social equilibrium, but this need leads to creativity.

This need begins to make an appearance in the final years of adolescence when young people are called upon to think of their vocation in life and to find a major outlet for their creative energies in their occupational life. Obviously the need for self-actualisation can be fulfilled to the extent a person is self-reliant, directing his own course, thinking and deciding for himself and striking out a course of action and life different from the group. He no longer cares what others think of him but ploughs his own lonely burrow. Teachers and parents should not curb any sign of independence on the part of the young to chalk out a career for themselves. Rather they should encourage and help them to find such outlets as will give them fullest opportunity for self-expression and self-actualisation.

11. Conclusion

These needs and motives are interdependent, and more than one need or motive may be satisfied by one act of behaviour. Man has a tendency to organise his behaviour in such a manner that he obtains the utmost satisfaction from it, that is he satisfies many needs by it.

The school should keep these needs in view and provide programmes and opportunities so that every student can obtain some satisfaction of his important needs. The stress should be on richness and variety of extra-curricular activities and participation in small groups. And whenever any student breaks away from the routine to behave in an unusual manner the teacher should try to analyse what important need the young person has sought to satisfy. This point of view will bring the teacher closer to the inner working of the mind of the young person and give him an opportunity to help him on the basis of this understanding.

Questions

1. Discuss the place of curiosity in education. How would you make use of this instinct in the education of the young?
2. Describe the essential features of the instinct of constructiveness. How could scope be given for it in the school? Discuss what provision the Wardha Scheme has made for its development.

3. What are self-assertion and self-abasement? What use should the teacher make of them in the education of children?
4. Select some prominent instincts and needs and show what are the best methods of educating them.
5. What do you understand by sex education? Should we encourage young people to read books on sex so as to give them knowledge? Describe some of the healthy ways of dealing with the sex instinct.
6. What type of teacher will succeed with the class? Analyse some of the qualities of an ideal teacher.

References for Further Study

1. Bernard: *Instinct: A Study in Social Psychology* (Henry Holt).
2. Bhatia: *What Basic Education Means* (Orient Longmans).
   Bhatia: *Craft in Education* (Asia Publishing House).
3. Dumville: *Fundamentals of Psychology* (Univ. Tut. Press).
4. Hall: *The Well of Loneliness* (Blue Ribbon).
5. Kalm: *Our Sex Life* (Knopf).
6. McDougall: *Outlines of Psychology* (Methuen).
7. Ross: *Groundwork of Educational Psychology* (Harrap).
8. Stuart and Oakden: *Modern Psychology and Education* (Kegan Paul).
9. Symonds: *The Dynamics of Human Adjustment* (Appleton).
10. Tolman: *Purposeful Behaviour in Animals and Men* (Appleton).
11. Williams: *Adolescence* (Farrar & Rinehart).
12. Wolf: *Drawn from Life* (Whittlesey House).
13. Woodworth: *Dynamic Psychology* (Col. Univ. Press).

CHAPTER NINE

Play

1. PLAY AND CHILDREN

If there is any characteristic so obvious in children it is their tendency to play. Every child plays and childhood is the playtime of life. Children would not be children if they did not play ; play is their chief business in life and if anyone wishes to understand their nature and needs, he cannot do better than watch them at play. Reading, writing or doing sums the child is apt to be artificial, he holds back his inner self, but at play he is himself and his inmost thoughts, feelings and attitudes find a free, natural and spontaneous expression. Therefore, it is in the many varied forms of play that we may see revealed the possibilities of his future development, his dominant interests at different ages, his preferences and aversions, and come to know his real needs.

2. THEORIES OF PLAY

But why do children play? To this question several and varied are the answers given by philosophers and educators and though none of them is complete enough to explain play fully, each of them emphasises some important aspect of play and helps us to understand children's nature and active life in play. Spencer urges that children play because they are so full of animal spirits, so over-charged with muscular energy. Just as lions roar when well-fed and birds sing, similarly children in their normal conditions have more energy than they need and indulge in play in order to provide an outlet for such surplus energy. But this theory is unable to explain why children play in just the way they do and why their play-interests differ at different levels.

Nevertheless, this view that play is 'an aimless expenditure of exuberant energy' is readily accepted by illiterate parents and fits well into their philosophy of life. If a boy has strength enough to run after a football, why not ask him to run errands? If he wants to play hockey why not ask him to beat dusty carpets or wash linen? What time and energy girls spend playing with a doll may as well be spent in looking after the baby at home. These things, it is argued, involve the same type of activity as play and at the same time lead to useful results. But do children get an equal amount of pleasure in doing them? If not, they will be poor substitutes for play. This theory misses the most essential aspect of play, the joy children get from their sport. Again, it cannot explain why children play when they are ill or tired, when energy is at a low ebb.

Groos regards play as a preparation for the business of life. According to him, in the various kinds of play children practise those forms of activity which they will need in later life and upon which their struggle for existence depends. Childhood and youth are periods specially provided by nature to enable young people to develop, mature and perfect those skills which they will need later. That is why boys play games that require hunting, attacking, running, defending, or play at soldiers, hawkers or railway guards and in games acquire group competition, co-operation, discipline and other social traits which will stand them in good stead in adult social life. Girls play with dolls and kitchen utensils, they practise being a mother, nurse or teacher. Their instincts and intelligence are being awakened, matured and perfected through play. Play thus becomes a preparation for the life we are to lead in mature years. But this theory, though readily accepted, does not explain how children, ignorant of adult needs, nevertheless prepare for them. Besides, if accepting this view we were to direct children's games accordingly, we would rob them of their freedom and spontaneity in play and introduce a seriousness which would be fatal to the very spirit of play.

Stanely Hall looks upon play as a group of bodily habits of the past persisting in the present. In play children recapitulate the entire history of mankind ; they go to play as if they remember a lost paradise. When children play at hunting with bow and arrow, go swimming and building caves on the sandy beach or enjoy playing with boats, trains and aeroplanes, they are repeating the main epochs through which human civilisation has passed.

McDougall traces all play to a motive of rivalry. No doubt, there is a spirit of competition in most games and without it much of the zest and enthusiasm in games would be lost, yet there are several types of play activity in which this element of rivalry is altogether absent. In the play of infants and in make-believe play there is hardly any competition.

Still another explanation regards play is an opportunity to relax and amuse oneself. Serious living calls for effort and concentration and leads to fatigue, therefore children as well as adults engage in play to refresh themselves. All play is recreation and relaxation, turning away from the serious business of life. Indoor games like chess, cards or carrom, outdoor activities like football, fishing or cricket, social engagements like going to pictures or clubs, are all means of play. This explanation may be true of adult play but does not explain the play of children for whom play itself is the most serious business of life and who cannot therefore be needing any relaxation from it.

All these theories emphasise different aspects of the value of play in child life and education. They tell us that play is the most sacred right of children and that both in the home and the school (the two chief influences in their education) frequent opportunities and facilities should be provided for wholesome play activities. No one theory contains the whole truth, yet much of what each says is true.

3. Characteristics of Play

Play is not easy to define, but going over the several definitions offered and examining the several forms of activity called play, certain general inferences may be drawn about its nature. In the first place, *play is instinctive*. Every child breathes, sucks, moves his arms, without trying to do so and at first without being aware of it. Similarly, he throws, runs, jumps, talks. All these activities are instinctive, children have a natural inborn desire and ability to do them and with practice their ability develops into skill. This strange desire to do things, to be active and to exercise as many limbs and muscles as possible is the origin and beginning of play. Placed in the strangest situations and with the strangest companions, children do not take long to overcome their shyness and indulge in wholehearted play even if they do not understand each other's language. Play is the most natural and spontaneous expression of child life. But though play is instinctive there is no special instinct which we can call the play instinct, for in that case all play must mean definite responses bound to definite situations. A cursory review of the play activities of children will reveal how varied and numerous are their interests, almost every kind of activity, impulse, mood, interest, instinct being tapped in play. Of couse, what impulses and interests are dominant at a particular age will determine the nature and form of play at that age, but all instincts find expression in play. Play is a general field for their exercise and development.

Secondly, *play is activity,* it is not idleness. Merely loafing away time or dawdling is not play, it is the absence and loss of play interest and spirit. Play is not limited to any one particular kind of activity. When children play hop-step-and-jump or at chasing and shouting, their activity is essentially bodily ; when they play at searching, pointing out distant objects or counting birds their activity is sensory ; and when they play at solving riddles, telling or listening to stories or reading nonsense rhymes, their activity is essentially mental. Or there may be a combination of all. Play is characteristic of the intellectual activity as truly as it is of the physical ; observation, attention, imagination, judgement, reasoning, are all used in play.

Thirdly, *play is marked by attention and interest of a strong all-absorbing type.* At play, children are so deeply absorbed in, and their attention is so deeply concentrated on, what they are doing, that they are hardly aware of what is passing just near them. Full of enthusiasm, inspired by a tenacity of will and purpose and forgetful of all else, they do not hear the mother's call or the school bell but merrily go on with their play. This attitude of mind found in play is the attitude which represents the greatest efficiency in all mental effort.

Fourthly, *play is engaged in for its own sake* rather than for any ulterior goal or end. It is its own reward. Play is freely chosen for its own sake and the gratification that is derived from it is immediate, ingrained in the very activity itself. The felling of joy and satisfaction found in activities called play is their sole motive. This does not mean that play is aimless and has no purpose. The purpose is self-prescribed and is a vital part of human nature.

To sum up, all play is activity promoted by a feeling of vigour. It is free self-expression for the pleasure of expression. It is a natural unfolding of the inner impulses from inner necessity, an act performed spontaneously, and for no conscious purpose beyond the activity itself. The pleasure results from the very exercise of the various mental and bodily functions.

4. Work and Play

Work is serious ; it is engaged in for some result useful to the individual or society. If there is any pleasure in work it is derived from a contemplation of the end it achieves rather than from the process of activity itself. Work is always carefully selected and done for some special purpose—hence it is always deliberate rather than spontaneous. It lacks the variety and vigour of play because the attention of the worker is divided between the work and its result. In work one has often to go on in the interest of the result even if one is tired. Hence work is never free and spontaneous like play. It is this attitude of mind alone that distinguishes work from play. The same activity may be work at one time and play at another. Boys engaged in building a make-believe house carry heavy loads of brick and earth and love to do it whether any house is actually built or not, but if they are engaged in regular building work they will shirk it and regard it an imposition. Their heart is not in it, they no longer do it in the play spirit and look upon it as drudgery. Again, if a spirit of competition is introduced they vie with one another and try to do more and more. Their attitude has changed into one of play. Thus the same activity may be called work or play according as the attitude of mind is one of free spontaneity seeking satisfaction in the activity itself or that of constraint going through activity somehow to gain an end outside it. From this it follows that work, to be more efficient and effective both for the individual and society, should function as play.

5. Values of Play

The values of play are varied and many. In the first place, it is a means of physical education. That children should play in order to achieve robust health and strong physique seems too commonplace a remark, but considering how little attention it has received at the hands of parents and teachers in our country, it will bear any amount of repetition. Play as a means of physical education is to be preferred to gymnastic or physical drill for two reasons. Firstly, play is so interesting that physical exercise is secured without compulsion. To take exercise at the parallel bars is tedious and requires great will-power even for adults. Young people cannot take it daily with as great a zest and enthusiasm as they feel for a game of football or hockey. Secondly, play affords exercise for all limbs. Work, however strenuous, cannot replace play. Play should enter the Indian home and the girls' school and there should be play centres for women and girls before we can reach our goal of national health.

Secondly, play is a great intellectual influence. It affords mental rest and recreation. Fatigue, sorrow, depression and ennui are worked off in play. Children tired from study, rush out of their rooms in the recess and come back refreshed and invigorated. Play also provides for a wide range of experiences. Children engage in a variety of activities, they come across a variety of objects and they meet a variety of people. Playing with marbles, blocks, paper or plasticine, young children explore new regions of sense-perception and acquire distinctions of form, shape, size, colour, sound and taste and acquire a practical interest in their environment. They come in contact with younger and older people and gain from their experience and thoughts. This exchange of ideas, learning other people's point of view and getting his own modified by the experience and thoughts of others, broadens the individual's mind and prevents him from growing one-sided and exclusive. His intellect is sharpened and stimulated. In play young people throw off all restraint and self-consciousness and can know and judge each other more correctly. They learn *from* their playmates and they learn *about* them, and this equips them to meet and deal with people in life. No wonder that great men like the Duke of Wellington proclaim that they learnt their first and last lesson in leadership on the playground.

Thirdly, play is a great training ground for character. It provides for the expression, exercise and growth along certain prescribed channels of the primary instincts and emotions of children. It regulates the thought, desires and actions of the child to form habits of conduct which determine his moral worth. As an individual the child needs for his success and happiness in life such qualities as courage, ingenuity, initiative, perseverance, self-reliance, self-control, thoroughness and aggressiveness; as a member of society in which he has to enter into harmonious relationship with others he has to learn to be fair, friendly, considerate and tolerant; and to be a useful citizen he must learn to be loyal to a cause, to acquire a spirit of co-operation and to learn to command as well as to obey. For the promotion and development of all these qualities play offers rich opportunities. Play offers such opportunities and activities as help to develop a democratic way of living and thinking.

6. Age Differences in Play

Since needs, interests, skills and abilities of young people change with age as they grow, the play activities for them should be changed to suit the level of physical and mental development at each age period. The child under three is mainly interested in sensory and motor-control plays. He likes to play with things that are brightly coloured, that produce attractive sound and that move quickly; he likes digging in the sand, scratching on any surface, rolling, kicking, moving and putting into his mouth everything he can lift, pushing, pulling and throwing small things—ball, stones, spoons and the like; building with blocks of wood, putting books, cups and boxes together in a line and pushing them. All his toys and activities are enjoyed because they afford opportunities for exercising his sense organs and limbs in them. Until six he is interested in imaginative and make-believe play with crude construction work. Play helps the child to work off excess energy. It gives his growing muscles the stretching and flexing they call for. The tendency to be active, to be always on the move is strong and the chief source of pleasure is in the variety of movements. Wading in shallow water, playing with swings, balls, sticks; imitating parents in farming or housekeeping ; playing at postman, soldier or guard; riding make-believe trains, horses or cars, make this stage.

Before the child enters schools the number of his companions is limited. At school he meets many new playmates and finds himself wanting their friendship and approval. To win them he soon realises that he must learn to share games and toys, to make turns, to give and take.

After six, imitation tends to be replaced by self-assertion and children begin doing things on their own initiative. Running, dodging, chasing and the like are more in evidence and self-assertion is so strong that more time is lost in disputing than in playing. Passion for self-display and pride in achievement is strong and interest in competitive games is entirely individual. It is just at this stage that the school and the home should co-operate to provide ample opportunity for individual contests in sports and in feats of strength and skill. Till twelve, the spirit continues to be dominant, muscular control and skill grow, interest in physical activity is vigorous and varied, and co-operation and team spirit begin to dawn though still at a low level.

After twelve, the child becomes more and more interested in organised games and cooperative play. Children will get together for a game of hide-and-seek, to produce a show in the backyard, to build a playhouse. The gang spirit begins to develop and team games are more popular. Groups begin to divide into teams, 'sides' and gangs, and individual competition makes way for co-operation and group rivalry. From pairs , 'sides' and teams grows the spirit of co-operation and fellowship, the subordination of personal glory to that of the team. Ideals of self-sacrifice and heroism appeal strongly to them and interest in club activities is sharpened. Group loyalty is strong and no sacrifice is considered too great to bring honour to the team or the school.

In later childhood the national games of hockey, football and cricket dominate the interests of many a boy. He plays them incessantly, saving his allowance to buy equipment, collecting pictures of outstanding players and identifying himself with the stars.

Girls almost give up playing as soon as they reach the age of twelve or so and some of them who come from progressive homes do take part in organised games like hockey and badminton in schools. But this is a very small number.

7. Sex Differences in Play

Sex too makes a difference to the play interest and habits of children. Quite early, boys show instinctive partiality for vigorous and active types of expression as is found in running, jumping, throwing, fighting, wrestling; while girls incline to motherly tasks, imitate their mothers in household duties and enjoy playing with dolls, in dressing and showing them off. Tradition also helps to widen the gulf between the play interests of boys and girls. In our country a girl's place is definitely in the kitchen and she cannot step out of the home freely. She has to help her mother in various ways, to dress, talk and behave with a certain restraint and decorum, and to curb her desire to indulge in free boisterous play. Custom invests her too early with clothes which obstruct freedom of action. Boys naturally leave her company and seek their opportunities for vigorous and aggressive play outdoors.

Girls cannot be as strong and skilful in physical activities as boys, but to a great extent the unjust taboos of social life are to blame for their weakness. The fair sex is the weak sex. No doubt, girls are handicapped by limitations of their physical growth and development, but whether the present condition of their physical health is not due to the nagging custom of purdah and other social evils is a question to be seriously considered. Girls have less endurance, strength and skill and seek rhythmic play like dancing, chorus singing, skipping, clapping or dramatising. The spirit of competition, the sense of co-operation and team loyalty which organised group play involves, are absent from their games. Considering how much of their interest and co-operation we need in the growing demands of social and civic life and how much they have to contribute to our tastes and happiness in life, it is very desirable that they should be allowed greater freedom in play. Of course, we cannot prescribe for them the same kind of play activities but if our programme can accommodate individual differences in the play interests of boys, there is no reason why the divergent interests of girls should not be provided for. At maturity the play interests of men and women have a tendency to converge and we find them enjoying the same kinds of games. It is only in childhood and adolescence that their play interests show marked differences, and a wise school will provide suitable opportunities for such differences. All that must be remembered is that in the interest of bodily and mental health and vigour, the need of freedom to play should be recognised and fulfilled. Any child, girl or boy, who does not play, not only misses much of the joy of childhood, but also fails to acquire the all-embracing benefits of play already described, and by failing to develop all that is best in him as a boy, or in her as a girl, fails to become the efficient man or woman nature has destined him or her to become.

8. Play and the Teacher

Should children's play be supervised? What is the part of the teacher when he joins their play? In infancy parents play for and with their children. Children are treated as playthings, they are rocked, pressed, smothered with kisses and not seldom thrown into the air or raised above the head. All this is bad. Infants play by kicking their arms and legs and by chirping and parents can help only by letting them to do so by themselves. Later, toys come in and parents play with them not only to initiate children into their right use but also to entertain and amuse them. This does help to cheer up the child but it should never be forgotten that he will enjoy much more playing with his toys himself than looking at others play with them. In every stage of life play is a great opportunity for self-activity and self-expression and whenever adults join young people in games, they should not usurp their right to act and play freely. The teacher should play with children by all means but he should be one among them. The teacher should come down to their level of self-forgetfulness and keep himself in the background to enable them to play freely. By no means should adults play for them and reduce active players into passive spectactors. The tendency to show off and overawe youngsters is all too common with most of us and we should guard against it when joining children at play. The benefits of play are reaped only by playing and not by looking on.

9. The Play-Way in Education

Play is free, spontaneous activity engaged in for its own sake and is marked by a complete absorption of attention and interest in the activity. The individual forgets his own self and intuitively follows the spirit which leads to the maximum of results with the minimum of effort. This attitude of mind which is found in all play is one which represents the greatest efficiency in all mental effort. Any work done in this spirit or attitude becomes an art, the work of a genius. The greatest achievements of the race in the field of science, philosophy, art, literature or industry have been reached by individuals who work in the play spirit. The great genuises are persons who have carried into their mature work the same forgetfulness, the same self-absorption in the activity in hand and the same following of the spirit. They are all grown-up children who have preserved the spontaneity and simplicity of their childhood. It is impossible to achieve anything great if the individual works with divided attention, if his initiative is borrowed from without and if he is bent upon reaching a result outside the sphere of activity. What would be the achievement of a poet, philosopher or artist if throughout his endeavour his attention is concentrated on the money that he is going to make by it or the renown that he will win ? The genius has always done his work in the play spirit, forgetting himself and identifying himself with the activity he is engaged in.

This aspect of play is a great asset to education and if at home or in the school, adult influence and teaching could be passed on to children through activities in which children have an all-absorbing interest and on which they concentrate attention with enthusiasm and joy as they do in play, education would be a task far less irksome and much more effective. Effective and fruitful education is as active as play, for children are better educated through what they do for themselves than what others do for them and play is the best opportunity for self-expression and self-activity in which the end is lost in the means. That is why modern education insists on what is known as the play-way method in school work. They are helpful to effective learning, eliminate drudgery and bring into serious work the eagerness and alertness of play.

Those who plead for play-way methods in education insist on children's needs and interests, try to adapt curricula, time-table, methods of instruction, school organisation and discipline to the demands of the child's nature, and to make the whole programme more flexible. The whole movement is based on a realisation that the centre of all educational effort and activity should be the child, that individual differences among children should be respected and provided for and that much of school work should be managed by children themselves. They elect prefects or monitors who organise and control all extra-curricular activities. The school is considered a self-governing and democratic community in which young people are allowed and encouraged to experiment with life and to experience the joy of adventure and self-expression as they do in play.

Most of the recent educational methods and movements emphasise the play-way in education. They work round the principle that learning should be a great adventure for children and the pleasure they feel in play should not be lost to them in instruction. The kindergarten of Froebel, the Montessori System, the Dalton Plan, the Heuristic Method, Scouting, all embody the play-way method in education. Let us describe them briefly.

According to Froebel, education means growth, and kindergarten, meaning children's garden, is a children's society engaged in play and in various forms of self-expression through which the child comes to learn something of the values and methods of social life. The child is primarily active and learns and develops mainly through activity, through spontaneous and free activity in play. Froebel devised and organised a series of playthings called 'gifts' from which children gain progressive series of sense impressions. The first of these gifts was a set of woollen balls of six standard colours; for the second gift he used the three fundamental forms, the sphere, the cube and the cylinder ; and so on. On the basis of play with those gifts Froebel expected to develop ideals of form, colour, dimension, number, line and texture which would find expression later in some kind of creative effort with plastic material.

The Montessori system accepts the general principle of the kindergarten but provides for greater individual freedom. In the 'Houses of Childhood' the child enjoys more unrestricted freedom as there in none of the class-instruction permitted by the kindergarten. Froebel's gifts are taken by the whole class at the same time and the teaching is collective. In the Montessori system each child is individually self-active, he continues his work independently of the teacher and his classmates. The responsibility of education lies on each child. The *didactic apparatus* which Madame Montessori has devised is more definitely and specifically adapted to the training of sense-perception than that of Froebel. And her system includes direct preparation for learning, reading, writing and arithmetic. In the perception of various forms and in the performance of various movements, children not only develop senses and limbs but also come to recognise letters painted in large scripts and, through pictures of objects whose names begin with those letters, are introduced to words. Writing is learnt through tracing and arithmetic through counting beads placed in jars or balls put on a string.

Another method which stresses individual activity and freedom is the Dalton Plan of Miss Helen Parkhurst. The various classrooms are termed *laboratories* equipped with tools necessary for the study of the several subjects. Thus the classroom for geography is supplied with maps, plans, charts, models and books. The teacher of the subjects instead of going round to certain classes at stated hour, according to the time table and giving lessons to the whole class, remains in his 'laboratory' ready to advise, guide and help when called upon by the pupils individually or in groups. The teacher is more a guide or tutor than an instructor. Pupils have complete freedom to come and go, as they think fit. On a particular day a pupil may like to study history rather than geography and may go to the laboratory meant for the study of that subject. He has to finish a certain amount of the syllabus in each subject in a particular month or term. The syllabus is generally divided into ten portions, one for each month, and the statement of each portion is called an *assignment*. Pupils cannot take up a new assignment till they have finished the previous one, but they have the freedom to do it at their own rate and as they like.

In the *heuristic* method the child is placed in the position of an investigator or a discoverer and is helped to obtain most of his knowledge inductively through question and answers. Children should be led to make their own inquiries and proceed to build general and abstract knowledge from simple concrete facts.

In Scouting the play impulse of children is used for their education. They live under discipline and obey the scout laws. Thus they learn social habits. They take journeys, organise rallies and campfires and help at public functions. All this has great educative value.

The play-way has entered the teaching of subjects, and lessons, instead of being dull and dry, have become interesting and meaningful. In the first place, an attempt is made to relate the subject matter to life situations and to show its practical importance in daily life. Secondly, the methods have employed some of the dominant natural impulses of children like competition, dramatisation or curiosity. In history, for example, visits to historical places are arranged and some important historical events are dramatised. In spelling, games of word-building and word listing are introduced. These help to sharpen the interest of pupils in their work and they do it with the same zest with which they play. The spirit of play has permeated every item of the school and promises a great future in making learning more effective. It becomes a motivating force for learning.

10. Dramatic Play

Dramatic play offers rich opportunities for recreation and self-expression. Dressing up and staging a play is great fun for children, and older children, too. Preparing it, rehearsing, costuming, and finally presenting it before an audience of friends from whose pockets are cajoled small money for some cause dear to young hearts will make life and work at both home and school far more enjoyable than it is today. For primary school children dramatics should be a weekly programme, a short fifteen to twenty minutes being reserved every Saturday for dramatising and staging an interesting story even from their own class reader. After a few weeks children may be encouraged to select their own story and do extempore acting. The impulse to impersonate is strong in early childhood and dramatics will offer rich opportunities for both impersonation and self-expression.

Many times a child's dramatic play helps him to work out his unconscious conflicts. Deeply frustrated by his inability to compete socially or physically with his playmates he can become a hero, sweeping all opposition before him in his imagination.

Many parents and teachers feel uneasy that some plays are too bloody, too rowdy and too noisy. They feel that dramatics involving fighting material like swords and guns in mock war may make gangsters and criminals of children. But experience has shown that dramatic play of the fighting sort has no such risks and psychiatry has confirmed that dramatic play even of the fighting sort is a natural activity of children all over the world.

QUESTIONS

1. Discuss the chief theories of play, and state how you would make use of the play impulse in the service of education.
2. 'Play is the training ground for character.' In the light of this remark discuss the moral value of play.
3. What is the play-way in education? Describe how it is being used in the Kindergarten and the Montessori schools.
4. Distinguish between work and play and discuss the question whether all work can be turned into play.

5. 'All work and no play makes Jack a dull boy.' Bring out the educational meaning of this remark.
6. What are the values of play? Should games be made compulsory in school?
7. What differences in games are due to age and sex? Should girls play football?
8. What do you understand by self-activity? What is its value in education? Describe how this principle is being used in the Dalton Plan.
9. What is the value of extra-curricular activities? On what principles should they be organised in schools?
10. What is the true function of the teacher in the class and the playground? Should games be supervised?

References for Further Study

1. Curtis : *Education Through Play* (Macmillan).
2. Dumville : *Teaching* (Univ. Tut. Press).
3. Johnson : *Education by Plays and Games* (Ginn & Co.).
4. Lee : *Play in Education* (Macmillan).
5. Montessori : *The Montessori Method* (Heinemann).
6. Norsworthy and Whitley : *Psychology of Early Childhood* (Macmillan).
7. Nunn : *Education : Its Data and First Principles* (Arnold).
8. Ross : *Groundwork of Educational Psychology* (Harrap).

Chapter Ten — Attention and Interest

1. The General Nature of Attention

Attention is always present in conscious life and is common to all types of mental activity—knowing, feeling and willing. It is the primary pre-condition of them all. We must attend before we know, feel or act. It is a characteristic of all conscious life. But attention is more essentially cognitive. It is the concentration of consciousness upon one object rather than another. Attention is the heart of the conscious process. When we are conscious of an object, it means that we are aware of its presence in the environment. To attend to an object means to be aware of it more keenly and intensely than of anything else, to hold it in the focus of consciousness. While we are conscious of every object we attend to, we do not attend to every object we are conscious of. Consciousness is a wider field and includes that of attention. We attend only to a part of the field of consciousness, the rest is not attended to. Thus there are two fields: one of attention and the other of inattention. The former coincides with the margin of consciousness. Reading a book I am conscious of a large number of objects in the room and on the table. I am conscious of the ticking clock, the table lamp, the pen-stand, papers, myself sitting in the chair and numerous other objects but I am more distinctly and clearly aware of the words and sentences that I read and of the ideas they mean. That is, I am aware of a large number of objects about me but I attend only to some of them. This may be illustrated by referring to a lighted room. Objects near the lamp are seen clearly and distinctly while objects removed from it are seen dimly and vaguely. Similarly the field of consciousness contains a central portion where objects are clearly apprehended and a marginal area of objects apprehended indistinctly. The former is the field of attention, the latter of inattention.

But though attention is the core of consciousness, it is not an end in itself. Attention is for the sake of something else. It is an attitude of readiness or preparedness for action. Woodworth cites familiar instances of it in the military command of 'Attention!' and the athletic call of 'Ready'. It is this sensitively conscious and preparatory attitude of mind which is characteristic of attention.

2. Marks of the Attention Process

Perhaps the nature of attention can be better understood by describing its general characteristics.

In the first place, attention is not a fixed state nor a faculty or power of mind. It is an activity, a growing process and like every mental act it cannot be centred round any one object for a long time. It is constantly shifting from one object to another. Even when we attend to the same object for some time, attention shifts from one aspect of it to another. In reading we attend to the changing, growing argument and different stages are attended to in quick succession. We have distinguished between the focus and the fringe or margin of consciousness, and the former we have called the field of attention. Now objects are constantly passing from the margin to the centre or focus. It is very common to compare the entire field of consciousness to a dome of stimuli trying to attract attention. To this dome there is a base and an apex. Objects attended to stand at the apex of the dome, while objects of which we are altogether unconscious lie at the base. The objects of attention stay at the apex or in the focus of consciousness for the shortest possible time and are displaced by others.

Secondly, the process of attention has all the three aspects of conscious life, knowing, feeling and willing. Not only does it help us to see and know objects clearly, but it is also a kind of striving and is accompanied by some feeling in the form of interest. We attend to reach a goal and because that goal is determined by our dispositions, instinctive or acquired, the idea of its achievement gives us pleasure and interest and the goal is seen and apprehended more clearly and distinctly. Attention is cognitive, conative and affective.

Thirdly, attention is selective. We do not attend to everything that comes our way. Only those stimuli which have some advantage are able to attract attention, others are ignored. The passage of objects from the margin of consciousness to the focus is regulated. Even when we attend to the same object for some time we attend to some aspects of it more carefully and clearly than to others. Attention represents a narrow field and is selective. Most of our achievements in life are due mainly to this selection. If we try to attend to everything without limiting our range, we will not be able to achieve anything.

3. The Importance of Attention

Attention is a preparatory attitude and involves important physical adjustments. Watch a student fully absorbed in listening to the teacher and you will have a picture of such adjustments helping the attentive process. These bodily adjustments are very necessary and bring out the value and importance of attention.

In the first place, attention increases efficiency. Before the race starts the runner is ready to jump off as soon as the signal is given. 'Are you ready?' is the signal which brings about an increased state of motor readiness and he responds very quickly to the second shout, 'Go!'.

Secondly, attention greatly improves sensory discrimination. It seems to have the effect of a bright searchlight throwing up the details of the whole landscape. It does so in two ways. In the first place, all objects attended to attain a degree of prominence in consciousness which they lacked before they were attended to. Attention to them makes them 'stand out' more conspicuously than the surrounding objects. Secondly, objects attended to are 'separately discerned'. We isolate them from the rest of the environment to examine and know them more comprehensively, and to realise some purpose with regard to them. Owing to attention our awareness of objects which was vague and indeterminate becomes distinct, definite and clear. That is why we speak of attended objects as having entered the 'focus of consciousness', or the field of concentrated consciousness.

Thirdly, attention is necessary as a meass to the acquisition of skill. The typist, the cyclist or the tennis player must attend closely to his hands and movements, to their coordination and control, and it is only when he attains proficiency that attention drops out.

Lastly, attention is very helpful to remembering. Those experiences which are carefully attended to are remembered more accurately and fully and those which we notice only cursorily are soon forgotten.

4. Conditions of Attention

Such being the value of attention, it is very necessary that it should be controlled; and one of the tests of sound education is that it promotes such control and direction of attention into desirable channels. Mention has been made of the fact that there are certain factors of advantage in the securing and holding of attention. Let us now discuss those factors of advantage or conditions which determine the passage of stimuli from the field of inattention to that of attention. Such conditions are of two kinds, objective and subjective, those that are found in the objects and those that lie within the person.

Of the objective conditions the first is *intensity* of a stimulus. Other factors being equal, a strong or intense stimulus will attract attention. A loud noise has the advantage over a low murmur ; a street band compels attention while a low hubbub does not. The second is *size*. A large building will be more readily attended to than a small hut. The advertiser uses large type in his notices to attract attention. The third is *change*. To attract attention the change should not be gradual but sudden. We do not notice the clock ticking on the wall but it arrests attention as soon as it stops. Fourthly, *repetition* secures attention. Objects presented again and again cannot help being attended to. The fifth is *novelty and contrast*. New objects or objects different from what we are used to attract attention more rapidly. We are aware how familiarity detracts attention. Common household objects are not attended to because they are too familiar.

The subjective conditions determining attention may be summed up in one word, *interest*. We attend to objects in which we are interested and we do not attend to those which do not interest us. Interest and attention go hand in hand. We are interested in objects to which we attend and we attend to objects in which we are interested. Interest means making a difference. We are interested in objects because they make a difference to us, because they concern us. Interest may be most safely defined as 'the felt value of an end', as the feeling which accompanies special attention to some object. It is obvious that the two factors, attention and interest, are inseparable and that they develop simultaneously. Ordinarily interest is less dependent on the objects outside than simple attention, it is more a function of the person himself. That is why interest has a more enduring and persistent quality that attention lacks. As education lays stress on stable and enduring aspects of experience, most of the teaching effort is devoted to securing interest rather than attention, and most of the useful material on the subject of attention is presented under the head of interest.

Interest is both cognitive and affective. When we are interested in an object, we observe and study it, we want to know more about it, it gives us a feeling of satisfaction and we may act to change it, or keep it unchanged. Since interest predisposes the organism to react in certain ways both to know and to act and is tinged with feeling and emotion, and there may be endless variety in these ways, we have begun to speak of *interests* rather than *interest*. But a pleasant feeling of satisfaction and a dynamic tendency to seek the object, to understand more about it and to do something with it always accompanies our interest or interests. Interest in history means one enjoys studying it, attending to facts and movements historical. A measurement of one's interests is also a measurement of what one will do or what one can do.

5. Sources of Interest

The primary source of all interest is to be found in our native desires and urges, instincts, primary needs and motives. Living beings are so constituted that they are interested in certain things from their very birth because they satisfy their natural desires and needs. The chicken is interested in pecking, the wasp in mudhouse building, the birds in nests, infants in bright moving objects, growing-up children in games and sports, because original nature has inclined them that way. A thirsty person does not attend to anything but water, a mother may be deaf to the noises in the street but she is alive to any sound howevery faint coming from the next room where her baby is sleeping, and children in a class prick their ears when the teacher says 'Let me tell you a story' because their interest in stories is natural and strong. To catch and hold the attention of children we arouse their curiosity, appeal to their love of mastery, make them compete and emulate. Instinctive drives are powerful motive forces in behaviour and give us a fund of interest to be directed into useful activities.

We have already listed a number of instincts and needs. They give the individual impetus to act which we call *drive*. A drive is an urge or push from within, it has no direction but is just focused energy but through learning the individual acquires goals and purposes which impart a direction to that fund of energy. Then we speak not of instincts, needs or drive but of *motives*. A motive is a drive which through learning has acquired a direction through aims and objects, goals and purposes. These motives are springs of interest.

But apart from primary needs we have psychological needs of security, affection, recognition, new experiences and self-actualisation. They are acquired through social experience and are learned. Since most of our activity has social implications these motives provide very strong interests for effort and attention.

Since acquired interests differ with different individuals a number of persons behave differently in the same situation. A professor, a confectioner, a bookseller and a child will behave differently when they are placed in a library.

The professor will select books for reading and study, the confectioner, if he does anything at all, may select books of large size thinking they would give him enough waste paper for packing sweets, the bookseller may start calculating how much profit he would have made if all those books had been bought at his shop, and the child will surely choose those books which either have brightly coloured covers or contain nice pictures. Such differences in attention and behaviour are due to differences in acquired interests.

Much of acquired interest may be traced to our sentiments and complexes. A person who has a sentiment of patriotism is likely to attend to everything that will affect the welfare of his country; if we have a sentiment of love for a particular person we attend only to his or her good points and fail to notice his or her faults. One who has an inferiority complex will readily attend to and mark the mistakes, weaknesses and faults of others and will fail to attend to their merit or accomplishments.

Our interest is also determined by our attitude and mood of the moment. If we have a friendly attitude toward a person or are in a cheerful frame of mind, we attend to his good points and emphasise them. If we are in a mood to worry, we try to find out things that will fill us with imaginary dangers.

Our interest also depends on our education and training. A tailor will notice the dress of the passer-by ; a barber, his hair; a boot-black, his shoes; a pick-pocket, his pocket; a tonga driver, his hurried pace and possible destination and so on. In the course of life and experience we all acquire goals and purposes, principles and ideals which determine what things we are interested in. Habits, attitudes, customs and the like limit the field of our interest.

6. Types of Attention

Attention is usually of two types, the *involuntary* and the *voluntary*. Involuntary attention is passive and free. It depends upon the striking qualities of the stimulus and the way in which the stimulus affects the person attending. Involuntary attention is given to an interesting object, as when a charming speaker holds us spellbound, or when a thrilling story absorbs us, or when we open the door to find out who is shouting. When we attend naturally, easily, spontaneously, without any effort of will, attention is involuntary. Any object will attract such attention if it is brightly coloured or makes a loud sound, if it moves quickly, or is repeated, or if it arouses our interest. When the teacher wants to attract attention he should present objects to pupils in such a way that they show these qualities. Attention is voluntary when it is given to uninteresting objects, when it requires some struggle, effort of will. It is sustained, active, forced. It is not given wholeheartedly, like involuntary attention, but under the stress of some problem, difficulty or end to be achieved, as when we go through a railway time-table to find out a suitable train, or try to understand a difficult argument or lesson, solve a sum in arithmetic, or check a bill. We prescribed ourselves a goal and to accomplish it we have to attend to it. In involuntary attenion, we yield ourselves to the stimulus, in voluntary attention we make up our mind to attend. Both types of attention are governed by the subjective and objective factors described above. But in some cases there is a fluctuation of attention between conflicting stimuli of which one is easier, pleasanter than the other. When we attend to the more difficult and uninteresting, attention is voluntary. Fortunately attending to an uninteresting object often makes it interesting if we succeed in our task and are satisfied, and voluntary attention is replaced by free, in voluntary attention. In teaching, attention in the beginning is voluntary, the teacher explains the value of the subject or the lesson and the pupils address themselves to understand it. But the aim of the teacher should be to make it effortless and involuntary by making the lesson interesting and by arousing the instinctive and acquired interests of his pupils.

7. Span of Attention

By the span of attention is meant the number of objects to which we can attend at any one time. Speculations in the past fixed the number at five or six but today we have experimental data. We can attend to only one thing at a time. This may be said to be contrary to common experience. In reading one can attend to many letters and also words. The span of attention with regard to vision is measured by an instrument called a tachistoscope. The subject is given a momentary glance at an irregular group of dots, and is required to report how many he has observed. It has been found that an adult can note at the most six dots. But they are not attended to separately but as a whole, as forming one single situation. We can attend to a number of objects only in so far as they form parts of a single complex whole. The object of attention at any one moment is a single one, though not a simple one. Where this unit is lacking we cannot attend to more than one object. The different facts fuse together and form one process. The man in the street will cite cases where two entirely different processes are carried on simultaneously. In all such cases either there is an oscillation of attention or the two are attended to as parts of one.

8. The Place of Interest in Education

Interest is the feeling which prompts us to spontaneous activity. It has been described as 'the felt value of an end'.

It is something urgent, active and stimulating. We have an interest in constructing things, in buildings, in telling, in finding out, in competing. We have already seen that our instincts are powerful sources of interest. There is a tendency among many psychologists to identify interest with instinct but there are important differences. Instincts are racial characteristics, interests are individual and subjective. It is possible to kill and root out interests without much injury to the person. A child's interest in harmful books is not difficult to eradicate but it is not desirable nor easy to root out instincts of curiosity or construction. Interest also grows out of acquired dispositions like tastes and sentiments, complexes and habits, moods and attitudes.

Interest is both an end and a means in education. From the point of view of the child, interest is a means, for with its help he is to acquire knowledge and realise his purposes. For the teacher, it is an end. Once interest is aroused in good conduct, studies, games or literature, the child will consider no sacrifice and effort too great to attain proficiency. Every wise teacher aims not at communicating knowledge to young people but at stimulating them to acquire it themselves. For him, awakening or building a strong wholesome interest in the subject is itself an end towards which all teaching methods and practices are directed.

The place and function of interest in education is the subject of a keen controversy. One view is that the school is a preparation for adult life and since adult life is full of bitter struggle whose knocks are hard and unrelenting, discipline in the school should be strict and merciless and the child's path should be strewn with trials and tribulations so severe that they teach him to face hardships and put forth strenuous effort against odds. Such an education will fit the child for life admirably. They condemn the 'interest school' as 'soft pedagogy' or 'sugar-coating' which will lead to flabbiness of character, killing effort and endurance among young pupils.

On the other hand, it is maintained that education is not a mere preparation for life, it is life itself and the joy which children feel in doing, constructing, collecting or finding out, should not be lost to them in the school. Interest is the pleasure tone of self-expression and self-activity and is a great asset to teaching and learning. Undue emphasis on effort makes the child work from a sense of fear and kills his spontaneity and initiative. It is psychologically false and morally wrong to turn the child's work into drudgery, and expect him to do his best.

Both these views are based on a misconception that interest and effort are mutually exclusive forces. They are neither mutually exclusive nor forces which influence learning and behaviour from without. Interest is not a quality which belongs to the subject-matter and which will solve all difficulties. It is something within the child, and the question is not how to make a lesson interesting but how best to interest the child in the lesson. Making lessons interesting does not mean making them easy and simple but arousing, stimulating or direct children's interests in the lesson. Interest is a subjective feeling and, when it is aroused for the achievement of a goal, the individual puts forth his greatest effort. Interest and effort are not opposed to each other. The promptings of interest lead to effortful striving. The end of interest is not entertainment or amusement but activity, effort, accomplishment. It has already been stressed in dealing with play-way methods in education in the last chapter that interest leads to effort and induces children to do their best from inner necessity. Again, things begun with effort soon acquire interest. Many schools make games compulsory for children and though children in the beginning do not like it, they develop an interest for them later on. When effort brings achievement and satisfaction, it inspires children with a new zest and enthusiasm and is converted into an interest. The child begins because he has to, but he continues because he wants to.

But if effort is to awaken interest and if interest is to lead to effort, the teacher should secure both through worth-while ultimate goals and not through immediate superficial objectives. Let children not be asked to work for prizes and marks, for cheap applause or even mere examination success, but for life purposes, chosen ideals, noble aims and aspirations. No doubt the former group have their place and value but they should be subordinated to higher aims and ideals.

9. How to Arouse Interest in a Lesson

Attention makes for great efficiency in adjustment and learning and one of the major problems of education is to secure the attention of the child to the lesson that is in progress. The objective and subjective factors on which attention depends have already been described and no doubt every teacher will bear them in mind in preparing and presenting lessons to his classes. All that is aimed at in this section is an emphasis on broad principles of teaching by which children's attention and interest can be easily secured.

In the first place, the teacher must recognise that children's interest varies with age, and he must know what differences in interest arise at different stages of their development. The centre of teaching is the child, not the lesson, and it is the lesson which is to be adapted to the needs and interests of the child, not the child to the lesson. At different stages of child life certain well marked interests predominate. The teacher should be familiar with them and should adjust both the subject-matter and the method to the capabilities and mental development of his pupils. The standard of teaching should not be so low that pupils consider it unnecessary nor too high that they consider it beyond their reach. It should be well within their power of understanding. For example, in the infant classes children acquire knowledge mostly through their senses, and systems of education like the kindergarten and Montessori have a greater appeal. Later, memory and imagination mature and the pupil cannot only remember well but also represent what he has read. Still later, thought and reasoning develop and he is interested in knowing the 'why' of things. Thus to expect small children to think and argue will be futile. Children's curiosity, a dominant factor in all learning, should be kept alive and the appetite for knowledge should not be allowed to run low.

This leads us to the second principle. Interest cannot be aroused unless we justify to the pupils the value and importance of what they are going to learn. It means that for learning a lesson pupils should have a motive, and this motive comes to them either in terms of the practical value of what is to be learned or in terms of the appeal the lesson may have to their urgent instinctive desires. Most teachers of science, grammar or arithmetic begin their day's work with a commonplace fact and lead the class to the lesson through stages which impress upon the class the need and value of the new knowledge. Such lessons are attended to with interest.

Thirdly, all new knowledge should be related to that which the class already possess. The teacher should know intimately what are the acquisitions of his pupils and plan his lessons in such a way that they appear to children as a continuation of what they have already learnt.

Fourthly, the teacher should avoid monotony, for that kills interest. Variety is a safeguard of interest and should be preserved by presenting lessons from a new angle. The subject-matter should be frequently re-cast and reviewed to provoke thought among pupils. Often a new point of view, an emphasis on a different aspect of the subject, a new organisation of the material, will arouse active interest.

Lastly, the teacher should approach the class and his work of teaching with great enthusiasm and interest. This fact about the teacher's attitude cannot be over-emphasised. A teacher who enters the class smartly, smiling and giving a good impression about his earnestness and interest in his work, will receive greater consideration, attention and interest at the hands of his pupils than the one who is listless, indifferent and tired. Interest is the feeling tone of conscious life and is contagious. The teacher has not only to take interest in his work but also show his interestedness. There are teachers who fill the classroom with an atmosphere charged with electricity, their mere presence sends a wave of enthusiasm among young pupils, and they are able to secure attention and interest by a mere look, a question or a gesture. Their vitality, sense of humour, interest and love for work, do the trick.

10. How Interests Expand

A commendable aim and means of effective education is expansion of the interests of young people. A plea has already been made that teachers should closely study the native interests of children and base their teaching programmes and efforts on them. This is not difficult and when taking children's interests as the starting point the teacher offers them experiences that have some immediate connection with them their interests will naturally grow and expand. There are endless ways in which this can be accomplished. For example children are very much interested in dogs. They may be asked to narrate what they know about them, to read about different breeds of dogs from books in the library, to collect stories about dogs and to write a composition about them, and so on. They will gather much more information in this way and the range of their experience, knowledge and interest will be greatly enlarged. William James in his famous book, *Talks to Teachers on Psychology* writes: 'Any object not interesting in itself may become interesting through becoming associated with an object in which an interest already exists. The two associated objects, grow, as it were, together; the interesting portion sheds its quality over the whole; and thus things not interesting in their own right borrow an interest which becomes as real and as strong as any natively interesting thing'.

Such enlargement of experience and interest is made possible because things in this world are closely associated so much so that one thing leads to another. Man, animals, plants, climate, soil, fruits, health, medicine, doctors, hospitals, social welfare are all bound together in one systematic whole and the teacher can carry children's interest from one item in that system to another. Here lies the great merit of the project method of teaching in which we teach through purposeful units of experience and work and the various subjects of study are inter-connected and taught through projects. Girls running a sweet shop at the school fair learn not only how to cook and make eatables but also how to sell them, to keep account and calculate gains. Boys running a school magazine will learn much about composition, printing, proof correcting, grammar, and business practice. Such activities and experiences will expand and enrich their interests.

11. Distraction

The absence of distraction is an important condition of effective attention. Distraction may be defined as any stimulus whose presence interferes with the process of attention or draws away attention from the object to which we wish to attend. Ordinarily, noise or absence of quiet is considered the main distraction, but the conditions of distraction are varied. Some seek solitude to concentrate attention, others find solitude itself a great distraction. Dead silence is not conducive to profound mental application; for one thing, it does not challenge the mind to greater effort to concentrate attention.

Of the conditions which hinder attention, the more common and prominent are abnormal temperature—too cold or too hot rooms, improper lighting, uncomfortable seats—the desk or the chair may be too high—ill-health, fatigue or worry, and the teacher wishing to control attention should try to remove them as far as possible. But very often the reasons we give for our inability to attend are only excuses. Students who complain of too much noise or of crowd in the library to read, hear no noise and notice no crowd when they are busy reading a letter or talking to a friend. He who is always complaining against distraction for his failure to study may be deceiving himself by offering lame excuses for his unwillingness to study. Distraction may be overcome in several ways. One is to run away from the distracting stimuli. If noise does not let us attend, let us seek a quieter place or time. Another is to get accustomed to the distracting factor. One may develop a habit of not attending to it. The roaring stream among the hills may prevent us from concentrating attention, may even prevent peaceful sleep, but we soon get used to it and carry on our tasks without feeling distracted.

Often distraction calls forth an extra mental effort to fix

attention and apply oneself to the task. Experimental studies have revealed that under conditions of distraction are often achieved best results in attention and learning, because the subject puts in greater energy to keep the objects before the mind. Under the stress of examination many pupils muster greater effort to overcome distractions and achieve higher aims. But this is not very desirable. They should work under conditions which do not require this necessary drain on their energies.

Finally, an alert, determined, hopeful attitude is very helpful to attention, and if pupils have developed a robust attitude to work and study, distractions instead of annoying and upsetting them will simply help to arouse them to greater effort or at the worst to adapt their routine to them. Interest, enthusiasm, confidence, smartness, in brief the mental attitude of the learner, is of primary importance in securing attention in the face of distractions, and the teacher's greatest problem and duty is to cultivate among his pupils a favourable mental attitude towards the school, the teacher and their work.

QUESTIONS

1. What is the relation of interest to attention? Discuss the criticism that the modern doctrine of interest leads to soft pedagogies.
2. What is the nature of attention? What are the objective and subjective conditions of attention?
3. What is the use of attending to things? Why do we attend to them? Do we attend to certain things instinctively? List some of them.
4. What is attention? How is it related to interest? Why is it important for the teacher to study the interests of pupils at different stages?

5. How should you discover whether a class of children were really attentive? What steps would you take to deal with habitual inattention?
6. Comment on the following statements:
   a) Attention is interest in action.
   b) Attention is interest dominating cognitive process.
   c) Interest is another name for attention.
   d) Attention is the heart of the conscious process.
7. Describe the main sources of interest and explain how interest is both an end and a means in education.
8. What steps would you take to make a lesson interesting? To what causes would you attribute the child's inattention to lessons in Class I? How would you prevent these causes?
9. Discuss the part that should be played by interest and effort in learning and teaching.
10. Distinguish between voluntary and involuntary attention and discuss their place in education.
11. What do you understand by distraction? How would you overcome it?

References for Further Study

1. Dewey: *Interest and Effort in Education* (Macmillan).
2. James: *Psychology* (Macmillan).
3. Poffenberger: *Applied Psychology* (Macmillan).
4. Ross: *Groundwork of Educational Psychology* (Harrap).
5. Sand: *Increasing Personal Efficiency* (Harper).
6. Stout: *A Manual of Psychology* (Univ. Tut. Press).
7. Stuart and Oakden: *Moden Psychology and Education* (Kegan Paul).
8. Young: *Motivation of Behaviour* (Wiley).

Chapter Eleven
Sense-Perception

1. What is Sensation?

All our information of the outside world comes to us through the sense-organs. They are described as the 'windows of the soul' or 'the gateways of knowledge'. Popular psychology speaks of five such organs, the eyes, ears, nose, tongue, and skin and through them we acquire knowledge of the conditions outside our bodies. The essential quality of a sense-organ is that it must have the property of responding to certain stimuli outside itself. Thus the eyes react to light and give us knowledge of brightness and colour; the ears respond to sound waves in the atmosphere and give us knowledge of noise and harmonious music; the nose tells us about smells, the tongue about tastes and the skin about temperature, contact and pain.

It is a characteristic of sensations that they come to consciousness by way of a special sense-organ. It is only when a particular sense-organ is stimulated that we have a sensation and we can define a sensation only by reference to the special bodily organ that gives rise to it and with which it is connected. A sensation is a response or reaction aroused in us by the stimulus. 'It is the stimulus that comes to us and the sensation is our own act, aroused by the stimulus.' A sensation is an act of the sense-organ which, when stimulated, sends nerve currents to the sensory centres of the brain, and the first response of the brain is a sensation. The activity of the nerve cells at the sense-organ does not by itself constitute the sensation.

A sensation is an elementary mental process. It is the simplest form of mental life. It resists analysis and cannot be reduced to anything simpler than itself. It is mental experience reduced to its lowest terms, and cannot be defined.

But a pure sensation, unmixed with memories and ideas from past experience, is seldom had. An adult practically never has one. It is in the very early days of childhood when the child's experience is almost nil, that he may be said to receive pure sensations. No sensations with which we can actually deal is free from being mixed with previous experience and ideas. Ideas about objects mix with our awareness of them.

2. Sensation and Stimulus

We get a sensation only when some sense organ is stimulated but it is not every type of stimulation to which a sense-organ will respond. Every sense-organ is so constituted that it will react only to a definite kind of stimulus. We cannot see with our ears or hear with our eyes or smell with our tongue. Within each sense-organ there are finely branched endings of sensory neurones to which the activity that is aroused in the sensitive tissue of the sense-organ is communicated and from which it is passed on to the central nervous system. Since each sense-organ has its own set of neurones and since these run to, or are connected with, a particular part of the brain, or spinal cord, it is possible to classify sensations according to the sense-organs in which they arise. The type of stimulus to which every sense-organ is adapted to respond is called is *appropriate* stimulus.

It is very common to say that in sensations we are entirely passive. External objects impinge upon our several sense-organs, arousing sensations. We only passively receive impressions determined by the stimulating objects existing independently of us. We do not act but are acted upon. And the character of sensations depends upon the physical stimulus. But this should not be accepted without qualifications. In the first place, as has already been shown, a sensation depends as much upon the brain response and the activity of sensory cells and nerves as it does upon the stimulus. We are not entirely passive in the sense of being inactive. Secondly, the stimulus is not always external, outside the body. Many of our organic sensations like hunger, thirst, are stimulated from within, rather than from without. The stimulus is external only in the sense of being other than, and independent of, the sensations to which it can give rise.

3. Sense-Perception

In psychology a distinction is drawn between sensation and perception and because the treatment of sensation precedes that of perception, the beginner is apt to get away with the idea that the child first has sensations and then preceptions. This is not true. Perception is sensation plus meaning. Sensations tell us of qualities like colour, taste, sound or smell and perceptions interpret them as objects. Preception is one process but it may be analysed into two factors. It involves a sensation through the stimulation of a sense-organ and an interpretation of the sensation. We sense qualities; we perceive objects. The two processes involved in perception stand out separately in daily experience. We hear a faint sound and for some time are not able to know if it is a buzzing bee, the sound of an aeroplane in the distance or of a car. Is the black spot on the tree a crow or a rag? Sometimes we interpret slowly and the perception is not complete till the sensation has been interpreted. We see a coiling thing on the floor and mistake it for a snake. What goes wrong is not the sensation but the meaning we give to it. Perception is sensation plus thought.

Perception is the true beginning of knowledge. Sensations

give us only the raw material of knowledge and perception is the first step by which that material is elaborated into a definite knowledge of the external world, the attributes and relations of objects outside us. It brings us in direct contact with things through their sensible qualities and connects them with previous experience so as to enable us to locate that thing in our system of knowledge.

Since the core of perception is sensation and since perception is an awareness of an object present to sense, for purposes of education it is not advisable to draw a sharp line between them. Education is not concerned with the mass of sense-qualities which are received through the several sense-organs, but mainly with the child's knowledge of the world of things and their relations and with how this knowledge grows. That is why we have preferred to combine the two into *sense-perception*.

4. What is Meaning?

Perception has been defined as the awareness of an object present to sense. Sitting in my room I hear a sound and at once conclude that it is that of the college bell. Now what is given is merely a sensation of sound, but because such a sound has been previously connected with a particular object, the college bell, I apprehend it to be that of the bell, though I do not see it. Thus when a sensation means an object we call it perception.

But what is this meaning? How is it acquired? The elements of meaning consist partly of the fusion of various sense qualities which are presented together in consciousness. I have a visual sensation of pink colour with a factual sensation of softness, an olfactory sensation of smell, sensations of form, shape and the like, all these sensations when given together form the perception of a rose. Partly this meaning consists of the revivals of past experiences which mix with the actual sense qualities presented. When these sensible qualities given together are repeated in experience, they get modified in the light of previous apprehension. I see, touch and smell a flower and also name it. When I see it again I do not say I see a patch of colour but that I see a flower. The fact that I see a flower which, strictly speaking, is a complex of sense qualities which cannot really be seen, is due to the fact that the patch of colour has acquired the meaning of a flower due to my past experience. Similarly, we speak of 'seeing the ground wet'. Now wetness cannot be seen but can only be felt by touch, but the reivival in thought of how the wet ground looks, suffices to make the present visual appearance mean wetness.

Every material thing is a unity of a very large number of attributes. Some of them are more interesting, more permanent and practically more important than others and we come to regard them as the essential constituents of things, others which are more fluctuating and less interesting, we regard as mere appearances of things. Psychologically speaking, so long as one of these attributes, when present to consciousness, stands for, and means, the rest, it is said to have acquired that meaning.

5. Gestalt View of Perception

That perception involves much more than sensation or even a combination of sensations was clearly brought out and experimentally verified by Max Wertheimer, founder of the Gestalt school of psychology. Gestalt means form or structure and this school of psychologists believe that they must deal with total structures, patterns or configurations, systems of internal forces rather than with parts and elements as analytical introspectionists and behaviourists do. Experience is an unanalysable whole that cannot be understood by breaking it into parts or components. The whole is always more than, and over and above, the parts. In looking at a square it is the total figure that makes it look square, not the parts. It is more than the four lines that make it. The four lines stand in a particular relation to make a square. It means that the four lines are not as important as the relation obtaining among them. Squareness depends on the relation and not on the lines.

Very early in his study Wertheimer discovered that if two slits in a screen were lighted for a fraction of a second alternately there would be an effect of movement as if light is moving from one slit to another. This is what really takes place in motion pictures which do not move but pass in quick succession to give an impression of movement. Therefore perception includes much more than is found in separate sensations. Mind works as a whole and responds to whole situations.

The work of Wertheimer was carried further by his colleagues Wolfgang Kohler and Kurt Koffka and this approach of Gestalt psychology did much to draw the attention of psychologists to larger systems of interrelated facts as an anti-climax to the too analytical approach of introspectionists on the one hand and the behaviourists on the other. It did much to popularise the notion that certain patterns of situations arouse certain patterns of responses. When we look out of the window the landscape is a composite scene, a distinct percept with a quality all its own. It is not merely made up of trees, houses, sky or the road but is something much more than that. The several items exist in some definite relation to each other. If the relationship is disturbed the quality of the whole suffers a change.

To show the importance of relationship Kohler carried out an interesting experiment with hens. Grain was placed on white and gray paper. If a hen pecked at the gray paper, she was permitted to eat and if she pecked at the white paper she was frightened away. After several hundred trials the hen learned to peck only at the gray paper. Then black paper was substituted for the gray paper and the hen approached it in 75% of the trials. This means that the hen had learned to respond to the relation 'darker than', not merely to the gray paper as such. The animal's perception was of the relationship between light and dark.

With numerous such studies the Gestalt psychologists are able to show that each of our perceptions is a unique configuration or pattern of relationships. It is a unique experience with qualities of its own. It is a whole made up of parts but it cannot be split into parts without affecting its essential quality.

6. Sense Testing

Accurate and efficient perception depends on the normal functioning of sense-organs and all good education should include a system of thorough health examination by which all weaknesses and defects in the sense-organs are detected. This needs all the greater emphasis in view of the farcical nature of the so-called medical examination in which the doctor taps the chest, looks into the mouth and ears and writes out the report. Parents and teachers judge children stupid or dull when in fact they may have some irregularity in one or more of their sense-organs. Often the child himself is ignorant of it and does not know that he is short of sight or hearing.

The school medical service should help to detect such sense defects among children and suggest remedial measures, and teachers should guard against strain by cultivating healthy postures and habits of work.

It is not difficult to find out the defects of sight. Every child who has habitually 'sore eyes', inflamed eyes or eyelids, who squints or blinks, who suffers from headaches, who cannot read from the blackboard, who must hold his book less than one foot from his eyes, must be promptly examined by a doctor. Some of the common defects are described here.

Myopia or short-sightedness is very common among children. *Hypermetropia* is long sight. *Astigmatism* is present if some of the lines of the same width drawn from a radiating centre look heavier than others. These three defects can be easily corrected with lenses. The prescription of suitable glasses is such a simple remedy that it is quite inexcusable not to apply it. The teacher should be on the look-out for symptoms of eye-defects, and should teach pupils certain simple rules of hygiene with regard to the use of eyes. They should avoid reading in insufficient light, or with glare directly in the eyes, with flickering light or while lying down on the bed. Proper methods of study and posture are equally important.

Defects of hearing are less common than those of vision but they prevent children from getting much of their knowledge, they are of no less importance. Children with defective hearing are habitually inattentive, have imperfect language development, are unable to enjoy the company of their fellow-beings and grow anti-social. The symptoms of abnormal conditions of the organs of hearing are earache or discharges from the ear both of which need prompt medical treatment. If there is defective hearing without these, it should be tested. Often deafness is caused by tonsils and adenoids and these should be attended to. If deafness is permanent, the child will have to be educated in a special institution for the deaf and on different lines.

Besides, tonsils and teeth should be periodically examined as their diseased condition is responsible for a number of physical and mental disabilities. In India malnutrition is very common and pupils and their parents have to be guided in matters of health and diet. An efficient medical service in schools with a follow-up programme to see that remedial measures are adapted is a crying need of the hour. Mental health and efficiency rest on physical health and efficiency and no school can afford to overlook it.

7. Sense-Training

The foundation of a great part of our knowledge is sense-perception and therefore, it is stressed, that education must train the senses. We are told that craft-work, drawing music, kindergarten, games are valuable because they train the senses. But what do we mean by sense-training? To many it means the improvement through exercise of such senses as eyes, ears, muscles, touch organs and the like. This evidently absurd view is commonly held by many superficial admirers of such systems as that of Madame Montessori though she herself is very clear about it. No amount of systematic stimulation of the sense-organs can develop them. Sense-training is a training of the mind, of its ability to discriminate and interpret whatever the sense-organs perceive. Thus the training of the ear by giving it practice in listening to music does not mean that the ear will become a better organ but the mind will become more sensitive to differences in tone. Drever says, 'The important thing is that through sensory experience sensory discrimination is developed.' Sturt and Oakden agree that 'the aim of such training is to make children discriminate between slightly different stimuli to the same sense-organ and to attend to sense impressions as well as to the objects for which they stand.'

The importance of sense-training has been recognised by all educators, past and present, but with Madame Montessori it rises to the position of a method. We have already outlined the main features of her system in the play-way methods of education. Here her emphasis on sense-training is considered in detail. Her famous 'didactic apparatus' consisting of coloured silks for discriminating colour, of pieces of wood for telling weight, height, thickness, size and shape, is designed to train 'sensory acuity'. She claims that it not only gives pleasure but also lays the foundation of aesthetic appreciation and leads to refinement in sense-perception. But it should not be overlooked that what is trained is the child's power of perceiving, discriminating and interpreting his sensations rather than his power of receiving sense qualities. However, Madame Montessori is right in stressing the importance of such a training in early childhood as it will pave the way for later intellectual development. Secondly, as Sturt and Oakden point out, mere sense-discrimination as an end in itself cannot be interesting for long. It must be connected with a purpose and must be supplemented by thought and study for the realisation of definite purpses.

But even if one does not accept the Montessori system sense-training is useful. It deepens knowledge and gives a more concrete and accurate insight into things. The more definite our perceptions are, the more accurate our thought and knowledge grow. Some time back I asked a high school class to give me the approximate height of the classroom. The estimates varied from nine feet to forty-one feet. Such loose estimation is the result of defective sense training. Young pupils know tables of weights and measures but they have no idea of the approximate height, length, breadth, or capacity of things. The reason is not very difficult to find. They have been taught words without thoughts and things. They learned words in tables and applied them in examples to obtain thought but seldom, if ever, reached things. The modern order in teaching is things, thoughts and words and hence sense-training and all that makes for acquaintance with the objective world is welcome.

Sense-training emphasises a wide sensory experience of the world. We know how city children are ignorant of plants, vegetable farms, dairies, streams, birds and the like and do not follow lessons dealing with them. Mere books and reading cannot achieve anything without actual sensory experience and teachers and parents should take children out as often as possible. School journeys and excursions not only provide a concrete background for instruction but also help children to develop an interest in the outside world and steer clear of a morbid interest in self-analysis and inner life.

8. Perceptual Development in Children

Perception is built up from experience and since experience varies, perception will also vary. Two persons may have the same sense-organs and these may be equally acute, yet they seldom form the same impressions. They attend to different aspects, interpret them in their own way, in the light of their own experiences and observe different things. The child whose experience is very scanty probably receives impressions quite different from what we get. It will pay us therefore to understand how children's perceptions grow and how they differ from those of an adult.

In the beginning the child has no experience and his sense-organs are very imperfect in perceiving qualities, things or relationships. His world is an 'undifferentiated mass of mental stuff' very much like the low level of consciousness felt in a slow awakening from sleep. James describes it as 'a great, blooming, buzzing confusion', in which sounds, colours and shapes stand in disorder, without meaning, vague and indefinite. Gradually through the activity of his sense-organs he is able to distinguish between things by analysing his environment, picking out certain qualities, locating them, associating them, through improved attention. The differentiation is very gradual and slow and there are marked differences between the sense-perception of adults and children.

In the first place, children's perceptions are less analytical and more indefinite than those of an adult. A young child does not distinguish between wire, hair, cord or ribbon, they are all strings. He does not distinguish between pen, pencil or a twig. In infancy he puts everything into his mouth as he is unable to distinguish between things. His perceptions of clothes, utensils, members of the family are vague and lack attention to actual detail. Their drawings of objects show how they leave out important details and do not mind. If they are shown a human head with eyes, ears or nose missing, they are not easily able to find it out, as the Binet texts reveal. The reason is that their experience is limited, their attention is fleeting, their power of interpretation is undeveloped and their perceptions are bound to lack richness of detail and definiteness, accuracy and logical organisation.

Secondly, the child requires much stronger stimulus to have a perception than a adult. He fails to see things which are not very bright or to hear sounds which are not loud. Often things have to be presented to him in bright light, and repeatedly, before they can be perceived. The child reads every letter to read a word and every word to read and understand a sentence.

Thirdly, children's perceptions are often confused with what they remember or imagine and adequately do not represent reality. For that very reason they are less serviceable. An adult perceives accurately and for a practical purpose. A child, having no idea of practical ends and means, is spontaneous and perceives what details come his way or attract him. Often his perceptions turn out to be fresh and even poetical because they are free from the mundane point of view of the adult.

9. Apperception

In every act of perception we interpret sense-experience in the light of our already acquired knowledge and experience. Perception is a process of 'taking in', of giving sensations a meaning. All perception is *apperception*, that is mental assimilation of a new presentation, according to William James. How a new experience will be assimilated depends on the stock of ideas already present in the mind Colours appear different to the plain man and the artist. Each perceives them in the light of his own past experience. The meanings acquired and the stock of ideas which help this recognition, assimilation and interpretation is called *apperceptive* mass and it differs with different individuals. Some treat this apperceptive mass as the active factor and the objects apperceived as the passive factor. But this is not really true. Not only is the new experience translated and transformed by the past experience, but the old is also modified by the new.

Understanding depends upon successful appreciation and if the new knowledge is to be readily and properly absorbed in the old, there must be sustained attention, previous knowledge must be wide, interest must have made us ready and receptive, and relevant ideas alone should be called up.

This has an important corollary for teaching. Every lesson should begin with a definite preparatory step. The teacher must never take the class by surprise with an entirely new lesson. He must lead up to new knowledge gradually from that which children already possess. He must inquire beforehand if children have in their minds a suitable body of ideas ready to receive the new facts which will be taught. Even in the course of the lesson attempts should be made to call up previous knowledge as often as possible by means of well-directed suggestions and questions. If this preparatory step is neglected, the new facts are isolated and soon lost and forgotten, attention is withdrawn and interest is killed.

But previous knowledge and past experience may also hinder pupils in seeing the desired relationship or element in a new situation. A teacher may have to break down old ways of seeing before he can establish new ones. At the same time he can be careful to build perceptions today that will help rather than hinder tomorrow's perception.

Prejudices, preconceived notions or habits of feeling about certain races or communities, about one's parents, one's ability to learn arithmetic may hinder a child from perceiving accurately. As a result of their past experience students bring prejudices, biases and past ideas to a new learning situation and this affects what they perceive and how they perceive. To a very significant degree we all see what we want to see. This is particularly so when the material presented is ambiguous. Students see things wrong or misinterpret them. So there is great need that the teacher should guide pupils to perceive and observe correctly and carefully.

10. Observation

It has already been stressed that sense-training cannot be an end in itself. It must have a purpose. It must lead to and cultivate observation. 'Observation', says Sully, 'is regulated perception. To observe is to look at a thing closely, to take careful note of its several parts or details.' Because observation always takes place with an aim, it involves ideas. Dumville defines it as regulated and concentrated preception, it is not aimless looking about. Passing through the street we look at hawker's shops, advertisement, signboards ; we hear sounds of vehicles and passers-by. All this is not observation, but a string of perceptions. When we keep looking at shops one after the other to find a particular shop with a certain name selling certain articles, we are engaged in a series of perceptions for a purpose. This is observation. Here perceptions have a purpose and follow a plan and an intelligent sequence.

Observation implies thinking and ideas. It aims not at perceiving a number of details but a few significant ones. It involves attention, selection, analysis, classification etc. Essential and differentiating marks are noted. The child who tells us that a chair has four legs, two arms and a back has seen much more than the one who says that its legs are unequal. But it is only the latter who has observed. In observation something vital and worth-while is perceived. Those who have read books dealing with the exploits of Sherlock Holmes must have realised that observation depends as much on imagination and reasoning as on sense-perception.

11. Training of Observation

The value and importance of cultivating the power of observation among young pupils cannot be overstressed. It not only exercises a voluntary control of attention and recognition of sensory qualities, but also helps better adjustment by providing ' explicit knowledge about significant characters and relations '. It is the basis of our ability for critical examination of arguments. It is not surprising therefore, that even the lay public expects the school to train children in observation.

It has already been pointed out that acuity of the sense-organs and sensory discrimination, though essential, are not sufficient for good observation. Pinsent tells us that in any given situation, other things being equal, superior ability in observation will depend upon three conditions: 'familiarity with the situation observed, knowledge about the situation observed, and interest in the situation and alert attending.' In the first place, children should be brought in frequent contact with the same situation so that they perceive characters and relations more easily and readily. The sailor's boy is able to discern ships in the distant horizon much more easily and quickly than one who is not used to it. Secondly, intimate knowledge is a great aid to observation. I see my typewriter every day, but when it goes wrong I observe a good deal less than the mechanic who straightaway finds out the defect. Evidently, his effective observation has been helped by his expert knowledge. One valuable aid to knowledge is an acquaintance with technical terms and names. Thirdly, interest and attention are essential to observation. What we do not need, what is not worthwhile, will not be observed. Most of the too familiar objects of daily use we do not observe. We do not observe the number of steps in the stairs, we do not know whether it was the left or the right arm that we pushed into the coat in the morning. Such information is of no practical use and interest to us.

Now of all these conditions children lack knowledge. They have a fund of curiosity and ask many questions. This leads people to think that children are good observers but this is hardly the case. Without sufficient knowledge and an adequate stock of ideas, they cannot apperceive and observe. The teacher should not tell them what they have to observe, but only, invite their attention to it.

What is not perceived or observed will not be learned.

Often because a relationship seems obvious to the teacher, he may point it out and pass on to the next point assuming that his pupils have followed him. But if the second point depends on the first, the learner will be lost if he has not understood the first point. So the teacher must check that pupils have perceived each link in the chain before he proceeds further. He must make sure that the first point has been understood or else go back and build readiness in the pupil to grasp the next point.

The observation lesson is to be organised with much insight and care. In the first place, the aim or purpose of the lesson should be clearly set out. The pupils should recognise it at the very outset. Secondly, observation being selective, children must be directed to osbserve only significant and vital details. Such details are not to be pointed out but the attention and interest of children is to be directed that way through helpful questions and suggestions. Thirdly, the observation lesson must always be followed by a discussion and study period in which the essential is distinguished from the inessential and books are consulted to verify and compare conclusions.

The best aids to the training of observation are school excursions, visits to museums, field trips, and films. They help the child to see things for himself. But they should be used after some planning. Casually used, they are only an expensive way of wasting time. The class should be placed in a questioning attitude before the start and some time should be spent after the trip or the film to answer some of the questions that arise.

Perceptions can often be sharpened by comparison of different points of view. The teacher who encourages students to observe and compare contradictory ideas is helping them to achieve more accurate perceptions.

12. Movement in Observation

All perception is movement. It is an act, a thing that we do. It has already been emphasised in the earlier part of this chapter that mind is not passive in perception and does not merely receive impressions. It is active and through activity acquires knowledge of the surrounding world. Perception is activity and muscular sensations play an important part in making perception richer and more definite. The child begins to discriminate between objects not only through sight and touch but also through movement, manipulation, avoiding, picking, pushing, pulling, throwing or striking against them. In observation we should appeal to as many senses as possible, the muscular sense is very important in so far as the child in early age is all movement and activity and movement gives him richer percepts. Playing with the rattle, the baby not only gets touch, sound and sight sensations, but also in turning it upside down, shaking, throwing, picking, biting it, he observes it from different angles and gets newer and more definite perceptions.

Handwork is given a very important place in modern education, not because we want to teach children manual skill, but because in measuring, cutting, moulding and making things, children observe them from different points of view and they convey to them a much more definite and richer meaning. The experienced man is always more proficient as he has actually been doing things and obtaining his knowledge in the most intimate and practical way. Teaching through doing, therefore, helps to increase the mind's power of observation. Handwork, clay-modelling, weaving, drawing, spinning, pottery and the like are, therefore, not to be additional subjects added to the curriculum, but methods or media of teaching and learning. The Wardha Scheme of education is based upon this cardinal principle of *learning by doing*. The traditional methods emphasise words and books and even in observation lessons the teacher is frequently suggesting words to express the results of observation. The result is that most book knowledge is useless for life. So strong is the reaction against this book-learning that many modern educationists suggest that in the first two or three years of school, reading and writing should be altogether banned. Others hold that handwork should be introduced into every subject. The Wardha Scheme is craft-centred and maintains that every school subject like arithmetic, geography, science, history and language should and can be taught through the medium of one craft or another. Considering how effectively we learn those games and tasks in which we have taken active part, the Wardha Scheme contains an important truth.

If observation is accompanied by movement of some sort, if the child observes while it moves, acts and makes, knowledge will be richer and more practical.

QUESTIONS

1. How far is sense-training a valid educational objective? Examine some of the well-known methods of child education in the light of your answer.
2. What is the meaning and value of sense-training? Discuss the place of sense-training in the system of Madame Montessori.
3. Distinguish between sensation and perception. Compare the perceptions of children with those of adults.
4. Distinguish between perception and observation. How can observation be made more effective?
5. Do you consider it necessary to train all children to observe? Why? Discuss the value and methods of training in observation.
6. Estimate the educational value of visits to museums

and school excursions. What steps would you take to make sure that pupils make the most of them?

7. Give some of the methods and aids for improving observation. What is the value of educational films and how would you use them in the school?
8. What do you understand by the statement that handwork is a method rather than a subject? Discuss the main principles of the Wardha Scheme of education.
9. 'We learn by doing.' Examine the statement carefully. Is real object-teaching and manipulation of objects essential in early education?
10. 'The starting-point of the education process should be the sensori-motor reaction.' Explain the psychological basis of the maxim and discuss the place of handwork in the education of children.

References for Further Study

1. Bayles: *Theory and Practice of Teaching* (Harper).
2. Bhatia: *What Basic Education Means* (Orient Longmans).
   Bhatia, H. R.: *Craft in Education* (Asia).
3. Bossing: *Progressive Methods of Teaching in Secondary Schools* (Houghton Mifflin).
4. Dexter and Garlick: *Psychology in the Schoolroom* (Longmans, Green).
5. Dumville: *Child Mind* (Univ. Tut. Press).
6. Dumville: *Fundamentals of Psychology* (Univ. Tut. Press).
7. Garrison and Garrison: *The Psychology of Elementary School Subjects* (Johnson).
8. Gates: *New Methods in Primary Reading* (Teachers College).
9. La Rue: *The Child's Mind and Common Branches* (Macmillan).

10. Mursell : *Development Teaching* (McGraw Hill).
11. Norsworthy and Whitley : *Psychology in Childhood* (Macmillan).
12. Parker : *General Methods of Teaching in Elementary Schools* (Ginn).
13. Pinsent : *The Principles of Teaching Method* (Harrap).
14. Reed : *Psychology of Elementary School Subjects* (Ginn).
15. Sturt and Oakden : *Modern Psychology and Education* (Kegan Paul).

CHAPTER TWELVE

Feeling and Emotion

1. FEELING

FEELING is an essential element of conscious experience. Without it there is no conscious experience. But the word feeling is used in many different senses and our problem is to know in what sense we consider it as an essential element of consciousness. In the first place, it is used for *touch* when we say that a surface feels rough or soft. Secondly, it is used for *sensations of temperature*. We say we feel cold or warm. Thirdly, it is used for *organic sensations*. We feel thirsty or hungry. Fourthly, it is used for *emotion*. We feel fear or anger. Fifthly, it may be used for *any mental state*. We talk of the feeling of doubt, certainty or confidence. Lastly, it is used for *feeling pleased or displeased*. It is in this sense that we speak of feeling as the ultimate mode of being conscious. The first three usages refer to sensations and mean the apprehension of a quality to touch, temperature, organic sensations. This is knowledge rather than feeling. Nor is feeling identical with emotions, for an emotion is a highly complex state and cannot be resolved into an elementary feeling of pleasure or pain. *Feeling or affection consists in being pleased or displeased with something, in liking or disliking it*.

Few objects can be counted upon as always giving rise to a particular feeling. Sweets, tennis, fine clothes, we may say, are always pleasant, but are there not times when we get 'fed up' with them? Often this feeling of being 'fed up' passes into a definite turning away, a positive dislike. No doubt they are more or less permanent and uniform sources of pleasure, but they may be pleasant at one time and unpleasant at another. Our attitude of being pleased or displeased is one thing and the objects which give rise to it another. That is why feeling is often described as *subjective*.

Feelings in children are expressed by the so-called positive and negative responses. The positive responses of moving towards the stimulus, to keep it before consciousness, to obtain, hold or possess it, indicate pleasure, satisfaction or pleasantness of the stimuli. The negative responses of moving away from the stimuli, to avoid or escape it, indicate annoyance, dissatisfaction or displeasure.

2. Sensation and Feeling

The contrast between cognition and affection, sensation and feeling, is well marked. In the first place, feeling is blunted by repetition. Objects lose their pleasantness or unpleasantness if they are presented again and again. The sweetest song repeated again and again becomes stale, quinine loses its bitterness if we have to take it every day. But the oftener the sensations are repeated the clearer grows our knowledge about their objects. Feeling grows weaker and weaker till it disappears altogether. Sensations become better defined and more serviceable.

Secondly, sensations are the objective, and feeling the subjective, elements of consciousness. Sensations to some extent are determined by the objects, but feelings are personal. They belong to ourselves in a more intimate way. We often talk of the object being blue or sweet, the sound being melodious, the surface being soft. But we talk of ourselves as feeling pleased or displeased. Feelings have no objective reference, they are purely subjective.

Thirdly, sensations can be easily attended to, selected and observed, and become clearer when so brought into attentive consciousness, but feelings tend to grow fainter till they disappear. The more you attend to an object, the clearer or sense qualities become, but the more you attend to your pleasure or displeasure, the more it eludes your attention.

Fourthly, sensations are ' localised '. Some definite object is presented and a particular sense-organ is stimulated. But feeling is diffused over the whole system. It is the entire person that is pleased or displeased, but only one sense-organ that gives us a particular sense quality.

Fifthly, distinct affective states cannot exist side by side in the same pulse of consciousness. Feelings get fused. We cannot be pleased or displeased at the same time. But two or more sensations may exist together in consciousness at the same time. This is because numerous stimuli may be present to a number of sense-organs or even one stimulus may give rise to a number of sensations. My cap gives me a sensation of touch, colour, shape, weight. But I cannot be pleased as well as displeased at the same time. Of the two opposite feelings, whichever is more intense will over-power the other.

Feeling is always present in consciousness though it is noticed only when it is pronounced. Often we say that we were neither pleased nor displeased. It only means that the feeling tone of our experience at the moment is so low that we are not even aware of it.

3. Emotions

An emotion is more than a feeling. It is a drive to do something—something that brings about a greater adjustment of the organism to its environment. An emotion is outwardly directed, it is the starting-point of an overt action, though sometimes the action is inhibited before expression. Feeling, on the other hand, is inwardly directed. The emotions of anger, fear, grief and the like are not mere pleasures or displeasures but tendencies to know and act as well.

Though everyone frequently experiences emotions, it is not easy to give satisfactory definition of emotional behaviour. We are all familiar with the common emotions of fear, anger, joy, sympathy, grief and the like, yet there are several theories regarding their origin. Some regard emotions as mere impulses to action ; others identify them with organic sensations ; still others define them as revivals by association of past pleasures and pains. Perhaps the best method of studying them is to take up characteristics common to all emotional behaviour.

In the first place, emotions have a wide range. They are present in all levels of mental life. From the lowliest organism to man it is the same fear or anger that is found. A dog may be angry because its bone has been snatched away, a child may be angry because his play has been interfered with or his playthings taken away, a man may resent being deliberately misunderstood. Emotions may be aroused in the young as well as in the old.

Secondly, emotions are capable of being excited by a large variety of stimuli. They have no specific stimuli which alone can arouse them. Any kind of obstruction may cause anger, any kind of danger may cause fear. Darkness, animals, memories, sounds, almost anything may frighten the individual. Stimuli causing a particular kind of emotion have a typical resemblance, there is a typical mode of behaviour to every emotion but the variety of stimulation is very great.

Thirdly, some emotions have a paralysing effect on voluntary movement. We know too well how anger gets the better of our intentions and renders us incapable for effective action. This paralysing effect is felt on thinking as well. Stricken with deep grief we are not able to think and know what to do. Some emotions lead to greater activity. William James describes the case of an athlete, who, when a boy, was chased by a bull and in his fright cleared a wall which he was never able to jump again till he had grown up.

Fourthly, emotions excite the vascular muscular apparatus which is connected with involuntary movements. That is why under the sway of emotions we act in a way which we ourselves in our quieter moments will find difficult to justify. How often in anger do we utter words which we are ashamed of later on? We never meant them and still we uttered them.

Fifthly, there are two sources of emotions. They may be aroused by definite perceptions or ideas, as when some good news excites joy, or they may be internally aroused by organic changes such as those which result from the use of intoxicants. It is too common a fact that a man's temper changes with the state of his health. Children with bad liver are peevish and obstinate and fret at everything.

Sixthly, emotions tend to persist and leave behind an emotional disposition or mood which makes the subject more sensitive to certain emotion. A mood is a heightened tendency to feel a particular emotion. A man in an angry mood frets at every object. His emotional disposition tends to fasten on every object that presents itself. Success fills young people with a confident mood and they are pushed on to try their hand at new and difficult things.

Seventhly, emotions have what Stout calls their 'parasitical character'. The occurrence of an emotion presupposes the existence of a conative disposition. The fear produced in birds by a shot presupposes the tendency to self-preservation. Beating another person's child is sure to arouse the anger of the parent because of the pre-existing parental instinct.

Lastly, emotional behaviour is made up of a number of bodily changes which are always present. We are only too familiar with the excitement which accompanies fear, anger or joy. Since this characteristic of emotions is the basis of an important theory we shall consider it in a separate section.

4. James-Lange Theory of Emotions

William James of America and Carl Lange of Denmark independently put forward the theory that an emotion is the awareness of the various bodily changes which we experience in anger, fear or joy. It is difficult to imagine the emotion of fear without the feeling of quickened heart-beats, shallow breathing, trembling lips, weakened limbs, goose-flesh, visceral stirrings. There can be no emotion of anger without an ebullition in the chest, flushing of the face, dilation of the nostrils, clenching of the teeth, an impulse to vigorous action. Commonsense believes that we lose our fortune, are sorry and weep ; we meet a bear, are frightened and run ; we are insulted by a rival, are angry and strike. James says that commonsense gives an incorrect order of things and the more rational statement is that we feel sorry because we cry, angry because we strike, afraid because we tremble, and not that we cry, strike or tremble because we are sorry, angry or afraid.

The James-Lange theory may be said to insist on two propositions ; firstly, that emotion is nothing but an organic sensation ; secondly, that bodily expressions and organic disturbances, which are said to be effects of emotions are really causes.

We all know that during profound emotion there are certain bodily changes, organic sensations, changes in breathing and heart rate without which the emotional state would be cold and dull. Nobody can deny that these form an integral part of emotional experience. But the question raised by James is whether bodily changes are the only constituent of emotion, and which comes first, bodily changes or emotion.

No doubt there is strong evidence in support of the theory. An actor may induce an emotion by portraying it. In trying to give just a mild rebuke we fly into a rage. In using expressions of sympathy and sorrow in the bereavement of a friend, we are led to feel great sympathy and grief. Whistling and humming a tune in the dark on a lonely road does help us to imbibe courage and confidence. Many people are able to experience emotions by acting the movements peculiar to those emotions. But evidence is not lacking to prove that there is more to an emotion than simple awareness of bodily or organic changes. Actors do not universally experience the emotion they portray. Organic changes can be artificially aroused without the emotion. The injection of adrenalin into the blood stream will induce the various organic changes peculiar to emotional behaviour without exciting any emotion. Sometimes emotion disappears while the organic changes persist. Walk ing on the road, I see a fierce dog and am very frightened. The organic changes and the bodily expression distinctive of the emotion of fear are aroused. But soon after I find that the dog is chained and cannot do me any possible harm, I feel joy but the organic changes of the emotion of fear still persist. If the emotion and the organic changes are causally related, or identical, how is it that the latter persist when the former has disappeared ? Again, it is not possible to deny that there are certain organic changes which are not emotional like those which accompany hunger or thirst. How are we to distinguish those organic changes which are emotional from those which are not ? James does not provide the answer. Lastly, it is very difficult to explain the large variety of higher and lower emotions from the simple bodily movements or organic changes.

The latter are few in number. Then there are a number of bodily changes which are common to several emotions. We do not always laugh out of joy nor cry out of sorrow.

Thus there is evidence both for and against the theory. But James and Lange have done great service in calling attention to bodily sensations as real constituents of an emotional state.

We cannot really define emotion. All that we can say is : emotions are complex affective mental states which presuppose a pre-existing conative disposition, they are always aroused by a situation, and not by an object, they are partly constituted by organic sensations in whose absence they would either disappear or diminish in intensity, but emotion as felt by us is distinct from the bodily expression and cannot in any way be merged or lost into it.

5. Thalamic Theory of Emotions

Walter C. Cannon studied the relation between emotions and the autonomic nervous system and showed that the central division of the nervous system controls bodily changes occurring in strong emotions like fear and anger. It speeds up blood pressure, palpitation of the heart and breathing and upsets digestion. When he studied brain action he found that a lower brain centre, hypothalamus 'acts in mediating' typical emotional responses. It controls emotions and is the seat of emotional experience. The bodily changes and emotional experiences are not causally related but both the changes and the experiences are simultaneously set off by this lower brain mechanism called hypothalamus. If this centre is injured accidentally in human beings emotional experience is lost. If this centre is electrically activated in animals, they show reactions which resemble emotional behaviour.

Cannon and later Bard developed a 'thalamic theory'

of emotions as alternative to the James-Lange theory. The thalamus they claimed sends impulses to our viscera by way of the autonomic nervous system and to the cortex and the muscles. This theory is generally accepted and emotions are accepted as brain functions rather than as caused by bodily changes.

6. Emotions and Instinct

McDougall maintains that all the specific human emotions are derived from instincts. Thus anger is due to the instinct of pugnacity ; fear to that of self-preservation. He says that each primary emotion is merely the affective or feeling aspect of an instinct and every instinct has its own peculiar emotion. A list of instincts with their distinctive emotions is given in the chapter on Instinctive Behaviour. McDougall thinks that all other emotions are blends of such emotions. Thus he explains awe as merely a blend or mixture of fear and self-abasement. Woodworth draws a distinction between emotion and instinctive behaviour. According to him the former is internal and preparatory, the latter is objective and directed towards an end.

7. Educating the Emotions

Emotions are the prime movers or motive forces of thought and conduct and their education and control is very important. Even the lay public expect that a person who has received some sort of education should be able to control his emotions. Those who take offence and become angry without sufficient reason, those who are elated by every compliment, those who go into raptures on every possible occasion or feel depressed at the slightest setback, or those who are frightened by the least possibility of danger, are described as lacking in self-control. To keep one's emotions under control and be able to hide them is considered a mark of strong character.

Individuals differ greatly in their power of self-control. Some are calm and placid, little moved by the ups and downs of life. They are reasonable men, who act thoughtfully, do not easily take offence or get quickly excited. They have emotional stability and balance. Others are always bursting into temper, getting upset about every minor circumstance. And there are many shades between these two extremes. There are others who feel insulted every time they are not consulted, and those who are absolutely unmoved by any reproach or insult.

Education should train young people to control their emotions and obtain a mental balance and stability which will make for individual and social efficiency and happiness. The older generation always insisted on self-control and poise. Children should never show anger or fear. 'Be a man', 'Count fifteen before you strike' and the like were the catchwords with which they made the young people suppress the emotion welling inside them. In the chapter on Instintctive Behaviour we have seen that there are four ways of treating native tendencies, through disuse, punishment, free-expression and sublimation and we found that the last is to be preferred. The same holds good with regard to the expression of emotions. It is not desirable to starve emotions by banishing from the life and experience of children everything that will excite emotions, for without emotions life is dull and unhappy. It is not desirable to suppress them through punishment for this measure is seldom helpful in cultivating habits of self-control. The child suppresses his emotions out of fear and when the source of fear is absent gives more free expression to them. Nor is it advisable to give free expression to every passing emotion. The best course is to direct their expression into healthy channels. Emotions are the spring-head of great motive energy for thought and action, and the task of education is not to get rid of them but to harness them for useful ways of thought and life. They are a powerful 'drive' for conduct and the cultivation of right emotional attitudes should be one of the major aims of the school. The young people should be taught to appreciate the beautiful, to see the perfect in Nature and art, to love truth and to fight for the right.

The most important factor in healthy emotional education is the teacher. If he is a person of poise and balance, his pupils will catch it. Emotional states are contagious and individual differences in emotional make-up can be traced to the parents and teachers with whom children had their first contact and experience.

Secondly, emotions cannot be cultivated directly. The teacher should never talk to pupils about the feelings they ought to have. Emotions are not felt or learnt through descriptions of emotions but through true and vivid ideas and right action. The school should provide opportunities favourable to the production of desirable feelings. It should supply new interests which open out fresh avenues of thought and conduct and give rise to new emotions.

Thirdly, the teacher should wait when there is a sharp and intense expression of emotion among pupils. He should be patient and sympathetic. Generally, the expression of strong emotions is short-lived and it is better to wait till it has blown off.

Fourthly, the teacher, should never utter biting remarks to wound children's feelings nor ridicule them, for that would kill their sensibility. It will injure their self-respect and one of the strongest motives for improvement will be killed.

Lastly, through stimulating teaching of literature, nature-study, drawing, music, games and dramatics, the school can and should promote the emotional development of the young; the subject will be discussed later in connection with sentiments.

8. Fear and its Control

The emotion of fear has been closely studied recently both by psychologists and biologists, and although there is no unanimity of opinion regarding its original causes and responses and the characteristics of the mental state, fear, knowledge about this emotion is much more definite than in regard to any other. Quite an interesting discussion centres round the question whether the child is instinctively afraid of darkness, loud sounds, animals or he learns to be afraid of them. If it is a part of his original nature to be afraid of certain things, what are these things?

J. B. Watson, the behaviourist, who has made extensive studies of very young children, tells us that the original sources of fear are two. In the first place, fear may be aroused by the suddenness or intensity of an impression and its unfamiliarity. A loud noise for which we are not prepared startles us with momentary alarm. Reverberating peals of thunder cannot help frightening most of us though we know that it is quite harmless; a mere clapping frightens the infants and the first response of many a child to a sudden appearance of the old man from the tin-box is that of fear. But it is not only the suddenness or intensity of an impression which causes fear. Mere unfamiliarity or strangeness may suffice to cause fear even in violent form. Apparitions are known to destroy presence of mind. Secondly, fear is caused by the sudden removal from the infant of all means of support. It is the fear of falling. The child catches breath, clutches wildly with his hands, tightly closes his eyes, puckers his lips and cries. Older children run away and hide themselves. Sometimes an infant is frightened by a sudden push or a slight shake when he is just falling asleep or is about to wake up.

Children are also afraid of darkness, but they have only learned to do so. Such fears Watson calls conditioned fears. For example, a child is awakened by a loud sound and by his violent muscular reaction his pillow falls off. He is frightened. If he is in the dark, fear is at once transferred to darkness itself. If there is a light and he is alone, the transfer may be to the feeling of solitude. If he is neither alone nor in the dark, fear may be transferred to the bed and he will cry when laid down next. Our fear of most other objects like dogs, soldiers, pain, death is because we have learnt to fear them due to bad training.

Such training in most of the homes is arrantly contradictory. Parents exhort their children to follow the example of courage and self-reliance set by heroes of history when it suits their immediate purpose, for example, when they want the child to fetch a book from a dark room ; immediately afterwards they frighten him by saying there is a bogey-man sitting in the dark, because they do not wish the child to get sweets from the same dark place. Such mixed motives in training have a very unhealthy effect on a child's character and conduct and they learn to fear many things which they should not be afraid of.

The feeling of fear is also related to the unknown. It is not noise in general that frighten children but an unexpected noise coming from an unknown source. They are afraid of thunder because they cannot locate its origin. Possibly the fear of darkness is due to this fear of the unknown. Even while moving in the dark the child's fear is that some unknown animal may fall upon him from an unknown corner. Such fears are not infrequently suggested and stimulated by stories of ghosts and robbers. Imaginative children suffer most from fear, for in their fancy they conjure up all sorts of dangerous situations.

The first appearance of fear is egoistic. The child fears pain to his body and personal loss. Gradually this fear is replaced by more social forms in which he prefers pain or loss to social disgrace and loss of prestige. This is a clear possibility for education to make a constructive use of fear, to sublimate it into nobler social forms and to cultivate a healthy attitude of courage.

Fear is a very real experience in child life, and when it does show itself, there are three important methods of dealing with it. The first is the example of others. The force of example is tremendous in inhibiting fear tendencies. As soon as a child hesitates in the doubtful situation of a new experience, the adult should jump at the opportunity to show that he does not feel any fear. The second is to associate with the fear-inspiring situation something which will afford greater satisfaction and thereby will lessen and gradually dispel fear. Many a thoughtful parent or teacher makes his children get rid of fear of darkness by telling him to get a sweet *ladoo* from the farther window in a dark room. What generally happens is that the child fixes his attention on the goal and has no time to think of the terrors of darkness. Great care should be taken that no suggestion is made about the darkness when the child is asked to get the sweet *ladoo*. The third is to appeal to the child's reason and knowledge and show him that what he fears is really nothing. When he sees that the shadows on the wall do not mean anything, he is no longer afraid of them.

As has already been stressed, great harm is done by laughing at the child's fear, as most of us do. Ridicule does not help to explain his fear. On the contrary it may cause the child to hide his fear, which is still worse.

Fear is commonly used to enforce discipline among children, both at home and in the school. But as has been pointed out before, discipline based on fear is external and short-lived. It has no permanent effect on the child's character except that it cramps his physical and mental growth and makes him long for an opportunity to overthrow it.

9. Jealousy

Jealousy is a late-appearing emotion and can occur only in social situations. Hence jealousy does not appear until a certain degree of social perception and participation has developed. Jealousy appears to be the opposite of affection in many cases, but the two are by no means mutually exclusive : one may feel drawn to an individual and yet be jealous of his achievements and honours.

Most often jealousy is the cause of much unrecognised conflict in early life. Not only does it stimulate anger, hatred, and inferiority in the child, but in later life it may so influence the conduct of the individual that he is always ill at ease with his environment. It lowers our self-evaluation and leads to humiliation, concealment and shame.

The jealous child is very miserable, he has failed, or thinks he has, to obtain the time, attention, and affection of some one about whom he is greatly concerned. This failure, real or otherwise, like other failures, lowers his self-esteem. He lacks confidence, feels inferior and is full of doubts and misgivings about himself. He becomes shy and diffident or angry, resentful, rebellious. He may not be able to explain his feelings and may not accept his feelings.

The jealous child is fretful and unhappy, giving and getting little out of life. He broods over his grievances until he feels that the whole world is against him. He is a source of great annoyance to his parents and teachers.

In the home it is generally the birth of a new baby that causes jealousy in the older child. The wise parent not only prepares the older child for the coming event but also gives him personal responsibilities in the care of the infant and extra evidence of love for himself. When the older child realises that the infant is not a threat but a pleasant experience, aggressive behaviour will usually disappear.

Our present-day world is largely competitive. In every area of life and work the ruling passion is to outdo others and in schools teachers arouse and stimulate rivalry and competition among children so that they make greater effort and achieve higher. These motives have tremendous power and in our age they make for the highest development. But how much heart-burning it produces and how bitter becomes the struggle to do better is perhaps never considered by those who resort to these motives to make young people do better. Jealousy is the outcome of selfishness and the individual is for ever resenting the success of others, cannot work with them and is constantly complaining that he is not being appreciated.

Too much emphasis on rewards and punishments, seating students in the class according to their examination score, grading them in every activity on the basis of some score, giving them graded badges and other measures by which young people are classified on merit for one thing or the other, all promote jealousy and increase bitterness. It is time schools saw that these things lead to uneducational results for a jealous child grows into a jealous adult and sows the seeds of unhappiness, selfishness and bitterness in society.

There are two things which schools can and should do. In the first place rivalry and competition in study, games and other activities should be toned down and students should be encouraged to improve upon their past achievement and thus compete with themselves. Secondly individual rivalry should be replaced by group rivalry so that while they compete with rival groups within their own group they are obliged to co-operate and work together for a common objective and group glory.

10. Anger

Anger means a large number of reactions from mild irritation, annoyance and resentment to violent rage and temper in which the individual seeks to break and destroy what has aroused his anger. Anger is aroused when a person is obstructed and thwarted. In early years any interference with the activities of the child makes him angry but as he grows up adult controls which he does not understand or like. his own lack of strength or skill, failure or defeat may cause anger. When he grows older and has formed certain goals and ambitions any thing or person which stands in the way of realising his goals or fulfilling his ambition makes him angry. Still later when he has developed a sensitive regard for himself and his prestige anything which threatens to humiliate or slight him makes him angry.

A person is more easily and readily aroused to anger when he is weak, tired, hungry, liverish or extremely sleepy. Or it may be that small pin-pricks have piled up and the last straw breaks the camel's back. Again unnecessarily strict control and discipline may cause resentment.

Often anger is displaced. It is aroused by some major situation but is sparked off by a minor incident. Snubbed by father the child does not speak out but breaks his shoe-lace or pen. Rebuked by the teacher he takes it out on his companion and quarrels with him.

The fact that one situation makes Madan angry but has

no effect on Manohar shows that there is something in the person himself which contributes to anger. One who is very sensitive about his self-respect feels slighted by a minor neglect but one who is thick-skinned or does not think highly of himself does not care.

Expressions of anger vary from simple crying to sneers and taunts. The child may just send out a shriek or resist and disobey. He may on growing up indulge in back-biting, cursing, abusing or ridiculing. In school children play truant, make noise in the class, pinch each other, spoil school furniture or disobey. Often young people express their anger by keeping mum and refusing to co-operate. Some of them develop negative attitude doing just the opposite of what they are told. Others develop feelings of revenge and hatred against those who have made them angry. Thus expressions of anger vary from person to person and situation to situation.

Anger disrupts the mind and does not let the individual act with coolness and consideration. Most angry people repent after their anger has calmed down. An angry person is not in a mood to pause and reason and is intolerant of what others may feel and think. But anger is a powerful source of energy. It is the angry people resenting injustices, exploitation of one class by another, corruption and other anti-social evils who have worked and achieved some degree of success in removing these evils. Eminent social reformers felt anger and worked hard to remove the tyranny of rigid social customs. At the social level anger is useful but at the personal level it causes undue distress to others and makes things worse for the person himself.

The school should cultivate among young people self-restraint so that they do not give way to rage unnecessarily. Situations which provoke anger should be avoided and the teacher should not impose undue restrictions or assign too difficult tasks. Tedious drill, asking children to write a misspelt word thirty times, making them stand with their face to the wall and the like should be avoided. Taunting, making fun, ridicule, reprimand and the like do no good. Perhaps the best way to avoid anger in children is to avoid anger in one's own life and behaviour. It is easier said than done, but it is still worth-while to remember that teacher's own example is a good deterrent to outbursts of temper. If he is usually calm and cool and keeps his balance even in trying situations pupils will follow his example.

Another very helpful device is to ask young people after their anger has subsided as to why they let themselves go like that. Such self-examination has great educational value.

Much anger is due to incompetence, lack of skill and understanding and fuller appreciation of the situation. With the growth and development of these the number of situations which will arouse anger will tend to decrease.

11. Emotional Stability

As has been pointed out above emotional control and balance is widely accepted as a mark of an educated person. Intense emotions are experienced by all but it is expected of an educated person that he should express his emotions in socially accepted ways without causing distress to others and without making a ridiculous display of himself. But perhaps the word control is negative and modern psychology prefers the words stability and maturity. Emotional maturity does not mean that emotions and feelings should be banished from life but that they should be experienced in their full range and complexity. They are the spice of life and make it worth living. Schools should teach young people to enjoy healthy pleasures, develop wholesome interest in games, art, music and companionship, and since education is life itself the school years should be made as happy as possible. But unless teachers themselves have this approach to life and participate in pleasurable activities they cannot encourage and stimulate young people to do likewise. They should at least refrain from frowning on those activities of young people which give them healthy joy and pleasure. Maturity means that young people should act, behave and feel as people of their age do. It does not mean that they should behave and feel like grown up people nor does it mean that they should feel and behave like a child. They should act their age. If a child of six does not run about and shout he is not normal ; if a boy of twelve does not cheer, shout and throw his cap in the air when his school team wins there is something wrong with his emotional development. Children should be children and boys should be boys and the tendency to impose on them adult standards of emotional expression is harmful.

Questions

1. What do you understand by feelings ? Why and how should feelings be educated ?
2. What do you understand by emotion ? What are its characteristics ? How far should the teacher encourage the expression and repression of emotions ?
3. What is the James-Lange theory of emotions ? Suggest some practical applications of the theory in the schoolroom.
4. Is the control of emotions necessary for the training of children ? How would you cure a child who gives way to fits of anger ?
5. Analyse the emotion of fear and show what steps you would take to help children to get rid of fears.
6. What is the place of self-control in life ? How would you cultivate it among children ? Would you let them express every emotion or repress it ?

REFERENCES FOR FURTHER STUDY

1. *A Handbook of Geueral Experimental Psychology* ed. C. Murchison (Clark Univ.).
2. Cannon : *Bodily Changes in Pain, Hunger, Fear and Rage* (Appleton).
3. Dexter and Garlick : *Psychology in the Schoolroom* (Longmans).
4. *Feelings and Emotions* ed. M. L. Reymert (McGraw Hill).
5. James : *A Textbook of Psychology* (Macmillan).
6. *Manual of Child Psychology* ed. L. Carmichael (Wiley).
7. McDougall : *Outline of Psychology* (Methuen).
8. Rivlin : *Educating for Adjustment* (Appleton).
9. Stout : *A Manual of Psychology* (Univ. Tut. Press).
10. Sturt and Oakden : *Modern Psychology and Education* (Kegan Paul).
11. Woodworth : *Dynamic Psychology* (Col. Univ. Press).
12. Young : *Emotion in Man and Animal* (Wiley).

Chapter Thirteen — Imagination

1. General Nature of Imagination

The layman connects imagination with building castles in the air or painting day-dreams. It is some uncanny power of the mind which makes things that do not actually exist. Sitting alone on the bank of a river we let our mind adrift and by a hop-skip-and-jump it wanders unchecked into fanciful worlds. We perceive in clouds forms of animals, birds and buildings. We exaggerate a common event into a story. All these are cases of imagination. But in psychology we need a more accurate definition.

Imagination consists of picturing objects in their absence. It is a process of forming images. We get a sensation or a perception of an object when the latter is presented to the senses but what we recall when we think of it without its being present to the senses is an *image*. Sometimes instead of the whole object, only one of its sense qualities is presented and there comes to the mind a more or less vivid picture of the object. This picture of the object, when the object is not present, is commonly known as an image, a mental image or a memory image. Thus, having seen a motor car and known the sound of its horn, I may have a mental picture of the car when I only hear the sound of its horn. An image is a mental counterpart of the object in its absence.

It is possible for every sensory experience to have its counterpart in an image. We may have images of lights, colours, sounds, smells, tastes, etc. After eating a hearty dinner we may have an image of the colour of dishes, the sounds we made while eating, its smell or taste.

Just as we cannot have a pure sensation but only a perception, that is, sensation plus the meaning it has acquired in the course of experience, so also we cannot have pure images apart from their meaning. We have *ideas.* Images are to ideas what sensations are to perceptions.

2. Sensation and Image

Images being incomplete pictures or copies of sensations are naturally inferior to the sensations ' both in the enjoyment they afford and in the uses that can be made of them . We will here consider the several ways in which they may be inferior to sensations.

1) Images are more fragmentary than sensations. The latter have a background which the former lack. They are continuous with the total mass of experience, but in an image, the background is lost. An image is more detached. When I see a flag flying on the top of a building, this sight sensation occurs in a context of other experiences made up of sensations of sound, smell and the like. Later, when I recall the flag in imagination, the image is cut off from the context in which the original sensation occurred.

2) Secondly, there is a difference in intensity. According to Hume, percepts differ from images ' in the form of liveliness with which they strike the mind '. The image called up of a fine picture or music does not possess the vividness or liveliness that characterises the actual sensation. Perceptions are aggressive, they ' strike the mind '. A very loud sound like the whistle of an engine or the flashing lights of a car has the aggressiveness in question. It sets up motor and organic sensations which are sure to be absent from an image. The image of such a loud sound or bright light will never be so disturbing as the original sensation is.

3) Another difference between a percept and an image is that of distinctness. Images are more sketchy and fainter

than sensations. They are more hazy and blurred. They lack in detail. Sensations are more distinct and full. It is because much of the detail which is present in sense-experience falls out from an image.

4) Images are apt to be unsteady and fleeting, as compared with actual sensations. So long as the stimulus continues, it keeps the sensation going. But in the case of an image, the stimulus being absent, it can only be kept before the mind by a persistent effort of attention. As attention flags from moment to moment, images come and go fleetingly.

5) Images are subjective, while sensations are objective, that is, they are caused by an external stimulus. The order of sensations is determined by the stimuli but images follow in individual's interest.

6) As Woodworth points out, images are inferior to actual sensations in their practical usefulness. In perception the object is actually present and we can by continued attention observe facts which we did not observe before. But we cannot utilise the image as a source of new information. We cannot observe facts in the image of a thing that we have not observed in the actual presence of a thing.

3. Individual Differences in Imagery

Individuals differ in the vividness of the image they can recall. Some report their images to be as real and full as the original sensation, while others deny that there is anything like the recall of images at all. They remember facts about past experience but are not able to form any mental picture of the events which those facts record. Nor can they enjoy the pleasures of imagination which poetry and fiction afford.

Individuals are also said to differ in the kind of sensations they vividly recall. Thus of the recollections of a theatre, some may have only pictures of brightly coloured dresses of actors and the lines and shades of curtains. Others may recollect only the speeches, songs and music. Others may have only images of dancing and movements. In psychology it is common to speak of ' imagery types ' or ' memory types '. We have visual, auditory or motor types according as the images are of sight, sound or movement. The most common of all is the ' mixed type '. Most individuals can recall a bit of light and colour and a bit of music and dancing. This is the only real and common type. Others are rare and exceptional.

Some time back the question of imagery types was considered very important in the education of children. It was believed that every one is strong in some one sensory field, his memory images are strong and vivid only in that direction and therefore he is able to learn much more through that particular sensory activity. The visual-minded child has to be taught everything by means of sight, the auditory-minded through sounds and the motor-minded through movements. This view is no longer credited and Pintner tells us : ' It is best for the teacher to disregard these distinctions, and it is almost impossible anyway to determine whether a child uses predominantly one type of imagery rather than another. Attempts at classifying pupils into image types should be abandoned. Material should be presented in the most effective ways in order to call forth the kinds of reactions which will be required later on by the child.'[1]

4. Differences Between Children and Adults

Differences in imagery also come in due to age. The differences between children and adults in respect of imagina-

* *Educational Psychology*, p. 148

tion are interesting and illuminating from the point of view of education.

An important difference between children and adults is the amount of use they make of concrete and verbal imagery. Children use more of concrete imagery and less of verbal imagery : adults use more of verbal and less of concrete imagery. Children tend to think in terms of objects and concrete situations, whereas adults are more inclined to use words. To a child the thought of a dog, a shop or a friend is a picture of the object, to an adult the thought of such objects is in terms of words. Children get most of their knowledge through sensations, nor have they acquired much of language. Therefore, their thinking is made up of pictures of objects. Adults get most of their knowledge through books and language and they substitute language symbols for things.

Verbal imagery has a distinct advantage over concrete imagery. A word gets associated with a large number of objects, has a richer and wider meaning and can suggest more than a concrete image of an object. It is only through verbal images that abstract thinking is possible and any speed in thinking can be acquired. This verbal imagery is more useful and economical. No doubt the ability to recall pictures of objects has a value of its own in appreciation, but thinking in terms of words and symbols helps to save time and energy and is a useful mental device which children must acquire.

Often, teachers, realising the value and use of verbal imagery, make haste to replace the object-image of children by the word-image. They rightly believe that effective thinking is not possible without verbal imagery. But their haste calls forth the rebuke of Rousseau ; ' The pedagogues, what do they teach ? Words, Words, Words '. It is because they try to cultivate verbal imagery without, and often independent of, concrete experience. Words without activity and experience are barren and should be taught and handled in close connection with actual experience. We have already stressed the need and value of activity in education but we should guard against the all too enthusiastic insistence on teaching through activity alone and without words. Without words the pupil cannot transcend his concrete, immediate perceptual experience and develop abstract ideas and general principles. At all times pupils should be able to generalise their experiences into symbols and words and when necessary, translate their symbols and words into experiences. What is objected to is the isolation of the one from the other.

Again, children are unable to distinguish between what has happened to them and what they imagine has happened, between reproductive and productive images. While reporting events that actually took place, their fancies, wishes and suppositions bring in details to garnish facts and the story grows in re-telling, particularly in the direction in which they would like it to happen. A child is afraid of dogs. Returning from school a dog just gives him an angry look. Reaching home he builds up such a story that he was attacked by a dog, nay, several dogs, they all barked at him and would have torn him to pieces but for his pluck in running away, climbing high ground and pelting them with volleys of stones. Such lies are not lies, they do not involve any intention to deceive. Children are unable to distinguish between memories and imagination, their hold on reality is weak and not only do they wishfully build stories but also believe them to be true. This accounts for excessive credulity among children.

Norsworthy and Whitley believe that 'the images of children tend to be more vivid, more intense, than those of adults. So true is this that there is a time in the mental life of little children when it is difficult, and sometimes impossible, for them to distinguish between memory images and the images of imagination. In some children the confusion goes even further, and they cannot distinguish between percepts and images '.[1] The latter part may be true but there is no evidence to show that children as a rule have more vivid images than adults. On the contrary they must have less vivid images than adults considering that their powers of observation are weak and their percepts are hazy and indefinite, and images depend on percepts. Vividness in imagery is an individual trait and belongs to children as well as to adults, and because adults have clearer and more definite percepts, their images should be more vivid than those of children. On the other hand, because children are interested in concrete things and their images are not mixed with associations and meanings, their imagery may be more vivid than that of adults. A very vivid type of image is called *eidetic* and it is rich and accurate in detail.

Lastly, phantasy plays an important role in children's imagination. Make-believe play helps them to build a fanciful world in which wishes revel and everything is readily supplied for the asking. Such phantasy is not altogether absent among adults but in them it represents an abnormal phase of mental life. With adults it is pathological, with children it is natural.

5. Forms of Imagination

Imaginative activity is distinguished into several forms and a knowledge of them will help the teacher in developing and training imagination among children. Usually imagination is classified into *reproductive* and *productive*. All imagination depends on perception and experience. When the product of imagination differs little from previous

[1] *Psychology of Childhood*, p. 159.

experience, rather it is a mere repetition or copy of it, it is called the product of reproductive imagination, as when we recall what happened yesterday in the college or the club or recall details of events of the last year. But when the past only provides the raw material for building a new structure, when images of the past experience are woven into a new texture, we speak of productive imagination. Stories, novels, scientific theories, poems are examples of productive imagination.

Productive imagination is further distinguished into receptive and creative. When the teacher tells the class of distant lands in geography or of distant times in history. the class tries to construct mental pictures on the basis of verbal descriptions given by the teacher. The imaginative activity of the class is guided by the teacher and each individual pupil is interpreting the clues to build a whole picture. This is called receptive imagination. On the other hand, when the author weaves a story or the pupils are called upon to describe an imaginary journey by plane or what they would do if they were a king, imaginative activity is essentially creative.

Again, creative imagination may serve an end or goal as when we make a programme or a general draws a plan of new strategy, the headmaster plans a school function; or it may be indulged in for the pleasure of it. The former type of imagination is called pragmatic, the latter aesthetic. But such a distinction should not mislead the reader into thinking that the latter is useless. Life would have been a dull drab affair if poets, novelists, painters, musicians, had not indulged in aesthetic imagination and, in their art, expressed, in an ideal form, the longings of man.

6. Significance of Imagination

Imagination bears on our everyday life in many significant

ways and is a very valuable activity. In the first place, it serves as a guide to action. It helps man to understand and grasp the possible consequences of his plans, policies and purposes. He is able to foresee what is desirable, what would work and how it would work. Thus, imagination is a great asset to an administrator, a scientist, a social reformer, a general and all those who are called upon to take decisions affecting the life and destiny of a large number of people. Secondly, without imagination there can be no human sympathy. People are sympathetic only because they can put themselves in the place of others and through imagination can understand and enter into their troubles and misery. In fact, much of the misery in the world is due to the fact that so many of us are unable to do this. Imagination makes for understanding and sympathy in human relationships. Thirdly, imagination is a powerful source of enjoyment. Contemplating the future we are able to visualise circumstances in which our ideals, dreams and wishes are happily fulfilled. Even if such circumstances never arise, the mere act of dreaming and imagining about them is a very enjoyable pastime. A man without imagination is unable to enjoy all that makes life worth living, literature, music, architecture, painting and friendship.

7. Dangers of Imagination

But like every other mental activity imagination is not without dangers. Excessive indulgence in imaginative fancies weakens character. A person who spends most of his time day-dreaming soon begins to fly away from reality and prefers satisfaction in fancy and imagination rather than in the world of concrete things and achievement. A distinction is very often drawn between imagination and phantasy, the latter meaning an abnormal, extravagant day-dreaming which may lead to a retreat from reality.

Imagination is healthy and helps us to adjust ourselves to our environment. Phantasy clouds the world with creations which have an emotional attraction and appeal to people who shut themselves away from reality. It has always an element of self-deception and that is its only attraction. Creative, constructive imagination in all spheres, whether of art or of human relationships, does not seek to replace life but to enter into the meaning and value of human experience.

Usually, children have an abundance of imagination and many educationists feel that they should be weaned of it as early as possible. Madame Montessori takes exuberant imaginative activity of the child as a mark of immaturity and thinks that in this respect the child resembles a primitive savage. From this she argues that all fairy tales and myths should be banished from the children's books. They only plunge the child into the supernatural and merely prolong the period of mental confusion, they develop his dread of reality and terror of the actual. Others object to the fairy tales because they teach a dubious morality often stressing the advantage of deceit and cunning or teaching that might is right. Adler also recommends that harmful, superstitious and immoral elements in fairy tales should be eliminated. Still others feel that stories of witches and wicked giants are likely to cause mental conflict and terror in the minds of young people and should be eliminated from their reading. But except Madame Montessori, the critics of fairy tales agree that the right kind of fairy tale will always have a place in education and instead of banishing it altogether, it should be reformed. Her conclusion about fairy tales follows from her general contention that imaginative activity must be based upon truth and reality as revealed in positive science but she overlooks, as Drever points out, that 'aesthetic imagination as phantasy corresponds to the real need of the child's inner life and without it there would be no artistic imagination.'[1] The fairy tale with its crude interpretations of Nature is in keeping with the child's mental development and reaches his imagination at a time when his own meagre experience cannot provide an adequate outlet for his growing wishes and desires.

But it should not be overlooked that phantasy becomes a danger only when it stifles effort and if the person, instead of meeting difficulties in the face, retires within himself to seek substitute satisfaction in a day-dream. He loses his grip on the real and becomes useless intellectually and socially. But day-dreaming has a great advantage. Apart from revealing the inner workings of the mind, it represents a mental experiment of a high order. Here 'we can split up a total experience, fix upon certain details, and combine these with details from other experiences, and do all this without the expenditure of time and labour which would be necessary to perform the operations in our actual work.'[2]

Phantasy is the source of all our ideals and 'is indispensable for individual and social progress.'

Another danger of imagination is that it intensifies our depression when we are placed in a world of sorrow and uncertainty. The more imaginative people are those who worry a great deal during days of anxiety and fear. With a crisis ahead or some esteemed friend in danger and unable to do anything, we worry. Parents worry about children, students about examinations. Some worry is normal. But there are people who worry excessively and this may be a symptom of excessive timidity, of lack of confidence, or of mental conflict. Some of them have a haunting fear of making mistakes or failing, others attach

[1] *An Introduction to the Psychology of Education*, p. 199.

[2] Pinsent : *Principles of Teaching Method*, p. 205.

so much importance to the opinions of others that slight criticism of their conduct sets them worrying. Some people worry a great deal about their health and this is called *hypochondria*. Worry is satisfying so long as it lasts. To others it offers positive pleasure because they are able to arouse pity among their friends and gain their attention. But excessive worry tells on health and like day-dreaming is a type of maladjustment. It is often an excuse for failure.

8. Development of Imagination

Imagination is no longer looked upon with suspicion. It is a normal process with a definite function and a significant value. We have seen above that imagination helps effective adjustment, and that all rational guidance of behaviour involves imagination of the possible results of the several plans of action. It plays an important role in self-development because through it ideals are formed, ambitions and hopes are entertained and means and methods of realising them are explored. The part played by imagination in the development of personality is clear. Imagination contributes greatly to the enjoyment of life. We select those experiences which please us and piece them together leaving out the unpleasant ones. The dangers of imagination arise out of its extravagant use and here as elsewhere too much of everything is bad. The problem for education is to cultivate and develop healthy forms of imaginative activity so that it becomes an asset to personality and avoid its growth into harmful channels.

By far the most powerful help in stimulating and developing imagination is given by play and the teacher who wishes children's imagination to grow should provide them with varied and numerous opportunities for free play. The play-situations call upon the child to imagine himself in several roles, in place different and remote and in pursuits different from the actual. One of the great things about children is that they are able to do this readily and realistically. Often they do not need any elaborate plaything or tools, they turn everything into a toy, weaving and draping it with fancy. Taking a stick, they push it in between their legs and ride it for a horse, they place it on their shoulders and it becomes a rifle, they scrawl with it figures on the ground and it becomes a pencil, they strike a ball or stone with it and it becomes a bat or a hockey stick. They conjure up all sorts of situations, things and persons and indulge in varied make-believe play. So long as such games last the child is in real earnest about them and accepts the whole situation as very real.

Almost every subject in the curriculum can be taught in such a way as to stimulate and develop imagination, though in some opportunities are greater and richer. In early years clay-modelling, drawing, paper-folding and colouring pictures with paints are useful. Even in the teaching of language, story-telling is a fruitful exercise and the teacher should not only tell stories himself but ask each pupil to bring up one. Every child is a great story-teller, and given proper encouragement, will build up several stories himself. Some of these stories may be dramatised so that constructive images of children in being worked out into action grow more definite and clear. History and geography when taught with the help of pictures and descriptions of detail will call upon young minds to imagine distant places and times. But the attitude of the teacher is the deciding factor. Later, lessons in literature and poetry can develop imagination through appreciation. The teacher should not merely make pupils understand meanings of words and phrases but help them to enjoy what they read. The poet or the novelist is a creator who writes for aesthetic enjoyment and invites us to share that joy with him by interpreting his pictures in terms of our own imagery. With this sympathetic understanding we all transport ourselves into new places and situations, play new roles, meet new people and enter into the imaginary world of the author. The study of science, too, affords opportunities for imagination. Investigating, observing, framing hypothesis, testing conclusions, all train imaginative activity.

Popular thought attaches a great value to creative imagination and expects the school to develop it. Most of the constructive work in life and society is done by persons invested with a high type of creative imagination and the school must address itself to its development. Creative work in primary grades is done in the several activities described above and later composition work in language, writing a story, a poem or a description, is mainly designed to encourage pupils to do creative thinking. Creative imagination means that images should be carefully selected and rejected in terms of a particular problem or goal and arranged in a meaningful pattern. Modern schools provide facilities for writing for a magazine, dramatising, organising social functions, discussion clubs, excursions, railway trips to industrial centres, historical places, museums and hills. All these are helpful in developing imagination for in the last resort the quality of imagination depends on rich opportunities for clear and accurate observation.

Children start with enough imagination, it needs only direction. The school should not kill it by too much formal work but should help it to grow to become a source of power and happiness to each individual child.

9. The Problem of the Day-dreamer

Every teacher often comes across children who do not concentrate attention on any task and do not make any effort to participate in active school life. They would rather spend most of their time in day-dreaming and their mental life is concerned with the most vivid and active imaginations. They find it difficult, sometimes impossible, to follow the daily routine of school work. They often understand the goal for they are intelligent enough but they lack the will to use the means for achieving it. They get more out of passive enjoyment than they do from active effort. Such children crave for mastery over their environment but unable to act they seek substitute satisfaction in day-dreaming.

Day-dream may take two directions. The child may indulge in extravagant phantasies as to what he will achieve in later life when he grows up. He dreams himself into some kind of a fairyland in which his craving for mastery is satisfied. This is an outlet for esteem-hunger. Often this fairyland is a very distorted version of the real world in which he has to live and move and therefore there is very little possibility of his dreams being translated into reality. Day-dreaming is a very poor training for the future and indulging excessively in them the child will retreat from reality.

Or he may build up fantastically happy glories of his past life and may invest his early days with such happiness and rosiness that may prevent him from taking any active interest with the present life and its responsibilities. He simply turns away from them.

As has been said above these children have been found to be intelligent and their intelligence test scores place them very favourably. The teacher need not doubt their ability but should try to dig deep into their domestic and social environment for signs of conflict and frustration. Such children usually have problems and difficulties of adjustment and it is the duty of the teacher to help them to solve such difficulties and overcome their problems. Without making them unduly conscious of their abnormality the teacher should use his influence to persuade them to join games and other physical activities of the school. In mild cases this advice has proved very useful. Hikes, indoor games, races, climbing trees and mountains and the like are good remedies. Taking part in group projects, social service squads, skits also help. Recently the introduction of compulsory craft work like woodwork, metalwork, clay modelling, tailoring and the like will further help to offset the tendency to dream time away in the school. Busy with concrete things and activities, with tools and materials, children will be weaned away from inner life and brought out into the open area of outdoor activity, pleasant company, fun, making and doing things. Meeting reality in the face will help them to avoid running away from it and seeking substitute satisfaction in day-dreaming or phantasy.

Abnormal extreme cases will have to be treated by a psychiatrist.

10. Dreams

Dreaming is simply imagining at night; it is a form of phantasy which, like day-dreaming, often gets its impetus from personal problems. Sometimes they provide a substitute for a desired goal. For example, a boy who is strongly desirous of buying a bicycle may dream that he has got an expensive bicycle and he is riding at top speed. Dreams may also provide wish fulfilment in a negative way. A student who is afraid of failing in the examination may dream that he is running on a railway platform to catch a train which is in motion and that he is unable to catch it. Such a dream symbolises his feeling of helplessness and anxiety. It is reasonable to believe that dreams are related to worries, wishes, hostilities, unpleasant memories, and the like. Analysis of dreams and other phantasy material offers an approach to studying emotional problems and personality because the themes of dreams are reflections or projections of our feelings, needs, attitudes and conflicts. But the interpretation of dreams is not an easy task. Dreams can be given a meaning only when one knows a great deal about the life and personality of the dreamer.

If young people are asked to describe a dream it will give important clues to their direction of thinking and personal problems, but the teacher need not put too much meaning into them as dreams are crazy, confused, irrational and bizzare, students' memories of their dreams are very vague and their descriptions of dreams are largely made up. Even then such descriptions will reveal much about the inner life of students.

Questions

1. What is imagination? What part does it play in education?
2. Distinguish between imagination and perception. How are the two related to each other?
3. Distinguish between reproductive and productive imagination and discuss the importance of each in education.
4. Distinguish between the imagery of a child and an adult. What is the place of language in the growth of thought?
5. What are the dangers of imagination? Distinguish between phantasy and imagination. What is the place of fairy tales in education?
6. What do you understand by training the imagination? How can it be done in the school?
7. What is the role of imagination in self-development? Does it weaken character? If so, how?

8. Show the several ways in which imagination can be developed in the teaching of school subjects.
9. What types of imagination are involved in reading a novel, writing a story, describing an event? Describe them in detail.
10. What is the place of day-dreams and worry in life? How should the school direct imagination into healthy channels?

References for Further Study

1. Drever: *An Introduction to the Psychology of Education* (Arnold).
2. Gates: *The Improvement of Reading* (Macmillan).
3. Green: *The Daydream* (Univ. of Lond. Press).
4. Griffith: *Imagination in Early Childhood* (K. Paul Trench Trubber & Co.).
5. Kilpatric: *Foundations of Method* (Macmillan).
6. Norsworthy and Whitely: *Psychology of Childhood* (Macmillan).
7. Pinsent: *Principles of Teaching Method* (Harrap).
8. Pintner: *Educational Psychology* (Henry Holt).
9. Stern: *General Psychology* (Macmillan).
10. Stout: *A Manual of Psychology* (Univ. Tut. Press).
11. Warren and Carmichael: *Elements of Human Psychology* (Houghton Mifflin).
12. Woodworth: *Psychology* (Methuen).

CHAPTER FOURTEEN

Memory

1. NATURE OF MEMORY

EVERYBODY understands that the term memory is used to mean an act of remembering some particular event and yet the formal definitions attempted by several psychologists do not agree with each other. The man in the street usually defines it as the power of reproduction or the faculty of remembering, but psychologically we have to analyse and understand what processes are involved in memory. Stout defines it as the ideal revival, so far as ideal revival is merely reproductive, in which the objects of past experience are reinstated as far as possible in the order and manner of their original occurrence. Some writers like Beatrice Edgell use the word memory as equivalent to retentiveness, the ability to retain being a step to reproduce and recall. Others use memory not only for acts of retaining and recalling but also for receiving impressions. Woodworth regards memory as involving learning, retention, recall and recognition.

We will not attempt any hard and fast definition but describe the main factors involved in memory. They are four : *registration* or the reception of impressions, *retention* or conserving of past experiences, *reproduction* or recall of past experiences and *recognition* or identifying the recalled ideas as known before in previous experience. Every one of these factors is equally important. Memory does not merely consist in reproducing or recalling previous experiences, as students commonly understand it. It involves all the four factors.

The first, registration, is merely the existence of experience; without having experienced anything it is absurd to try or presume to recall it. Experience is the first precondition. Secondly, such experiences must be retained or conserved in some form or the other. The mind must hold experiences in its grasp as it were, before they can be reproduced or recalled which is the third element in memory. Fourthly, on recall, such ideas and images must be recognised as our own. Finally, as Stout emphasises, memory should specially refer to those cases in which the power of retentiveness gives rise to the definite revival, reinstatement as he calls it, of some portion of past experience, in the form of ideas and images. Thus a person will not say that he remembers how to ride a cycle or play tennis, for here a reference is made to acquired dispositions which do not form a part of his immediate experience. He can say that he remembers the last occasion when he rode a cycle or played tennis.

2. Individual Differences

There are very great differences of memory among individuals. There are persons who work hard to learn and remember only to be disgusted that they forget immediately after learning, and there are fortunate people who acquire easily and retain for long and with accuracy. Some acquire readily but also foget quickly, others acquire with great difficulty but, once they acquire a thing, they never forget it.

Some people have a good memory for names, figures and dates and can remember them well; others can learn languages better; still others have a very good memory for faces, scenes or places. Most people can remember very well in the line of their special interests, but some people can remember anything that comes their way. We have prodigies and geniuses whose memory can work in a marvellous way in a restricted sphere like mathematics, music or languages.

Again, there are memory differences at different stages of mental development. How often do old people complain that their memory is not as good as it used to be. In extreme old age the ability to remember new impressions becomes definitely very weak, but the events of childhood and youth are still clearly remembered. Certainly, in childhood, memory for learning lines of poetry, nonsense rhymes, dates and the like, is greater. Memory is said to develop up to the age of 25 after which it remains what it is.

3. Signs of Good and Bad Memory

But what constitutes a good or a bad memory? What distinguishes the one from the other? Stout describes four marks of a good memory. The *first* is the rapidity with which the power of recalling an experience is acquired. People with good memory are able to learn quickly and easily. The *second* is the length of time during which the power of remembering lasts without being refreshed. A person with a good memory should be able to recall the details of an incident long past, without having for once gone over them in his mind. The *third* is the rapidity and promptness with which things are recalled. Some people go on feeling for long on their tongues the details to be recalled. Others can recall easily and quickly. The *fourth* is the accuracy of what is recalled. A person with a good memory will be accurate in what he recalls. To these may be added the *fifth* mark, the serviceableness of what is recalled. A person with a good memory will recall or remember things which are relevant to the occasion. Many people commit things to memory but cannot recall them when they are needed. A good memory should be serviceable. Many students who cram for examinations fail to recall, in the examination, thoughts and words they had committed to memory.

Thus a good memory will help a person to recall relevant details, with speed and accuracy.

4. Conditions of Good Memory

What are the determining factors of good memory? What are the general conditions favourable to effective remembering? A detailed discussion of the factors which may improve memory will follow later. Here we turn to a consideration of the general factors only.

In the first place, good health helps memory. We have seen that every mental process means the formation of certain brain-paths and memory is in a broad sense retracing those brain-paths. How long these traces will remain depends upon heredity and our inborn capacity to retain. But poor health will definitely diminish this retentiveness and good health will take it to its height. In order to make the most of our power to retain, we must keep good health. Students during examination days neglect health and suffer for it. Mental vigour, freedom from fatigue and fresh air, help us to remember better. Students often appreciate the value of this suggestion when they study their difficult subjects and topics in the morning hours.

Another most important condition of a good memory is attention. One author has remarked wittily, 'Interest is the mother of attention, and attention is the mother of memory; if you would secure memory, you must first catch the mother and the grandmother'. The student who has no interest in what he studies, and goes through his task inattentively, does not acquire much and retains very poorly what little he acquires. There are students in every school who cannot recall even a single theorem of geometry, are very poor in recalling facts in history or geography, but who can recall very minutely even small details of almost all the matches played during the season. This is essentially a question of the differences of interest and attention. Irksomeness and superficiality of acquisition are natural accompaniments of this lack of interest and attention. The person who is not deeply interested in the task that is before him constantly wanders away to more alluring fields, attention is scattered, and recalled ideas are vague, confused and fleeting.

Thirdly, impressions received more vividly and distinctly are better remembered. The more intense and vivacious the impression, the longer it is remembered. The details and dates of tragedies and fatal accidents are remembered perfectly because of their powerful impression.

Fourthly, repetition of even ordinary experiences helps us to remember them. Lessons frequently repeated are at our finger's end. But mere repetition will not suffice unless it is frequent, recent and regular. This factor comes into play so often in education that it needs a more detailed treatment.

5. THE VALUE OF REPETITION

Many pupils and teachers believe that the best way of remembering things is ceaseless repetition. Frequent conning over lessons, cramming or mugging is still a very popular method of learning and the teacher unhesitatingly recommends that answers to questions should be memorised verbatim so that they can be effectively reproduced. Repetition means bringing into attention again and again the items with which we wish to be associated and exercising that association. Experiments have shown that items repeated more often are remembered longer than those repeated less often. Repetition helps the pupil to make the material his own.

Children have a strong impulse to repeat rhymes, tables and lessons from their readers and one frequently meets a young child who knows his primer by heart. The teacher should certainly make use of this impulse and make children learn a number of useful things. But not infrequently one comes across pupils who can repeat lessons without understanding a word of them and many grown-up pupils are chagrined on the examination day to find that items memorised through repetition cannot be recalled. It is because mere repetition is not enough. It must be accompanied by understanding and interest, there must be motive to learn and a concentration of attention on the subject. The old method of drill was ineffective because in it repetition was not meaningful. The teacher should encourage pupils to understand things clearly and then leave them alone to find out what degree of repetition each one of them will need to learn any item. Some pupils need less time, others need more organisation of the subject-matter and so on. The length of repetition will depend on the individual pupil's span of attention. If he is not able to attend to an item for long, repetition will be useless.

Should repetition be spaced? Experimental studies show that a daily programme of short periods in which topics can be repeated frequently is better than a prolonged single period. The teacher who has to give six hours a week will gain by devoting one hour daily than by giving two hours on three days. Two periods of thirty minutes placed independently in the daily time-table will be still better. Attention will not flag, impressions will be clear and more lasting. Fatigue will be avoided and a fresh start every time will insure interest.

Woodworth describes an experiment on part and whole learning. In committing a poem to memory is it more economical to learn it part by part or go through the whole poem again and again till it is mastered ? The experiment he describes favours the whole method. A young man took two passages of 240 lines, both from the same poem and studied one by the whole method, the other by the part method in sittings of about thirty-five minutes each day. One passage he read thrice daily, and doing three readings of the whole, could recite it in 10 days, taking in all 348 minutes. The other passage he learnt by parts memorising 30 lines till the whole could be recited to 12 days, taking about 431 minutes. Thus by the whole method he could save 83 minutes, that is, 20 per cent of the time.

Woodworth goes on to emphasise that the factors of advantage involved in memorising are interest, attention and confidence, recency of experience, meaning and organisation of subject-matter. They should supplement repetition.

6. Registration or Fixation

For an accurate and detailed analysis of the act of remembering and for a consideration of the important question of improving memory we must examine the elementary processes involved in it more closely.

In recording experiences or registering verbal material there are certain principles which make for better reproduction and longer retention. The most prominent of them such as good physical health, freedom from fatigue and anxiety, interest and attention, vividness of impression, repetition, giving experiences and verbal material, rich meaning, spaced repetition and memorising by the part or the whole method have already been dealt with. All that is attempted here is an emphasis on some classroom practices which may help fixation.

Before undertaking to memorise, it is advisable to determine whether the material is to be learnt for permanent or limited recall. There should be a definite purpose in all learning and memorising. Most students learn for a limited recall for use in the examination. They put off the entire learning till the last day or hours just preceding the examination, but only to find that they have made a hopeless mess of it. The best method is to have spaced recitations of the material sometime before the examination until it is fairly well learnt, and then to have a final practice just before the examination. In learning for permanent use the matter should be repeated very frequently, repetition should be done for a long period of time and associations among the items to be learnt should be developed.

It has already been emphasised that vivid impressions last longer but effort should be made to prevent trivial things from occupying too much attention. As we shall see later, unless we withdraw attention from unimportant, irrelevant items we cannot concentrate on the important ones.

Repetition, too, has already been stressed. In the class every student should think of the answers to the questions asked of his classmates. If he knows the answer, he is getting a review; if he does not know, he will be able to learn when his classmate repeats the answer. Many students repeat gists of what they learn or repeat orally by closing their books. Others read rapidly and then note down the main points of what they have read to see if they have missed anything important. Some students in colleges listen to the lecturer attentively and take down notes with the help of textbooks on reaching home, others take down notes in the class-room and develop them at home with the help of a number of books. All these devices are helpful.

Some pupils outline their reading matter and count the sub-headings. Others learn the first letter or word of every line of a poem. Others organise their matter into logical heads and learn the order of those heads.

From the point of view of the teacher the lesson to be

learnt should have a multiple sense appeal. We have already seen in sense training that stimuli which appeal to more than one sense-organ are perceived and remembered better. In teaching new words the teacher not only pronounces the word, he spells it, asks the class to pronounce and spell it, he writes it on the blackboard and asks the class to transcribe it. Thus children have seen it, read it and written it, and their impression is visual, auditory and muscular. The multiple sense appeal helps effective fixation.

James says, ' All improvement of memory consists in the improvement of one's habitual method of recording facts '. These methods may be *mechanical* as the intensification and repetition of the stimuli. They may be *judicious* as remembering things by arranging them logically, classifying and placing them under general heads. They may be *ingenious* as remembering things by fancifully connecting them with other things.

7. Retention

As already mentioned differences in retention are due to heredity. The ability to retain rests on traces left in the brain-paths, that is, on physiological factors which are beyond our direct control. Anything that is retained in the mind persists in the form of dispositions. Individual differences in retentiveness have already been described and the factors which influence it are age, fatigue, illness, poisons and drugs that is, all that affects the health of the nervous system.

Many charlatans exploit the credulity of students by selling them drugs which are claimed to improve their retentive power. But the best thing to do is to improve the general bodily tone.

Retention is very difficult to improve by practice. It is a case of dispositions and the strength of dispositions depends upon an individual's brain. The capacity of retention is native and cannot be improved by training. But what help the teacher can give to ensure retention of learned material will be discussed in the next chapter.

8. Measurement of Retention

In experiments on retention the subjects are asked to master a certain learning task. The task may be motor or verbal or both. After some fixed time the amount of learned material that the subjects have retained is measured. In some cases it is done soon after the learning period and in other cases an interval of time is allowed between learning and testing. The interval may be days or even weeks. This is usually what the teacher also does, first teaching, then allowing pupils to learn and then testing them after some time, but his practice is neither methodical nor standardised

There are four common methods of measuring retention in the laboratory. The first is the *method of recall* in which the learner recreates from memory what he has learned. Any deviation is counted as an error. May be there is only one answer to the question and the learner may get it right or wrong. But the teacher may expect originality of interpretation and expression in which case there may be degrees of recall. If the recall has to be verbatim the score is usually lower. But a pupil may not be able to recall though he can recognise in which case we can say that the method of recall is not perfect.

The second *method of recognition* is used very extensively in psychological testing. A number of answers are given to a question and pupils are asked to identify or recognise the correct one.

The third method of measuring retention is that of *reproduction* or *rearrangement*. Here the subject has learned material in a certain order, he is given that material in a mixed up form and he is asked to organize it into the original form or order.

The fourth method of measuring retention is that of *savings* or *relearning.* It is assumed that a person never completely forgets anything he has learned, and here the subject is asked to relearn the same material. The difference between the time taken in the first learning and that required for relearning to the same degree of proficiency is a measure of the subject's degree of retention from the original learning.

Only the first two methods are used in the classroom but all four methods are used in laboratory studies of retention.

9. RECALL

Recall is the mental revival of past experience. Of all experiences retained only some can be recalled and psychoanalysts tell us that even those which are not recalled influence our present behaviour, likes and dislikes. But here we are concerned with the factors which influence the revival of most pertinent memories.

The past is reproduced or recalled to make an adjustment to the persent condition but often we cannot make the proper recall. The thing just escapes us. It may be the name of the friend, a place or a town and however we may cudgel our brains, it gives us a slip. What are we to do under such circumstances ?

Recall is of two kinds, spontaneous and deliberate. We have seen how in a reverie one idea leads to another and a long string is made up without any effort on our part. After-dinner hours are generally filled up by such recollections of old long past experiences, hopes, disappointments, joys and sorrows. One picture fades into another. This is spontaneous recall. But on other occasions we are called upon to meet a new situation, to solve a new problem or make new adjustments. We recall our past to help us, but in reproducing we select those experiences which bear on the present. From the host of memories that arise only a few are chosen to solve the problem or to make a proper adjustment. This is deliberate recall. The need of the moment seems to attract and pull out of the past into the present such memories as are in tune with it. Taking an examination, a pupil recalls facts pertinent to the subject in hand.

For improvement of recall or reproduction the following suggestions are helpful:

i) An attitude of confidence is essential to recall, anxiety, fear or diffidence will prevent the recall. Those students who enter the examination hall in an attitude of excessive anxiety are sure to spoil their work. Doubt blocks reproduction. He who thinks he can, does succeed in recalling.

ii) The stimulus should be given a good chance. Look squarely at the person whose name you wish to recall, and you will soon be able to recall it.

iii) If there is any difficulty in recall, drop the matter for the time being and come back to it afresh. Sometimes we are unable to solve a problem and give it up Later when we try to tackle it, the solution flashes into consciousness readily. It does no good to keep doggedly hunting for a name you are not able to recall. Half an hour later it may enter your mind without the least trouble.

But what can the teacher do to help efficient recall? The first thing the teacher can do is to help students to see meaning in what they are learning and find value in it for themselves and their problems. A student's interest is the key to his learning. If the teacher can capture his interest he will work with persistence and imagination and learn with remarkable precision and detail. Pupils should be given a chance to share in the responsibility for their own learning. The teacher should not do all the planning, execution and evaluation ; if he does so pupils will lose interest. Students' participation in teaching and learning is helpful in building up their interest and in recalling what they learn. Secondly students should be helped to organise their learning so that they find out what they have learned and what they have left out. If they are continually helped to recall, draw inferences or establish relationships they will be actively involved in the task of learning and will recall better. Thirdly multiple approach through group discussions, talks and writing will help fixation and recall.

10. Association of Ideas

The association of ideas is a well-known principle by which one idea calls up another or others that have been previously experienced. Peacocks shriek when clouds thunder, children are afraid when they spill milk, dogs run away when you raise your arm to strike. It is because these experiences recall others to mind and arouse original responses. Animals are trained to make certain movements at the bidding of their masters. A particular sign awakens thoughts of previous behaviour which is reproduced. It is a type of conditioned response.

Human experience is continuous and can be marked out into wholes. The thought of one fact or element of experience brings to mind others experienced along with it. As I sit, reading at my desk I suddenly hear a whistle. I think of the engine that has produced it, the train, the crowd, the scene at the platform. It leads me to think of the last journey I took by train, the circumstances under which it was performed, the people I met, the places I visited and a host of things and details. A string of ideas flashes across my mind and I find myself in a new setting.

Such an association of ideas is governed by certain factors. Of a large mass of experience and thought only a few are recalled. It depends on *recency*, *frequency* and *intensity* of experiences or on the *mood* or *attitude* of the person. If you ask a person the first word that comes to his mind when he hears the word *day*, most often he will respond with *night*. This association is determined by frequency of connection, but if the *day* has been hot or it has been an unusual summer, he may respond with *hot*, in which case. the association will be based on recency or intensity of the connection. Again, in a happy frame of mind we recall bright sunny thoughts and in a depressing state our ideas tend to be gloomy.

There are two ways in which different things may be associated so that recalling one leads to the recall of the other. In the first place, things may, in some way, resemble each other. One story may remind me of another with the same plot, one face may lead me to think of my friend who has a similar face; some dogs remind us of a fox, others of a wolf. This is *association by similarity*. But the story may remind me of the persons who described it last week. the face of a man may lead me to think of the party where I met him some time back, a dog may remind me of the child bitten by another dog and so on. These associations do not depend upon similarity but on *contiguity*. Facts experienced or thought together are so associated that the thought of one leads to the other.

Associative thinking opens up a large vista of past experiences and thoughts and its value depends on the worthwhileness of connections between ideas. If the aim of education is to establish useful links among ideas, young people should have a wealth of primary experience with life and the things that are to be linked together should be presented together. Healthy interests and a variety of social contacts will be helpful. In teaching a language words should be associated with actual things and experiences. If the two are presented together, the one will spontaneously recall the other.

Relationships or associations make ideas, things and events meaningful. A new topic taught will be meaningful to pupils to the extent that it is rooted in their own experience of making different kinds of associations under different circumstances. School learning is often condemned as barren because dates, names, definitions, rules, multiplication tables and so on have been set before the learners to be learned verbatim without any meaning to the learner or relationship to his previous experience. They are retained as they are committed to memory through drill and verbatim but they can be recalled usefully in any context of their need only if they are associated with concrete situations in which they are going to be used or applied. But only a part of the meaning to be found in associations lies in the material itself. The other part lies in the relationship of associations to the learner. The new ideas or material to be learned becomes all the more meaningful and clear to the learner if they are related to his needs, interests and abilities, if they are useful, threatening or satisfying to him, and if he can relate them with things he has already learned.

11. Recognition

To recognise is to identify an object and place it in one's system of memories. It is knowing the object again and there is an awareness that it is being known again. There are degrees of recognition. There may be a vague feeling of familiarity; we are conscious that we have been there before or have seen that person though we may not be able to give any details. Or there may be a very definite identification of the object, we are able to place it in our past experience. Walking on the road I see a moving object in the distance, I may recognise it as a dog. I may not have seen that particular dog but I am able to place it in a familiar class. But I may also recognise it as a terrier or better still, as a terrier belonging to a neighbour. Recognition in all these cases is the same, it differs only in degree, in specific details which place it more definitely in my past experience.

The feeling of familiarity is basic to recognition and plays an essential part in all acts of recognising. But the act of recognition is more than this feeling of familiarity. It is not complete till the object recognised is definitely placed in our past experience. Recognition is easier than recall ; we may recognise a person without being able to recall his name. Repetition leads to greater familiarity and finally to recall.

Recognition is so prompt and spontaneous an act that it is very difficult to say if it can be improved.

12. Forgetfulness

A seemingly paradoxical statement that to remember well we must forget a great deal is very often made. Forgetfulness is very essential. If irrelevant details are forgotten the relevant ones are remembered better. In economical learning we must select. Instead of memorising details we should select the significant factors and large concepts, and try to fix these in mind in discarding the mass of details which can be filled in if those large concepts are recalled. If after reading a chapter you try to classify your material under selected class-heads, it will be easier to recall and reproduce the substance of that chapter. Attention which is basic to all retention and reproduction is by its very nature, selective and our ends and purposes determine such selection. Every moment of our waking or concious life is replete with teeming details of experience and it would be embracing a sheer catastrophe to try to remember each one of them. We must select a few and forget the rest.

Forgetting is the failure of the individual to revive in consciousness an idea or group of ideas without the help of the original stimulus. Forgetting is not abnormal and we are often able to recall experiences which we failed to recall previously. Doubt, distraction, fatigue and emotional disturbances are some of the common causes of forgetting. How well prepared lessons are forgotten in tests or under the stress of fear and anxiety due to excessive punishments in schools or due to domestic worry is a common experience of every teacher and it is his duty to smooth over such situations and inspire confidence and trust among his pupils.

Unpleasant experiences and thoughts are often forcibly suppressed and banished from memory. Such troublesome ideas are said to be 'repressed' but though forgotten they continue to influence behaviour and personality. Psychoanalysis is one of the best methods of bringing into consciousness such forgotten experiences. The person is allowed to throw off all moral restraint and to talk of his vital interests freely. A detailed discussion of the method will follow later.

13. Why Do We Forget?

There is no single or simple answer to the question : Why do we forget? A pupil learns the English equivalent of a Hindi word, he is introduced to a new class-mate and later addresses him by his name, he masters the formula that $(a+b)$ into $(a-b)$ is equal to (a^2-b^2). Why should any of these fail on a future occasion?

One reason could be that the occasion in fact is different. The class-mate was met in school and in the market his name could not be recalled, the translation of the Hindi word was learned in a context that has changed. Another reason could be that much has happened between learning and recall that has interfered with the retention of the original experience and its reproduction. It is the latter which concerns us more.

A common answer is that with lapse of time what is learned tends to be forgotten if not used. *Disuse* accounts for a good deal of our forgetting. We talk about memory 'fading' or being 'a little rusty'. It is assumed that as flowers fade and iron rusts if we are not careful similarly things learned decay and disappear if they are not properly practised and used. Many things learned in the school are forgotten because they are not put to any use or thought of after leaving the school. Just as unused muscles atrophy so unused learnings fade away.

Another cause of forgetting is *interference* with what is learned by other experiences. If other activities intervene between original learning and recall they affect retention and recall. In an experimental study two groups were taken, one learned a certain material and then went to sleep and the second learned the same material and then took part in other activities, learnings and experiences. In the test the first group did better leading to the conclusion that other experiences interfered with and impaired the recall.

Interference between old and new learning may work in either direction or both. Suppose a class is taught two stories one after the other, an important way of testing what they have learned is to ask them to identify the characters of the two stories and describe their plot. Often pupils will mix one with the other. If details of the first story are confused or interfered by those of the second we call it *retroactive inhibition* or backward-working inhibition. What is learned in the second task interferes with the retention of the first. But if the memory of the first interferes with the recall of the second, it is *proactive inhibition* or forward-working inhibition.

Experimental studies have shown that there is considerable evidence to support the concept of interference as a major cause of forgetting. These studies have shown that interference in learning increases with the increase in the number of competing associations, interference is greater when the two learning tasks are very similar and when the learning is not complete, and in either case it suffers from interference by material learned before and after it.

These conclusions are drawn from the laboratory studies but there is general agreement among educational psychologists that subjects very similar or bodies of material closely resembling each other should not be taught in close sequence, that is, immediately after each other. Also pupils should gain a fair mastery of one before another is taught. Incomplete learning is more liable to interference. These precautions will help to differentiate and reduce the chances of interference.

Another cause of forgetting, as has already been pointed out, is *repression*. We forget what we want to forget. People with emotional conflicts tend to *repress* thoughts and memories which are particularly unplesant, embarrassing and threatening, thereby avoiding those conflicts. A husband frequently forgets to bring things from the market because he himself dislikes them. We frequently tend to forget the names of persons and places we dislike. We forget appointment which we had no wish to fulfil, we forget to post letters we did not like to write. We forget things, places and events about which we have had intense anxieties. The subjet will be discussed in detail in a later chapter.

Finally forgetting also depends upon our *set*. Set is readiness or interest with which we remember and if the set is changed or is in incorrect direction we may fail to remember. The set is a property of the learner but varies with surroundings, instructions to, and preparations of, the learner. If in seeking to recall a name we insist that it begins with P, the search may be confined to names beginning with P and all other directions or alternatives for searching the name will be neglected. When the correct initial letter is found the name may be recalled.

14. The Problem of the Bad Memoriser

Memory is the name we give to processes by which images and ideas are registered and recalled and now and then teachers come upon pupils who cannot memorise, recall and reproduce, anything which they are taught in the class. Such pupils are often dismissed as wicked, incorrigible, dumb or dull and allowed to please themselves as back-benchers. But the educational problem is to find out what is wrong with them and help them to learn better and more effectively.

Bad memorisers are of several types. Some of them have only immediate memory and are able to recall details soon after they are learned. They are not reliable retainers. Such memory is good for such work as that of a telephone operator. It has already been pointed out that the power to retain is native and cannot be improved much. In the power to retain as a permanent possession all that is learned young children have an advantage over grown-up adults. Retentiveness increases upto the age of eleven or twelve and then starts diminishing. Therefore there is some justification for the plea that the matter which has to be retained through one's life should be learned in childhood. That is why multiplication tables are expected to be committed to memory in primary schools.

One cannot recall without registering and there are several pupils in every class who fail to register. There may be faults of observation and attention but there may also be utter indifference to the work in the classroom. They are not at all interested in what is going on, they do not understand the meaning and purposes of teaching and learning, and they themselves have no goal or purpose. Most of these pupils have experienced gross neglect at home, nobody has taken any interest in their life and work and the necessary affection and love has been denied to them. Often rehabilitation in the family and restoration of affectionate ties have improved their interest in their memorising.

It is a commonplace to stress that schools do not teach children how to attend, observe or study. Often children do not know what is expected of them. Just to shout ' attend to me ' is not enough. Teachers must help children to develop habits of close attention and observation and regular study. If details are attended to carefully, if they are registered accurately they will be remembered better.

Often the inability to attend and observe carefully is due to some physical defect or ailment. Bad teeth, short sight, earache or digestive disorders may be preventing concentration of attention and detailed medical check-up may be of help.

The important thing for educational psychology is what the teacher can do to improve retention of material learned in school. In the wake of experiments made by Ebbinghaus several studies have been made of memory and out of them have emerged certain practical suggestions for teaching.

In the first place the teacher should provide sufficient

motivation, that is, provide incentives to secure and maintain interest in learning. He should make sure that material to be learned has meaning for pupils, seeing meaning in material to be learned aids learning and retention. Nonsense figures and syllables are soon forgotten. Pupils cannot remember for long the figure 48163264128 but if they see that the figure goes on doubling the first number they will see meaning in it and remember it. Much of the learned material taught today is lost because the stress is on words, barren verbalism is not retained unless pupils see the meaning and value of the material in life and work.

Secondly the *presentation of material* should be made in such a manner that details to be memorised receive due emphasis and in a manner familiar to the children. They should have opportunity to get a whole view of the material before studying the parts. Those items which are to be remembered together should be presented together in close association.

Thirdly the teacher should help pupils to develop efficient ways of going about their study and learning. This is a very neglected aspect of school work. Too often teachers stress hard work, memorising and nothing more, for a large majority of them studying means memorising verbatim and they insist on drill and recitation. Any variation on the text is discouraged. This does not help. To promote long term retention stress should be laid on defining, organising, comparing, analysing, questioning, interpreting and evaluating searching actively for meanings and relationships. Such a study is active and creative and what one learns becomes truly his own.

With a slight variation on the first suggestion learning and remembering are both helped if the learner has a conscious *desire and intention to learn* what he is studying. Whether his intention is to show off to the class, to impress the teacher, to gain mastery, to solve a puzzling problem or score high in the examination, his desire to retain is an important factor in stimulating his effort and attention and thus securing retention. In one study it was shown that the group of pupils who were anticipating future use for the material learned retained longer than the group who saw no purpose in learning.

Again the *first impression* should be very vivid and accurate. If there are errors they should be corrected immediately and on their first appearance. Use the whole method for short lessons and the part method for long lessons, and there should be intensive practice, keeping the above considerations in view. Practice, however, should be carefully distributed avoiding fatigue and boredom.

Lastly, after learning encourage understanding of the material by relating it to previous knowledge and practical situations, *reviewing* the material frequently and expecting pupils to apply it in new situations. Review need not wait till learning is completed. Study may be interruped frequently to review the parts covered. Tests too are very effective means of review.

Questions

1. What is memory? Analyse the processes involved in memory.
2. What are the marks of a good memory? On what conditions does a good memory depend?
3. Show how improvement can be made in the several processes involved in memory.
4. If pupils complain of lack of memory, could the teacher help to remedy it? How could a lesson be taught to facilitate memory?
5 Is repetition the best method of remembering? If not, why not? Give reasons.

6. Analyse the mental process called 'trying to remember.' What factors help it?
7. What should the teacher do to help long-term retention of material learned?
8. How will you deal with the problem of the bad memoriser?
9. Why do children forget what they learn? What will you do to help such children?

REFERENCES FOR FURTHER STUDY

1. Bartlett : *Remembering* (Macmillan).
2. Bentley : *The New Field of Psychology* (Appleton).
3. Bird and Bird : *Learning More by Effective Study* (Appleton).
4. Catty : *The Theory and Practice of Education* (Methuen).
5. *Elementary Educational Psychology* ed. C. E. Skinner (Prentice-Hall).
6. Gates: *Educational Psychology* (Macmillan).
7. James : *Principles of Psychology* (Macmillan).
8. Simpson : *Fundamentals of Educational Psychology* (Lippincott).
9. Stout : *A Manual of Psychology* (Univ. Tut. Press).
10. Trow : *Educational Psychology* (Houghton Mifflin).
11. Woodworth : *Experimental Psychology* (Henry Holt).
12. Woodworth : *Psychology* (Methuen).

CHAPTER FIFTEEN

Learning and Fatigue

1. THE LEARNING PROCESS

ALL living is learning. If we compare the simple, crude ways in which a child feels and behaves with the complex modes of adult behaviour, his skills, habits, thought, sentiments and the like—we will know what difference learning has made to the individual. The individual is in active relations with his environment. He not only changes and modifies his environment but is, in turn, changed and modified by it. The modifications of behaviour which result from this interaction, from activity and experience, are what we understand by learning. Learning is change. It is change of behaviour influenced by previous behaviour. It covers all those processes by which individuals acquire new forms of thinking, feeling and willing. It is more than school learning. It means all knowledge, skill, habits, virtues, vices, beliefs, attitudes, in brief all that makes up our character and personality. It is any activity that leaves a more or less permanent effect on later activity.

In all learning either the innate, inherited modes of behaviour are modified or new forms of behaviour are acquired. Most learning in children consists in modifying, adapting and developing their original nature. In later life the individual acquires new forms of behaviour. All this is done to meet new situations, to adjust to a changing environment. That is why learning is often described as adjustment. Learning is universal. Every creature that lives learns. Insects behave in a very uniform way, they cannot readily adjust themselves to new situations. The extent to which they can adapt themselves progressively to new situations is small. Higher animals like a dog or horse show greater adaptability. They learn more than insects. If the mud-house of the mason-wasp is broken, it flies away to build elsewhere but if the tail of a dog is pulled, it may kick, bite, bark or run away or it may start wagging it all the more, licking your hand or cringing. It will depend on how it has responded in the past. All living beings learn.

But of all creatures man learns most. Human children have the longest period of immaturity and helplessness and hence the longest period and opportunity for learning. They are unable to stand on their own legs for a long time while the young ones of other species have to look after themselves almost immediately or soon after birth The human nervous system is very complex, so are human reactions and so are human acquisitions.

Learning is growth, but it is a never-ending growth. There is hardly anybody, man or animal, who has no more to learn. At each stage, the learner acquires new visions of his future growth and new ideals of achievement in the directions of his effort. Every achievement made becomes the basis of a fresh endeavour and thus the constant urge of his soul to newer and higher ideals of work and achievement is progressively fulfilled.

But should this learning be haphazard and aimless? Should there be no direction to the learning process? Young people may learn bad things as well as good, they may acquire vices as well as virtues, inefficient ways of acting and wrong modes of thought. It is the responsibility of education to direct them into desirable and efficient learning and in this book we have indicated how the teacher can help them to make the most of their powers and develop all that is best in them.

2 THE NATURE OF LEARNING

What elements are common to various types of learning? We have seen that all life is learning and people do not learn simply by growing older. They pass through experiences whether of listening to parents and teachers, reading books, working with others, practising on a typewriter and their learning activities include some perception, observation and knowledge, some manipulation of ideas, some feeling and some motor activity. As this perceiving, observing, knowing, thinking, feeling and doing took place some changes took place in the learner's ways of perceiving, observing, knowing, thinking, feeling and doing. These changes we have called learning and they are relative to the past experience of the learner, his needs, his present abilities and his feelings and skills. Learning, therefore may be defined as changing one's ways of perceiving, thinking, feeling and doing through experiences partly motor, partly perceptual, partly intellectual and partly emotional. It has not been possible so far to find out what changes in the nervous system accompany learning. But we may mention some of the important general characteristics of the learning process.

In the first place learning is *many-sided.* As indicated above learning is always multiple involving perception, knowledge, thinking, feeling and doing. Psychologists may for purposes of close study distinguish learning into motor, emotional and intellectual but these are only several aspects of one process of learning. In doing craftwork a pupil acquires motor skill, the best way of handling tools and moulding and changing material; he may also be acquiring knowledge about the nature of raw material, where it grows and the like; he may be enjoying or disliking his work, companions and the teacher. Thus learning has many facets.

Learning comes only through *experience*. Learning is not what parents and teachers can do for the children nor is it something they can give him. Even knowledge cannot be given directly, it is the result of the child's own perceptions and thinking. He can learn only through what he experiences. This is the basis of the common phrase ' learning by doing '. In India we often speak of knowledge as a gift from the teacher but it comes about through the learner's own experiences, his own effort and attention and intellectual activity. Learning cannot be imposed from outside, the teacher can control it to the extent he controls experience. Even such things as making decisions, co-operating or controlling the expression of strong emotions children can learn only through facing situations in which they must take a decision, co-operate or control their emotions, certainly not by simple advice or reading, about them.

Learning is always *purposeful*. It is only in the satisfaction of their needs and interests that young people learn. They have had certain experiences and on their basis they have acquired goals and purposes, ideas about their own abilities and proficiency, about what is expected of them by their parents, teachers and class-mates. And it is in their light that they work and learn. They work hard willingly only to fulfil these expectations, goals and purposes, because it is satisfying for them in some manner giving them a sense of accomplishment and power. In the several studies made of learning processes in the classroom and laboratories by psychologists there is no evidence for the common belief that the more bitter the medicine the better it is for the patient.

3. Types of Learning

Learning covers a wide range. It is present in simple

forms of animal behaviour as also in the complex types of adult human behaviour. The difference between the simple and the complex is not one of kind but of degree. Let us describe the main types of learning.

Learning by Conditioned Response. The simplest and the most rudimentary type of learning is that of *conditioned response*. It has already been described in a previous chapter as a process of substituting the original stimulus by a new one and connecting the response with it. A child's face shows fear when his mother approaches him with a bottle of medicine. Fear was originally aroused by the bitter taste of the medicine but now after some association the appearance of the bottle is enough to excite fear. The bottle has taken the place of the bitter taste and is effective in causing fear. Fear is now conditioned to the bottle and the child has learned to fear the bottle. The animal trainer raises his stick as he puts the paw of the monkey on a hot plate and allows it to raise the paw. The monkey responds to the hot plate by raising and removing its paw. After some repetitions the monkey learns to raise its paw when the stick is raised and the animal trainer has taught the monkey to salute in response to the stick. The response which was originally made to the hot plate is now conditioned to the stick through repeated associations. The mother threatens, shouts and beats the child who cries in pain. After a number of experiences the child begins to cry even when the mother shouts or assumes a threatening posture. The learned response is called a *conditioned* response because it is dependent upon conditions and the process is referred to as *conditioning*.

In learning by conditioned response repetition of the association between the new stimulus with the response is necessary and much time should not pass between the presentation of the stimulus and the response. In course of time the stimulus is generalised. In the examples given above the child may learn to fear anything similar to the bottle and later the word bottle may be enough to rouse fear. Learning by conditioning is learning by association.

But in learning by conditioning there is no choice or freedom nor is there any consideration of the use or good of learning. A good part of the learnings in early childhood are the result of conditioning. It is very fortunate, however, that learning through conditioning is waxing and waning all our lives and does not persist for long. Practice and repetition strengthens the bonds of conditioning and the lack of it weakens them.

Learning by Trial and Error. This is anotner simple form of learning. Placed in a new situation the individual makes a number of random movements, those which are unsuccessful are eliminated and the successful ones are fixed. A child learning to open a new box makes a number of blind efforts. He does not deliberate, he tries one and then another method till he hits upon the right response. It is a hit or miss method and the animal like a rat or a cat when placed in a cage tries to get out by the same method. It is as characteristic of the man as of the animal, of the adults as of the child. The baby learning to eat with a spoon, to walk or put on shoes, the adult learning to drive a car, to play tennis or give a knot to his tie, the rat trying to get into a tiffin box, the dog learning to open a gate or the cow getting over a fence into a green field, are all following the method of trial and error. They try one way, then another and then still another till they hit upon the right course.

The random movements are not eliminated at once. In the first attempt their number is very large, in the second the number of errors diminishes and the range of activity becomes narrower. Gradually the individual learns to proceed straight to the goal without any error. Improvement generally takes place through repetition.

Although this method is very common, it is not economical. It is slow, tiresome and aimless. It needs a far greater energy than higher types of learning. But it has been the chief method of man in his race toward civilisation and he has been trying out devices, principles and methods in discovering and building up the vast storehouse of modern knowledge and industry.

The essential nature of trial and error learning is that the learner is unable to foresee what movements are essential and what is the right way of making them. It is learning by blundering, by trying something and succeeding or failing. The learner fumbles about a great deal and by chance hits upon the right course. Secondly, at least among animals the element of deliberation is absent though there is considerable trial and error activity in thinking itself. In the solution of problems we often follow the try out method in reasoning. Thirdly, the learner has greater freedom in this type of learning, he can move about at will and go at his own pace, and when he is unable to solve the problem he is quiet and normal. Fourthly, he learns by doing, through activity and self-direction. This is a very effective manner of learning, actually living through experiences. Lastly, the presence of goals and purposes, drives and motives, stimulates the process of learning.

We may sum up : in the trial and error learning the learner has a motive, the motive leads to varied types of activity in which the learner tries various types of responses, some of them later are rewarded with success and the satisfaction of the motive and the responses not leading to success are discarded while that leading to success is established.

Learning by Insight. Some animals and all men learn in a fewer trials. They use their sense along with motor activity. *Learning by observation is learning by insight*, learning by perceiving the relationship in the scene and understanding the situation. After looking over the whole situation the learner strives to make some sense out of it, and it gives him clues regarding the way he should proceed to solve the problem, the method he should pursue, and a general awareness of the consequences of performing an act. This type of learning is obviously more efficient for here the learner consciously perceiving the relations which a problem involves passes from helplessness to a mood of confidence and grasp of the problem. Woodworth does not favour its description as learning by insight and prefers to call it learning by observation, because insight implies some penetration into the true nature of things. Even this word is too strong, he says, as it suggests deliberate effort to observe. All that is meant is that the animal or man applies his past experience to a problem, perceives the significant characteristics of a situation and connects the right response with the solution.

Do lower animals learn by observation? There is no unanimity among psychologists. Thorndike thinks that one cat did not profit by watching another cat get out of the cage. Woodworth, on the contrary, describes the case of a chimpanzee who, having first learned to use a stick to pull a banana on the floor, was given two sticks of bamboo, one small enough to fit into the open end of the other, and the banana was placed too far away to be reached with either stick alone. After some unsuccessful attempts he could join them and at once jumped to secure the banana. Evidence is conflicting but it is safe to assume that higher animals learn by observation.

Learning by Imitation. We assume that children will

copy both important and trivial characteristics of adults. They learn the language and ways of thinking of the family in which they are brought up and they walk with their hands behind their back as their father does. Imitation is an important way of learning not only among human beings but also among certain birds and animals. Parrots learn to reproduce certain sounds including some words of human speech. Nightingales fail to learn the song of their species if they are brought up alone, they seem to learn it from the older members of their class by imitating them.

4. Animal and Human Learning

A comparison of animal and human learning will help towards a better understanding of the learning process. In the first place, trial-and-error method is common to both animal and human learners as we have seen in the examples cited above. Secondly, in both, the presence of rewards and punishments works as a strong incentive to the learning process. Household pets learn a number of things because their attempts are rewarded and children learn better when they have an interest in things to be learned. Learning is effective when it has an incentive. Thirdly, both build habits and show progressive improvements. Lastly, both profit by their experience of similar situations in the solution of new problems. If an animal has tackled a maze or cage once, it will be able to manipulate the second maze or cage more rapidly.

But most of the animal learning is confined to sensorimotor responses. No doubt man employs trial-and-error method but unlike the animal he is not limited to it. He makes use of language and employs verbal aids in fixing details. His imagery helps him to plan and visualise. And he is able to generalise on the basis of his past experience and obtain general principles for future guidance. Imitation which plays a very unimportant role in animal learning is very vital to human learning.

5. The Laws of Learning

Thorndike has put forward three laws which govern the learning process among animals and men. They will be of great help and guidance to the teacher as they govern learning among children.

The first is the *law of exercise*, use and disuse. Whenever any given activity is repeated it becomes prompt, easy and definite. We re-read lessons a number of times to master them, we play a musical tune a number of times to be able to play it accurately and easily. Repetition and drill fix facts and activities to be learned. Skill in games, music, craft, typing, and every human endeavour is gained by constant exercise and practice. Practice is the price we pay for being perfect. This is the *law of exercise*, the *law of repetition* or the *law of use*.

It is the most common law and is widely used in both life and education. We have already noted in the last chapter the place of repetition in education.

But we know that lack of practice weakens the quality of what we have learned. How often we apologise for our poor performance on the tennis court, at a musical instrument, in diving, swimming or rowing by saying, 'I am sorry, I am out of practice.' An activity that is not used, repeated or exercised for a long time tends to be forgotten. We learn and retain by use and forget by disuse. This is known as the *law of disuse*. A good part of what we learn is lost because we do not get any further opportunity to use it. Forgetting is largely the result of disuse.

Use and disuse are two aspects of the law of exercise. But as we have seen mere practice or repetition is not enough and the law must be qualified by other laws like that of interest.

The second is the law of *readiness*. If the learner is ready to act or to learn, he will learn more quickly and effectively. Readiness or preparedness for a task is half the battle and if the pupil's mind is set on a lesson he is disposed to work at it and master it. If a person is not ready to act, it is annoying for him to act ; if he is ready to act, it is annoying for him to be prevented from acting. Woodworth uses the word *mind-set* for this preparatory attitude.

Much of the waste in education is due to the teacher's neglect of this principle. Pupils are not prepared for the lesson and they do not learn it easily. They go through their studies in a routine indifferent manner and much of the effort of the teacher and the class is wasted. Often pupils' interest and curiosity are aroused by some event or news, they are ready to learn more about its background, but the teacher simply brushes it aside as a distraction. A wise teacher will exploit a solar eclipse, the death of a great statesman, an earthquake shock or even a railway accident to teach very useful facts of history, geography or industry. Moments of mental alertness are valuable opportunities for directing the pupil's interest and effort into desirable channels.

The third is the *law of effect*. This law is based on feeling and has already been referred to in different forms. Activities which are accompanied by a feeling of pleasure or satisfaction are more readily and effectively learned than activities which are unpleasant or annoying. Feeling plays an appreciable part in the learning process and all factors in learning are subordinated to this law. Trial-and-error needs incentives which means seeking satisfaction ; repetition without motivation is ineffective ; readiness is not possible without interest. If children succeed in doing a thing, in solving a problem or meeting a situation, they are pleased about their achievement and this feeling of satisfaction spurs them onto further effort. Success leads to further succss and failure often is a fore-runner of further failures. The system of rewards and punishments in schools is based on this law. Patterns of behaviour which are rewarded are fixed and those which are condemned or punished tend to be eliminated. It has, therefore, to be carefully noted by all those who are responsible for the education of children that they should never associate good and useful things with something annoying. A detailed discussion of the nature and place of pleasure and interest in education has been given in the chapters on attention and emotions.

6. Efficiency in Learning

What are the general conditions on which efficient learning depends ? In our previous discussion we have emphasised the part played by good working conditions like fresh air, light, comfortable surrounding, health, equable temperature, absence of distractions like noise, worry and fatigue. Besides, we need vigorous application, concentration of attention, habits of hard work at a fixed time. Interest and effort are equally necessary. They spring from strong motives and desires and he who wishes to learn effectively should not only have the desire and intention to learn but must also form definite aims and ideals which stimulate him to achieve greater heights. We have also emphasised such principles as learning by doing and spaced periods of practice. A common experience in learning is that after a period of satisfactory progress there comes an interval of little or no improvement. Such periods of stagnation are called *plateaus*.

When the plateau appears, it may be that the interest has slackened or weakened or a limit of progress has been reached and there is need of consolidation before further effort can be made. But plateaus discourage the learner and prevent steady progress. They are found much more frequently in complex skills and the best way of overcoming them is by a judicious distribution of work and rest periods. Rest periods not only help to avoid fatigue but also provide opportunity for assimilation. An important duty of the teacher is to fix the amount of time for which a pupil can study any one subject. Individual variations in the capacity and interest of pupils have also to be considered.

7. Motivation in Learning

We have been stressing in this book that practice and mechanical drill are of no avail if they do not fulfil some need, interest, desire or goal, that is if there is no motive for it. Motivation is the heart of all learning, it is the condition which increases the vigour of activity, it initiates and sustains behaviour and it is the reason why we do what we do. A motive implies a need and the direction of behaviour toward a goal. Often teachers exhort pupils to apply themselves and work hard but such advice will be effective only if pupils want or have a desire to learn. Without this desire to learn no amount of inducement will have any effect. So teachers should make pupils want to learn for with a desire to learn there is almost no limit to what the teacher and the class can accomplish.

Some teachers use the fear of punishment to make children learn, others ignore them altogether and let them do what they like, and still others are just requesting them to learn. All these attitudes are fruitless. Successful teachers implant a desire in the minds of pupils to learn and accomplish what tasks they give them, they are able to create in them a motive for learning. By expecting them to work they impart seriousness to their programme and pupils are never allowed to think that schools are for any other purpose but learning. They themselves are earnest and serious in giving lessons and assignments, now and then ask questions and give interesting information. Such teachers believe that in general children like to learn and given right kind of guidance and help will take to their work with zest. We all respond to what others expect of us and young people are the more ready to do so once they are made to realise that work and learning is expected of them.

Rewards and punishments are also used to motivate learning. Pressures of success and failure, promises of enjoyment and fear of disappointment, are powerful motives. Rivalry and competition also provide the motivating power. But all of them may be over-employed to produce real anxiety. Every teacher knows how examinations cause tension and how fear of failure renders many pupils incapable of any effort. But making learning satisfying through teacher recognition, class praise and parental pat on the back will spur pupils to do better work. Every teacher will have his own device of achieving this. Readers are referred to the chapter on interest and attention.

But motivation is not only the teacher's responsibility. It also depends on what needs, desires, interests and goals the pupil brings to the school and its work. A hungry, thirsty or sleepy child will not apply himself to any task. If he has not had anything to eat at home, if he had no sleep the previous night he will not attend to the teacher nor learn. Grown-up boys and girls are often detracted by the opposite sex and cannot concentrate on their work. Apart from these drives the need for activity is urgent and has to be satisfied. A teacher who does not work himself and does not provide work for children, and a school which has no provision for games and sports, cannot help young people to learn. Then there is the need to explore and manipulate, to go and search for things from books. The teacher must use them to motivate learning.

Usually children have enough motivation but they are motivated in different directions, and the direction of motivation will decide the direction of learning. They should be encouraged to work for self-esteem, self-advancement and self-actualisation. Wise teachers are able to build a self-image among their pupils and stimulate them to dream of what big things they can accomplish, what talents they have, what use they can make of their talents for their own good and for the good of society. It is obvious that different children will have different ideas and motives and their goals in life may also be different. The teacher will place a whole view of life before them with a large variety of objectives for which men and women work and live and let young people choose what goals they may. Such goals may frequently be reviewed to inspire and induce children to work harder and learn better. The goal of preparation for the future is most appealing to those who come from middle class homes. A learner working for a goal puts forth maximum effort, is imaginative and creative, takes more responsibility for his learning and is more likely to retain and harmonise new learnings with what he already knows.

8. Need for Guidance in Learning

It is possible for the teacher to make sure that his teaching programme offers sufficient scope, sequence and continuity within a subject and is in harmony with children's level of growth. Readiness for learning is necessary. Children should have reached a certain level of development, acquired certain skills, abilities, interests and attitudes but this readiness is not enough by itself. Some teachers do believe that once children have developed readiness and interest for a subject their job is over and they can leave children to their own effort and themselves relax. Once children mature mentally and emotionally for reading all that is necessary is to surround them with books in a pleasant friendly atmosphere and they would get on with reading. But a large number of teachers will agree on the basis of their experience that this is not enough and young people must be guided in learning. A few suggestions are made here for such guidance.

1. He must carefully assess the readiness of the class, individually and collectively, for the new learning. For this he may have to contact parents to know the cultural background, to study their previous records, to talk, work and play with children, and to test them. Often careful observation of children in and outside the class will give enough knowledge of their development level, their abilities, skills and interest. In some cases he may have to make the child break from his past experiences and learning and in some cases to use those past experiences and learnings as a bridge for new learning.

2. There should be enough flexibility in the class work so that all kinds of abilities are encouraged. Let each child feel that he has a contribution to make and should do his best. The class should not be made to work at a uniform pace in the interest of some arbitrary standard.

3. If possible the class may be divided into smaller groups for instruction and each group may be given different assignments to work at their own pace and level. Such groups should be flexible and no attempt should be made to class them as bright, slow and the like. Of course some teaching and activities will be common to the whole class.

4. Through such group work the teacher should ensure the participation of every pupil in learning tasks.

5. Every new lesson should be related to what pupils have already learned, to their previous knowledge and learning so that the new learning does not appear unfamiliar and strange.

6. During the entire programme the teacher should be for ever looking out for opportunities to clarify children's ideas, to define goals and encourage them to do their best. Children's progress has to be maintained by such help as the occasion demands, looking over children's work and offering corrections, stimulating their interest by words of praise and indicating various steps in the task. Children who are slower may be helped with patience and brighter ones may be given deeper and broader understanding of the topic. Stressing the sequence of steps in learning the teacher will maintain continuity with what children have already learned in the last class or session and what they are going to learn in the next class or session. Simply failing pupils because they are not upto the mark and giving them a bad report is no answer. The teacher should help the child to make up through easier assignments and remedial teaching.

9. Transfer of Training

Do abilities acquired in one situation help in another ? Does training in one kind of performance lead to improvement in some other kind of performance ? Many controversies have been waged over the influence of learning one thing upon the learning of another. Some believe that memorising words in language, dates and events in history or the multiplication table in arithmetic train the memory so that one can remember other things, such as names of places and persons, better. Others argue that the study of science trains the powers of observation so that one can be an accurate observer in social and personal relations as well. Training is transferred from one skill or mental power to another. This is known as the doctrine of *formal discipline* or *transfer of training*. Older psychology analysed mind into separate watertight compartments of faculties and held that powers like memory, imagination, observation or reasoning are strengthened through exercise and can subsequently be used with equal advantange in any situation. Certain subjects like Latin, Mathematics and Logic were considered to have a higher training value and pupils doing well in them were supposed to do well in other spheres of life.

Obviously the problem has an important bearing on school work. Only such subjects are to be included in the curriculum as have disciplinary value and they are to be taught in such a way that this value is secured.

Faculty psychology on which this doctrine of formal discipline is based is entirely rejected nowadays. If thought, judgment, memory, reasoning, observation and the like are independently functioning units, how can any transfer be possible? And yet many eminent philosophers and psychologists have believed that some kinds of training build up a general power that may be used with advantage in any life situation. Plato and others thought that the study of Mathematics sharpens the pupils' power of understanding and reasoning. The whole practice of mental testing assumes that there is a general intelligence which is measured by standard tests, which takes part in a large variety of actual performances and which determines a pupil's rate of progress in education and undestanding. The supporters of the doctrine of transfer of training cite a large list of eminent administrators, doctors, educationists and public men who were reared on Latin and Mathematics and given a liberal education in public schools, and who did remarkably well in life. It is claimed that this is the result of general training. This argument is easily refuted by the critics of the doctrine. They contend that these men are the result of selection, not of training. They come from better homes and were critically selected by the school committees. They are not the result of Latin or Mathematics. Sir John Adams clinched the argument by asking why apple-stealing does not rank with Latin and Mathematics as mental exercise when it involves the same caution, observation, judgment and reasoning.

Fifty years ago William James made an experiment with learning. He committed some lines of Victor Hugo's *Satyr* to memory and then portions of Milton's *Paradise Lost*. Later he went back to Hugo's *Satyr* to see if he could memorise more rapidly than the first time because of his practice on *Paradise Lost*. He found he could not. He contended that there is no such thing as transfer of training.

Recently scores of elaborate experiments have been made to determine the extent of transfer. Two groups of persons, usually school children, are chosen. Each member of one group is matched by a member of the other group having the same age, sex, race, training, intelligence and the ability to be tested. The particular ability is first tested, then trained and then tested again. The other 'control group' does not take the training but is given the final test to see what difference training has made to the other group. Such experiments have tested the transfer of memory for nonsense syllables to memory for numbers, letters or words; of judgments of areas and weights to widely different sizes; of sound intensities to light intensities. In practically all these experiments the group which received training has shown a small improvement over the control group.

Some have developed a general principle that in subjects

of identical elements or having identical methods of study, there is small but real transfer. The more we know, the easier it is to learn similar things. Past experience and knowledge to help future learning and if the subjects are altogether similar, there may be a hundred per cent transfer. If the subjects are altogether different, there may be no transfer at all. It is claimed, not without plausibility, that learning Mathematics helps in the mastery of Physics and students proficient in their mother-tongue are good in English too. People who can play tennis well can learn cricket more easily and it should be easier for a typist to learn to play on a harmonium. But the best way to learn anything is to concentrate on practising the very thing rather than anything similar to it. Nevertheless, to get the most out of any subject of study the teacher should point out its relation to others, and encourage pupils too to find out such relationships. This is called positive transfer and can be explained by Spearman's Two-Factor theory of intelligence. The learning of anything exercises the pupil's general ability as well as his specific ability. There is no transfer in special abilities but there is some in general ability.

But skill in one field may hinder learning another skill. People who can play cricket very well are unable to play the measured strokes in tennis and many a good student of Hindi brings in vernacularism in English. This is called negative transfer. Running in football may inhibit running in basketball.

Though recent experiments have shown that the doctrine of formal discipline cannot be accepted yet it is not without an element of truth. The problem for education is to inquire into the extent to which learning anything in one situation or context helps learning in another and what conditions are necessary to that end. Some transfer is possible when the two situations have identical elements as has been already stressed. Secondly, the teacher can help this transfer if he stresses the general aspect of all that is learned. If experience and learning are generalised in such a way that what is done in one context is recognised as applying a principle which can be differently applied in another situation, if relationships and implications are clearly brought out and if the teacher takes pains to integrate different items of the curriculum so as to bring out their affinity, some of the advantages claimed on behalf of the doctrine of formal discipline may be secured.

10. Fatigue

An important factor which causes loss of efficiency in learning is fatigue. When any activity, bodily or mental, is continued beyond a certain limit, the individual feels tired. At first there is loss of interest, followed by a positive aversion for the task in hand. Then there is strong desire for a change and if the activity is still continued, there is headache and pain in the limbs. In extreme cases, mental and bodily activity is much lowered and one is incapable of doing anything. Efficiency in learning depends on fresh air, good health, strong motives, clear aims, intense interest and the like and the absence of any of them will hamper learning. But even when all of them are present, fatigue may prevent attention, reduce the output of work and hamper any learning.

Many parents and teachers naively believe that children are never tired, they play all day long and have an inexhaustible fund of energy. This is quite incorrect. On the other hand, children are much more readily tired and the teacher should know what causes fatigue, how it can be prevented and what steps are necessary to cure it when it comes on.

Fatigue should be distinguished from a state of mind which passes for fatigue but is not really fatigue. In this state we simply 'feel' tired. There is no depletion of nervous energy, there is only lack of interest, a general *ennui* or boredom. A change of occupation often cures it.

Fatigue is said to be of two kinds—mental and bodily. Mental fatigue is caused by changes in the brain due to persistent mental work, and bodily fatigue is due to changes in muscles caused by continued mechanical work. We also speak of brain and muscle fatigue. A distinction is also drawn between local and general fatigue according as a particular part of the system or the whole of it is exhausted. In writing for a long time hands are tired because their muscles are engaged in one type of movement. Fatigue is confined to hands only. Or it may involve the whole nervous system. Local fatigue can be cured by changing work.

But what causes fatigue? What changes take place when we are tired? Within the tissues of the body there are two different metabolic processes going on—a process of decomposition, tearing down or consumption when energy is being used up in some form of nervous or muscular activity, and a process of composition, building up or rejuvenation when tissues absorb food elements and oxygen brought to them by fresh blood supply. If the body is to maintain health, keep fit and function normally and harmoniously, there must be a balance between these two processes of tearing down and repair. In the process of decomposition certain waste products are thrown out. They are poisonous and are called *toxins.* When they are so large and numerous that they cannot be counteracted by oxygen and carried away by fresh blood, we have fatigue. In other words, when activity is continued rapidly and more energy is consumed than what is built up, that is, when the process of repair cannot keep pace with that of tearing down, more toxins are thrown off and the capacity for function is reduced in the organism. This is the physiological explanation of fatigue. In complete exhaustion due to prolonged vigorous activity without rest, these toxins completely poison and paralyse the whole organism.

Mental fatigue is closely related to muscular fatigue, the one induces the other. When the mind is too tired, say after an examination or continued work at the desk, it is not possible to undertake any physical work, and after too strenuous a game or tiresome a journey, it is difficult to concentrate on any mental work. That is why some writers do not accept the distinction between mental and bodily fatigue. Of course when one is only slightly tired, one can and should shift from mental to bodily work and vice versa to obtain rest.

11 Remedy for Fatigue

Children are more liable to fatigue and the younger the child the sooner he is tired. Hence it is clearly the duty of the school to provide against fatigue. Let us first deal with general cures before we take up specific measures to be adopted in the school.

Apart from the normal conditions of work such as fresh air, enough light, equable temperature, freedom from fear and anxiety and the like which have already been stressed and which prevent fatigue, there are some general remedies for fatigue. The most important is *rest*. Drowsiness in fatigue points to the need for rest and sleep, the two help to repair our broken spirits. During rest and sleep new tissues are built up, depleted energy is replenished and the organism feels fresh and vigorous.

A second remedy for fatigue is *change of occupation*. In local fatigue it has been pointed out that using different activities gives rest to the tired parts. In mental work certain parts of the brain are exercised. If later manual work is taken up different centres become active and the former get rest. Many great men like Gandhi, Stalin, Churchill were able to do intensive mental work with the help of a programme of many-sided activities in which they shifted readily from one to the other.

Thirdly, strong *interest* cures fatigue. Interest is a great dynamic force in life and work and if we cultivate in ourselves an abiding interest in the work that has fallen to our lot, we can to a very considerable extent avoid real fatigue in the sense of tiredness from mental exertion. As the examination approaches how earnestly students burn the midnight oil and pore over their books, how zealously they sacrifice all comfort and luxury and take to the dull, mechanical task of mastering their notes! It is simply because their work is shot through and through with genuine interest in success. Could they do all this without interest ? The presence of interest is a powerful factor in dissipating fatigue.

Fourthly, *nourishing* food helps to recover from fatigue. Milk, fruits and food containing sugar are specially useful. Tea, coffee and cocoa remove fatigue for a time. A number of schools are introducing midday refreshments for pupils. Many people eat short meals at regular intervals to avoid fatigue.

Fifthly, *quick and rapid performance* within certain limits is less tiring than slow and lock-step work. Just as the amount of gasoline consumed by automobiles on the city street and in slow traffic is considerably greatler than it is when they are driven at a greater speed on an open and free road, so rapid performance is less tiring than slow work. It is mostly because in quick work there is better adjustment and the possibility of obtacles or distractions is either completely ruled out or considerably minimised.

Of course it does not mean that we should force ourselves to excessive performance beyond our capacity.

Lastly, we should get used to our work as quickly as we can by building up *habits*. Work that is unfamiliar and new and in which we have not acquired any proficiency is more tiring than the one to which we are accustomed and in the performance of which we have acquired necesary habits and adjustments. Habits diminish fatigue of body and mind by dispensing with random and preparatory movements and effortful attention, by giving mechanical facility in behaviour and by ensuring greater speed.

12. Fatigue in the School

These conclusions are significant for the school. If younger children are more quickly tired, their lesson periods should be shorter and they should be given more frequent pauses between them. In primary schools there may be more than one interval for recess and frequent periods of play should find a place in the regular time-table. Many teachers believe that changing from one subject to another alone is sufficient. But considering that all work of one kind or the other means expenditure of energy, refreshment that results from such changes is only psychological, not physiological.

Secondly, it is desirable that there should be frequent changes from intellectual to manual work. Agility exercises, gardening, craft-work, drawing and music provide a welcome and useful change from languages, mathematics and history. The classes should change rooms for different subjects of the day's time-table. Such changes also keep up interest. An hour for the library comes in handy. Monotony should be avoided and the school should be a happy place with beautiful and cheerful surroundings and the time-table should be punctuated with interesting adventures into study and creative work.

Thirdly, certain subjects on the curriculum make greater demands than others upon the learner. Mathematics and exercises in recitation are more fatiguing than drawing or poetry and there is an urgent need that in framing the daily time-table the headmaster should take due note of these facts. Such subjects may be placed earlier in the day when pupils feel fresh or have just warmed up for work. The easiest subject should come at the close of the day.

Fourthly, if continuous work is required, care should be taken that the rate of work is well within the capacity of the learner. Not only periods of relaxation should be permitted but the rate of work should not be forced. Each child has its own speed of work and the teacher may expect him to do his best and not to do it at the fastest rate.

Lastly, individuals differ in their capacity for work. Some tire much sooner than others. The teacher should be on the look-out for symptoms of fatigue among his pupils. He should also understand that worry and fear are powerful causes of fatigue and should infuse a spirit of cheerfulness and freedom in learning.

QUESTIONS

1. ' All the conditions, physical and mental, which favour attention, also tend to delay the onset of fatigue.' Discuss this, and show how far and by what methods, fatigue can be avoided or delayed.
2. What are the main characteristics of learning ? Explain and illustrate the laws of learning.
3. In what respects and for what reasons is human learning superior to animal learning ?
4. Explain the dictum ' practice makes perfect '. Point out, with examples, some of its limitations.
5. What arrangements would you make in the school timetable to avoid excessive fatigue ?

6. Explain : Transfer of Training, Trial-and-Error, Mind-set, Plateau.
7. Discuss some of the general factors which bear on efficiency in learning.

References for Further Study

1. Averill : *Elements of Educational Psychology* (Harrap).
2. Berrien : *Practical Psychology* (Macmillan).
3. Dewey : *Experience and Education* (Macmillan).
4. Dumville : *Child Mind* (Univ. Tut Press).
5. Gilliland, Morgan and Stevens : *General Psychology for Professional Students* (Harrap).
6. Kingsley : *The Nature and Condition of Learning* (Prentice-Hall).
7. McGeoch : *The Psychology of Human Learning* (Longmans).
8. Poffenberger : *Principles of Applied Psychology* (Appleton).
9. Ryan : *Work and Effort* (Ronald Press).
10. Starch : *Educational Psychology* (Macmillan).
11. Thorndike : *Educational Psychology* (Col. Univ. Press).
12. Woodworth : *Psychology* (Methuen).

CHAPTER SIXTEEN

Habits

1. THE NATURE OF HABITS

ONE immediate result of a process of learning is the ease and facility with which acquired actions are performed. Actions which at first appearance require effortful attention come to be performed without that effort and attention, if they are repeatedly performed under similar conditions. Such actions are called habits, they become automatic and mechanical and have a quickness and accuracy which the first performance of an action lacks. Thus habitual actions are a form of the learning process or rather habits are the final stage of the learning process. It is that mode of behaviour which, through repetition, has become so perfect that it neither requires nor undergoes any further adaptation. We enumerate the characters of habitual action.

(i) It is acquired through repetition. Thinking and acting in the same way a number of times makes that thought and action recur whenever the circumstances of its original occurrence are repeated.

(ii) It is semi-mechanical and automatic, that is, it does not require any effort and attention once it is acquired.

(iii) It can be performed only under similar circumstances.

An Indian who is in the habit of eating with his fingers goes to England and begins to learn to eat with a knife and fork. At first he blunders but gradually he begins to perform the action with the ease and grace of an Englishman. It is because the use of knife and fork has become habitual. Previously he had to concentrate all his attention on the fork, how it is held and moved, and how it is taken to the mouth. He could not talk while he ate, because he could not attend to two acts at the same time, but now eating, having become habitual, is done automatically in a stereotyped way without any effort or attention, and he can talk or think while eating.

It is usual for psychologists to give physiological explanation of habit. The law of habit as known to physiology may be stated thus: Whenever a nervous current travels from one centre in the central nervous system to another, it leaves the path modified and thus facilitates any future overflow of energy along the same path. Thus when a nervous current passes from centre A to B, it leaves behind a channel or path, such that when a new current starts, it has a tendency to flow to B rather than to any other. In this way each time a current passes from A to B, the tendency becomes more and more strengthened.

Speaking psychologically, habits are acquired dispositions and depend upon retentiveness.

Habits are not confined to bodily action alone, we may have habits of thoughts as well. The suspicious person is one who is in the habit of suspecting others. Some persons have habits of punning, of replying to letters the day they are received, of back-biting and the like.

2. Habitual, Reflex and Instinctive Actions

While dealing with instincts we studied the difference between reflex and instinctive actions. Let us study the relation of both to habitual actions.

In the first place, reflex and instinctive actions are native. They are ingrained in our mental and bodily constitution and inherited from our parents. They are innate and inborn. Habitual actions are acquired through repeated performance of the same type of action under stereotyped circumstances. Some psychologists maintain that all habits are modifications of instinctive behaviour but it is difficult to find habitual modes of behaviour which cannot be traced to any instinctive tendency.

In the second place, they all resemble in being prompt, automatic, fixed and definite. The habitual response is made as regularly as the reflex or the instinctive. But there are fundamental differences in their origin and development. Habitual and instinctive actions are psychical and conscious, they are mental phenomena. But reflex actions like the beating of the heart are bodily. Again, a reflex action is incapable of any modification, development or change. Instinctive actions are capable of being infinitely modified and developed. Habitual actions are the result of such modification and learning, and through the final stage of the learning process, they are capable of change and cessation.

Thirdly, instincts and reflexes are universal characters found in every member of a species. Habits are individual and specific.

3. Practical Results of Habit Formation

One great advantage of the formation of habits is that the performance of habitual actions costs no effort. It reduces the amount of conscious attention to an act. Let us take, for example, the habit of study. One may have a very keen interest in the subject he takes up in the college, but may lack the habit of regular study. He has no fixed time-table of studying his subjects. In the beginning of the year when the examination is yet far off, work gets neglected. He always intends to work, but having formed no regular habits of working at a particular hour, the future always seems to be the more appropriate time for work. And when the projected hour of work arrives, the pleasant occupation of going to a cinema show or reading a novel proves too congenial to discard. If the student does give up such occupations, it can only be at the cost of much struggle and effort. The student who has formed regular habits of study, gives up his novel at the proposed hour with the same ease and absence of effort with which he enters the morning bath.

The child learning to write is very painstaking. He has to attend to the formation of each letter, to spell his words and to go over each of them a number of times. He has to give his concentrated attention to every part of the act. But with what ease and simplicity the teacher writes a sentence on the blackboard! Adult writing has become automatic.

Habitual actions have been called secondarily automatic. This only means that habit is a great conservative force and leads to the economy of mental and bodily energy. It diminishes the conscious attention with which acts are performed. This has certain corollaries which may be brought out in detail.

i) Habit reduces fatigue. The first day we play any new game tires us much more. As we get used to it, it tires us less. The first day you begin to learn typing or playing on a harmonium, it gives you finger-ache. But when it becomes a matter of daily routine it is easier to do.

ii) Habit makes movements simpler. A beginner has to perform a number of preparatory, random movements before he gets to the correct ones. Watch a person trying to learn riding a bicycle and compare his blundering attempts with the simple grace of an expert who simply gets on to the seat and starts pedalling.

iii) Habits make our movements more accurate. The harmonium player or the typist makes no mistake in handling the several keys. The novice usually touches the wrong ones and only after months of practice achieves efficiency as a result of habit formation.

iv) Habits ensure greater speed. What we are used to we can always do more quickly. The child takes an aggravatingly long time to write a sentence while we do it with great speed.

Thus habits make for a greater ease, simplicity, accuracy and speed of movement.

Another great advantage of habit formation is that petty actions of daily life are mechanised and higher powers of thought and intelligence are released for superior adjustments and endeavours. Through habit formation it is possible to do more than one thing at a time. As the habitual action does not need attention of effort, it is left free to be devoted to some other work. Women spin while they talk. It is because spinning no longer needs conscious effort and attention is free to be fixed upon talking. To use our intelligence to better results, we must make habitual as many of the tools of writing and thinking as possible. Multiplication tables, rules of grammar, correct spelling, facts of history and geography, laws of science must be mechanised so that our understanding and thought may be free to seek new spheres. Habit formation helps to save our energy from being frittered away in a tiring search for items of information. Thus some fundamental knowledge and skills must be made habitual and drill must be given some place in education.

But habit which has been extolled as 'second nature' is not without its limitations. Habit is mechanical, stereotyped, and therefore not adaptable to new situations. Whenever a changed objective requires a changed mode of behaviour, it fails to achieve the end towards which it is directed. One who is habituated to the cosy chair of his study finds it very difficult to meet the living facts of a new vocation. Habit is the conservative factor in life and character and, with all its advantages, acts like a clog to the wheel and retards the quick flow of mental energy into new channels, for the adaptation of new means to ends. Those who live by habits alone have wooden and mechanical characters. It is this mechanising tendency of habit which has led some philosophers to condemn habit as the negation of life.

Habit is considered to be opposed to intelligent behaviour so much so that Rousseau insisted that the only habit a child should be encouraged to form is that of forming no habits. Initiative and resourcefulness which generally go with problem-solving in both school and outside life have no place in the character of a person who lives by habits alone.

Habits are both good and bad and once bad habits are formed, it is difficult to get rid of them. Those who have acquired habits of smoking, drinking, sleeping with the light on or writing with the left hand and the like, know too well how hard it is to escape the bondage of habits. They can only be gradually supplanted by other habits.

Most habits are formed in childhood when there is little or no discrimination between desirable and undesirable habits, and when discrimination comes in later life, habits are too firmly rooted to be easily supplanted.

Habits kill feeling and make us indifferent to what may concern us most. Behaviour and experience that have become habitual bring little emotional stirring. The farmer is blind to the beauty of Nature around him, the soldier is so used to maimed soldiers in the field of battle that he pays no heed to them. Habits make our blood cold as it were and stories that rack the human heart are just incidents to a magistrate who is used to them.

Thus habits have their merits as well as dangers.

4. The Role of Habit in Life

Life is a tissue of habits and the health, happiness and efficiency of an individual depend on what habits he has acquired in the course of his experience. A man is lazy or industrious, selfish or generous, cold or shy, honest or dishonest, sympathetic or callous in the several relationships of life largely because he has practised being that and not something else. His viewpoints, his tastes, his like and dislikes, the use he makes of his ability, material resources and social status, the ease or otherwise with which he makes friends and fits into their life, the joy and satisfaction he gets out of his patterns of life, in fact a thousand and one other traits, qualities and relations in their several shades and degrees are to a very large extent matters of habit. He who abounds in vigorous health and succeeds in maintaining it for long; he who always takes a sunny view of things, readily co-operates with others and is intent on making the best of whatever is thrown in his way ; the good craftsman who executes his work skilfully and quickly ; the open mind that can see virtue and commend it wherever it is found, irrespective of caste, creed or person; the cyclist who pedals his machine along a line on the road with ease and skill—all these owe their achievement, health, happiness and efficiency to the great power of habit. Our manner of speaking, walking, writing, playing, sitting; our hours of rising, bathing, eating, working, sleeping; our beliefs, prejudices, opinions, faith; our hopes, fears, enthusiasms, these and numerous other items of life are reflections of our habits. Whatever we do and think tends to become habitual and we are what we tend to do and think. An individual truly is a bundle of habits and his character and personality loses its content and cannot be visualised if you strip him of his habits. ‘ Personality is clothed in habits. Habits are the very garment of the soul.’

This ability to form habits is the most striking and useful characteristic of man, whether we see him as an infant, a child, a youth or an adult. Whenever any action is performed by him several times it becomes easier to carry it out, and if it is continued it becomes so easy that the muscles and the nerves employed in carrying out the action do so with very little effort from his conscious will. He may, in fact, not know that he is performing the action until it is nearly, or quite, completed. This action has become habitual. The habit-forming ability is very useful in so far as it eases the burden on the hard-working executive part of our minds and leaves it free to carry out new and unaccustomed types of action. When a four-year-old child tries to lace his shoes for the first time, he is awkward, makes many unnecessary movements, puts the laces in wrong holes and seems somewhat ill at ease in the situation. But after some months of practice he will lace his shoes correctly in a fraction of the time previously taken. Still later he will lace them with ease and automatically, and when he grows up he laces them so mechanically that he is hardly conscious of having performed that act, so much so that even after five minutes he will not be able to recall as to what foot, left or right, he laced first and will be able to carry on active thought or conversation while performing the act.

Good moral character is also a matter of habit. The honest man is he who habitually practises honesty; faced with tempting and difficult situations, he has not to weigh the pros and cons of his course of action and decide as to which he should follow. The habit of honesty he has formed facilitates his decision, he acts without a moral conflict, in fact with the same ease with which he slips his foot into his shoe. On the other hand, one who is not habitually honest and with whom other considerations also weigh, has to make an effort, to fight an inner struggle with his conscience, to expend considerable thought and attention to the advantages and disadvantages or the alternative courses of action open to him before he makes a choice. And if he ever decides in favour of the honest course, it is at the cost of a great mental strain and he feels as if he has made an uphill effort and great sacrifice of other things that matter to him.

In view of the powerful role played by habit in life, the aim of all education, as of all instruction and discipline, both at home and in the school, should be the inculcation of right habits. If habits make the man, if they constitute and lie at the basis of his character and personality, if they ensure his health, happiness and efficiency, every objective which the agencies of home and school set themselves to achieve would be measured in terms of what it contributes to the cultivation of desirable habits in young minds. James thinks that the cultivation of proper habits is the sole aim of education.

James stresses the social significance of this tendency to form habits thus : ' Habit is the enormous fly-wheel of society, the most precious conservative agent. It alone keeps us all within the bounds of ordinance and saves the children of fortune from the envious uprisings of the poor. It alone prevents the hardest and most repulsive walks of life from being deserted by those brought up to tread therein. It keeps the fisherman and the deck hand at sea through the winter ; it holds the miner in his darkness, and nails the countryman to his log cabin and his lonely farm through all the months of snow. It dooms us to fight out the battle of life upon the lines of our nurture or our early choice, and to make the best of a pursuit that disagrees, because there is no other for which we are fitted, and it is too late to begin again.' Obviously James attaches too much permanency to habitual modes of behaviour. Though there is a strong resistance habits do change and people have changed their ways of living.

Through habits we meet our needs and the demands of our physical and social environment. We have the habit of wearing clothes to cope with extremes of heat and cold and the demands of our culture. Culture is just a body of habitual responses to meet basic human needs, the ways of eating, dressing, child rearing, working, recreation and the like. Cultural norms express themselves in the personal habits of the individuals who are members of that culture. An American habitually holds his cigarette between the second and third fingers while a European holds it between thumb and first or second finger. This is learned from other members of the culture and is one of the numerous ways of sharing that culture. But here too variations in the habits of individuals are noticed quite often.

5. How Habits are Formed

Let us inquire what principles should be followed in the cultivation of desirable habits.

i) In the first place, in the cultivation of good habits we should begin very early. The child begins to form habits very early and the tendency of habits to be firmly established is stronger in early years of childhood than in later. The younger the child the more receptive and plastic will be his mind. Not having acquired any habits as yet the organism and mental structure of the child is weak enough to yield to influence readily. Childhood is the impressionable or formative period of life. The modes of behaviour in both thought and action have not become fixed or unalterable, and it will be easier to form good habits. The advice to begin early is the advice to begin on a clean slate. ‘Just as the sapling is bent, the tree is inclined.’

ii) Secondly, habits are formed by frequent repetition and it takes time. Thinking and acting in the same way for a number of times makes that thought and action recur whenever the circumstances of its original occurrence are repeated. Every time a child in a Hindu family enters the kitchen he is asked to take off his shoes. Constant insistence on this action builds in the child a habit in the course of time, so that he no longer needs any admonition from his elders to take off his shoes. As he reaches the door of the kitchen the shoes take themselves off, as it were.

The fact that habits are formed by repetition and practice has been made out into a law by Thorndike. He calls it the 'Law of Exercise' and we have dealt with it in the last chapter. This repetition or exercise takes time. We cannot form a habit in a day, not even in a week. Opportunities must be repeatedly given for the exercise of a certain type of behaviour before we can hope that it should become habitual. It is an uninterrupted continuity of performance under similar circumstances which tends to strengthen particular modes of behaviour. Therefore, patience and perseverance should be the key-note of the attitude of the teacher.

This is a principle which is too obvious to deserve discussion. We learn to swim by swimming, to run by running and to write by writing. And yet many teachers expect habits to be formed by a top-hattrick. They would not admit this, but what else do they mean when by sheer coaxing, preaching and exhorting they expect children to acquire desirable habits? Unless opportunities for doing and repeating things are afforded to children, it is futile to expect them to form habits. Sermons and exhortations may help children to acquire a moral vocabulary but not a moral character. Precepts uttered in moments of annoyance will not help in the formation of habits unless children are afforded actual practice in those modes of behaviour.

iii) Form habits as they will be used. Children should repeat and practise actions in the same situation in which their habits when acquired are going to be helpful. For example, it is no use asking children to con over the several letters in a word and thinking that they are learning to spell. The need of correct spelling arises in writing and it is in writing alone, and not in oral speech or reading, that they should repeat correct spelling. Habits are highly specific in operation. They do not extend beyond their sphere of action, beyond the particular situations which are apt to call out their activity.

iv) We must start with a strong emotional stimulus. An appeal to feelings conveys greater force than that to reason and that is why we find an emotional public orator making a greater impression on the audience than a philosopher. Starting in a mood of enthusiasm the former appeals to the emotional susceptibilities of the crowd. James advises : launch yourself with as strong and decided an initiative as possible. Half-hearted appeals do not avail. This principle justifies public pledges which give us strong motives. Even when a start has been made, appropriate emotional attitude should be maintained during continuity of performance.

v) In the formation of a new habit there should be no exceptions and the action should be persistently performed without a break. One exception will destroy the effect of long practice. Never say 'I will let you off this time but you must never do it again'. By letting him off this time you are making him do it again. You are not merely neglecting the particular habit that you wished to encourage but actually encouraging some counter-habit that you wished to suppress. Most people who start smoking or drinking think that doing it just once will do no harm and the first drink or smoke breaks the barriers of inhibition.

vi) Another useful maxim is to seek the first opportunity to act on a new resolution. A single right act is better than many pious resolutions. Most of us keep putting off our resolutions but the best time to carry them out is the moment they are formed.

vii) The formation of good habits among children should be rewarded. Children seek pleasure and avoid pain Conduct which gives comfort, pleasure and satisfaction tends to be repeated and that which is followed by pain discomfort and punishment is avoided. 'Reward all good impulses and punish bad ones', says Thorndike. But there must be a much more rational use of rewards and punishments than is made by an average teacher. Some make too frequent a use of punishment, they are always criticising, ridiculing or condemning their pupils' efforts. Such pupils grow shy and diffident. Some teachers go to the other extreme of rewarding every effort made by their pupils in the hope of encouraging them to better effort. But this indiscriminate use of rewards may never let them know their mistakes or defects. In many schools pupils are asked to do extra exercises after school hours as a punishment for negligence. This is harmful as it builds in them an aversion for the task and hardens their habit of negligence.

6. Breaking Bad Habits

But with the best of training, care and intentions, children often develop undesirable habits owing to influences over which teachers have no control nor are likely to have any. In fact, the formation of bad habits is so common that with most of us the chief concern is not the cultivation of good habits but the 'breaking' of bad unhealthy ways. Now this 'breaking' task is full of pitfalls and many a young child hardens into a callous 'delinquent' beyond any hope of reform simply because of the mistaken attitude and measures taken by teachers.

In the first place, it should be recognised that most bad habits are acquired unconsciously and the teacher should try to know how they are acquired. He must look for the cause and try to remove it. One common cause is that a lower standard was expected of the child, or a lower achievement was accepted from him and he did no better. The most important thing in the re-eduction of such children is to prescribe right standards and ideals, set a worthy example and show the right way. But weakness in training may not be due entirely to lower standard of expectations of parents and teachers. It may be the result of physical weakness. Some children have a bad habit of bending over their desks while writing or bringing a book too close to their eyes while reading. Remedial measures in such cases will mean enlisting the aid of the school medical service and providing correctives such as glasses in the case of defective eyesight.

Some bad habits are the result of emotional instability such as nail-bitting, pen-chewing, nose-picking. It is not quite correct to speak of them as habits for they are not acquired through repetition. They are an expression of some inner conflict and unrest. They are often described as 'nervous' habits. Children who are frequently abused, teased, punished, frightened or cautioned at every step develop a feeling of insecurity and anxiety, and these nervous habits are but an outward sign of the inner emotional unrest. Remedial measures for such undesirable habits should never be direct. The child should never be told that he has such bad habits nor should he ever be punished for them. The former will only make him more self-conscious and increase his sense of guilt and shame, the latter will intensify his fear and anxiety. In either case his trouble will be aggravated even though he may give up biting nails or picking his nose in the presence of teachers. The best treatment lies in ignoring the habit, avoiding every possibility of further conflict and unrest and restoring confidence, poise and self-esteem in which the child has suffered. It may be pointed out that quite a large number of children have these habits and grow out of them. Positive guidance towards healthy goals, improving the physical condition of the child and providing opportunities for vigorous games often helps. In all cases the treatment should be directed to the underlying cause rather than to the symptoms.

Knight Dunlap suggests a new method of breaking bad habits. He himself had the bad habit of typing '*t h e*' as '*h t e*'. By deliberately practising the wrong spelling '*h t e*' he fixed his attention on the wrong spelling and got rid of the habit. If a child given to thumb sucking is reminded and asked again and again to put his thumb into his mouth even when he is not doing it in course of time he will stop doing it altogether. Many children can be induced to drop the bad habits of nail biting, stuttering or nose picking by being asked to practise them deliberately and consciously. This may seem strange and contrary but this negative approach gives children insight into their bad habit, they begin to understand its nature and undesirability and drop it. This method of breaking bad habits is one of punishment because the child does feel that others do not approve of his habit and it is really bad.

Secondly, there is no such thing as 'breaking' a bad habit, if by that phrase is meant a rooting-out of any trait. The problem is not to displace a bad habit, but to cultivate a good counter-habit so that the former has no scope for expression and exercise and falls off through disuse and neglect. The child who has developed the use of bad language when he is annoyed is not allowed to be annoyed for several days and consequently to use bad language. In course of time the bad habit dies a natural death though nothing was done to 'break' it directly. Good habits expel bad habits. Slovenliness and negligence are stamped out by neatness and care, diffidence by confidence, lying by truth-telling. The latter simply replace the former and if teachers wish to break some bad habit they should work for the cultivation of its better counterpart so that bad action becomes more difficult to perform than the good one. Therefore, to a large extent principles for the 'breaking' of bad habits are the same a those for the cultivation of good ones.

Questions

1. How would you define habits ? How is a habit formed ? Make a list of your own habits.
2. What is the place and value of habits in life ? Describe some of the laws of habit formation.
3. Discuss and criticise the following statements :
   a) Man is a bundle of habits.
   b) To form habits is to fail.
   c) Habit is ten times nature.
4. How would you proceed to break a bad habit among students in a school ? Describe some bad habits among children in the primary school.
5. How are habits related to school discipline ? What is the responsibility of the teacher in building useful habits ?
6. Compare habitual action with instinctive action. What laws of psychology and physiology govern the formation of habits ?
7. What habits should a child of eight have formed ?

8. What are the dangers of forming a habit of all things that we are called upon to do?

References for Further Study

1. Allport: *Personality: A Psychological Interpretation* (Henry Holt).
2. Bode: *How We Learn* (D. C. Heoth).
3. Catty: *The Theory and Practice of Education* (Methuen).
4. Dexter and Garlick: *Psychology in the Schoolroom* (Longmans).
5. Freeman: *How Children Learn* (Houghton Mifflin).
6. Hollingworth: *Psychology: Its Facts and Principles* (Appleton).
7. James: *Principles of Psychology* (Macmillan).
8. Kilpatrick: *Foundations of Method* (Macmillan).
9. Thom: *Everyday Problems of the Everyday Child* (Appleton).
10. Woodworth: *Psychology* (Methuen).

CHAPTER SEVENTEEN

Thinking and Reasoning

1. The Nature of Thinking

MAN is commonly described as a rational being and his rationality consists in his ability to think and reason. His superiority over other animals in learning and adjustment lies in his capacity for better thinking. The great edifice of civilisation and culture which man has built up during centuries of effort and struggle, the systems of science, philosophy and religion, the works of art and literature, the elaborate technical inventions and social institutions bear testimony to the great human efforts at clear and bold thinking. The progress of the individual as well as of society depends on the human tendency to think and break away from the habitual and customary modes of life. It is the independence of thought that has killed magic and superstition and set man free from the influence of charms, incantations and fetishes. The uplift of humanity lies in developing the capacity of man for free and independent thinking and no education is worth the name if it does not include among its objectives the development of children's capacity for independent and creative thinking.

In a broad sense thinking includes all forms of cognition, perception, imagination, memory and conception. But in a restricted sense it means either imagination or reasoning. Woodworth aptly describes the former as mental manipulation and the latter as mental exploration. In imagination facts previously observed are recalled and these images are combined and manipulated into new patterns. In reasoning we mentally explore new relations actually existing between facts. Both are independent of the present and seek to meet a possible situation in the future. In actual experience it may be difficult to separate the two, but when we think without images or mental pictures and in terms of words alone, the activity is described as pure thought. But both lead to solutions of problems we anticipate. In imagination, however, there are a number of possible solutions, and in reasoning there is just one solution that is to be found and that is considered adequate for a solution.

Popular psychology believes that thought is some inner kind of mental process in which mental contents follow one another and which can be studied independently of the needs, motives and desires of an individual. This view shall have to be amended. Thought is a type of behaviour, aroused by stimulus present or absent and satisfying an immediate or remote practical need. If man has survived and built a civilisation, it is because his needs have been served by the complex process of thought. The new attitude in psychology is to stress this relation between thought and practical needs.

When it gets dark we turn on the light; when we feel cold, we wrap ourselves; when there is a car coming, we move to one side of the road. These are adjustments to meet the practical needs of a situation. Similarly, thinking is conative in character, it arises in situations which upset or disturb our routine and call for a new adjustment. Thinking is often described as adjustment to a hypothetical situation. Placed in a difficulty animals try one course of action and then another to find out the best method of meeting it. A rat trying to get out of a cage, an ape trying to secure a banana beyond its reach, a dog trying to open a gate, all indulge in a number of wasteful trials before they hit upon the right method. But man, when faced with a difficult situation, sits down and thinks. He goes over in thought the several possibilities of action, tries them out in imagination and selects one for action. Thinking is a delayed response in which an absent or a future situation is responded to.

In all forms of thinking the items within the stream of thought cohere by virtue of some type of association. In the chapter on memory, the meaning and role of associative thinking has been dealt with in detail. Even animals and children are capable of it. But man is not a mere victim of such associations, he does not always let his mind go adrift. When he is said to reason, argue, make a point or solve a problem, there is a selection and orderliness in his ideas which may be contrasted with day-dreaming and reveries. This selection is made not on the strength of any similarity between ideas nor on the basis of any spatial or temporal connections recognised among them. We only pass from the acceptance of one idea to the acceptance or rejection of another. In reasoning, association between the several thought items is controlled. There is a definite problem and in its light the contents of experience are broken up into their component parts and regrouped into a fresh pattern. The situation which calls for adjustment is analysed and the relation of the parts to one another and to the whole is clearly seen. The analysis brings out common elements of several situations and these are grouped into a new whole which is general and abstract. To understand this complex process of thought fully, we must study the processes through which concepts are formed judgments arrived at and reasoning carried out.

2. Conception

What distinguishes man from animals is his ability to form concepts. He not only retains mental pictures of concrete objects and experiences, but also builds on their basis general ideas denoting classes of objects. These are called concepts. After having seen a number of horses we come to form a general notion about their common qualities, characteristics and relations. This is a concept or idea of a horse in general. When we use words like 'horse', 'man', "soldier", we mean that cluster of qualities which is common to all horses, men or soldiers. A concept is a system of meaning.

The basis of concepts is perception. The several perceptions are compared, their common qualities are emphasised and abstracted and a general idea which does not correspond to any one subject but is the cumulative result of many, is formed. Concepts are the result of comparison, relation, abstraction and generalisation. The wider the experience, the richer the concepts. A child sees a person in a uniform, with a gun, sword, military hat and belt and is told that the man is a soldier. Next, he meets a cavalryman, an artilleryman or a foreign soldier and is told that despite apparent differences they are all soldiers. He begins to recognise the essentials and later when he sees pictures of soldiers from other countries, he calls them soldiers. The general idea of a soldier which does not correspond to any one particular individual is a concept and the mental activity through which it is obtained is called 'conception'.

Concepts make for mental economy through organisation. They give us the power to think of the many into one. They help to organize knowledge; separate, isolated facts of experience and knowledge are combined and retained under general heads. It is easier and more economic to use general ideas than to deal with each individual object. Concepts make possible abstract thought and reasoning and the system of science is just classified knowledge, knowledge built into concepts which apply not only to the past and the present but also to the future. When the child calls persons, differently dressed and equipped just soldiers, he is referring to essential qualities which will help in future classification and distinction as well.

Concepts are formed with a purpose, an end in view. They are tools of thinking and since different individuals use tools for different purposes, the meaning of concepts differs from individual to individual. The selection of essential qualities is relevant to the purpose and what is essential from one point of view may not be so from another. Not only are our concepts of abstract general qualities like honesty, decency, justice or health, widely different, but even our concepts of such concrete things as paper, oil or shoes have different essences. For example, paper may signify different things to a student, examiner, merchant, manufacturer or chemist.

Concepts may be of objects, relations or qualities. Horse, cap, table, etc. are concepts of concrete objects. Honesty, redness, taste, punctuality, etc. are concepts of qualities. Bigger, higher, smaller, etc. are concepts of relations. Concepts of abstract qualities and relations are acquired by children later and the main care of the teacher should be that they acquire most of their concepts themselves. He should make them discover relations and common qualities, and then supply the name.

Words play an important role in conception. With their help children are able to concentrate attention on general ideas. They help clarity of thought and the precise and accurate use of language goes with clear and definite thinking.

3. JUDGMENT

Concepts do not hang alone, they are always related to one another. Whenever two ideas are connected and a relation of agreement or disagreement is asserted between the two, we have a judgment. To judge is to discover the relationship between two ideas. 'The house is burning', 'A horse is a useful animal', 'Honesty is the best policy', are examples of judgment. The ideas related may be concrete or abstract. The common meaning of judgment as decision is true: we decide about the relation between ideas on the basis of perception and our interpretation of what we perceive.

Conception and judgment involve each other. It is only for the sake of distinction that they are treated separately. In forming concepts, percepts are compared and this comparison involves judgment. Most often such judgments are not expressed but they are understood. In comparing different kinds of soldiers and discovering the essential qualities common to them, the child does arrive at relationship between the several qualities and types of soldiers. He does judge. On the other hand, all judgment involves conception. Ideas previously formed are used and in judging relationship between ideas, ideas themselves grow richer, more accurate and better defined. Fresh qualities or relations are recognised among concepts and new meanings are added. Making new judgments about education, war, peace or planning, our ideas about them grow richer.

Some judgments are made spontaneously and immediately; we call them intuitive judgments, for example, *the child looks ill, telling lies is bad.* Intuitions are judgments made instantaneously without any effort of thought. When judgments are the result of reflection and deliberation, they are called deliberative, as for example, *every man is equal before the law*; *rest is necessary during examination days.*

Judgment enters into every aspect of mental life. Every one of us is called upon to judge every moment of our waking life and it certainly is one of the main objectives of education to teach children to judge correctly. Most often teachers pass on ready-made judgments to pupils and thus unconsciously breed, among them, a habit of depending upon the judgments of others. Cultivating the right standards of judgment and healthy habits of acting according to their own judgment has very great value. It makes pupils efficient, self-confident, self-reliant and intellectually independent. In an enlightened community each member should be a law unto himself, adjusting self-interest and social service by his own trained judgment.

But judgments often go wrong unintentionally; it turns out that we are honestly mistaken. What are the common causes of failure of judgment ? The first is lack of experience. When all the facts are not observed, when evidence is insufficient or when same data is neglected, judgments go wrong. Secondly, it may be due to lack of reflection. All the implications of facts may not have been fully thought about. How often we repent for making snapshot judgments, jumping at conclusions or expressing opinions thoughtlessly. Thirdly, emotional prejudices like jealousy often mar our judgments. We all view the world from our own angle and our judgments are faulty to the extent to which we let our feelings play with them. Lastly, the mental habit of depending on others or of borrowing opinions and echoing them is fatal to independent judgment. Blind acceptance of judgments from others makes mental parrots of us all.

The teacher's responsibility in training children to judge for themselves is great. He should not only help them to acquire knowledge but also to turn it into wisdom by guiding them to attend to the bearings, the relationships, the applications of facts. Young people should be encouraged to think independently. They should be asked questions which demand earnest thinking. The aim of the teacher should be 'not uniform knowledge, but multiform thinking'. Much of our common teaching is mere telling either by the teacher or the texbook. What is needed is the creation of such social situations as the solution of an urgent problem, discussion of a burning topic, the criticism of a story written by a pupil and the like, so that pupils may have no other alternative but to search their minds and form judgments. In the study of science they should discover facts for themselves or verify those already known; in literature, biography and history they should judge motives and conduct of the characters studied ; in art and music they should distinguish between the beautiful and the ugly, the harmonious and the jarring. Good taste and love for truth will stimulate independent judgment.

4. Reasoning

Reasoning is the mental activity used in argument, demonstration or proof. It consists in making a new judgment on the basis of judgment or judgments already formed and is commonly defined as 'perceiving relations among judgments' or seeing agreement or disagreement among judgments already made. Reasoning is generally associated with formal rules and formulae of logic, but all people, even young children, reason without consciously realising that hey are doing so. When the child runs towards the door on hearing a hawker, when a dog comes back on seeing the master enter a car, when we put off an engagement or thank a friend for a favour received, reasoning is involved.

Reasoning is a process or adjustment to a new situation and at a somewhat higher level aims at the solution of a problem. Dewey analyses it into five steps. In the first step a difficulty is felt or a problem is realised. Unless a problem is felt we do not reason. The second step is to examine the object or the situation carefully. Often the problem is stated in the form of a judgment or a series of judgments. Thirdly, an attempt is made to solve the problem or explain the puzzle. Possible causes of difficulty and the several possible solutions are explored and developed. Fourthly, one very probable solution is provisionally accepted, and an attempt is made to verify or test it. All implications are examined and compared with facts. In the last step, on the basis of proof one solution is finally accepted or rejected. This may be described as taking a decision or making a judgment.

Let us take an example. On reaching home the mother finds that the baby is crying bitterly. Her peace of mind is disturbed. This is the presentation of the problem. Next, she examines the baby carefully to see if it has been hurt or is hungry. She observes it from head to foot and there is no mark of injury. She puts the baby to breast, but the baby does not stop crying. Next, she is convinced that the trouble is internal. But what is the trouble ? Next, she supposes it to be pain in the stomach. If this is true, a pinch of soda should set it right. To test and verify it she gives the baby a pinch of soda. Next, the baby belches and stops crying. The mother has accepted finally that the baby was crying owing to pain in the stomach.

This decision or final judgment has been reached through a close examination of facts. When a universal judgment is thus arrived at, on the basis of particular facts, the method is called inductive, and when we start with a general truth or statement and proceed to apply it to particular instances the method is deductive. The mother proceeded to find out inductively what the trouble with the baby was. She formed a supposition or hypothesis and proceeded to verify it but she may have started with a general brief that babies cry only when they have pain in the stomach and then may have proceeded to prove it by applying it to her baby. The first approach is inductive, the second is deductive.

In induction we start with a few observed facts, compare and classify them, try to observe some common elements in them, form a hypothesis about their explanation, verify that hypothesis for final acceptance or rejection. If the hypothesis is verified, it is accepted as explanation. Thus induction tries to discover universal relations among facts on the basis of what is observed and experienced. It passes from the particular to the universal truth. In deduction we start with a universal proposition and proceed to prove it by applying it to fresh instances. Induction is a method of discovery and research, deduction is a method of application and proof. The two start at the opposite ends and move in different directions, but they are not opposed to each other as is commonly supposed. They are two processes in the same activity called reasoning or they may be considered as two aspects or phases of the same process.

Though it is possible to analyse reasoning and indicate its most essential steps, people not only do not analyse their reasoning but also resent other people's effort to do it for them. They reach conclusions by processes which are largely unconscious, or simply jump at conclusions.

Reasoning is a valuable mental activity and in the solution of problems is far superior to the method of trial and error. In the latter the material must be present, but in reasoning the material need not be present. The commander plans strategy from the headquarters, hundreds of miles behind the front, and since the several alternatives are mentally tested, it saves great time and energy. The administrator can find out by reasoning the effects of a change in policy before making the change, the engineer can plan a building less costly and more commodious, the educator can choose between policies and methods before putting them into practice by a process of reasoning. Reasoning solves problems and can use the experience of others. Reasoning leads to cultural progress and is a source of individual efficiency and well-being.

5. Conditions That Stimulate Thinking

These may be traced to the environment of an individual or his personality. In the first place there are some types of situations which compel thinking. Face to face with rapid and far-reaching changes as our own times are witnessing, thinking is an imperative necessity. In any democratic country considerable premium is placed on thought and it is a common belief that only through reflective thinking people can meet the challenge of social and political problems. But in communities where custom and tradition hold full sway over the life and thought of the people, thinking is looked upon with suspicion. So is the case with communities in which religious or political dictatorship prevails. The school is a community and if the pupils are not hedged in by too many rules, if the teacher, instead of giving too much guidance, presents situations in which pupils are called upon to decide for themselves in matters of discipline, organisation and social functions, they will develop habits of self-reliance in thought and reasoning. The teacher should have a progressive attitude, and should be constantly presenting problems to their classes for effortful thinking.

Secondly, thought is stimulated by contact with people of different views, habits, beliefs and culture. Today our cosmopolitan neighbourhood has brought us very close to different parts of the world. Radio, newspapers, travel-books should figure prominently in the life of the school as also visits to other lands and peoples. Travelling should be encouraged and subsidised by the school in collaboration with the state.

Thirdly, in the development of thought, language plays

an important role. It is not merely a means of communication, a medium of social intercourse, but also a tool of thinking. Thoughts and words are so closely connected that the one nearly always tends to call up the other. 'The word thus becomes a sort of handle to the idea.' Ideas are elusive, they quickly fade from consciousness and if we wish to organise ideas to a high degree of complexity and subtlety, we can do so by organising our expression in language. Words act as pegs on which we can conveniently hang out ideas and come back to them ; they are vehicles of meaning and often bring back to consciousness the corresponding ideas. Many sciences like mathematics would not have developed without language.

6. Training in Thought and Reasoning

In modern education nothing is considered more important than teaching children to think and reason for themselves. Stress is laid on the all-round changes taking place in our manifold environment and on the impossibility of educating the younger generation for adult social living whose pattern is uncertain. The best that can and should be done is to equip children with an ability to think for themselves and successfully meet the changing situations of a changing world.

The teacher has to play a more difficult role in achieving this aim. He is not to be an initiator, a leader into whose mental footsteps children are to walk, but throwing himself into the background, he is to stimulate them to become their own leaders, to meet each difficulty as if it were a battle to be won. Young people must be encouraged to stand on their own legs, to be self-reliant and resourceful in study and thought. Teaching must be dynamic, presenting new material and a new standpoint and challenging the young intellect. No ready-made definitions, rules of thumb or 'tabloid thinking' will help. Pupils should be guided to think and study. Study periods in which they study by themselves at the suggestion of the teacher should be carefully organised and frequent classroom discussions of an informal type on topics already studied should be held.

Should teaching be inductive or deductive? Should the teacher start with a particular instance and, through comparison, help pupils to obtain general rules, or should he give them the rule or definition straightaway and ask them to apply it to particular instances? Older teaching was mostly deductive. The teacher offered the rule or definition, asked the class to commit it to memory and then gave examples to illustrate it. Definitions of parts of speech, rules of grammar, rules for multiplication of decimals and the like were boldly printed in textbooks, transcribed on the blackboard and ceremoniously repeated by the teacher so that the pupils may memorise them for mechanical application. This method was no doubt economical for both the teacher and the taught, but it gave no opportunity for independent thinking. The lesson lacked vigour, the concepts formed were not so rich and the general rule acquired was not so suggestive. On the other hand, the method of induction takes the mind through the same steps which it would follow naturally if left to itself. It helps to establish intimate contact between study and experience. The teacher takes half a dozen sentences of daily use. He presents each sentence one by one and asks what person or thing is talked about in it. Often he gives a couple of sentences about the same thing or person to emphasise his point. Then he tells them, 'What we talk about is called *subject*', and calls upon individual pupils to frame a definition that the part of sentence that tells what we talk about is called the *subject* of that sentence. The class feel that it is by their own effort that they achieve the rule and develop skill in the use of knowledge. But the inductive method is long and, with complex topics, may prove cumbersome and confusing. And when a heavy syllabus is to be covered within a prescribed period of time, the deductive method has to be used without apology.

The best method of teaching is neither the inductive nor the deductive, but a wise combination of both. Nor do the two exclude each other. The teacher should use the inductive method to make knowledge vital and objective and the deductive method to make knowledge systematic and comprehensive. All subjects can be taught both ways and each should be taught to some extent in each way.

7. Creative Thinking

We all set much store by creative thinking because only those capable of it have contributed to human progress and civilisation. Once it was believed that only talented people and geniuses are capable of creative thinking. Today we hold that all individuals are creative in varying degrees. Not all of us have the originality of Raman and Tagore but we all do have new ideas and insights from time to time and vary our ways of doing things. Every idea that is original is creative from the point of view of the individual no matter how often others may have had a similar idea. Creativity is seeing or expressing new relationships. Creativity is possible in all areas of life, thinking, working, playing or social interaction. In almost everything we do we can change old relationships into new arrangements, add new items or forms to the old structure. Each of us is doing almost everything in his own way. When habits do not help we change our approach, inquire and explore the new situation and look for new relationships and strike a new line of thought and action.

Creative thinking generally passes through four stages.

The first is *preparation* in which the individual tries to relate facts in various ways, there is much trial-and-error. The second is *incubation* in which there is no overt activity and the individual may engage in activities like taking a walk or playing cards which have nothing to do with his problem. The third is *inspiration* when new ideas or solutions flash across the mind after a period of incubation. A new idea may occur even in a dream. The fourth is *verification* or testing in which the bright idea is tested or revised. The last stage is necessary in research or invention.

8. Creative Thinking and the School

What can schools do to foster creative thinking? The common belief is that creativity cannot be taught and nobody can make another person more creative. It is an innate natural power which will assert itself whatever the nature of environment. But several studies made of creative people in various areas of work show that the role of the teacher in stimulating and encouraging creative thinking is not negligble. At least several creative thinkers have paid glowing tributes to their teachers and it is an argument for recruiting the best men and women into the teaching profession. It is common knowledge that a teacher who bullies and ridicules his pupils is a greater damper of the pupils' spirit and efforts than the one who with affection and understanding encourages and stimulates them. Let us consider some of the ways which help foster creative thinking among pupils.

In the first place the atmosphere in the schools should be wholesome and encouraging. Young people should be assured that if they think and express themselves in new and unorthodox ways they will not be condemned or ridiculed, their wild ideas will be judged on merit and the teacher will not fly at them for saying things which are not to the liking of the teacher. Very early young people come to understand that their teacher likes and dislikes and they start doing and saying things which fall in line with his ideas, and which are trite and commonplace.

Secondly, the teacher instead of expecting dead uniformity should encourage and commend variety and originality. One of my teachers used to insist ' Write an essay on " Under a Tree " and I want that each one of you should write his own individual and unique experience and thoughts. ' The best essay went into the college magazine. Differences of opinion and approach, variety in treatment and expression, should be praised and expected. But if pupils are expected to conform to an established pattern there is no room or reason for doing creative thinking.

Thirdly, to be creative in thought one must be creative in observation, in seeing and listening. The same teacher used to advise : ' Before writing your essay "Under a Tree ", go and sit under a tree and see what you never saw before, look around for new things and relations. ' Going out on a hike young people should be expected to note down in their diary some very remarkable things they saw which probably others did not see. Alertness, activity and flexibility in day to day observation reveals many new things even in familiar surroundings, and give us food for creative thinking and expression. Such observation is sure to be selective, if young people distort facts let them do so within limits adding or changing details here and there, after some time they will learn to be objective.

Fourthly, the teacher should give exercise in divergent thinking in all subjects. What would have happened to India if there had been no Himalayas ? If Mahatma Gandhi had not been assassinated how would it have affected the course of events in the country ? What would you do if you were the Prime Minister of India or the headmaster of your school?

Lastly, build up in young people the maximum of self-confidence and self-trust. A harassed, worried child cannot create new ideas. Nor should he be overawed by the greatness of his teacher or by the great masters he reads. Let the atmosphere be realistic, allowing reasonable criticism and comments on everything that is done, thought and taught in the school. This will imply that the teacher himself must be a creative thinker who has kept alive his youthful curiosity, who still wonders at the world and who wants young people to join him in the enjoyable task of studying and teaching as willing partners in a zestful game.

QUESTIONS

1. What are the various steps in a complete act of thought? What are the causes of poor thinking? How can children be trained to think efficiently?
2. Describe the relation between thought and language and the significance of this relation for teaching.
3. How do concepts arise in the mind? What is the significance of concepts in education? How can the teacher help the child in forming concepts?
4. What are the conditions which stimulate thinking? How far do they affect thinking among Indians?
5. What processes are used in reasoning?
6. Explain and illustrate the inductive and the deductive methods of teaching and discuss their relative merits.

REFERENCES FOR FURTHER STUDY

1. Cohen and Nagal: *An Introduction to Logic and the Scientific Method* (Harcourt Brace).
2. Dewey: *How We Think* (Harrap).

3. Dexter & Garlick : *Psychology in the Schoolroom* (Longmans).
4. James : *Principles of Psychology* (Macmillan).
5. Judd : *Education as Cultivation of the Higher Mental Process* (Macmillan).
6. Kingsley : *The Nature and Conditions of Learning* (Prentice-Hall).
7. Piaget : *The Child's Conception of the World* (Harcourt Brace).
8. Rignano : *The Psychology of Reasoning* (Harcourt Brace).
9. Thouless : *How to Think Straight* (Simon & Schuster).
10. Wallas : *The Art of Thought* (Harcourt Brace).
11. Wertheimer : *Productive Thinking* (Harper).
12. Woodworth : *Experimental Psychology* (Henry Holt).
13. Woodworth : *Psychology* (Methuen).

CHAPTER EIGHTEEN

Sentiment, Will and Character

1. THE NATURE OF SENTIMENT

THE early life of children is essentially instinctive and their emotions arise largely from the principal instincts we have already described. Such instincts and their accompanying emotions are aroused by a large variety of objects. Thus anything which obstructs a child makes him angry; it may be a table, dog, door or father. Anything strange and new arouses his curiosity; it may be a book, bird, flower or engine. Sometimes one single object arouses more than one instinctive tendency and different emotions mix with each other to form complex emotions. Thus a child feels fear, admiration and respect for his father; this blend of emotions we call *awe*; he feels fear and disgust at the sight of a frog and this blend of emotions is called *loathing*. Thus, in the course of experience, emotions come to be organised round a variety of objects and a number of emotional attitudes are formed about them. So much so that when an object is presented, or even when an image or idea of it occurs, the whole emotional blend so organised is aroused. The object becomes the centre of an emotion or of a system of emotions. Such an organised system of emotional tendencies and attitudes is called a *sentiment*. 'A sentiment', says McDougall, 'involves an individual tendency to experience certain emotions and desires in relation to some particular object'.[1] It is an emotional disposition, a group of attitudes and interests organised around a certain object.

Let us examine the typical sentiment of love between a

[1] *Social Psychology*.

man and his wife. In the begnning, interest in her may have been aroused by sex attraction. She looked young and beautiful. Later, he finds that she looks after his comfort and strives to secure and promote his well-being. The emotional attitude is further strengthened when he enjoys her company, shares with her his experiences and thoughts as also the burden of domestic responsibilities. He feels lonely in her absence and secure in her presence. Later, they have children and she is looked upon as the mother of his children. Thus the sentiment of love grows and matures and in its formation and maturity the instincts of sex, self-preservation, gregariousness, self-assertion, self-abasement and parenthood play an important part. The sentiment has grown from the instinctive nature of man into a form which cannot be easily traced to any one of those instincts.

Thus sentiments are more or less permanent emotional attitudes ; they are built up round particular objects, they take time to mature and if they die, they do not die in a day, and they are based on certain instinctive tendencies.

If we have sentiment for a thing, we tend to feel more strongly for it than for other objects of the same kind. We all develop a sentiment for a certain room in which we work, for our pens, schools and favourite authors. We feel a thrill of pleasure when we return to our room after a period of absence, find our pen after having lost it, pay a visit to our old school or talk about the merits of our favourite author. We do not experience such emotions for rooms, pens, schools and authors in general.

Sentiments may also be developed for abstract ideals such as justice and truth. Childhood quarrels were solved by giving every child his due ; parents, distributed sweets toys and other things equally : teachers awarded marks, according to merit. Fears and jealousies were set at rest by our idea of justice and we felt a sense of security and protection in the idea. Later, we treated others fairly, demanded justice for the oppressed, and applauded all those people in fiction and real life who dealt with others in a just manner. The idea of justice came to be charged with strong emotions. It began to be frequently appealed to, spelt with a capital letter and worshipped like a deity. A strong sentiment had been developed round the general idea or ideal of justice.

Sentiments may be centred round a concrete particular object as I may have a sentiment of love for my child or round a concrete general object as love for children in general or round abstract objects as love for truth, justice or virtue. This is the order in which sentiments grow and this is the basis on which they are commonly classified.

2. Sentiment, Emotion and Mood

A sentiment should be distinguished from an emotion. A sentiment is a permanent disposition, a more or less permanent attitude of the mind towards objects, while emotion is something immediately experienced, a transitory passing state or process of mind. The former is a fact of mental structure, the latter a fact of experience. A sentiment is not an actual experience, but an emotion is. A child feels angry because he cannot do what he likes and his anger is an emotion. So also is the anger of a lover towards his rival trying to do harm to his beloved. The anger of the child is an emotion attached to his instinct, while the anger of the lover is an emotion attached to his sentiment of love towards his beloved. Both the states of anger are actually experienced but not the instinct of the child nor the sentiment of the lover. A sentiment is an attitude of mind, while an emotion is an experience in which that attitude is expressed.

Nor should a sentiment be confused with *mood.* A mood is a mere emotion long drawn out for some time, but a sentiment is a permanent attitude. A mood can be experienced when we get angry at every object that comes our way. It has less objective reference. When we are in a mood of anger every object will invariably excite the feeling, but we know too well that we cannot love each and every objcct. Sentiments are aroused only by a definite class of objects.

3. Sentiments and Habits

All our sentiments form for themselves certain habitual modes of expression. If such habitual modes of behaviour do not grow up round any one of our sentiments, the sentiment gets relatively neglected, becomes spasmodic in its operation, and may gradually die out. Thus the man who has no regular habits of association with his family, no habits of customary forms of public worship, or of studying and participating in national activities and interests, cannot possibly have any sentiment for family, religion or country. He is moved to all these forms of activity by sudden outbursts of emotion and his emotional excitement does not lead to any constructive and continuous flow of energy in any particular line of action. In the absence of habits his emotions grow less frequent and the sentiment gradually dies out. Habits bring stability, strength and regularity to sentiments.

4. The Growth of Sentiments

Early life of instinct is impulsive and only gradually comes to be controlled and modified into an orderly and well-organised life through the growth and development of sentiments. When a sentiment has grown up round a specific object, the impulses of the individual with regard to the object come to be controlled by that sentiment. Such impulses as are in harmony with it are strenghened and those in conflict with it are restrained and modified. The early reactions of children to their toys and hobbies are sudden and irregular and they are accompanied by stray emotions. But gradually order and continuity is restored when a sentiment is developed. The angry child hits or breaks the object, stamps his foot, clenches his teeth, abuses and indulges in some form of hostile action towards the object or person that has aroused his anger. But the man who has developed a strong sentiment of revenge plans to do injury to the enemy, he spends untold time and thought to carry out his plan. In the early years a child has outbursts of affection for his mother, he embraces her plays with her and does a score of other things as she ministers to his needs and pleasures. If she thwarts him, he becomes angry with her, he does not speak to her or may even tear her clothes. Such reactions are spasmodic and irregular. But consider the love of a grown-up young man for his mother, there is a quiet feeling of respect and consideration for her. Through conversation and behaviour he reveals his sensitiveness for her feelings and comfort, her faults are changed into her merits, everything he does is seen and valued in terms of what it would mean to her. The sentiment of affection for the mother has now broughs unity, order, stability and conitnuity into the life and behaviour of the young man.

Just as the growth of an individual sentiment transforms the life of instinct and impulse into one of order and harmony, so the sentiments themselves are organised into a hierarchy or an inter-related system. Such organisation is brought about on a dual basis. One sentiment may control another either on account of the greater intensity of the impulse to which it gives rise or on account of the greater generality of the object towards which it is directed.

As an instance of the first, we may take the love of Romeo for Juliet. Romeo had many sentiments before his love for Juliet grew up ; for example, the family sentiment and the sentiment of rivalry. These sentiments were opposed to the sentiment of love, but in course of time they all had to be subordinated to it. Love became the master sentiment and all instincts and impulses prompted by minor sentiments could not function independently of the master sentiment. If they are opposed to the master sentiment, they are restrained and checked, if they are in harmony with it, they are further strengthened and encouraged. All the other sentiments thus come to be controlled by this sentiment and in so far as the behaviour of the living organism is ruled by this master sentiment there is a greater uniformity in it than if the various sentiments functioned separately.

The development of the master sentiment is relative. But at different times in our life some sentiment or the other becomes the ruling passion of the day. The school boy buys a cycle, and eating, walking, reading, all his life for the time being is centred round it. Whenever he has to go out for a short or long distance, to see a match or run an errand, he thinks of his cycle and rides it. Later on something else turns up, say a trip to the hills, and his thoughts, feelings and actions are all directed to the proposed trip. At several periods of his life, something or the other becomes the centre of a strong sentiment and rules his life. So through the whole course of life new love, ambition, a hobby or an ideal becomes the ruling passion of the day and gives a semblance of unity to all that we think, feel and do.

Secondly, the organisation of sentiment may take place not under a strong sentiment but under a more general one. The more abstract, the more general, the more inclusive a sentiment is, the more it takes up, within itself, the restricted sentiments. The love of a child may fall within the sentiment of love for the family as whole, which may in its turn be overpowered by a love for the community and later, for humanity.

It is obvious that if the growth and development of sentiments proceeds on a more rational and moral basis there would be a greater concord and happiness not only in the life of the individual but also of the society to which the individual belongs. But our moral life is seldom thus organised. Most often several sentiments dominate at different times and there is a danger of conflict. When two or more partially opposed sentiments are excited together and there is no principle of harmony, there is strife between them involving pain and misery.

5. The Sentiment of Self-Regard

But there is one sentiment which possesses concreteness, generality and all-inclusiveness. This is the sentiment of self-regard. It is a system of emotions, impulses and desires which grow up and become organised about the idea of self. The sentiment of self-regard grows out of a series of experiences relating to the prestige of the individual and to the goals and ideas pursued by him. ‘ I am not the person to cheat’, ‘ I belong to this or that type of family ’, ‘ What will my friend say ?’, and so on. These thoughts and feelings contribute to our idea and ideal of ourselves around which a sentiment comes to be organised. The sentiment dominates the mind in all normal people. It is concrete and particular because it is a sentiment for self. It is all-inclusive and general because all other sentiments are parts of myself and in a sense this sentiment is directed towards all of them. It is the ruling and master sentiment of all.

A child begins early to distinguish himself from the things and persons around him, to know what he can feel and do and what is beyond his capacity. Then he becomes conscious of himself as a living being and later begins to reflect on and criticise his conduct. His friends praise or blame him and his social experience makes him realise that he is not only an object of thought but also a thinker. Gradually self-consciousness grows and he identifies himself with certain likes and dislikes, thoughts and ideas, feelings and emotions, skills and abilities, tastes and pattern of living. He forms definite ideas of himself as being a person of such-and-such a charater. How he is treated by his friends not only helps him to know what he is but also what he ought to be. This is very important from the point of view of education. Young people should be helped to form a better picture of themselves. If they are persuaded to think themselves as honest, truthful, reliable, hard-working people by being treated as such, they will be filled with shame when it is pointed out to them they have shirked work, told a lie or let down a friend. A boy who has come to regard himself as a wicked, worthless fellow, will look upon his faults and misdemeanours as a confirmation of what opinion others and he himself told about his character and merit. 'A decent man does not do that', 'A Brahmin or Rajput does not behave like that'. 'The son of so-and-so has never stolen', 'A student of this school has always been a good sport' and the like, emphasise different aspects of the self and heighten the regard which young people should have for themselves. They build his prestige, self-respect and character. He tries to live up to this idea first by cherishing and worshipping the ideal self and then by obeying its dictates in daily life.

Thus grows the sentiment of self-regard which gives unity and stability to his whole life.

The fulfilment of his loves and hates evokes elation, and the failure and frustration of them evokes disgust. So keen may be this disgust and the disapproval of society that life does not seem worth living. At first the social reference of the sentiment of self-regard is to the family. As our love is confined to this circle, it is there that we are elated and depressed. The circle widens and it is in the presence of his equals that the schoolboy feels abasement and elation and so throughout our lives we seek the approval of our peers The man of letters refuses to be judged by the vulgar herd.

Gradually we come to look to the ideal self for approval or otherwise of our conduct. With the growth of moral sentiments the individual becomes a member of an ideal society and it is to the approval of that society as represented in our own higher self that we attach the highest worth. When the stage is reached we arrive at the limits of self-development. Now all impulses are controlled and directed by the ideal self. This is what is meant by self-control. But such control is won through and after long training during which the ideal self grows and develops. With most individuals such a stage is aspired to but seldom achieved.

6. Voluntary Action

Self-control of the type described above has direct reference to what is generally called *will*. Will is variously defined as the power of sustained voluntary activity, the capacity to regulate conduct, as persistence or concentration of effort. But these definitions are either moral or partake of 'faculty psychology' which we have carefully avoided in our treatment of mental life and behaviour. The best course would be to analyse and describe voluntary activity or volitional actions rather than enter into a speculative discussion of the power of willing and making an effort.

A voluntary act like instinctive action is purposive and is directed to the attainment of ends. But there is one difference. A voluntary action is preceded by a full foreknowledge or pre-vision of what we are going to do. The outward bodily movements are the same, but they are accompanied by a desire and pre-knowledge of the nature of our activity as well as of the purpose going to be served by it. This future end is present from the beginning in the form of an idea, and this idea rouses a wish and suggests to thought means for the realisation of the end. The idea of the means and the end along with a desire on the part of the self to achieve it distinguish the voluntary action from others. It is an act performed knowingly, deliberately, with desire, decision, precision and free choice of both the ends and the means. It is action mediated by ideas.

A voluntary action is opposed to the involuntary or impulsive action. The difference is that an impulsive action is isolated, it is not the type of action we usually perform and it is not accompanied by any pre-knowledge of the end and the means to its achievement. Reflex, instinctive and habitual actions are involuntary because they are performed more or less automatically. In a voluntary action the means and the end are 'first considered in their relation to the total system of impulses included in the conception of the self.' When two impulses leading to the opposite courses of action are present simultaneously, we have a conflict followed by inaction, temporary or permanent, but when the two voluntary acts oppose each other we consider their respective advantages or merits. As Stout remarks, 'Voluntary action does not follow either of the conflicting tendencies, as such, it follows our preference of the one to the other. It is the conception of the self as agent which makes the difference The alternative is not 'this' or 'that' but 'shall I do this?' or 'shall I do that?'. Each line of action with its results is considered not in isolation but as a part of the ideally constructed whole for which the word 'I' stands.'[1]

7 DELIBERATION

When an action follows the bare presentation of an idea of that action, we have an *ideo-motor* action. We think of a particular movement and our muscles carry it out, though we may not have meant to do it ourselves. While we are watching an athletic contest our leg automatically moves with that of the athlete who is trying to clear the pole vault and whom we wish to win. There is only one idea in the mind and we act on it. But often the mind has many thoughts before it. Some favour one line of action, others inhibit it. Action is arrested and the mind is said to deliberate. Several objects occupy attention and we review the merits of the opposing courses of action. Whenever any one of them issues into movement we are said to have decided or declared in favour of one of the alternatives. The considerations strengthening or opposing the different alternatives are termed *reasons* or *motives*.

The process of deliberation is capable of great complications. The alternative may be simple, doing a thing or not doing it; or there may be two incompatible lines of action equally attractive. The mind hesitates and vacillates, there is a sort of mental see-saw. Now one alternative, and now another, is brought before consciousness. There is a conflict of motives. The two courses of action are weighed and considered in all their possible advantages, merits and drawbacks. This state of disturbed equilibrium may last

[1] *Manual of Psychology*, p. 630

for weeks and months, occupying the mind at intervals. Today one set of motives or reasons appears stronger, tomorrow another set. The self is inclined sometimes to one and sometimes to another.

8. Decision

How does decision arise in a case of deliberation ? How is suspense and hesitation translated into resolution and action ? This may happen in many ways. It may be that we decide very rationally after weighing arguments for and against a particular course of action. In such a case it appears as if the arguments themselves have settled the issue and we ourselves are passive. Decision seems to flow from the very nature of things. Sometimes there are no strong reasons for one course or the other and we decide by some accidental circumstance. We let ourselves be guided either by such a thing as a throw of the coin or by a passing fancy. In a come-what-may attitude we act abruptly without caring for the consequences. Such decisions are determined by passions and are not of great moral worth.

But there are some cases of conflict in which it seems that a decision has been reached by an effort of will. When we follow the path of austere duty sacrificing all sorts of rich and mundane delights, when we resist temptations to act on a moral principle, when we repress our strong feeling and expose ourselves to danger or social disagrace for the sake of an ideal that we cherish or a moral principle that must be upheld, we feel like *acting in the line of the greatest resistance* and speak of conquering and overcoming our impulses and temptations. Whenever a rare and more ideal impulse prevails over one of an instinctive and habitual kind, we feel that we ourelves, by our own wilful act, inclined the beam, that we added our own living effort to the weight of the logical reason, which, taken alone, seems powerless to act. There is a feeling of effort and the self appears to have made a creative contribution to decision.

Our impulses have stronger motives being habitual as well as emotional, while our ideals have weaker ones. When the latter overpowers the former it does so through the reinforcement it has received from this effort. The strength or amount of this effort varies with the amount of resistance it has to meet from the impulse. 'And if a brief definition of ideal or moral action were required, none could be given which would better fit the appearances than this : *It is action in the line of the greatest resistance.*'

'The fact may be most briefly symbolised thus, *P* standing for propensity, *I* for the ideal impulse and *E* for the effort :

$$\frac{I + \text{per se} < P}{I + E > P}$$

In other words, if *E* adds itself to *I*, *P* immediately offers the least resistance, and motion occurs in spite of it.'[1]

Whence comes this effort ? What decides the struggle is not any separate power but merely the sentiment of self-regard. If this sentiment is satisfactorily developed the ideas of a person's position in the world, his status in society, his ambitions and aspirations along with the emotions and impulses associated with them will be capable of reinforcing the ideal motive. As McDougall says, '*The conations, the desires and aversions, arising within this self-regarding sentiment are the motive forces which, adding themselves to the weaker ideal motive in the case of moral effort, enable it to win the mastery over some stronger, coarser*

[1] James : *Principles of Psychology.*

desire of our primitive animal nature, and to banish from consciousness the idea of the end of this desire.'[2]

9. Self-Control and Character

The meaning of self-control has already been explained. It is the control of the lower impulses of undeveloped instinct life by the ideal impulse connected with the self-regarding sentiment. Our effort to follow the arduous path of duty is merely the strength or power of the impulses connected with this sentiment and we may define all *volition* or *will* as conative activity aroused within the sentiment of self-regard. Hence to live a moral and rational life is to have developed a strong sentiment of self-regard to the level described here.

But it is possible to develop a very strong sentiment of self-regard apart from the activities to which it would have given rise. Thus a person may have very noble and exalted ideas of his duties and yet may be very poor so far as action, practice and life are concerned. Such persons have frequent weak moments when they cannot act up to the ideas which they have prescribed for themselves. They have strong sentiments no doubt and in their thoughts they have never succumbed to the lower motives, but in the absence of strong conative habits, they are led astray by powerful emotions and impulses. Hence arises the need and value of forming habits to strengthen sentiments. Habits stabilise the control of actions by the ideals within the sentiment of self-regard.

Character is the sum of all those tendencies which an individual possesses. It is based, in the first place, on heredity, the innate inborn instincts, the native mental capital of the man at his birth with which he starts life. This be-

[2] *Social Psychology*, p. 213.

comes modified in the course of experience by his social circumstancs and is replaced by habits. Character is often described as a bundle of habits, but it is more than this. For habits are mechanical, automatic ways of behaving in certain definite situations while life is seldom so automatic and mechanical. There must be some powerful agency behind them which controls them and constantly takes them out of the rut to meet new situations. Such factors are the sentiments and dispositions and their systematic organisation under one sentiment. Character thus includes acquired tendencies built upon the native basis of disposition and temperament ; it includes our sentiments and our habits in the widest sense of the term, and is the product of the interaction of instinctive dispositions with the physical and social environments under the guidance of intelligence.

Character is through and through social, its need and value arises in society and it is the result of social growth. How an individual behaves toward others, how well or ill he gets along with others, how sensitive he is to what others say and do, and how closely his behaviour conforms with what is generally considered moral and good, reflects his character. These traits are developed through social experiences living and working as a member of a group understanding the social heritage of that group and acquiring patterns of conduct which conform to that heritage. Character is the result of social growth and in its turn promotes further social growth. Character implies three things : it means habits of thought and action which are considered good or bad ; there is an element of consistency in character, good character usually behaving in a good way and bad character in a bad way; and character means harmony between inner and outer conduct, between ideas, thoughts, purposes and the like on the one hand and outer behaviour on the other.

10. The Self-Concept

An individual's efforts and goals, his strivings and aspirations are largely determined by how he perceives himself and his surroundings. His view or picture of himself is his 'self-concept'—who and what he is. It includes all those aspects or areas of life in which he is personally involved, his family, his group, his school, his community, his clothes and the like. As a child grows, he also grows in self-understanding and self-respect for the way he feels about himself will have much to do with the kind of learning he can achieve and how he will conduct himself in any difficult situation or in meeting a conflict and taking a decision. A child who feels wanted and loved for his own sake, feels free and self-confident to learn to adjust to the physical, social and emotional demands of life. But a child who is ordered about too much and who is very much afraid of failure will feel uncertain, diffident and inadequate and will not decide what he wants to do or learn by himself.

Thus every young individual faces his future in terms of what has happened to him in the past. For most of them the future always promises more than the past has offered. His level of aspiration reveals his past. One who has always succeeded in most of his efforts will aim much higher and one who has been failing most of the time will aim lower to make sure of his success. Some boys want to score first or second division while others would thank their stars if they just got through. It all means what estimate they have formed of themselves, their abilities and learning.

There are four dimensions of the self: 1) the individual's perception of his abilities and his status and roles in the world, including other people's reactions to these, 2) the changing perception of the self at one moment in any particular situation, 3) the social self as the person thinks others see it, the opinions of his peers and teachers about him, 4) the ideal self that is the kind of person the individual aspires to be. The self-concept changes in the course of development, depending largely on social relations, the kinds of experiences in the family and the school, the culture to which he is exposed and the like. But by far the most powerful influence is the teacher who not only translates the curriculum into concrete experiences but also whose opinion and judgment about the pupil lasts and whose estimate of his success goes far to form the child's self-concept. The teacher can change the self-concept in desirable directions. The child should accept himself but he should have a fairly accurate picture of himself to accept. With feelings of adequacy and confidence the young individual will address himself to the problems of life hopefully and take decisions consistent with his idea of himself.

11. ATTITUDES

An attitude is more than a state of mind. It is a generalised tendency to think or act in a certain way in respect to some object or situation, often accompanied by feeling. It is an enduring predisposition or readiness to behave in a particular way toward a given object or situation. 'He would not allow children in his garden'. 'His father does not want Mohan to become a teacher'. 'The headmaster will not allow any student to write a bad hand'. These are examples of attitude which lead an individual to choose one type of behaviour instead of another. Two observers watching the same event may perceive different things if they have different attitudes. Seeing half a glass of water the optimist observes that it is half full and the pessimist observes that it is half empty. A boy devoted to study and anxious to do well in the coming examination feels that *only* six months are left but one who is otherwise inclined feels that there are *still* six months in hand.

Attitudes may be classified in a large variety of ways Usually we divide attitudes into favourable and unfavourable but do we not speak of other people's public and private attitudes, general or specific attitudes, temporary or permanent attitudes?

Attitudes are built in many ways. They may originate in a single dramatic experience such as great emotional shock. One who has seen a person drowning in a river or sea may develop an attitude of hatred and fear for water. Or they may arise as the result of accumulated experience as many teachers who have monotonously taught classes for years are anxious to escape into other professions. Or they may be taken over ready-made from parents, teachers, friends and others in the group. Each individual starts life in a certain culture pattern made up of institutions, traditions, customs, fashions, laws, language and ways of thinking, dressing, behaving and living. This is an obvious commonplace fact and yet all that we are and all that we hope to become is to a very large measure determined by this simple fact. This social framework is being brought to bear upon us by our parents and teachers every moment of our life.

Many emotionally toned words and phrases are acquired from people around us quite unconsciously. The child not only learns the words 'Harijan', 'Pandit' or 'Bhagwan' but also imbibes the emotional tone of hatred, love or respect associated with these words.

Attitudes are usually expressed through opinions and attempts have been made to measure attitudes through opinions. Three methods are used to measure them. One is to obtain census or poll of opinions as Gallup poll of views on current questions. Another is the questionnaire method in which a carefully devised set of questions are asked on any subject. A third is to prepare tests methodically so that fewer but more representative questions are used along a scale.

Attitudes are not usually consistently maintained. A business magnate may have one moral attitude while presiding over the managing committee of an educational institution which he himself has endowed and quite the opposite when doing business on the stock exchange. A child may have one attitude to discipline at home and quite the opposite to discipline in the school.

Some attitudes go with certain personality traits. Individuals inclined to radical views on social or political reform are generally more intelligent, persistent, less suggestible and more steadfast in action. Religious minded people are idealistic, tender, sympathetic and devoted.

Attitudes are frequently modified by experience, suggestion or propaganda. Dictators before the war succeeded in changing and directing the attitudes of their people. The devices of the advertiser and the propagandist are varied and numerous and the appeals are both rational and emotional.

QUESTIONS

1. Define a sentiment and show how it is related to habit.
2. Discuss the influence of praise and blame on the development of a child. What steps should parents and teachers take to build a healthy sentiment of self-regard ?
3. Describe the several stages in the growth of the sentiment of self-regard and show how it brings about unity and stability in mental life.
4. Explain self-control and 'action in the line of the greatest resistance'. What happens when temptations are overcome ?

5. What is meant by character? What part do instincts and habits play in it?
6. Explain the nature of will and compare it with other types of action. What are the several ways in which an individual passes from a state of deliberation and hesitation to a state of decision?
7. What do you understand by 'attitude'? How are they built and changed?

References for Further Study

1. Allport : *Personality : A Psychological Interpretation* (Henry Holt).
2. Charters : *Teaching of Ideals* (Macmillan).
3. Hadfield : *Psychology and Morals* (*Methuen*).
4. Hollingworth : *Psychology and Ethics* (Ronald Press).
5. James : *Principles of Psychology* (Macmillan).
6. Klein : *Mental Hygiene, The Psychology of Personal Adjustment* (Henry Holt).
7. Langer : *Psychology and Human Learning* (Appleton).
8. McDougall : *Social Psychology* (Methuen).
9. McDougall : *Character and the Conduct of Life* (Methuen).
10. McKown : *Character Education* (McGraw Hill).
11. Murray : *Exploration in Personality* (Oxford Univ. Press).
12. Newman : *Lives in the Making* (Appleton).
13. Stout : *A Manual of Psychology* (Univ. Tut. Press).
14. Thorndike : *Psychology of Wants, Interests and Attitudes* (Appleton).
15. Travis and Baruch : *Personality Problems of Everyday Life* (Appleton).
16. Weatherhead : *Psychology in the Service of the Soul* (Epworth Press).

CHAPTER NINETEEN

Conflict and Repression

1. THE UNCONSCIOUS

UPTIL now we have described mental life in terms of perceptions, memories, feelings, thoughts and emotions of which we are conscious. We have direct access to them and can study, observe and analyse them through introspection. They are generally described as the 'contents of consciousness'. But a little reflection will convince us that many human thoughts and actions have no connection with conscious processes and their causes are hidden from our 'introspective gaze'. We are ourselves surprised at thinking and behaving in a particular manner. We do not know the origin or source of such thoughts and actions. Then there are sudden disconnected thoughts and actions which we cannot explain. They belong to the sphere of the 'unconscious', the sphere of memories and desires which are prevented from entering consciousness.

Mental life is usually distinguished into three levels ; the conscious, the sub-conscious or the foreconscious, and the unconscious. Consciousness consists of that small part of mental life of which we are conscious at the moment. It is a series of immediate experiences of which we are fully aware at any time of waking life. But there are certain ideas, feelings, and memories of which we are not conscious at any time but which may enter consciousness whenever we happen to need them. Facts of history, the multiplication table, our engagements for the year, can be easily brought into consciousness. They are at the foreconscious or the sub-conscious level. There is no special barrier to prevent their coming into consciousness. Lastly, there is a region of the mind normally inaccessible to consciousness and this is called the unconscious.

'The unconscious', says Ross, 'differs from the conscious not merely in degree, but in kind, denoting facts of structure, not of experience or functioning.'[1] It consists of those psychical determinants of experience or conscious life, which from their very nature, can never become conscious. The unconscious is a mental structure and at birth consists mainly of instinctive dispositions which determine and influence behaviour though the individual is not conscious of them. It has two general characteristics, the horme and mneme. In its hormic aspect it is the source of all energy and activity. We have already seen that human behaviour is directed from within, the organism is the centre of internal energy, the unconscious is the springhead of the life-force or libido or whatever else you may call it. In its mnemic aspect the unconscious conserves the past experience either as traces of after-effects or as memories. The unconscious is not static, but like all living and mental structures grows and develops. Every experience leaves behind an after-effort or engram and these are not 'dead deposits, but active constituents of the unconscious' entering into and modifying the structure that is already there. This growth and modification of the unconscious is called the *endopsychic process* and the individual is wholly unconscious of it. To Freud and his disciples like Jung, Adler and Rivers belongs the credit of laying bare the nature of this process.

But if we are not able to introspect the contents of the unconscious or to know how they are formed, what makes us think that they are there at all? How do we know of their existence? The plain answer is that we know them

[1] *Groundwork of Educational Psychology*, p. 39.

through their effects on normal behaviour. One person is abnormally afraid of darkness, lonely places or heights. Another shuns the society of women, forgets engagements, thinks that the whole world is against him or loves to advertise his troubles. Such people admit that their behaviour is irrational and yet they are unable to explain why they do it. There is evidence to show that there are certain thoughts, feelings and desires which do not form a part of our normal life so as to be clearly observed at the time of their experience. Many of our thoughts and wishes have to be given up because their occurrence is extremely unpleasant, because they conflict with the sentiment of self-regard and are embarrassing and distressing, because physical and social environment will not allow immediate satisfaction or because our wishes contradict and conflict with each other. Such thoughts and wishes as are repugnant to what we like to think of ourselves or are too charged with emotion to be endured are forced out of consciousness. They are said to be repressed. Sometimes, however, wishes are too strong to be permanently suppressed. They are simply put off and remain dormant. Freud and others of the school of psycho-analysts say that they enter into the unconscious while still remaining active. Some of them find gratification in dreams, others burst into normal mental life and cause mental disorders. It is the unconscious which causes dreams and Freud has succeeded in giving a psychological explanation of them. Unfulfilled wishes emerge in a disguised form in dreams and find their symbolic realisation. Dreams are just a ghostly realm of outlawed ideas and wishes, a sort of no-man's land where wishes and thoughts, buried alive into the unconscious, rise and run riot.

Many human thoughts and actions have no consecutive antecedents in the stream of consciousness. They seem to be produced by causes which have arisen from some other source. Sometimes the source is easily, and sometimes it is only vaguely guessed and sometimes the causes of our thoughts and actions defy all introspective effort on our part to grasp them. How often do we make an effort of deliberation to bring into consciousness a name we have half-forgotten? Cudgel our brains as we may, it is just on the tip of our tongue and yet eludes our grasp. We drop it in despair, and a little later, we find it flash into consciousness all of a sudden. Again, we are all familiar how disconnected ideas crop up in our mind all of a sudden and seem to have no reference or relation with our present line of thought. Such phenomena are accounted for by the unconscious.

Thus the unconscious mind contains the springs of most of our behaviour. It is the 'lumber room' of all our repressed wishes, tabooed impulses and forgotten memories which are supposed to have been lost. These cause dreams, slips of pen and tongue, irrational fears, feelings of unrest and the like in normal life, and most of the mental disorders can be traced to them.

2. Conflict

We have already seen in the last chapter how we are unable to decide and act when more than one idea or impulse tries to lead us to opposite courses of action. There is a conflict between the two followed by inaction, temporary or permanent, and the mind is said to deliberate as to their respective advantages or merits. Conflict with its indecision, hesitation and anxiety is painful and exhausting. 'The mind divided against itself cannot hope to stand up successfully to a difficult environment.'[1] The psycho-

[1] Ross: *Ground work of Educational Psychology*, p. 157.

analysts use the term conflict to describe those struggles between the individual's instincts which result in the repression of many desires, fears and the like into the unconscious. Instinctive urges point one course of action and the sense of self-respect or social standards prescribe another or even opposite line of conduct and there is a conflict. The state of conflict in the unconscious is equally uncomfortable and exhausting and there is a strong general tendency to avoid it.

We have already pointed out that in mental life harmony among motives, drives or instincts, though very desirable, is rarely found. Often environment arouses more than one of them and there is a conflict as to which should issue into action and which should be suppressed. The young child wishes to handle fire but the instinct of self-preservation checks him. Curiosity and manipulation are ranged against it resulting in a painful emotional state called conflict. Whenever the expression of a tendency is blocked or thwarted, the individual makes an abnormal adjustment. The child wants to catch the burning stick, he is afraid to handle it, he grows emotional, grieves and worries. He is forced to give up his desire, even to repress it. The result is a conflict. Tensions over sex, self-assertion, friends, work, relatives and the like cause conflicts.

With children, as with adults, quite frequently this conflict is bearable. They simply turn away, yield to persuasion from others, worry or cry a little and soon take to something else. But in some cases the struggle is very complex and keen. In describing living behaviour in earlier chapters it was pointed out that the human organism is a highly differentiated system and is called upon to react to a highly complicated environment so much so that a complete co-ordination of tendencies to action is very difficult if not impossible. In early life the several instincts come into conflict by being simultaneously aroused and in adult life the several sentiments lead to contradictory conations which are often pursued alternately. We have already seen how one master sentiment tries to bring in unity and harmony among the several sentiments, but this unity and harmony is seldom achieved to a desirable level. Conflicts are the rule rather than the exception and life is full of contradictions, indecisions, compromises and sacrifices. We cannot be both generous and hospitable as well as stingy and selfish. We cannot both drink in a public house and maintain our self-respect. Young people cannot gratify their sex urge as it arises in puberty, for society does not permit it. Constant conflict is going on in the inner life of every individual. There may be conflict between one natural impulse and another; curiosity prompts us to move towards, and fear makes us move away from, a new strange object. Self-assertion tells us to throw away our job when we receive a rebuff but self-preservation warns us against a hasty step. Conflict between two opposing impulses leads to the suppression of one of them. Conflict also arises, as has been shown in the last chapter, between our desire to gratify our natural impulses and our keenness to follow certain moral and social standards of conduct. Man's dynamic urges do not readily accept the restrictions of social conventions and taboos, and there is a conflict between one's *ego* and *super-ego*. The primitive urges make up what Freud calls *Id* and the *ego* is constantly defending itself against the instigations of the *Id* as well as against the reproaches of the punishing conscience. History and literature are full of illustrations of such conflicts and their devastating effects on the mind.

3. Repression

Conflicts, whether at the conscious or the unconscious level, cannot continue indefinitely and the mind makes every effort to put an end to the exceedingly uncomfortable, even agonising emotional tension that is involved. One very common way of getting rid of a conflict is to forget forcibly the offending impulse. What is unpleasant, obnoxious, embarrassing or offensive is banished from consciousness. It is said to be *repressed* and enters into the unconscious. It is not destroyed, but eliminated or deflected; it is forced out of consciousness, but continues to influence our behaviour.

Some forgetfulness and repression is common enough in everyday life. Memory is selective and a large number of useless details of our daily experience are forgotten with advantage. But if strong and powerful emotional impulses are altogether repressed and become completely unconscious, their effect on mental health is very injurious. They upset the balance of mind and the individual may develop hysteria or some type of insanity. Numerous cases are reported from the frontline of soldiers who collapse mentally because of the repression of fear. To show fear is a great military sin and yet it is very natural, and the soldier in order to save his face tries to repress it. The strain of repression unhinges his mind.

Repressed memories influence conduct though we may not be conscious of it. A young child comes to hate milk because his mother once forced it down his throat. In later years he is unable to recall the particular circumstances under which he acquired this dislike, but the sight of milk arouses aversion. Many of adult tastes, likes and dislikes are formed in this way and become a part of our personalities. We are not conscious of how we acquired them.

Some of the repressed wishes seek expression in many devious ways. They may be realised in a dream or they may undergo a change and emerge as fear or anxiety. The poor child who cannot afford sweets or toys turns away from them, but the wish is fulfilled in dreams when he sees heaps of them. Or he may feel nervous or anxious that others should not mention toys or sweets in conversation or that he should not meet children who have plenty of both.

Because psycho-analysts have stressed that unwelcome ideas and wishes are repressed to the unconscious, they have been misunderstood to consider all repression as unhealthy. What they do maintain is that repression is an ineffective solution of the difficulty. It is not only a failure to solve the problem but is also dangerous to personality. The wish merely assumes another form, the tension set up is injurious to health as the effects of the emotional drive cannot be eliminated by refusing to recognise it and the ultimate form of expression may be very undesirable.

4. Complexes

The repression of a strong wish is one of the factors leading to the development of a complex, a term basic to psychoanalysis. The complex is an idea or a group of ideas strongly tinged with emotion that is repressed by the individual because his standard of moral life and the customs of his community do not permit its expression. It is so powerful in the unconscious that it exerts an important influence on personality and behaviour even when the person does not know of its existence and is altogether unaware of its effect. The complex best known in popular thought is that of inferiority. The individual possesses an ill-recognised feeling that he is incapable or less capable than others, of meeting particular demands of life. Physical defects, favouritism by parents and teachers, ridicule by friends, being too much reproached for minor faults, are some of the causes which produce an inferiority-feeling. The person is always thinking of failure and allows others to take a leading part. Whenever a new task is undertaken he points to difficulties and dangers and stresses the chances of failure rather than of success. What makes matters worse is that he may believe that he has some defect when he has none. A bright child may believe that he is dull, or a really good child may believe that he is wicked. Lack of self-confidence due to this inferiority complex is a common experience of parents and teachers.

Not all complexes are undesirable. They are emotionally toned thoughts around certain objects and situations and may be beneficial, useless or harmful to one's personality. Our hobbies, obsessions and professions may become complexes. Every stimulus may remind us of them and arouse the particular complex. A research student in Botany may be so fond of his work that he develops a complex for the subjects. His thought and life may be dominated by a passion for this study. Going out for a walk, visiting friends' gardens, receiving and presenting flowers, purchasing fruits and vegetables, he thinks of the family names of plants and their peculiar features. Such complexes are valuable for the individual and society and human progress is due mostly to people who develop complexes about social or political reform, poetical expression or scientific discovery and invention. Ideas about these crowd out all others and make them concentrate all effort and attention on one thing only.

5. Repression in Children

Children are helpless and dependent and in their effort to adjust themselves to a complex environment are frequently called upon to banish from conscious life a number of unfulfilled conative tendencies or wishes. Repression is frequent and common in the life of both children and adults, and such wishes as are repressed, are by their very nature, not accessible to introspection. They are said to lie in the unconscious. Now it is claimed that repression is the root cause of a number of mental disorders and we may here deal with some ways in which repressed wishes show themselves. Repressed wishes frequently express themselves in dreams. At night self-control and social check is at the lowest and these wishes get an opportunity for free expression. Some of our dreams shock our moral sense when we recall them during the day. Some of these wishes are disguised in dreams and when we dream of a king, we mean father; when we dream of missing a train, we mean missing useful opportunities; a falling dream may be a symbol of falling in self-respect. Freud, Jung and others have emphasised that an intelligent meaning can be given to our dreams. Walking and talking in sleep is also a symptom of mental conflict and repression.

Mannerisms like frequent scratching of the head, movements of legs while talking or reading, twitching the face, shrugging shoulders, stammering, winking too frequently, perpetual worry, morbid fears of lonely or dark places are all symptoms of acute mental conflicts. Freud tells us that frequent slips and omissions are not due to chance but to conflict, and have their origin in the unconscious. Frequent spoiling of exercise books, breaking of pencils or forgetting to bring homework or the textbook to the classroom, may be due to the child's unconscious attitude of hostility to the teacher or the school.

Much of truancy and delinquency among school children is due to repression. Children steal not because they need the things stolen, but often because that is one way of fulfilling their repressed desires of revenge against either the school or their companions. They stay away from the school for a similar reason.

Many children are extremely absent-minded, inattentive

or moody in the classroom. They are irritable, fail to attend to what is taught, look gloomy or break all rules of discipline. These are symptoms of inner conflicts and children themselves do not know what is wrong with them.

Abnormal forgetting and unusual zeal in any one direction are traced to repressions. Things we forget are those whose memory is unpleasant. If we do not wish to write a letter, we forget to post it when written. In the school some boys are morbidly interested in certain activities like scouting, games, social services and these are outlets for compensation of interests denied expression in normal life.

Repression has been over-emphasised as the source of terrible troubles. Repression is an essentially normal necessity and if we wish to escape conflicts and maladjustments, to avoid repression becoming harmful to the individual and society, we should make children stand up to difficult situations rather than forget or evade them. We should effect some sort of a compromise between conflicting tendencies and maintain our mental balance. A person who can keep his conflicts in the open and on an objective level has the best chance of reaching emotional stability and balance. He who expresses and airs his difficulties and failures frankly to his friends without exaggeration and without feeling ashamed or small about them, can relieve himself of conflicts and complexes. His mind will move upward towards increased knowledge and power. Conflict is the father of progress in character formation.

The personality of the teacher and the attitude of parents is the most helpful factor. If both meet the problems of life frankly and humanely, without either hypocrisy or listlessness, and try to help children in a friendly and sympathetic manner, the emotional problems of young people will be better solved. If they are sure to expect fairness and consideration from parents and teachers, they will trust them and confide their troubles to them. In doing so they will destroy their complexes. On the other hand, teachers and parents who are always pointing out what children should not do, who make a moral issue of every little problem, who approach children with an infalliable authority and who surround them with inhibitions and taboos, only serve to increase the emotional tension among them. The best atmosphere prevails in the classrooms of those teachers who talk to their pupils in an informal humane way, who let them express themselves freely and who place frankly before the class all the aspects of a situation so that they may make their own decisions.

The teacher should realise the grave danger of repression. 'The attempt to force all children into one mould, without regard to the individuality of each, is foredoomed to failure. And not only will such attempts merely fail, in some cases they will cause serious harm. A child who is coerced and overwhelmed by repressive treatment may appear externally to have submitted, to have become obedient and tractable, and to be progressing satisfactorily in his educational development. But this is often secured at the expense of a scission of his personality. Outwardly he is tolerably obedient and industrious, though lacking in energy and force. But deep down in his nature the wounded Titan rages and plots, consuming in vain and futile phantasies the power which might have been usefully employed in the services of society. At best, such a child may develop into an inefficient and listless member of the community ; at the worst, he may become neurotic and even insane.'[1]

6. Mental Hygiene

Life calls for continuous adjustment to changes in the

[1] Dumville : *Child Mind*, p. 224.

physical and social environment. The individual, the environment and the relation between the two, are constantly changing, and therefore this adjustment is a complex and continuous process depending on the growing organism that a person is, the changing situations that our environment presents and the ever-changing relations in which the two stand to each other. Through adjustment the individual in a way maintains a balance between his needs and the circumstances in which those needs are usually satisfied. These circumstaces are not always favourable and the individual has often to change the circumstances or modify his needs. Obviously even though individuals have similar needs and are placed in similar situations, their adjustments will not be similar. Some are able to make effective adjustments enjoying life and making a success of what they attempt, others make very ineffective and inadequate adjustments, feel and spread discontent and failure and do not find life worth living. Thus adjustments differ very widely and those which yield neither pleasure nor satisfaction of needs are called *maladjustments*. Maladjustments vary in degree and importance as the strength and imporance of the needs varies.

Our emotions are the prime movers of behaviour and there is a wide range of behaviour problems in which emotions are involved and in which the individual fails habitually to make happy or satisfactory adjustments because of emotional inadequacy. Such maladjustments are found in the experience of all of us and deal in fact with every phase of our lives. Men and women, young and old, are continuously distributed over a scale of increasing adjustment. At one end are a few seriously maladjusted and at the other end a few very well-adjusted while the majority are found scattered between the two extremes. Moreover, the same individual may be adjusted at times and not at others, or to some types of situations and not to others.

Obviously such maladjustments are extremely various in kind and degree. We have minor fears like the fear of darkness, animals or teachers and acute phobias like intense fear of water, height, closed space or loneliness. While seeking to fulfil his desires each individual inevitably experiences frequent thwarting, defeat, failure and disappointment but some develop a defeatist attitude, a frustration complex or strong diffidence. We have passing confusions and indecisions and persistent emotional instability. The child who plays truant, the child who has temper tantrums, the 'shut-in' child, the young bully and the like are examples of maladjusted children. Often these maladjustments are no more than a personal inconvenience, but too often they upset our major adjustments in study, games, marriage society and occupations. Children are equally prone to maladjustments. Before they enter school, environment in the home and the community provides for their needs for affection, belonging, protection and self-esteem and continue to influence them even after they join school. Such influences may be good or bad and although it is desirable to recognise both good and bad influences, an understanding of the latter is more important for effective correction and mental health.

Mental hygiene is the science and art of avoiding mental illness and preserving mental health. It is a branch of psychology, related to psychiatry and influenced by psychoanalysis. It is concerned with the development of well-adjusted personalities and with the correction of maladjustments. In so doing it is inevitably drawn into the determination of causes of maladjustments which often have their roots in the early experiences of children. Therefore mental hygiene has to handle the education of children intelligently so as to discover maladjustments in their earliest forms and to provide for their early correction. If a child is to be treated for extreme shyness, for example, it is necessary to find out how he got that way. This will lead to a study of the entire background of his experience, of what pressures of environment, what influences in the home and the community and what episodes of childhood are at the root of the trouble.

Hygiene ordinarily refers to the prevention of physical illness and preserving bodily health. Similarly, mental hygiene is the attempt to reduce the prevalence of mental illness or emotional maladjustment by pointing the way to the development of habits and attitudes conducive to good mental health. Mental hygiene is not concerned with the treatment of serious pathological conditions. Just as the teacher's advice regarding the care of teeth is different from the dentist's treatment of the decayed teeth so there is a difference between the teacher's practice of the principles of mental hygiene and the psychiatrists' remedy for a specific mental disease.

Today our knowledge of maladjustments and personality is growing very rapidly and we are able to trace most of them to early pressures like poverty, lack or an overdose of parental affection, favouritism in the home, unduly high moral tone in the family, conflict between parents and the like. If mental hygiene has to attend to preventive measures, these must be applied in the early years of childhood when emotional disturbances are just taking root. A wise teacher will catch the incipient symptoms, study the home influences and initiate suitable adjustments in the life of the child. In progressive countries help of trained social workers and clinics is available to repair the damage done and thus many maladjustments which otherwise might have developed into serious neuroses are nipped in the bud, and through re-education or re-adjustment a normal healthy life is assured.

The whole development of mental hygiene indicates a new and important responsibility of the school, and the fact is being increasingly recognised. We are reviewing our common school practices in terms of good pupil adjustment. For example, we have begun to ask: Does not excessive competition breed indifference to the welfare of others and to abnormal self-interest? Does the curriculum satisfy the vital needs of the young people? Are teachers over-strict? Are the teachers themselves property adjusted persons? Should not schools provide for a programme of mental hygiene? Though schools in our country will take some time before a provision for corrective mental hygiene is made, there is a growing awareness of the need of such provision.

Mental hygiene has revised our entire attitude to 'discipline'. We no longer believe that children are not good because they are incorrigibly bad, and with a humane and reasonable understanding of the role of emotions our ideas of punishment and correction have become much more sensible Let us study some important emotional needs of children which must be suitably adjusted in the interest of mental health and the problem of freedom and discipline in this background.

7. Security and Achievement

Two emotional needs, the desire for security and the desire for achievement, are very significant from the point of view of mental hygiene and bear closely on the problem of discipline in the school and the classroom. They are fundamental to the behaviour of every individual and their appropriate satisfaction makes for healthful adjustments. Every individual craves for security. He keenly wants to belong to someone and in some place. Security is used in the sense of 'belonging' to a class, group or community. All of us want to be missed when we are absent for we want to feel that we have a function and a place in our spheres of work and life. At home the affection of father and mother gives the child a feeling of security and if the home is happy and harmonious in which members young and old live in sweet accord he feels perfectly at ease and secure in the world. But if members are vying with each other for the child's affection, if there is jealousy, discord and hatred in the family, the child lives in a world of uncertainty and emotional insecurity.

When the child joins the school he has to face a period of re-adjustment. It is a trying experience for him and a wise teacher can smooth over things by making him feel at home in the class. If the teacher helps him to talk and say things out, if he by little acts of kindness wins his love and confidence and if by carefully offered incentives he can induce the child to activity, he may succeed in bridging the gulf between the home and the school and reduce the tension which the new entrant to school feels. Teachers who are constantly threatening punishment or dire consequences, induce undesirable rivalry among boys of the same class or are prejudiced against the pupil or the group to which he belongs help to charge the classroom atmosphere with unnecessary strain and unhappiness and add to children's feeling of insecurity. There are others who bully, make fun of or constantly criticise children for one thing or the other. Such teachers are temperamentally unsuited to the teaching profession and the authorities are taking undue risk in entrusting children to their care.

One of the important responsibilities of the teacher is to make his pupils feel at home in the classroom and with its routine. Let them feel that they are engaged in a worthwhile task and that they can do it. Let every child feel that he can do things as well as others, that he is as capable, smart and effiicient as his classmates. Failure may not be condoned but it should not bring irrevocable censure. The pupil should feel that what advice and criticism is being offered is in the best interest of his welfare and progress. A teacher who is a hard taskmaster, a tyrant and a merciless critic will not succeed in stimulating children to do their best for he is robbing them of a feeling of security so essential for their mental health.

Another fundamental need is the desire to achieve or accomplish things. The urge to do things, to make or build things, to create, construct and accomplish things is almost universal. It makes life worth living and adds respect and value to our life and personality. However limited our talent may be, each one of us seeks satisfaction in accomplishing things which others appreciate. Therefore it is the duty of teachers and schools to provide for ample scope and opportunity for children to succeed in one field or the other. In all progressive institutions there are so many activities in and outside the classroom that every pupil is able to accomplish things and stand out in one way or the other. This is very conducive to mental health and individual efficiency. 'Nothing succeeds like success' is a sound psychological advice. The taste of success stimulates even a backward or maladjusted pupil. He is able to breathe greater self-confidence and to overcome his frustration. A wise teacher will assign tasks which are well within the reach of pupils and lead them from success to success.

In the present condition only pupils who excel in games or examinations are recognised. The ability to take part in debates is also recognised to a lesser degree but what pupils are able to accomplish in reading, writing, dramatics, social ease, regularity in attendance and work and a host of other minor accomplishments do not find suitable recognition and appreciation. The school exists for all and must succeed in providing opportunities to all its inmates to accomplish things and acquire a sense of achievement during their stay in the institution. A good school provides for the cultivation of hobbies and numerous extra-curricular activities so that each pupil may have something to excel in. Each of these activities should have an equal amount of social prestige so that pupils taking part in them should get satisfaction out of their activities and efforts.

But all this is possible if the headmaster and the teachers act as fountain-heads of inspiration and encourage even pupils of small talent to do their best. Whatever the merit of their success such pupils will not have any maladjustments and will enjoy vigorous mental health.

8. Freedom and Discipline

While the need and importance of discipline in education is recognised, there is nothing like agreement as to the purpose of discipline, its nature or the method by which it is to be attained. Discipline means, of course, the capacity for self-control, but parents and teachers often understand by it things directly conflicting.

Every child loves freedom, he wishes to have his own way and to behave as it occurs to him. He is a creature of impulse and has no thoughts ideas or purposes. But he has to live in a social order and before he can be admitted to adult society he has to learn manners and etiquette, to follow certain rules and customs and to act up to certain traditions and ideals. He has to learn to respect the needs, opinions and efforts of his fellowmen so that his own freedom does not interfere with the freedom of others. The child knows nothing of social needs or of the needs of his personal welfare. But teachers and parents conscious of such needs and anxious to secure his welfare, cannot let him do whatever he feels like doing. They wish him to exercise control over himself, his actions, his speech and his feelings. The conflict, between what the child wants to do and what the parents' experience and conditions of life require that he should do or avoid doing, is at bottom the problem of freedom and discipline.

Again, it is necessary for each child to learn to do skilfully and cheerfully many things that he cannot do untaught. He has to learn to dress himself properly, to lace his shoes and button his coat, to learn reading, writing and many other things which demand an effort and which are not quite agreeable to him. It is only through discipline that he can learn them.

Lastly, our culture demands that children should acquire a civic sense, a social spirit, habits of co-operation and fellowship. But children as a rule are very selfish and care most for the satisfaction of their own desires. It is only through discipline that we can educate them to understand, appreciate and realize the needs of civic society.

But discipline is not only a means of education but also its end. It stands for such qualities as self-control, emotional balance, intellectual sanity, respect for the rights and feelings of fellowmen, a sense of responsibility and respect for law and authority. And it is the duty of homes and schools alike to work for, and through, discipline.

Our traditional ideas of discipline are those of threat, rigid obedience, disapproval and punishment. From the dim dawn of civilization comes the proverb 'spare the rod and spoil the child' and to this day many a wise teacher makes the rod the symbol of discipline. The demand for discipline is the demand for rigid obedience. It is for the child to obey and for the teacher to order. No punishment is considered too severe for any act of disobedience or for flouting the authority of the parent or the teacher. At home the mother is continually shouting 'Don't do this' and 'Don't do that' and in the school the teacher surrounds him with rules and prohibitions. If children sit as still as parcels in a railway godown, in compulsory goodness, both the teacher and the parents are highly pleased. Children must keep quiet, they must work and move about in silence and as they are told, they must always be good which means they must be obedience and passive. And if they rebel they must be broken with the rod even as the horse is.

But discipline based on severe and frequent corporeal punishment defeats its purpose. In the first place, it degrades the child to the level of a brute and kills those finer feelings which are found in every human being. A child which is treated like a brute is sure to behave like a brute and this treatment instead of improving his character demoralises him. Secondly, it breaks the spirit of the child, it destroys so much of healthy freedom that is his birthright and makes him more and more cowardly, more and more afraid of the blows. Thirdly, corporeal punishment blunts his sense of shame and soon he grows so used to it as to be altogether indifferent. And lastly, it leads to conflicts, repression and complexes and destroys any hope for the child to acquire mental balance and emotional stability.

Nor is rigid obedience a very commendable type of discipline. It makes the child think that to be good is to give up, to surrender his right to choose and act for himself, and the highest virtue is to do as he is told by others, to be a mere sheep, a dumb driven cattle pulled and pushed about by others. In India, the virtue of obedience to elders has been so extravagantly commended as to demoralise us into a helpless mob of servile yes-men, favourities of our superiors but incapable of any initiative.

Equally harmful is the attitude of the new parents and

teachers who shrink from their duty as disciplinarians. In their effort to break away from the harsh severity of the old discipline, they go to the other extreme of allowing children full freedom bordering on licence. They are afraid of losing the affection of their sons and daughters and try to satisfy their every whim and fancy. Children are allowed to follow the line of their natural interests and in order to avoid repression and conflict anything that interferes or thwarts is condemned. But when freedom degenerates into licence, children become selfish and domineering.

What is the best method of teaching children discipline and self-control? Parents and teachers expect that the recent advances in psychology will be able to give them certain prescriptions or rules of thumb. Discipline is a matter of human relationship and human relations are so complex that they cannot be regulated by any simple rule or formula. All that is possible is to make some general suggestions for teaching children discipline.

Discipline is self-control, it is self-determination through self-direction, and since the young child has little knowledge of his capacity or of his needs, it is only gradually that he can acquire a sense of responsibility and judge and act for himself without interfering with the rights and feelings of his fellowmen. Self-control is slowly acquired in the course of experience and education, and all those influences, domestic and social, which help its achievements, constitute good discipline and all those which interfere with it are questionable.

Since discipline is only gradually acquired it must be a different thing at different ages. Young children need outside direction from parents; to them parents will be the interpreters of law and authority and no parents should fail to get obedience from them. As children grow, parents and teachers should understand them and through guidance and reasoning should educate them into young men who can be relied upon to do most of the things by themselves, who have a sense of responsibility and who do their best to act up to social forms and ideals. A few suggestions are made to help such training.

i) Study each child individually and treat him according to his age, disposition and temperament. For Mary just a hint is enough to secure the best results, to John I have to give a definite order and insist that he must obey, and to Amin I have to explain and argue things.

ii) Guide their interest in wholesome pursuits. Whatever you want them to do should have a purpose which they understand and in which they are interested.

iii) Let children learn things by doing them. If the mother always laces the shoes for her five-year-old child, always buttons his coat, always does this and that for him she may do a somewhat better job than he does, but she is robbing him of the opportunities for experience. Children must have ample opportunities for experience, choice and action.

iv) Encourage good habits for they are the basis of self-control and discipline.

v) Discipline should be positive and not negative. The child wants to do things, encourage him to act in his own way. Do not surround him with a series of 'don'ts', give him positive guidance about what he should do. If he rebels, let him do so within limits. If he makes mistakes, let him do so and learn by them. If his mistakes happen to be more serious, treat him with patience and good humour. Remember that children do make mistakes and parents and teachers do correct them. And whenever situations arise which demand disciplinary steps, act promptly, intelligently and firmly. Vague threats and warnings do more harm than good.

But when all is said and done, it is the personal example of the parent and the teacher which matters most. Children learn by imitation; parents and teachers are their first models and it is very important that the first model should not fail. If in the home parents treat each other and their children with kindness, respect and frankness; if in the school teachers set an example of consideration, self-control and courtesy, these qualities will be readily reflected in children and the problems of discipline will be solved. Discipline will become a case of a spirit speaking to another spirit, a life educating another life.

Questions

1. What do you understand by the unconscious? What influence does it exercise on behaviour?
2. Explain conflict and repression. How should the teacher try to avoid the evils of repression?
3. What are the common dangers of repression? How will you guard against them in the home and the school?
4. In dealing with children, would you emphasize freedom or repression? Give your reasons.
5. What do you understand by discipline? Is obedience the best method of securing it?
6. Discuss some of the factors which make for healthy discipline in the school.
7. What do you understand by 'Mental Hygiene'? What steps would you take to provide for mental hygiene in the school programme?

References for Further Study

1. Allport: *Personality: A Psychological Interpretation* (Henry Holt).
2. Averill: *The Hygiene of Instruction* (Houghton Mifflin).

3. Brown : *The Psycho-dynamics of Abormal Behaviour* (Mcgraw Hill).
4. Dumville : *The Child Mind* (Univ. Tut. Press).
5. Fisher : *An Introduction to Abnormal Psychology* (Macmillan).
6. Freud : *Pyscho-pathology of Everyday Life in the Basic Writings of Sigmund Freud* (Modern Library).
7. Green : *Psycho-analysis in the Classroom* (Univ. of Lond. Press).
8. Hart : *The Psychology of Insanity* (Macmillan).
9. Horney : *New Ways in Psycho-analysis. The Neurotic Personality of Our Time* (Norton & Co).
10. Maslow and Mittlemann : *Principles of Abnormal Psychology* (Harper).
11. McDougall : *Outline of Abnormal Psychology* (Methuen).
12. Morgan : *The Psychology of Abnormal People* (Longmans).
13. Rivlin : *Educating for Adjustment* (Appleton).
14. Ross : *Groundwork of Educational Psychology* (Harrap).
15. Shaffer : *The Psychology of Adjustment* (Houghton Mifflin).
16. Symonds : *The Dynamics of Human Adjustment* (Appleton).
17. Transley : *The New Psychology* (Allen & Unwin).

CHAPTER TWENTY

Stages of Development

1. MENTAL DEVELOPMENT

EACH child is constantly changing, growing and developing. Today he is different from what he was yesterday and will be still different tomorrow. We may not be able to describe exactly what such differences are, but nobody can deny them. No doubt there is a sense in which each child preserves his identity but his interests, games, play, companions and the things to which he is sensitive are constantly changing. Stimuli which appeal to him at one time may not appeal to him at another. Perceiving, imagining, remembering, feeling, willing and the like are not stationary processes but activities continuing in time.

While the fact of physical growth is commonly and readily recognised, that of mental growth is not so clearly understood. Many parents and teachers treat the child as if he were miniature adult. They interpret child behaviour in terms of adult motives. How behaviour is subject to growth, how children differ from adults not only in degree but also in kind and how human life can be marked into certain well-defined stages, has been stressed in earlier chapters. In chapter six the broad features of human growth and development have been described in detail and its physical, mental, social and emotional aspects have been treated at length so that readers must have by now a clear understanding how a child grows and develops from birth to youth. What is here attempted is a detailed treatment of certain characteristic mental traits which are peculiar to each stage so that the teacher may understand his pupils better.

There are four stages of mental development. The first stage is infancy; it lasts up to the age of six. The second stage is called late childhood and closes at about twelve years of age. Then comes adolescence which lasts up to the age of eighteen. The final stage is maturity which goes on after eighteen and ushers young people into adult thought and activity.

But it should not be supposed that these stages are very sharply marked off from one another and that the characteristics of one period are entirely absent from others. Only such characteristics are likely to be more prominent and to dominate the life of the child in that period. Nor do they show themselves suddently. Each characteristic in its turn gradually stands out distinct from the whole mass of thoughts, feelings and actions of the child in that stage. Nor again should it be supposed that the change from one stage to another occurs at exactly the time mentioned. Individuals differ in their physical and mental make-up and in the rate at which they grow and develop. There are a number of powers and traits and their growth is influenced by a number of factors, inner and outer. It is very likely that the growth of an individual may be accelerated in one direction and retarded in another. All these considerations make it difficult not only to determine what the normal stages of development are, but also to determine the causes of peculiar or abnormal traits among individual children.

The discussion of the characteristics that mark each stage of development does not prescribe what every child should do nor describe what any particular child has done. It is just an account of average, normal children at successive stages to enable the teacher to stimulate desirable types of conduct on its basis.

2. Infancy

The period from birth to six years marks a gradual progress from complete dependence on the mother to the beginning of independence of the pre-school years. The infant can sit, stand, move and run about by himself. He learns to help himself with food, drink, clothes and other daily needs. He has learnt to communicate and developed skill in manipulating common things. In the beginning, he had to look up to his parents for all his physical needs. But intellectually and emotionally his dependence continues. He still craves for love and attention from parents and wishes to monopolise it. He inquires about his environment and accepts answers from parents uncritically. Many grown-up people continue to depend on their parents for any major decision to be taken in life. But if successful living consists in developing initiative and self-reliance young people should be weaned early from this attitude of dependence on their parents.

Another important feature of infancy is egoism. The infant loves to be the centre of all activities in the home and expects others to applaud everything he does. His self-assertion expresses itself in unqualified self-interest and he desires to snatch and possess everything that catches his fancy. He is jealous of his brothers and sisters and even of his father for taking most of the time and attention of the entire family including the mother, for he wants all their time and attention for himself. Infancy is a period of solitary play and the infant when placed in the company of older children is a nuisance to them for he takes up their playthings and obstructs their play. He is too self-centred to share his playthings with others or to join others in play.

Infant behaviour is mostly instinctive and the impulse to seek food and pleasure is the most dominant. Food is taken whenever hunger is felt and whatever is at hand is swallowed. The instincts of curiosity and self-assertion are also strong and so also the instincts of construction and acquisition. It is a period of rapid growth and the several instincts are always clamouring for expression and satisfaction. In the absence of knowledge, experience and thought, they are satisfied as they are aroused and there is no restraint and no inhibition. The infant has no sense of shame, no self-discipline or self-respect. He is a creature of impulse, he has not yet discovered himself and is at the lowest stage of moral development where physical pain is the only check on his conduct. It is only later on that he learns to be social and moral. Rewards and punishments are the chief influences under which his moral development takes place.

The period of infancy is a period of fertile imagination. Fantasy, make-believe play, day-dreaming, fairy tales and the like play an important role in the life of an infant. He is continually imagining himself in the role of a father, a soldier, a teacher or even a horse. The topic has already been dealt with in detail but it may be recalled here that imagination helps to compensate for the harsh realities of life in which the child cannot get what he wants. Most parents and teachers fear that children will not be able to grapple with the problems of life if they are not able to get rid of imagination and fantasy. This is not correct. An average child does grow out of it and what is needed is a due recognition and appreciation of the place of imagination in life.

Infants have a tendency to repeat common movements and sounds. Whirling round and singing common words and nursery rhymes show a positive love of repetition of the familiar among children. 'The crude repetition which forms the salt of so many childish amusements becomes, when elaborated and refined, the rhythmic repetition of the dance, the song, the ballad, the ode and other forms of art.' [1] Repetition and rhythm satisfy a deeper hunger of the organism and should be used by the teacher to play an important role in the cultivation and development of aesthetic sensibility, ideals of conduct and social manners and habits of order and grace.

The infants are supposed to have no interest in sex, and some time back this was considered to be an important aspect in which they differed from adults. But recently the studies of psycho-analysts have revealed that sex plays an important part in the life of an individual and is dominant at all stages of mental and physical development. In the ordinary use of the term *sex* the infant may seem to be free from desires and interests that are strictly sexual, but feelings and impulses which become clearly related to sex in later life have their beginning in the infant. The small baby is sensitive to every kind of contact and derives pleasure from the mere touch of any part of the body. Certain parts of the body like the lips, the genitals and the anus are particularly sensitive and here contacts arouse a large amount of pleasure. The infant is very much pleased also when he is handled, tickled or kissed and when he is sucking a nipple or his own thumb, or is passing urine or stools. Gradually, such pleasures are differentiated and he seeks specific ones.

The several stages in the growth and development of the sex instinct have already been described in chapter eight. The infant is auto-erotic; he loves himself. This is called Narcissism from the mythical Greek boy Narcissus, who fell in love with his own image seen in water. Normally, infants outgrow it, but in some exceptional cases it may

[1] Nunn: *Education, Its Data and First Principles.*

linger on till later childhood and adolescence and even maturity.

For a detailed study of this stage the reader must also refer to the treatment of such instincts as construction curiousity, acquisition and self-assertion in chapter seven.

3. Later Childhood

Later childhood is a period between six and twelve years of age. The child spends it mostly in the primary school, and though the health factor is also important, the main task of the school is mental and social development of the child. From the point of view of the teacher it is the most formative period. The child makes his first contacts with persons outside his family, faces serious tasks and makes adjustments to a wider environment. Physical and mental growth is rapid, but at the end of this age consolidation begins and there is stability and adaptation in the behaviour of the child. He feels quite at home in his small world.

The instincts in evidence in early childhood continue to be as dominant. Curiosity grows with the birth of thought and ideas and the development of language. The questions of the child are more definite and inspired by a genuine effort to learn and understand things, and the teacher should answer them in the light of what the child has already thought, experienced and learnt. Children's questions should be linked to useful knowledge. If the child asks where tea comes from, he should be told more than the mere name of a country or two. Tell him that getting tea means industry, trade and navigation and the hard work of thousands of men and women, and make every question worthwhile for the child.

Children between six and twelve are able to remember their past experience and language also helps them in acquiring knowledge from experience and their questions are no longer of the nature of 'What is this?' but of the type 'How has this happened ?' and 'Why is it so ?' This is a very significant turn that curiosity takes in intellectual development and the teacher can keep alive the desire for more and more knowledge by supplying the information sought and suggesting that more accurate and fuller knowledge can be gathered from other sources. If children lose their curiosity at this stage through repression or negligence, they will not be able to develop any originality, adventure or initiative in the field of knowledge and thought at any later stage.

One of the most well-marked characteristics of this stage is gregariousness. The child no longer enjoys his solitary play ; he wants to play with others. He is susceptible to the influence of his fellows. In early years he sought the company of others so that they may be spectators of what he did. He used the members of his family for his own gratification. But now he seeks the company of others like him to share his thoughts and experiences, and plays with them. He invariably becomes a member of some group, team, gang or club. Members are usually of the same sex, and organisation differs in definiteness from group to group. Some are closely knit, select and rigid in their membership, so much so that they have a definite place and time for the meetings, a fixed name with rules and a pledge of secrecy. Others are loosely organised and of short duration. Most of them have leaders, captains or commanders and the most self-assertive or one physically strong is chosen to lead.

Many parents complain that their boy does not pay any heed to them and does not respond to their call while he hears and responds readily to a shout from one of his friends. They must understand that this is a very healthy way of growing and the child's interests are no longer confined to the home but are taking a social and outward turn.

Organised groups and gangs bring in their wake some important social qualities. Obedience to the captain and loyalty to the group are strictly enjoined. An attitude of sympathy, helpfulness and co-operation towards members of one's own group and of deceit, enmity and opposition to those outside it, is very much commended. The conduct of the child is largely determined by anticipation of social approval or praise and disapproval or blame at the hands of his group, and severest punishment that can be awarded to a child at this stage is exclusion from the gang.

This socialisation of the child is not without its moral bearings. The gang loyalty is by no means a loyalty to individuals only ; it is a loyalty also to ideals. Not that every gang must have an avowed ideal, but its members are inspired by a group consciousness which by itself is of great moral value. The boy does not 'squeal' under pressure, does not sneak or tell against his fellows. He persistently refuses information to the headmaster, partly because he has to protect his friend, but mostly because it is against their moral code. The school authorities should appreciate it. It is better such boys should go unpunished than that they should violate a code which they hold sacred. Quite often the boy belongs to a number of groups and loyalty to one requires treachery to the other. Boys cheat parents, steal from home and do a number of other things against the school, to gain the good opinion of their gang. Their morals are governed by public opinion of the herd. Teachers and parents should strive to understand such conduct and treat boys sympathetically with a view to helping them out of undesirable gang behaviour. Any coercion will confirm young people in their secretiveness and force them to persist in their behaviour.

Scouting is based on very sound psychology and every school should provide opportunity for organising scout troops. Hunting packs, wolf cubs and the like will employ the gang spirit for desirable ends.

Civilised life is community life and the most urgent need of our times is to learn to live with others. The world has grown smaller with improved means of communication and transport and our cosmopolitan neighbourhood brings us in contact with people of many kinds, people with divergent interests, outlooks, ideals and values. To secure lasting peace and prosperity on this planet the next generation must be educated into healthy ways of mutual understanding co-operation and helpfulness. Competition, self-assertion and national or communal loyalties need not be eliminated but we must also learn when to yield and how to yield gracefully, to the rights of others people, both individually and collectively. The spontaneous association of children into groups is a significant opportunity to be exploited for healthy social education.

Another marked characteristic of children at this stage is their outward look. They grow externally minded, they are active, energetic and interested in things outside. They do not brood or sit in a corner to dream, but are expressive and sociable. Psychology terms such a characteristic *extroversion*. The child in this period is an *extrovert*. He is deeply interested in practical outdoor activities, in running, climbing, jumping, swimming, games, camping and the like. He revels in boisterous company and thinks less of himself than of objective environment, of things and persons other than himself.

Naturally such children cannot have any thought of sex and this period has no sex problems. Even their love for their parents yields to their love for friends and many psychologists are of opinion that the sex impulse lies dormant in this period.

4. Adolescence

The period of adolescence is the period during which a child develops into an adult. It is a stage of development that comes between childhood and adulthood. It varies in length and in the age of its onset. Some children show signs of its coming as early as the tenth year while in others it does not manifest itself till the fifteenth or the sixteenth year. It makes its most obvious appearance at puberty and the familiar physical signs are the growing of hair at the armpits and about the pubes, and in the case of the girl, the onset of the first menstrual flow. In a warmer country like India adolescence begins at about twelve or thirteen in boys and at about eleven among girls, but there is a wide range of difference among normal individuals in the age of puberty. It is easier to indicate the beginnings of adolescence than to find the point at which it ends and adulthood begins.

Early writers were prone to regard this period as a 'critical' one in which psychological upheavals of a far-reaching importance take place. Stanley Hall, in his book *Adolescence*, made much of puberty as a period of great stress and strain, storm and strife, and pleaded that incidents occurring in this period might be of extremely great importance in moulding the whole career and personality of a youth. Recent writers are inclined to think that important changes do take place as a result of changes in glandular functions, but they are not of so critical and disturbing a nature as is commonly believed and that they pass unnoticed in societies where young people are less inhibited. M. Mead's studies of the inhabitants of Samoa and New Guinea are now very well known.

Samoans live in large families, their attitude to sex was very liberal, there were very few taboos and inhibitions, and they were very well adjusted. Adolescence among them was not a period of stress and strain.

Some describe adolescence as the ' awkward ' period, in which the young person is uncertain about himself as he is no longer a child and not yet and adult, but the awkwardness lies in the attitude of adults who are taken by surprise when they see that boys and girls have emerged so rapidly into distinct personalities who cannot be ignored nor treated as children. Failure on the part of parents and teachers to recognise and appreciate this fact makes young people look awkward.

Many people look back on the years of adolescence as some of the happiest years of their life, and also the most distressing. It is an age of revelation in awakening emotions and newly discovered capabilities, but it is also an age of anxiety and moodiness. One may describe it as the joy and pain of growing up.

Let us describe some of the changes which take place with the onset of adolescence.

Physical changes. Adolescence is first and foremost a physical change and can be recognised by a sudden acceleration of growth both among boys and girls. Sex glands or gonads begin to function for the first time and secrete into the blood what are called hormones or life ferments. These are responsible for the growth of boys into manhood and of girls into womanhood. There is a noticeable increase in height and weight. Often this growth is very uneven, growth in one direction is not matched by a similar growth in other directions. The boys may add as much as three inches to their height in one year. Bones and muscles increase to the greatest possible extent leading to a great increase in motor activity. The strength of boys doubles from twelve to fifteen, but girls show less increase in strength. The internal organs and systems of organs, like the heart and the circulatory system, the lungs and the respiratory system, the liver, the stomach and the digestive system, also grow and fill the trunk. At the same time other changes are taking place. In the boy the sex organ develops, pubic hair appears, the shoulders, broaden, the voice deepens and the beard grows. In the girl, the breasts develop, pubic hair appears, menstruation begins, the hips broaden and the body takes on rounded contours.

This growth has been described uneven for not all parts of the body grow at the same rate. Feet often get too big, and arms and legs too long. Gain in height is not accompanied by a proportionate increase in weight. Bones and muscles, too, show disproportionate development, often muscles fail to keep pace with bones and ' growing pains are experienced. Usually there is some drop in blood pressure as the heart is slower in growing.

Some scholars think that this unevenness in growth is the cause of awkwardness in the teenagers. They become unusually self-conscious, move and walk in jerks, stumble and drop things. This clumsiness makes him or her all the more self-conscious and adds to the awkwardness. In motor activity too there are periods of over-activity and laziness. These ups and downs may be due to uneven growth. With rapid growth the young boy and girl is too easily tired.

With the advent of puberty there is a distinct change in voice. Earlier the voice of boys and girls showed no marked sex differences, but in adolescence the high pitched voice of the boy becomes deep and sonorous and that of the girl remains shrill.

Since girls mature on the average about two years earlier than boys, this means that there will be a period of a few months when girls are likely to be taller and heavier than boys. The average girl is growing most rapidly at 12.6 years, as contrasted with 14.8 years for the average boy.

Sex development. With the maturity of sex organs sex consciousness dawns. To most parents and teachers adolescence is essentially the period when the sex urge is active and strong, and exerts a powerful influence on the emotional and intellectual life of young people. The sex urge is linked with an enormous fund of energy and with its stimulation the individual grows restless, his or her imagination runs riot and his or her interests, speech and behaviour become romantic. If the urge is left uncontrolled and undirected it leads to a train of evils like unhappiness, weakness, disease and degeneration. Therefore, the growing adolescent is to be supervised carefully and judiciously. Most parents and teachers are inclined to shirk their responsibility. Tradition shrouds sex with a nimbus of mystery, secrecy and delicacy and an attitude of silence and indifference is deliberately cultivated. But more harm is done by ignorance than by knowledge.

Often ignorant young boys and girls are surprised and shocked by the physical changes, and if false modesty on the part of parents does not let them know about sex functions, they pick up such crumbs of knowledge as the irresponsible neighbourhood provides. Vague and mysterious ideas and habits of frequent self-inspection, masturbation and other practices develop. These weaken both body and mind. The person looks pale, feels listless and is unable to exert physically. His intellect grows less sharp, he is haunted by sense of sin; fear, anxiety and depression prey upon him and he falls in his own esteem. He develops many complexes and thinks himself beyond redemption.

Instruction in matters related to sex is commonly advocated and certainly knowledge is always better than ignorance. But the problem is full of danger. Sex knowledge without self-control may do more harm than good. Considering, however, that the acquisition of some information is inevitable, we have no choice as to whether sex instruction is to be given or not. Our choice is limited to how it is to be imparted, who is to do it and in what attitude and spirit it is to be done. One fundamental principle, however, is not to be overlooked. The instruction should be idealistic, positive and constructive, not negative, morbid or fearful.

Sooner or later children begin to ask questions and parents should never let this opportunity slip from their hands. Realistic, frank and straightforward answers should be given with regard to facts. Later sane and healthy books may be made available. If the parents do not lose their children's confidence and themselves take a rational view of the place of sex in life and if whatever instruction young people get from them and books avoids 'the degrading implications of the irresponsible gutter' on the one hand and 'the fears and repugnances of the serious minded and well intentioned but ignorant puritanism' on the other many of the trials and tribulations of adolescence can be avoided or softened.

Emotional development. Emotionally, the adolescent is restless and unstable, his moods fluctuate between quite opposite impulses. At times he is active, hilarious and exalted and then passes into a dull state of lassitude, moodiness and lack of motive power. There are days and weeks when he takes to his games with vigour, plays admirably, works hard at his books and does not sleep as much as he should. New interests make him almost a maniac. And there are days and weeks when he is indifferent to everything, play or study, feels tired, sleepy, languid and inert. He has moments of extreme selfishness to be followed by a wave of altruistic conduct. This drift into opposites is particularly marked in adolescence. On the one hand he becomes more aware of the needs and feelings of other people, but on the other hand he also develops a kind of anxious self-concerned.

He also grows in empathy, in the ability to put himself in other people's shoes, in the willingness to admit that there are points of view different from his own and to value and understand the feelings and attitude of others. When he develops satisfactory relations with his peers he is sure to develop a certain degree of empathy. But he may also feel a good deal of insecurity in his relations with others, particularly adults. In the process of nearing adulthood, the adolescent has to learn new roles, new ways of behaving, adult ways and standards of living, but his behaviour does not satisfy every group of adults. Some consider him too presumptuous if he dares to put on adult ways, and if he behaves submissively as a junior they criticise him for being childish. This fills him with self-concern, insecurity and anxiety.

His self-concern makes him highly sensitive about his appearance. He is always anxious to know how he looks to others. How he thinks he looks and how he feels about it is very important. His acute sensitiveness and self-consciousness makes any change in his body, dress and appearance a crisis. Somebody calls him a flat foot and he goes on worrying about his feet, looking at them from various angles and comparing them with others. He has had big ears, high nose or large hands from his very birth, he has known it all along his years of growth, but it is only in his teen years that he has become sensitive about them. Sex too is a source of great anxiety and tension for the adolescent. Most of them are ready by the time they reach middle teens to perform the sexual functions of adults, yet society expects and demands that sexual expression be put off till marriage. Also society does not speak with one voice, nor does it always speak clearly. Sex is an indelicate and embarrassing subject in our society, all talk about it is a taboo and yet it is a very real thing for the adolescent. Wanting to know and not getting any knowledge or answers to his questions fills him or her with uncertainty and anxiety. Such anxiety is much greater among girls.

A Spirit of Independence. There is also a growing spirit of independence manifested in all his or her interests. Self-assertion is strong and the adolescent wants to free himself from all adult restraints. There is a marked tendency to rebel against authority and this independence of outlook shows itself in all spheres. Curiosity of early childhood is re-awakened in a stronger form and takes on a more scientific tone. It is not the *what* that is sought but the *how* and the *why* of things. He is more interested in the ways of adult living and is anxious to be initiated into them. Habitual obedience to parents and elders is replaced by a spirit of criticism and revolt. There is a keen desire for free self-expression and self-improvement. The adolescent wants to be an artist, a hero, even a genius. He begins to assess his parents critically and often there is an estrangement in the home. Psychologically the child is being weaned away from parental control.

The Need to Belong. Because of intense feelings of insecurity the adolescent has a strong need to belong, to be like everybody else. He is a member of several groups and follows them in dress, the mode of wearing hair, the slang words they use and the like quite slavishly. He will blindly do what others of his gang are doing. He or she wants to join as many groups as are available and enjoys being in a crowd. He desires companionship and widens his circle of acquaintance. He is getting socialised and initiated into adult ways. The social structure in the school is a very powerful influence and teachers him or her the ways of social adjustment.

The Search for Values. His social contacts will impress upon him or her the need of desirable patterns of behaviour. What is acceptable to his group, what others do, etiquette and manners, social norms and standards of conduct confront him at every turn and to be at peace with himself he arrives at his own code of conduct. Some just follow what others do, some grow idealistic and set themselves very strict standards and others learn to talk things over with their parents or companions. Social and moral problems are taken seriously and under the need to grow up and mature he tries to arrive at a reasonable solution. But may be that he is made to feel by his environment that nobody cares and that he should have unrestricted freedom.

Adolescence is also 'the great birthday of religious emotions'. These find expression not only in various forms of worship, including song, prayer, ceremony, but also in the expression of love toward other persons, missionary zeal, and altruism toward all mankind.

Imagination and Intelligence. Adolescents have an exuberant imagination like children in early years, but it is no longer fantastic or of the make-believe type. Tales of adventure, accounts of travel, history, biography and the like replace the fairy tale, and there is a growing tendency to identify oneself with characters described in such literature. Hero worship is common, heroes and ideas are freely chosen and the pattern of later adult life is visualised.

Intelligence grows to a maximum, and its sceintific, philosophical or humanistic interests begin to take shape.

Poetry, science and critical thought monopolise the adolescent mind and there are vague doubts and questions arising in his or her mind about the constitution of the universe and society.

5. Educating the Adolescent

The changes that set in during adolescence are many and of crucial importance. Therefore, education both at home and in school has a special responsibility in dealing with adolescents.

Rapid physical growth needs abundance of nourishing food and restful sleep. The food should be bulky rather than fine. Healthy outlets for the rapidly growing bodily energy should be amply provided through vigorous games gardening, cold bath, swimming, boxing, riding, climbing and for the right cultivation of physical habits and manual adjustments, formal gymnastics, athletics, organised games, craftwork, instrumental music, cycling and the like are very necessary. Correct posture and modulation of voice should be pointed out and insisted upon.

There is a spurt in physical growth but the range of individual differences is very large. Some grow early and some grow late, and these variations affect the adolescent's attitude toward himself as also other people's attitude toward him. A boy who grows late is certainly at some disadvantage. He may be called a midget or 'shortly', may withdraw from competition, become submissive and self-effacing and suffer from feelings of inferiority. He may be rejected by his group and dominated by his bigger classmates. He may develop hostility to the school or he may compensate by being too noisy and naughty. At home parents may coax him for not growing up properly or for not taking enough physical exercise and doing jobs which boys of his age do. In the school the teacher may coax him for not eating really nourishing food to grow properly. Thus he may develop negative feelings toward both the home and the school. On the other hand the early maturing boy is at an advantange, he plays an adult role and dominates his fellows. He breathes greater self-confidence and independence, he tends to be tall for his age and his size and muscular strength helps him to positions of leadership and responsibility in the class and in games. Thus such differences in physical growth may create problems for both parents and teachers. Both should realise that bodily growth cannot be forced and therefore they should adjust their demands and expectations to the level of the physical growth and strength of each adolescent. Body size has great psychological significance and parents and teachers should not only be conscious of them but also try to help adolescents to get over their difficulties arising from such differences in bodily growth.

The strength of the sex urge has been sung in story and song and demonstrated by experience. The traditional attitude is to withold information about sex and maintain a ' conspiracy of silence '. It is being replaced by one which encourages knowledges and enlightenment. Correct information is less ' dangerous ' than silence and mystery. The latter leads to all sorts of fears and worries and consequently to greater harm. As soon as enlightenment is sought, true knowledge should be imparted frankly and simply. In a number of schools in the West, instruction in sex hygiene is given and a beginning should be made in Indian schools as well. Provision should be made for the development of natural relations between boys and girls in work and play, and coeducation can do it. There is a deep-seated prejudice in India against mixed schools, particularly at the secondary stage. Nowhere is coeducation free from problems and difficulties, but in a progressive community in which relations between men and women are both liberal and based on mutual respect, and with a mixed staff, its advantage to the adolescents cannot be overestimated.

As adolescents become more independent and self-sufficient, they have less need of care, direction and attention on the part of their parents. Parents not only need to face this fact and accept it but also to seek new roles and interests in their sons and daughters. Usually this is not done and there is a conflict of approach between parents and adolescents. The latter want more freedom, less direction and control than their parents think desirable, and at the same time want the former to tell them what to do. Parents too want more direction and control, but at the same time want them to learn how to think and act for themselv es This inconsistent attitude on the part of both parents and adolescents is often a cause of deep conflict which can be smoothed over by sympathetic understanding and frank talk. Parents should not be over-strict lest adolescents should rebel and over-react and break away from home in any violent manner. It is a period of transition from control to independence and parents should recognise its dangers. Often, teachers can help ; most of them are not emotionally involved with their students, and their objective approach allows sufficient independence to high school boys to work by themselves and yet obtain the teacher's guidance. Often the adolescent is easier to live with in school than he is at home. He often responds better to group situation in which he is free to form attachments on equal footing and is accepted in his own right.

The adolescent has a great need for acceptance and recognition at the hands of adults, and should be dealt with sympathetically. His sense of self-respect should never be injured by rebuking and snubbing him publicly. Every effort should be made to share with him the conduct of the home and the administration of the school. Many parents and teachers start addressing boys and girls as if they were already grown up adults. This helps to inspire them with a keener sense of responsibility, greater self-respect and self-control, and joy at being initiated into adulways.

The emotional restlessness and instability of the adolescent can be safeguarded by providing numerous and varied opportunities for social intercourse through extra-curricular activities. Every school worth the name has dramatic societies, debating clubs, art, music and hobby classes, sports and games and the like, and these serve to sublimate emotions into healthy channels.

The library and the study circles help to satisfy the intellectual hunger, the school excursions and trips provide for the wander lust and the thirst for adventure, and the school ceremonies and functions provide for a good training ground for the social spirit. In a number of schools students are encouraged to help social service, rural uplift and adult education organizations. Scouting with all its programme of healthy group life is a very great advantage and deserves the popularity it has attained in our schools.

Most of the Indian schools provide for religious instruction. If this could be made less sectarian, less polemic and less negative, if the stress could be shifted from the ritual to ideals, if the universal element in all religions could be brought out and emphasised, and if with the examples of saints and prophets from all religious lessons of ideal living could be more forcefully brought home to young people, the needs and interests of adolescents would be better served. Through hero-worship they will be led to concentrate on the good qualities and ideals of their heroes and imbibe some of their spirit.

There is much sense in the tradition found alike in the East and the West that the adolescent should be fruitfully employed in varied activities all the time he or she is awake. A hard and busy routine is prescribed. Rising early he or she is called upon to undertake strenuous mental and physical work, build up the power of resistance and go to bed duly tired. But all this regimen is negative treatment. What we need is a positive programme of healthy and interesting pursuits so that even in leisure, he or she would have abiding interests to engage him or her.

6. Conclusion

Our educational system is being based on a clear recognition of the needs and dominant interests which a child has at each stage of development. We are beginning to have nursery and infant schools dealing with early childhood. After seven or thereabout children go to primary schools where they remain upto the age of eleven. For the adolescent there are hardly any definite kinds of schools. The upper middle and the high schools may be said to cater to their needs, but only a small percentage of our youth can benefit by them. Most of them go adrift uneducated. In fact, educationally, India is one of the most backward countries, provision of educational facilities is small and poor and the percentage of literacy is not more than 24.57. To talk of adapting the educational system to the needs and interests of children may seem ridiculous, but careful attention to aims and objects of educational effort is necessary.

Questions

1. Trace the development of social traits in children dur-

ing infancy, childhood and the pre-adolescent period. Give concrete examples from experience.

2. What are the main stages in the growth of a pupil? What is their educational significance?
3. What tendencies would you expect to find most active among children at the age of ten? What provision will you make in the school for their education?
4. What are the mental and physical characteristics of boys and girls during the period of adolescence? Discuss their bearings on the principles of education at this stage.
5. Why is adolescence described as a period of 'stress and strain'? How should the adolescent be emotionally educated?

References for Further Study

1. *Child Psychology* ed. C. E. Skinner and P. L. Harriman (Macmillan).
2. Fisher and Gruenberg: *Our Children* (The Viking Press).
3. Furfey: *The Growing Boy* (Macmillan).
4. Gesell: *Infancy and Human Growth* (Macmillan).
5. Gessel and Thompson: *The Psychology of Early Growth* (Macmillan).
6. Hall: *Adolescence*, Volumes 1 & 2 (Appleton).
7. Hollingworth: *The Psychology of the Adolescent* (Appleton).
8. Isaacs: *Social Development in Young Children* (Harcourt Brace).
9. Jones: *Development in Adolescence* (Appleton).
10. *Manual of Child Psychology* ed. L. Carmichael (Wiley).
11. Ross: *Groundwork of Educational Psychology* (Harrap).

CHAPTER
TWENTYONE

Social Behaviour

1. SOCIAL NATURE OF BEHAVIOUR

BEHAVIOUR has been defined as adjustment to environment or as an individual's responses to the world. Since the world or the environment consists of persons as well as things, our behaviour has a social aspect which cannot be ignored. We eat to satisfy our hunger, we put on clothes to cover our bodies and protect them from extremes of temperature ; we sing to express our joy, but we eat, dress and sing in a manner approved by our fellow beings. All behaviour has a social side. No doubt some instinctive urges and bodily needs provide only for the upkeep and welfare of the individual but even their mode of expression and fulfilment must follow the norms laid down by our society and be restrained by the urges, needs and interests of our fellow men. It is commonplace to describe man as a social animal. He lives, moves and has his being in a group. He cannot live alone, in a vacuum, cut off from other members of his community. The urge to seek companionship, to compete, co-operate and enter into a variety of social relations with others, is natural, inborn, universal and strong, and, by his original nature, man is obliged to live in particular relations with his community, and, consequently, to modify the expression and fulfilment of his needs, urges and interests to suit the convenience of his neighbours. For example, it is very natural for a child to cry for food when he is hungry, but in a well regulated home he waits for the mealtime and even then does not start eating till everybody has been served. Such changes in original behaviour take place under social pressure and are common. Folklore, traditions, customs, fashions, language, laws, institutions and the like are all evidence of man's need and desire to live in groups and enter into many relations with other members of those groups.

The problem for educational psychology is to bring out basic factors in social behaviour, the type of common social relations, the nature and extent of various groups influencing the social growth and development of the child, the type of group or community the school is, and to suggest ways and means by which young people can be helped to function as group members better and more effectively and the school can be organised into a wholesome community with healthy ideals and aims and with individuals happily adjusted within that community.

Wise men and women all over the world are agreed that in the face of weapons of wholesale destruction and massacre developed by advanced nations the only hope for the survival of mankind and civilisation lies in the study and improvement of social relations, and since the foundations of our social relations are laid in the formative school years, educational psychology must provide to the teacher under training an elementary knowledge of such relations, and how best to improve them.

2. Socialisation

A child becomes a 'human' being by living with other human beings, through the relationships and experiences he has with other humans and what he learns from those experiences. We have already discussed the several stages of social growth through which a child must pass before he is assimilated in adult society. This process of socialisation or social learning is largely determined by the culture of the group in which the child lives, the customs, traditions, conventions and the like obtaining in the family.

the neighbourhood, and the community. All those among whom he is brought up and educated have keen interest in his behaviour, particularly when it does not conform to their expectations, and they communicate their reactions to his behaviour.

The family is the major agency for socialising the child and it is here that the child has direct, person-to-person relations. The child lives with his parents and other members of the family in the most formative years of infancy, he is with them all the time and their impression on him is most effective and crucial. To begin with, the child is egoistic, caring only for the satisfaction of his own needs and whims but gradually he is compelled to learn that the best way of enjoying his toys is to respect the property of others. Through smiles and frowns, cuffs and caresses the child is slowly and gradually domesticated to the requirements of group living and to mind other people's interests and needs as much as he minds his own. In the family he learns many basic skills like sitting, walking, eating and the like, he also learns his characteristic ways of adjusting to obstacles, restraints and frustrations ; he may cry out, throw up a temper tantrum, sulk and withdraw or quietly accept his position.

The family is called the cradle of culture because it is here that the child acquires the cultural heritage of the group. Interacting and communicating with his family most of the time he learns their specific ways of thinking, feeling and doing. He also learns the folkways, how to eat with his fingers or with knife and fork, how to wear shoes and take them off before entering the kitchen, how to address the people around him. Gradually he learns manners, codes of etiquette, what things to avoid in food, what words to avoid in speech. The mores and the taboos of his social heredity are transmitted to him through the family. He begins to love and like things and persons his family loves and likes and to dislike and hate what and whom they distlike and hate. Thus enthusiasms and prejudices of the family are passed on to him.

This process of socialisation and transmission of culture leads to an overall similarity of social habits in any community. Thus class differences, prejudices, and habits of thought and action associated with the income and occupation of parents are perpetuated. Such differences become obvious if we compare the social habits of children from families of officials, teachers, businessmen or priests. But this does not mean, however, that there is no room for individual differences. On the contrary it is in the family that a child finds the first outlet for the expression of his personality.

The family is able to exercise social control too. It is a group with a common purpose and every member has to work with others to realise that purpose. The family is an institution with its organised routine and ways of thinking, feeling and doing, and the members, young and old, have to conform to those ways. They learn to obey the head of the family. Such obedience is made easy because all the members depend on the father and the mother for the fulfilment of their basic needs. They also learn to fear him. The social relations in the family are personal and constant, there is an intimacy and emotional attachment in any family, young people imbibe the religious and social attitudes of parents, their faith and their morals. This instils in them some sense of responsibility for the family. Their attachment to the family does not let them tolerate any adverse criticism or hostility to their family, and they generally work for its welfare and prestige.

3. Basic Processes of Socialisation

There was a time when psychologists explained all social phenomenon by referring it to the instincts. Some instincts like self-preservation, construction and curiosity were considered primarily individual modes of behaviour while those of self-assertion, self-abasement, sex, parental tenderness, fighting, repulsion and gregariousness were considered social. Nobody can feel proud and indulge in self-display unless there are people who look on. It is only before the admiring gaze of others that we stand and walk erect, speak with dignity, put on our best clothes and try to maintain a high standard of living. Humility and sex presuppose group living ; motherly tenderness is not experienced without children and nobody can fight by himself. The fact of community living is common enough and civilisation is nothing but growing interdependence of individuals. The more civilised we are, the more intimately related we must be. We are partly co-operating with others and partly competing with them.

Some writers like Hobbes think that rivalry is inborn and natural, and co-operation is acquired under conditions of fear of authority. Others believe that man's co-operation is what he shares with lower animals and is truly instinctive, while his competitive spirit is acquired as a result of the economic struggle found in society. Still others like Trotter are inclined to the view that the entire social behaviour of man is due to a single instinct called the 'herd instrinct' or gregariousness. But considering that human society is a complex thing and that man's social behaviour is woven into numerous and varied relationships, it is difficult to accept that the general instinct of gregariousness is responsible for it. Human community living is rather the result of a number of different urges and drives working together and modifying each other. In chapters seven and eight a detailed treatment of such urges and drives, needs and motives has been given, and all of them come into play in the various institutions and groups in which men live and work. These urges and needs are not of one type and they undergo numerous kinds of modifications, and so our responses too are quite varied and numerous. This is conclusive evidence that our social behaviour is the result, not of one, but of a number of native urges, primary and secondary needs, acquired motives and ideals.

The basic process of socialisation is social interaction and communication between one individual and another, one individual and a group, and between one group and another. The behaviour of the child is influenced by the facial expression of the mother, this is individual to individual interaction. How a child responds to any threat to his family or behaves in a team or a class, and how the family responds to the call from the head or the class responds to the call of the teacher or an audience responds to a speaker are examples of individual to group and group to individual interaction. And communal riots, inter-school prejudices and racial segregation are examples of group to group interaction. We shall have occasion to refer to them again in later part of this chapter.

In this social interaction the mechanisms of imitation, suggestion, sympathy, social facilitation and inhibition, competition and co-operation play a very prominent role and to them we now turn our attention. Older psychologists termed imitation, suggestion and sympathy as general tendencies and T. P. Nunn speaks of these three as *mimesis* to denote the general tendency of the individual 'to take over from others their modes of action, feeling and thought'. Modern social psychologists are inclined to hold that there is no drive to imitate and behaviour described as imitative can be explained in a number of ways as satisfying our basic needs. In any case they urge that imitation is not so pervasive and in most cases it is selective imitation. But they are useful concepts in educational psychology and we may deal with them in detail.

4. Imitation

We all, consciously or unconsciously, imitate the actions, manners, gait and ways of our fellow beings. A child learns to talk, to walk, to button his coat, to lace his shoes, to hold the spoon in very much the same manner as his parents or the nurse does. This type of imitation is largely unconscious and the adult nearest to the child is taken as the model. The child copies the intonation of his parents and adopts most of their habits and even mannerisms. It is very essential, therefore, that the first model, that is the parents, should be worthy of imitation.

But imitation should be conscious and deliberate. The child may wish to acquire a mode of action because he has to achieve the same end as his model or because he admires the person whom he imitates and wishes to be like him. In learning drawing, music, high or long jump and several other forms of skilful activity, the child has an idea of the end to be achieved and tries to follow the manner of the teacher. Very often the latter asks the former to attend to his movements and imitate them, but if the child really desires the end, learning by imitation will become effective and easy. Wherever and whenever demonstration has to be given with a view to teaching any skill it is very important that those for whom the demonstration is meant should clearly understand and enthusiastically desire the end of it.

Secondly, we imitate what we admire in others or copy the style and manner of those whom we love and admire. The spread of fashions in society shows how the lower ranks are always imitating the leaders whom they envy and admire. Children learn most from teachers they like and married people tend to grow like each other not only in likes and dislikes but also in thought and expression.

Imitation is a powerful source of much we all learn. Our habits, good and bad, our manners, or postures, our conformity to social standards, are all the result of our tendency to imitate those about us. ' Each man is his brother's keeper ', unconsciously shaping the destinies of those who come in contact with him. Imitation is a great socialising agent, through it an individual is initiated into his social heritage and acquires the fruits of the entire past experience of the race. Our customs, ideals, modes of thought and behaviour, and the entire culture is conserved through imitation. It gives us a common basis of customs, ideals and language and produces a social uniformity which makes community life possible. Thus imitation is a great social bond, a means of uniting a large number of individuals into one group.

From the point of view of education it is a distinct advantage to urge the child to imitate commendable social ways of thought and behaviour which our past and present culture emphasises, and the teacher should always be ready to point those out to the child and also to set a good model himself.

The educational and social importance of imitation has been only recently recognised. Many still believe that imitation is a low order of learning, something slavish and unworthy, and is characteristic of the raw and the immature. Others think that imitation kills originality and initiative ; that to originate and initiate is to create and lead, to imitate is to follow. Thus imitation is fatal to creativeness and progress, and leads to stagnation. If individuals and groups only follow blindly the actions and behaviour of others instead of thinking for themselves and striking out new and better ways, there woud be no real improvement. But hardly any modern teacher will accept this view. On the contrary, he believes that imitation is one of the most fundamental and important means of learning. 'Only the imitative individual is capable of learning and the most imitative is the most educable.'[1] In the first place, there is always an element of choice in every act of imitation. There are numberless activities about us, each worthy of imitation, and each one of us chooses some of these for imitation and neglects others. The teacher may present several models, but each pupil will make his own selection. In this choice there is an expression of personal preference and originality. Secondly, no imitation is an exact reproduction. However detailed and accurate may be the instructions to a child, his 'copy' will not be free from the impress of his taste, genius and personality. Some of the details will surely be changed. These deviations may be put down to disobedience or negligence, but the truth is that the child cannot help being himself and his individuality is expressed in all that he does. No imitation is an exact reproduction nor can it rule out an element of original creation.

But to ensure these values for imitation the teacher should never expect an over-exact reproduction. He should rather use imitation to stimulate choice and preference. This can be easily done by presenting a number of models so that every pupil makes his own choice or by urging children to imitate the spirit rather than the mere form of a model.

5. SUGGESTION

Suggestion means accepting ideas from others or adopting other people's ideas. But this general sense is qualified and

[1] Bolton *Everyday Psychology for Teachers*, p. 218

the term is used now for the process by which an attitude towards a system of ideas or beliefs is conveyed from one person to another, in the absence of any adequate grounds or without any rational analysis and persuasion.

Suggestion plays a very important part in social conduct for both good and evil. All forms of propaganda are rich in suggestions, and they are successful because human beings have a strong tendency to believe anything they are told or given to read. Hitler used to say that a lie, if repeated often enough, is accepted as truth. It is found that if a statement is repeated frequently and with confidence, it is likely to be accepted or the command it contains is likely to be obyed, even though there may be no logical ground for it. The process is unconscious on the part of one who accepts the suggestion, and may be conscious on the part of one who makes it. A good example of suggestion is to be found in the old story of the Brahmin who threw away a goat because a number of people told him it was a dog. How often do we feel depressed if we are told that we look pulled down or feel elated if told the opposite. Some people are more suggestible than others and a number of studies have been made recently to estimate the suggestibility of various people. Seashore asked a number of people to hold in their hands a wire which was to be heated by switching on electric current. The switch was kept away from them and they were expected to report as soon as they felt the wire becoming warm. Many, including adults, reported it to be warm before the current was switched on.

Suggestibility depends on age, intellectual development, knowledge and beliefs, temperament and the source of suggestion. Children are far more suggestible than adults. The fact is not difficult to explain. They are less critical and more credulous than adults and, in the absence of fuller knowledge, accept what their parents and teachers have to teach them. Little children can often be led aright and their faults can be easily corrected by the mere suggestion that such things are not done, that people of their age, family or school are seldom guilty of them, or that their class-fellows and teachers think better of them. Through judicious suggestions they can be brought to submit to, and respect, the public opinion and traditions of the school. With their entry into adolescence, young people develop independence of outlook and begin to criticise and the teacher should cease to mould them through suggestion.

Some people are temperamentally more suggestible than others. People who are less self-assertive and self-willed are more suggestible. The docile type of 'good' pupils are able to learn more from teachers, but they are less stable and reliable as they may easily be carried away by the opinions of others.

People who have knowledge and have formed definite opinions and views on the basis of their study and thought are less suggestible than those whose knowledge is insufficient. Finally, we accept suggestions more readily from people whom we recognise to be superior in one way or the other than from those who are our inferior or equal. This is 'prestige suggestion' and comes commonly to children from their parents and teachers, to people from their social and political leaders, from experts and prophets they admire, from their favourite authors and journals. The teacher who enjoys the confidence and respect of pupils can easily and quickly mould their thoughts in desirable directions. But the teacher should not abuse his superior position by choking all independent thinking among them. No doubt many of our ideas are only irrationally acquired from others whom we worship, but education should be on the side of rational thinking. The teacher should give the benefit of his éxperience, knowledge and wisdom to young, immature minds, but he should encourage free and independent thinking rather than give ready-made thoughts. He should guide them to arrive at right thoughts, to learn and acquire right ideals and habits. If he himself stands for fair play, toleration and intelligent thought, he will soon help his pupils to acquire these qualities. As soon as children grow up, they should be allowed to learn more from each other and the teacher should function more as a friend and guide than as an arbiter of the life and opinions of his pupils.

Generally, what the majority thinks and believes is readily accepted by individuals and the teacher in association with senior boys should set a healthy tone in the school and build up useful traditions. If the atmosphere of the school is good, discipline is easy to maintain because children readily share ideas and ideals accepted by the school community.

Sometimes children not only resist the suggestion made by the teacher, but do just the opposite of what he suggests. This is called *contra-suggestion* and is frequently found in the class of a teacher who is either too aggressive or too incompetent. The personality and attitude of a teacher often arouse discontent among pupils and they may act and think in the prohibited direction. This opposition is unconscious in contra-suggestion. A persistent attitude of contra-suggestion is called *negativism* and many children, when too frequently scolded and ordered about, take to negativism.

6. Sympathy

Sympathy is fellow-feeling or feeling with others. When two or more people are together there occurs a spread of emotion and they share each other's feeling. How readily panic spreads in a crowd when there is a cry of fire, how easily a mob is infuriated and people begin to fight and destroy things, how a number of babies begin to cry because one of them did so, are examples of the contagion of feeling in a group. It is not necessary for each of them to be conscious of the cause of the emotion before experiencing it. The expression of the emotion in others is enough to excite that emotion in him. Everyone seems to ' catch ' the emotion. When individuals run away in panic, they do not perceive the cause of fear. They cry and run away because they see others doing it.

Sympathy is unquestionably a powerful source of much social solidarity. The strength and effectiveness of a social group depends on the extent to which its members are sensitive to the feelings of others. It is only when anger, fear or distress of some members leads to group anger, fear or distress, that social behaviour can be whole-hearted and the members of the group can be closely knit into a powerful organised community.

Sympathy plays a very powerful role among animal herds. It makes their actions harmonious and helps them to profit from each other's experience and knowledge. The human child also enters into other people's feelings and makes the right kind of response in a social environment. Thus sympathy makes up for intelligence.

This type of sympathy is described by McDougall as passive. Distinguished from it there is ' active ' sympathy by which we actively try to arouse in others sympathetic reactions to our feelings and emotions. Beggars and orators practise it as an art. Certain children and adults are always whining and complaining, weaving a long list of misfortunes, imaginary and real and describing them to everybody to win their sympathy or to excite pity for themselves. Such an over-development of active sympathy is a fault and leads to anti-social behaviour.

The teacher is responsible for the emotional development of his pupils and should arouse their sympathy for the right things. If he himself approves smilingly of good things and expresses resentment at wrong ones, he will be able to rouse similar emotions among his pupils. His own emotional attitudes towards life will infect his class. A cheerful, smiling teacher inspires good cheer and hopefulness and a sullen and grim face will depress them.

In building up discipline among his classes the teacher may be strict, but he should not lose the sympathy and goodwill of a majority of them. If in punishing the wrong-doer, he makes the class feel the justice of it and the severity of his punishments does not turn the class against him, his discipline will be effective and wholesome. He must be firm but kind.

Teachers of history and literature who deal with persons and incidents with a view to judging them should take care that their enthusiasms and admiration are for the right sort. Otherwise their teaching will degenerate into mere propaganda.

7. Social Facilitation and Inhibition

The above processes of imitation, suggestions and sympathy describe person to person interaction, but the individual may interact with a group and engage with other individuals simultaneously in similar activities and his performance may improve or be impaired as a result of working with others. When the individual in a group situation exceeds the performance level which he usually reaches when he works alone we have *social facilitation*. The sight and sound of other people working with him stimulates him to do better and more. In company people eat and drink much more than they would do alone. Working in a group young people work with greater ardour and put in more labour. In a classroom if the teacher is able to make all the pupils busy in similar assignments their efficiency and speed will increase. An individual does more in a group situation.

In other cases the quality of performance may go down as a result of working with others. Many people eat less in a party or eat wrong things which do not suit them. This is *social inhibition*. The presence of others stimulates and strengthens our motives but too often disturbs accurate discrimination and thinking. Some individuals are too sensitive and shy, and their performance is inhibited by the group. Others are afraid of competition.

8. Competition and Co-operation

It is common knowledge that people work better when they are inspired by a spirit of competition and a desire to excel and surpass others. Our educational programmes and classroom practices make full use of the motivating power of competition. Young people are for ever exhorted to do better than their peers, to 'beat' them, to score higher grades and marks. Prizes, marks, divisions, honours, badges, lavish teacher-praise are some of the common incentives to whip up the spirit of competition and force learning at a much greater pace. 'Who will finish first?', or 'Let us see who does most and fastest,' are some of the common devices to force learning. Classroom seating, games and sports, tests and examinations and the like sharpen the competitive spirit and raise the level of performance. But do teachers and parents ever realize how much it adds to the anxiety and fear of failure among young people? Over-emphasis on competition breeds egoistic impulses and the same are carried into adult life. One of the great ills of modern civilisation is the abnormal cut-throat competition among individuals and groups, countries and nations, adding to conflict and misery. And it goes against the progress of able students who, complacent about their high achievement, rest on their oars and dono more, while what is needed is that everybody should do his maximum.

Competition breeds heart burning. When some students make high scores others look bad and an unfair conflict is unnecessarily created. Therefore, educationists all over the world stress the need of cultivating a co-operative spirit among young people. There is a strong tendency among students to itdentify themselves with each other and this should be used to foster among them a spirit of working together, to give and take, and to help each other. Group work in which each pupil contributes his share will foster healthy attitudes and promote mutual regard and happiness. Young people will feel that they are working for the good of the whole and the welfare of the group is almost as important if not more than the good of the individual. If competition is at all brought in, let children compete with their own past achievement and try to excel it.

A discussion of these elementary forms of social behaviour in the last five sections has made clear the meaning of the term ‘ social interaction ’.

9. Kinds of Groups

Human groups are of many kinds. *Primary groups* are small and its members have face to face intimate contacts with other members. The family is the universal primary group in which members act, think and feel together and make sacrifices for each other and share responsibilities and co-operate with each other. Play group is another primary group. These groups are called primary because they are first in time and importance. Their effect on human personality is most lasting. *Secondary groups* are marked by casual, abstract, less intimate and indirect relations among its members. The school, the class, political party or religious body are all secondary groups. No doubt members are emotionally attached to each other and work hard for the aims and objects of the group. Some secondary groups have long time programmes, frame rules and regulations for their work, have well defined roles for its members and persisting for some time become institutions.

Some groups are casual and transitory such as those that meet in a waiting room, a railway compartment or in a street. They have no unity of purpose, no common ways of thought, feelings and action. Many groups are what may be called struggle groups. They come into existence for a short time, to gain a goal common to members. Trade unions, rate-payer's associations and the like achieve organised and unified behaviour for a short time through a community of interests and goals. Their strength depends upon the intensity of their struggle against a common enemy and for a common aim. Then there are groups of a more permanent and stable nature. They have a past and a future, a number of common interests in the form of customs and traditions, common modes of living, and a common cultural heritage. India abounds in such small and large well knit communities and castes. A nation ought to be such a group, only it should have, besides, a comprehensive common purpose through which each individual may achieve complete self-realization.

10. Crowd Behaviour

It is commonplace that individuals behave differently in

crowds than when alone. One condition is essential for crowd behaviour—individuals must be together. When people are together in a group they react to situations which cannot exist when they are alone. No doubt they do not give up individual traits when they are together, but group behaviour is not merely an aggregate of individual behaviour. New stimuli, new arrangement of stimuli, new forces and new influences are at work when individuals are together.

In a general way a crowd is an assembly of people at a particular place, it has no organisation, there is no division of labour, no leader and no structure. It is a temporary assembly with no past or future. There is shoulder to shoulder relation among the members of a crowd and they may act together.

In a crowd people are more disposed to accept ready made conclusions and to think less. Crowd decisions are always less intelligent than those of individuals comprising the crowd. Individuals in a crowd are less responsible, more impulsive and suggestible, and more given to uncontrolled expression of an emotion either of destructive or of ecstatic nature. It is so because crowd behaviour is determined by the highest common factor among its individuals and this is always lower than the intellectual development and emotional stability of some individuals. If a professor, a doctor, a stationmaster, a farmer and a merchant were to talk together, the standard of their conversation would be intellectually much lower than that of a group in which all are professors or doctors. They often talk like children, because they have nothing in common except the primary needs of living beings. The larger the crowd, the more emotional and irresponsible its behaviour is. The fact that they will not be found out makes individuals throw off all restraint and behave irresponsibly, violently and irrationally. A crowd may turn into a violent mob. The individual would normally not *think* of looting a shop, much less do it. But when others are looting he may join them. The idea that 'everybody is doing it' and the feeling that he cannot be singled out and punished for his acts are in part responsible for this change.

Nowadays even school students have begun to indulge in violent agitations, strikes and rioting. They break school furniture and destroy school property. It is difficult to control student mobs. But the best thing to do is to forestall their assembling and bring their leaders or prominent members to a free discussion of their grievances. Frank, face to face dialogue in the early stages of an agitation is more effective than a later attempt at resolving the conflict. But in a school where teachers inspire respect and win the trust of their students through personal interest in the welfare of their students and sympathetic understanding of their difficulties students never indulge in violent agitation.

11. Class as a Social Structure

A very important and influential environment for the child is the classroom in which he lives a good part of the day. His relations with his teacher and his class fellows are two major aspects of his school environment. These relations have a variety of important meanings for the child : 'Am I liked by others ?', 'Does the teacher like me ?', 'What is expected of me ?', 'What children I like most ?', 'Who hates me most ?', 'Who is the most favoured pupil in the class ?', 'Who is the most intelligent pupil ?' 'Who is the most naughty ?'. Answers to such questions give a stable structure to the class as a group. What pupils are at the top and what at the bottom, who come from rich homes and who from poor homes, and the like questions about the role and position of several members of the class not only build up a picture of the class as a socio-emotional structure but also help to determine the exact position and role of each member, his mental health and adjustments, his enthusiasms and devotion to work and his participation not only in learning programmes but also in the social life of the class. The teacher has a great responsibility. He should help young people to develop healthy social attitudes and relations, wholesome group standards in inter-personal dealings and in behaviour patterns toward pupils with low social or academic status and thus avoid serious dangers to the mental health and harmony of his class.

12. Group Mind

The presence of highly organised communities has led certain psychologists like McDougall to postulate the hypothesis of a group-mind. If the individual mind is a system of mental factors like thinking, feeling, memories and sentiments, the group-mind may be attributed to highly developed communities which have common customs and traditions, common beliefs and practices, common history and culture, and common aims and ideals. Such communities or nations are highly self-conscious and know and plan for their destiny. Most of the modern nations do not merely drift with the current of circumstances but plan their future. They are keenly drawing up short and long-term programmes for their economic, social, educational and political improvement and uplift. Of late Indians, too, have become very self-conscious, they are realising more and more, their needs and interests, they compare their lot with their neighbours and strive for what they have not got, they are making greater sacrifices for the realisation of their aims and ideals and we often do speak of awakening the soul of India or of rousing her spirit. To attribute a group mind to such growing communities is only to recognise their unity and continuity, and a collective self-consciousness on the part of its members.

Such communities always grow and function through their leaders who, by their intelligence and wisdom, guide the destinites of their followers. They raise the level of group behaviour by their own example and direct it towards worthy ideals. Leaders make or mar the progress of a nation, and many a country has been saved from utter ruin by the wise statemanship of its leaders. The world today is becoming increaingly small, remote countries are becoming neighbours, and if they are to live together in a world federation in peace and plenty, they must have leaders inspired by such an ideal and willing to work wholeheartedly for its realisation.

No doubt individual behaviour calls for an individual mind, but does social behaviour call for a group mind? If by a group mind is understood something which has thoughts, experiences, and volitions over and above those of an individual, it is entirely unnecessary because facts of social behaviour can be intelligibly interpreted without it and there is no evidence for it. For one thing, there is no group apart from the individuals who make it up. It can only be accepted as a convenient concept for emphasising the social side of human behaviour.

13. Studying Inter-Personal Relations

There are two important methods of studying interpersonal relations. One is sociometry which has been described in detail in the second chapter. The second is *social field analysis* of the type which led Kurt Lewin to speak of *social dynamics*. Lewin found that interactions are not based upon objective facts alone but upon how they are perceived by interacting individuals, and each in his own way. He put forward the concept of *life space* meaning the individual and his environment as perceived by him. There is a difference between environment as it is physically and as it is in the eyes of the individual who behaves in it. Two individuals in the same environment may psychologically be in very different environments. The *social field* means the social environment consisting not only of other persons present but also of those persons who may be physically absent but symbolically present. A son is aware of his mother's reactions to what he is doing even though she is not with him. A wife may picture her husband doing things even when he is physically far away. He is a part of her social field. The life space includes the social field. In the analysis of social field people have mutual expectations and if these are not fulfilled there is conflict. These expectations are in terms of what each party perceives in any situation.

In group dynamics small groups are subjected to different kinds of leadership and later their behaviour is studied in terms of productivity, morale, and attitudes of members toward their leader and each other. Experiments have been made with small groups of boys engaged in specific projects after the school. These boys were similar in intelligence, socio-economic status and the like. Leadership was given by adults who were trained to lead in three ways. The *authoritarian* leader did not share their work but ordered policies and programmes himself, dictated orders and expected rigid obedience. The *democratic* leader discussed policies and programmes with others, himself joined work and worked through advice and suggestion. The *laissez faire* leader allowed members to work as they liked and when they liked. He gave no advice or information and members had full freedom. Each group worked on the same project under different leaderships. The same person worked as different types of leader and the same group of boys was asked to work under different types of leadership. The *group climate* or *group atmosphere* differed with the type of leadership. There was nothing favourable under *laissez faire* leadership. Under authoritarian leaders boys who were submissive did better and worked more, but only when the leader was present. Under democratic leaders boys went on working even when the leader was away and their morale was high. They were less hostile and aggressive toward each other and their leader.

From these studies Lewin drew an important conclusion. Situations in which there are oppotunities for members to get involved in what is going on, to share in decisions and actions, have greater advantages than those in which members were just passive lookers on. In the lecture method people only listen, take notes and work passively, but in the method of group discussion they actively participate in deciding and implementing their decision, they feel as if they are responsible for the decision, they are involved. Group discussion has proved more helpful when any new change has to be made in industry and in higher education where group participation means preparation, study and thinking for group discussion and lecture method has proved very ineffective in comparison. Even in day to day programmes of the school when and if students' participation is assured through group discussion of the various items of any project they feel involved and work more wholeheartedly and with greater devotion and interest. A wise teacher always invites suggestions before, for example, organising a hike, a dramatic show or a social function. Once students feel that it is their responsibility they put in their best.

14. Educational Application

Educational theory and practice stress the need of understanding individual children and providing for their individual differences, and in this book such differences have been pointed out in connection with each mental activity of the child so that the teacher may keep them in mind in dealing with his classes. But he should not think on that account that the ideal educational system would be one in which each child has a teacher or teachers all to himself. This chapter must have shown him that man is essentially a social being, that he shares his thoughts, feelings and actions with his fellows and that if he is to achieve his cherished ideals, he can do so only in society, in cooperation with others. There is no contradiction between the claims of the individual and society. Keeping in view all those traits which make an individual different from every other of his group, we can help him to make healthy adjustments to others and work in co-operation with them for the realisation of common ideals.

This is possible in a well-organised community to whom a group-mind may be attributed in the sense discussed above. The group should have common ideals and strive for higher things through its leaders. Every notable teacher or headmaster has worked to build up such a community in his school, and to stress the tone and spirit which prevails or should prevail among his students. Let us study some of the conditions which are conducive to the promotion of such a spirit.

In the first place, the school community must have a continuous existence. This means that not only the staff should continue but the students, too, should remain at the institution for a reasonable time. Such schools as have only three or four classes cannot claim to build up a body of healthy traditions. Security of tenure for the teachers is of great advantage to the school as they help to keep alive the spirit and the tone of the school.

Secondly, both teachers and pupils should have an adequate idea of the aims and ideals of the school. Through extra-curricular activities, group meetings, celebrations of anniversaries of national leaders, morning congregations and lectures, a sentiment for the name and prestige of the school should be built up. What the school stands for is often expressed in a number of maxims painted on the walls, in the school motto prominently printed on exercise books used by pupils, in the school uniform which is made a symbol of something noble, in the college crest or the daily prayer. A sentiment for the school community is strengthened by having an old boys' association, common dinners for the whole school, prize distribution ceremonies and the like.

Thirdly, by entering inter-school tournaments or inter-school debates and competitions, pupils develop group self-consciousness and pride in all that their school does and achieves as a community. Healthy rivalry among schools, classes, hostels or groups formed on other bases heightens group feeling.

Fourthly, each school must have a body of traditions which its inmates must guard jealously. Some good schools have lists of distinguished old students put up on the walls of the main hall and the teachers frequently describe how some of them distinguished themselves in public examinations, sports, social service, recitation and debating contests and the like. Others invite eminent old boys to preside at school functions and thus heighten pupils' pride in their school.

Lastly, it is essential for a well-organised community like the school to have intelligent and socially inspired leaders.

A number of extra-curricular activities will call forth secretaries, presidents, captains, prefects from among students, and if the staff help the general body of students to make a wise choice, they will not only have a band of young enthusiasts ready to share their responsibilities, but also cultivate a healthy social spirit among their pupils. Of course, it is possible for the teacher to assume the role of a leader, and he may be able to fill that role very successfully, but generally students do not accept him as such for the gap in age is too wide. A student leader can be a more effective guide, particularly among grown-up pupils, for they learn more from their own companions than from their teacher.

Such schools are an asset to the country for they cultivate a healthy social spirit in which competition and co-operation are happily blended and which readily transforms itself into the national spirit. Discipline among such schools is easy and presents no problems. A residential school has an advantage over a day school where pupils meet each other and the teachers either in the class-room or on the playground. If hostels are close to the school and if every student lives in the hostel, there are larger opportunities for organising group activities and more common interests.

QUESTIONS

1. 'The tone of the school is the most important thing. Explain this remark and show what you will do to develop a healthy tone in your school.
2. What are the psychological characteristics of a well-organised social group? What would you do to secure social spirit in your school?
3. What do you understand by a 'group mind'? How is it helpful to the teacher?

4. How does a crowd differ from a community? How would you build a well-organised school community?
5. What are the basic instinctive factors in group behaviour and how should the teacher use them for the moral education of children?
6. Suggestion is an influence which may harm or benefit children. Discuss what use the teacher should make of it.
7. Discuss the role of imitation in education.
8. What is social climate? How would you improve the social climate of your class and school?
9. Discuss the role of competition and co-operation in education.
10. Discuss the role of teacher as a leader of his pupils. What sort of leader should he be and how should he proceed to improve the tone of the school?

REFERENCES FOR FURTHER STUDY

1. Allport: *Social Psychology* (Houghton Mifflin).
2. Bernard: *Instinct: A Study in Social Psychology* (Henry Holt).
3. Brown: *Psychology and the Social Order* (McGraw Hill).
4. Drever: *Introduction to the Psychology of Education* (Arnold).
5. Freeman: *Social Psychology* (Henry Holt).
6. Marshall: *Freedom to be Free* (John Day).
7. McDougall: *An Introduction to Social Psychology and Group Mind* (Methuen).
8. Murchison: *A Handbook of Social Psychology* (Clark Univ. Press).
9. Murphy: *Human Nature and Enduring Peace* (Houghton Mifflin).

10. Nunn : *Education, Its Data and First Principles* (Arnold).
11. Ross : *Groundwork of Educational Psychology* (Harrap).
12. Trotter : *Herd Instinct in Peace and War* (Fisher Unwin).

CHAPTER TWENTYTWO Intelligence and its Measurement

1. INTELLIGENT BEHAVIOUR

EVERY teacher is conscious of individual differences in intelligence among his pupils. Some are bright, others dull. Some adapt themselves to new situations easily, while others experience difficulty ; some are quick, others slow ; some learn with little effort, others with much painstaking application. Some solve problems directly and quickly, others fumble over them for a long time. The teacher understands that these are differences of intelligence and though he teaches them all alike, all pupils do not derive the same benefit from his teaching.

If one were to consider the behaviour of intelligent people either by careful observation of pupils in one's class or by a study of eminent people's biographies, one would find a number of traits peculiar to them. Such people are able to adjust themselves to changing environment with greater ease, efficiency and speed. They are alert and their sense organs are quick to perceive clearly. The assimilate new impressions and are able to retain and recall them better. They have a fertile imagination and in meeting new situations are able to manipulate ideas actively. They move about, with confidence, have strong interests and are able to review, criticise and improve upon, their achievements. They are able to rise above their physical weaknesses or social handicaps and are sensitive to changes in their environment. They take delight in thinking and acting in new directions and solving baffling problems. They have helped to change the course and direction of human life and history and our achievements in art, culture, philosophy, science and industry are due to them.

2. Measuring Intelligence

That there are levels of intelligence has been recognised ever since man began to be educated. There are degrees of resourcefulness, alertness or intelligence and some are believed to be more gifted than others. Every teacher ranges his class in order of merit and his judgment is based on observations of pupils under varying situations. But even long acquiantance does not provide more than a rough basis for judgment. In the first place, the teacher's observation is not varied enough, and in the second, he often takes into account qualities like cleanliness, manners, the colour of eyes and the like which have nothing to do with intelligence. His judgment, therefore, remains unscientific.

The first successful attempt to measure intelligence was made early in the present century by Alfred Binet, a French psychologist. He was asked by the school authorities of Paris to devise a way of distinguishing the bright pupils from the dull. Is there any way of telling which children cannot profit by the ordinary kind of teaching so that we can pick them out and place them in special schools where they can be taught what they can learn and not hamper the progress of others ? This was the problem which Binet undertook to solve. He saw that in order to distinguish intellectually normal children from the sub-normal, he must find out some means of measuring intelligence, that no single test would do, and that children increase in ability as they grow up. With these assumptions he devised with the help of Simon, a number of tests, graded in difficulty according to age and requiring information of a non-scholastic nature which every normal child of a particular age could be expected to possess. He had to try these tests on a large number of children of different ages to standardise them, that is, to make sure that they suited children of a certain age level. Thus these tests had to be tried again and again and revised frequently before they could be offered as an accurate measuring device. The scale of tests is known as the Binet-Simon scale. The first one was put forward in 1905, the second in 1908, and the final in 1911.

Binet observed that older children are, on the average, more intelligent than younger children ; a five-year-old is more intelligent than four-year-old. With this yardstick he proceeded to find out what children of different ages can know and perform. As many as 200 children were studied in the first examination in order to get an idea of what children of a given age can do. Later these tests were given to a large number or children between the ages of three and twelve and a fairly satisfactory evidence was acquired about what the average child of Paris of any age could do. Now with a knowledge of the average it was easy to find out if a particular child was above or below it. The more widely these tests were applied, the more they were standardised.

Binet's pioneer work in this direction was immediately taken up in other countries and his tests were translated, modified and revised in America by H. H. Goddard and L. M. Terman, in England by Cyril Burt. The best revision is that of Terman.

3. Intelligence Tests

A few samples of tests are given for the benefit of the reader.

Binet Scale Tests

Three years

1. Pointing out nose, eyes and mouth.
2. Repeating two numbers.

3. Enumerating the objects in a picture.
4. Giving one's own surname.
5. Repeating a sentence like : ' It is hot, let me go. "

Five years

1. Comparing two weights.
2. Copying a figure, a square, for example.
3. Repeating a sentence of ten syllables.
4. Forming a triangle from two triangles.
5. Counting four coins.

Eight years

1. Finding omissions in a picture.
2. Counting backwards from 20 to 1.
3. Giving differences from memory.
4. Repeating five digits.
5. Giving the date, month and year.

Terman's Stanford Revision Tests

Three years

1. Pointing to parts of the body.
2. Naming familiar objects.
3. Enumeration of objects in pictures.
4. Repeating six to seven syllables.
5. Giving the family name.
6. Giving sex.

Five years

1. Comparing weights.
2. Naming colours.
3. Aesthetic comparison.
4. Giving definitions in terms of use.
5. Putting 2 triangles together to make a rectangle.
6. Performing a triple order : Putting a key on the table, shutting the door and bringing a book.

Eight years

1. The ball-and-field test.
2. Counting backwards from 20 to 1.
3. Comprehension, *e.g.*, what will you do if a playmate hits you without meaning to do so ?
4. Giving similarities.
5. Definitions superior to use.
6. Vocabulary, 20 words.

The Stanford revision, first published by Terman in 1916, has been most popular. It included six tests at each age level from three to ten, eight at age twelve, six at age fourteen, and six each at the 'average adult' and 'superior adult' levels. In 1936, Terman and Merill brought out an improved version of the scale. The new tests cover a wider range, provide a richer sampling of abilities and include non-verbal test situations, particularly at the lower ages.

4. Mental Age and Intelligence Quotient

The usefulness of the method of intelligence testing has been greatly enhanced by the concept of mental age. The tests were framed on the examination of a large number of children of different age levels, for example, tests framed for four-year-old children were those passed by a typical four-year-old child. If a test was passed by 60 to 90 per cent children of a given age group, Binet assigned it to that age. A child who passed all the tests upto and including those of age five and no more was said to have a mental age of five years, no matter what his actual chronological age may be. If he is five years old he is normal. If he is only four years old but can nevertheless pass the five-year-old tests, he is much brighter than the average and the normal. If he is six years old but cannot pass beyond the five-year tests, he is backward. Thus an eight-year-old may have the mental age of six or a six-year-old may have the mental age of eight. Mental age, often expressed as M. A. represents the level of mental development attained by a child, as expressed in terms of the average mental development of children of a given age. The concept of mental age is an important contribution to the psychology of mental development and individual differences.

Three children whose ages are six, seven and eight years, may have the same mental age of seven, and yet the first one is bright, the second normal, and the third back ward. How are we to distinguish between the three having the same mental age? This is done by obtaining the ratio of the chronological age to the mental age of the individual, that is, by finding the so-called Intelligence Quotient or I. Q. The mental age is divided by the chronological age and the result multiplied by 100 to avoid decimals, and this gives us the I. Q. Thus the child whose chronological age is six and mental age nine, has an I. Q. of 150, but a child with the chronological age of twelve and the mental age of nine has an I. Q. of 75. The child whose C. A. (chronological age) is the same as his M. A. (mental age) has an I. Q. of 100. It is expressed in the following formula.

$$\frac{M.A.}{C.A.} \times 100 = I.Q.$$

The concept of Intelligence Quotient was devised by Stern, a German psychologist, but its popularity is due mainly to its adoption by Terman.

For the purpose of calculating mental age, if there are six tests to a given age level, each test scored means two months added to, and each failure, two months subtracted from, the mental age. For the purpose of calculating the I. Q. 16 is treated as the highest chronological age and in testing the intelligence of an adult, his chronological age will be considered as 16 regardless of his actual age. The reason is that experimental studies have shown that basic intelligence does not increase appreciably after 16. This means that mental ages of adults are not as meaningful as those of children.

From the above account it would be clear that children of the same mental age may have different I.Q.'s and children of the same I. Q. may have different chronological ages.

5. The Distribution of Intelligence

There is a wide range of differences in intelligence. At the lowest end of it are the idiots whose Intelligence Quotient does not rise above 25, and at the highest end are those very bright geniuses whose Intelligence Quotient rises upto 150. A large majority of the people have an I. Q. ranging between 90 and 110. They are the average and normal people. Terman classifies human intelligence in terms of I.Q.'s as follows :

Above 140	Genius or ' near ' genius
120—140	Very superior intelligence
110—120	Superior intelligence
90—110	Average or normal intelligence
80— 90	Dull, backward
70— 80	Dull, feeble-minded
Below 70	Definitely feeble-minded
50— 70	Morons or high class imbeciles
25— 50	Imbeciles
Below 25	Idiots

Psychologically, 60 per cent of the people are regarded as average, having I.Q.'s from 90 to 110. About 14 per cent are of superior intelligence and an equal number is of the dull, backward type with I.Q.'s between 80 and 90. Those with I. Q.'s between 120 and 140 are balanced by those whose I. Q.'s are between 70 and 80, for both are 6 per cent of the population. Those with I. Q. below 70 are 1 per cent as are those whose I. Q. is above 130. Nature seems to have balanced the sub-normal with the super-normal.

6. Types of Intelligence Tests

As has already been pointed out, a large number of extensions and revisions of the Binet-Simon scale of tests have been made in many countries, and hundreds of intelligence tests are in use. These can be classified in many ways. According to form we may classify them into *verbal* and *non-verbal* tests, according to the number of subjects that may be tested we speak of *individual* and *group* tests or we may classify them according to the ages or grades of children and speak of *pre-school*, *primary*, *secondary* or *college* tests. There is a good deal of overlapping among these types but the first two bases of classification are usually accepted for purposes of study.

The Binet-Simon tests, even after several revisions, are individual tests. They can be given only to one person at a time and usually require forty to sixty minutes for testing each child. It means that only a very limited number of children can be tested at any one time. In the beginning these tests were used only for exceptional individuals and therefore offered no difficulty, but with their growing popularity and a general acceptance of their usefulness, quicker methods are needed. Secondly, these tests are largely linguistic. They consist of 'verbal questions and verbal answers', as Ross puts it, and cannot be used with illiterates or with those who for one reason or the other have language disability. They take for granted an average ability to understand, speak and read a language, and this ability is not universal. Thirdly, these tests are instruments only when administered by trained examiners. A trained examiner must have, besides considerable general tact and skill in handling individual children, special insight of the tests and the scale as a whole. He must be familiar with the several parts, how each part is to be given, how the attention of children can be secured and by what standard their reactions are to be measured. Such trained examiners are not to be easily employed in every school, and therefore the use of individual tests such as the Binet-Simon scale provides is not as general as one would wish it.

The second type of tests are called *performance* tests because the child responds by performing a muscular action. What he is to do is indicated by the tester either by oral instruction or by pantomime or signs. They are devised to measure intelligence without the use and aid of language. There are fifteen form-board tests in this scale which may be used for children from four to sixteen years. The form-board test is one of the commonest types of performance tests and calls for fitting blocks of different shapes into corresponding holes. It is, therefore, a test both of perception and of correct motor response. In other tests the child is asked to assemble parts of a picture or solve a mechanical puzzle. Scoring is done on the basis of time taken and the number of unsuccessful attempts before final achievement. The most widely known is the Pintner-Patterson Performance Scale. Another is the Arthur Point Scale of Performance Tests. Suitable for approximately the same age range, it consists of form-boards, picture completion, block design and other assembly tests. All performance tests demand ability to see the situation as a whole, besides perception and motor accuracy. They are mostly individual tests and are not used as a substitute for the Binet-Simon scale but as supplements except in cases where a language difficulty, deafness or other handicap, makes the use of Binet-Simon scale uncertain, difficult or impossible.

The third type of tests are *group* tests. They can be given to a large number of persons at the same time and usually consist of a series of tests to which responses can be recorded on paper by the children. The testing material is in the form of sheets of paper or a booklet distributed to children or adults and they are required to give their answers either in *yes* or *no*, or by underlining portions of tests, or in brief verbal replies and the like.

1) Underline the word which is most nearly *opposite* in meaning to the word in capital letters.
WISE....clever, angry, foolish, slow, rough.
2) Complete the following
   a) A cow gives....
   b) A fan gives....
   c) A lamp gives....
3) Under line the best answer.
Cats are useful animals because—they eat mice, they are afraid of dogs, they are gentle.

In an hour the child can deal with eight or ten items in each of a dozen or so tests. By means of such group tests thousands of children of a given age may be tested at one place at the same time. These records are also very easy to value ; the correct answers are supplied by the examiner or the psychologists and the valuation can be done by teachers. Before giving the tests the group of children are given detailed instructions about the procedure.

World War I provided an urgent need for means of testing many persons in a short time and the psychologists devised the Army Alpha test, a group examination which was administered to 1,750,000 men between September, 1917 and January, 1919. Since the war a large number of improved group tests have been constructed. Dr. Ballard's and Professor Thompson's group tests are quite well known.

Usually individual tests are regarded as being the most accurate tests of intelligence. The examiner comes in close personal contact with the child and can observe his total reactions. He may find out if the child is shy or forward, if he is willing to co-operate or inclined to hold back, if he can give sustained attention, if he is quick or slow. He may learn a great deal about the child's temperament and character, his habits of work and his social attitude. A trained examiner will try to understand the background of each child, to arouse his interest and to help him to do his best. But individual tests may fail with a child who is highly emotional or unstable and who gets nervous. Such children can be more reliably tested in groups where they can work on their own without any self-consciousness.

Testing can become a very serious matter when parents and teachers take test scores too literally or mis-interpret them. Only trained persons who have the patience and ability to gain the confidence of the child are qualified to administer tests and get meaningful results for they can ensure standard conditions for the test. Nor should a final judgment be passed on the brightness or dullness of a child on the results of one single test.

7. Wechsler-Bellevue Intelligence Test

Besides, the limitations of the Stanford-Binet scale given above it is inadequate for use with adults. Terman's research had led him to conclude that intellectual growth slowed down at age 13 and stopped altogether at age 16, and all adult I.Q.'s calculated on the basis of his test assumed a chronologoical age of 15. The material contained in the Stanford-Binet tests was meant for children alone and was criticised as looking 'babyish' to many adults. To meet the need for an adult test D. Wechsler, a clinical psychologist of Bellevue Hospital in New York City, presented the Wechsler-Bellevue Intelligence Test : a Semi-Performance Scale to measure the ability of persons from ten to sixty years of age. Later he developed Wechsler

Adult Intelligence Scale (WAIS) and Wechsler Intelligence Scale for Children (WISC).

Wechsler's full scale consists of five verbal tests, five performance tests and a vocabulary test which can be used as an alternate. The verbal scale has sub-tests dealing with general information, comprehension, arithmetic, memory for digits and vocabulary, and the performance scale deals with picture arrangement, picture completion, block-design, object-assembly and digit symbol.

The performance of the individual taking the test is measured in terms of the number of points for each sub-test and scaled scores for each sub-test. The total scaled scores obtained on 'verbal' and 'performance' sections of the test may be converted into I.Q.'s based on the norms for persons of his age, and an I.Q. can be obtained from the total scaled score of the test.

It is interesting to note that the correlation between the full scales of Stanford-Binet and Wechsler tests is as high as 86.

8. Standardisation of Tests

Tests are said to be standardised when they have *objectivity, reliability* and *validity*.

A test is said to be objective when it is free from the personal factor of the examiner. His predilections should not spoil the test. The usual methods of marking pupils have been under fire because they are subjective, that is, the same answer would score differently with different examiners and there is no universal criterion of judgment. It is not unusual, for instance, for a teacher to overestimate the intelligence of a talkative child and underestimate that of a quiet child. A clean and courteous child would be rated higher than a shabbily dressed impudent child. Older children are judged to be more intelligent than younger children. Such estimates based on the mood and preference of the teacher or on the qualities of the pupils may or may not have any relation with intelligence or attainment. What questions should be asked? How important are they? How should they be worded? What marks should be awarded for various degrees of imperfections in answers? The whims, fancies and liver of the examiner have much to do with the success of pupils. When examination work has been marked by a number of examiners, quite an amazing divergence has been found, ranging from 30 per cent to 90 per cent marks.

This difficulty is met by new types of objective tests such as the *multiple choice test* in which a pupil has to choose one right word out of four to make the right answer, for example :

1. Akbar was the son of...........
   1. Bairam Khan; 2. Humayun; 3. Babar; 4. Timur.
2. The river Nile falls into........
   1. The Arabian sea ; 2. The Mediterranean ; 3. The Persian Gulf ; 4. The Red Sea.

Then there are the *true-false tests* in which a number of statements are made and the pupils are asked to mark the correct ones ; the *best answer tests* in which four short answers are given to a question and the pupils are asked to pick out the best answer ; and *matching tests* in which pupils are expected to match definitions to correct words, and the like. In all these tests the system of scoring is agreed on beforehand and the differences in the working of a paper are not so great.

A test is said to be reliable when it yields the same results on repetition. If it yields different results from time to time, it cannot be accepted as reliable. The reliability of intelligence tests is measured by correlating the scores obtained by a number of applications of those very tests to the same children at different times. Of course, much time must elapse between these repetitions. The bright child will continue to score high and the backward child continue to score low. Often duplicate testing is possible when two distinct tests are available and their reliability can be measured by correlating them. The 1937 Stanford revision of the Binet-Simon scale is available in two forms and the scores obtained from them can be correlated. Theoretically, the *coefficient of reliability* should be 1.00, but in practice it varies from .85 to .95. If the correlation is not high, either one of the tests is unreliable or if the same test is repeated, the test may be unreliable or the method of administering it may be faulty.

A test is said to be *valid* when it does measure what it purports to measure. But how are we to know whether a test measures intelligence? This can be determined by finding the correlations between the test and some independent criterion. Thus the validity of a new test of intelligence would be determined by correlating it with some recognised group test, or better, with the Stanford-Binet tests, with the estimates of intelligence given by a reliable teacher or with school marks.

9. What is Intelligence?

It is easier to measure intelligence than to define it and phychologists have spent more time in devising intelligence tests than in defining the term intelligence. And those who have made an attempt at definition do not agree. It is more helpful to describe the chief characteristics of intelligent behaviour, as has been done in the beginning of this chapter, than to seek a hard and fast definition. Let us study some well-known definitions as well as theories of intelligence.

Binet defined intelligence as 'judgement or common

sense, initiative, the ability to adapt oneself, to judge well, understand well, reason well.' According to him there are three phases of intelligent behaviour: the ability to take and maintain a definite direction, the ability to make adjustments for the attainment of a goal and the power of self-criticism. Terman says, 'An individual is intelligent in proportion as he is able to carry on abstract thinking.' Stern thought of intelligence as 'a general adaptability to new problems and conditions of life.' Thorndike considers it 'as the power of good responses from the point of view of truth or fact.' Woodworth identifies it with general adaptability, the ability to adjust means to ends and to reach a goal. Many psychologists have defined it simply as the ability to learn, but most are agreed that it helps us to meet new situations, to adapt ourselves to changing environments and to solve problems. It is a composite function of the mind and is innate. It is mental alertness.

We may distinguish four distinct views about the nature of intelligence. In the first place, there is the popular view describing intelligence as a general 'all-pervading mental power' which helps us to solve problems and make successful adjustments to new situations. It is 'all-round mental efficiency' which enables people to do equally well in all types of work. Spearman calls it the *monarchic* view as it takes one supreme power directing the rest. Opposed to it may be considered the *anarchic* theory of Thorndike which regards intelligence as a general name for a number of specific abilities. They have some common elements but these common elements do not make up the whole of intelligence, nor is all intelligence of the same kind. All specific abilities are independent of one another. Knowing a person's ability in one direction, we can infer absolutely nothing of his ability in other directions. If a child is good in history, absolutely nothing can be judged from it about his achievement in chemistry, music or painting. This is an extreme form of the *oligarchic* view which accepts a limited group of abilities and regards each mind as a sample group. Binet, as we have seen above, emphasised three distinct manifestations of intelligence, and Godfrey H. Thomson urged that in any mental activity a number of mental qualities come into operation. The latest theory is that of Spearman and is known as the *Two Factor Theory*. He believes that a general intellectual factor which he calls *g* for abbreviation, influences to a greater or lesser degree all mental activity, but it does so in co-operation with a number of specific factors which he calls *s*. The general factor *g* is constant for any one individual, but the specific factors *s* vary in any one individual, for example, talent for music, ability in mathematics or facility of expression, and so on. The different intellectual performances of any one individual have a positive relation to each other and this grouping is due to the presence and working of *g*, the general factor. But each type of performance is determined by the specific factor *s*. There are many *s*'s but only one *g* for one individual. Although the *g* factor is present and working, in every ability, its influence may not be equal. All behaviour involves some amount of *g* and the general quality of an individual's performance inany direc tion will tend to be high or low according to the amount or degree of *g* he possesses. That is why people who show ability for one thing are likely, on an average, to show ability in other directions as well. If a person is inferior in one line, he is likely to be so in others too, as he has a low degree of *g*. But, besides, mental activities derive their special characteristics from various kinds of special abilities or qualities known as *s* factors. The reason why some people are superior in one line and inferior in another is that while their *g* is constant, their *s* factors are variable and uninfluenced by *g*. Spearman's two-factor theory is called *eclectic* because it seeks to harmonise all the others.

10. Limitations of Intelligence Tests

The commonest and also the weakest objection raised against intelligence tests is that they seek to measure intelligence about which there is no agreement among psychologists. It is futile to measure a power or function about which there is lack of definite understanding. Such an objection may seem to upset the very foundation of intelligence tests, but it does not. For do we not measure electricity by what it does, though there is no universally accepted definition of it? Mind, life or matter cannot be expressed in any hard and fast definition, but is it any argument against the study of psychology, biology or physics?

Again, it is objected that tests measure intelligence only indirectly, through language spoken or printed. Children from better homes are likely to score better than those from poor ones. Psychologists admit the force of this objection, but think that home conditions do not modify the result to any serious degree. No doubt environment may stimulate or discourage intellectual activity, but tests can be slightly modified to suit changes in environment.

Intelligence tests are also not adequately standardised and do not predict with absolute certainty success in school or industry. They are not perfect measures of intelligence, and in several types of work intelligence alone does not make for success. A typist may be more intelligent than other typists in his office, but may not be a good typist. A man may be intelligent enough to succeed in business and yet his moral standard may stand in his way. It is man's total personality which should be measured and it is on such measurements that our estimate of his future success should be based. Finally, while correlation between intelligence and achievements in such subjects as arithemetic, history or reading is high, the correlation in the case of manual skill, music or drawing is often low. All this means that intelligence tests must be supplemented by tests of other special abilities, attitudes and personality traits. Happily, workers in the field are conscious of these limitations.

11. Values of Intelligence Tests

In the first place, as Ross has pointed out, intelligence tests have helped us to reach certain broad conclusions about human nature and its growth. Even though psychologists are not agreed upon any one definition of intelligence, they accept that there is 'some intellective quality' which can be tested. Secondly, this quality is so widely distributed and the range of individual differences is so large that the fact cannot be ignored by education. The psychology of individual differences has influenced educational practice. Thirdly, the mental age of a person does not normally continue to grow after the age of sixteen. The Stanford scale puts the mental age of an adult at sixteen and a half and subsequent studies have confirmed his conclusions. Fourthly, the intelligence quotient remains practically the same throughout the period of growth and is not affected by schooling. 'To call any one a " born fool" is at least sound psychology, if it is deplorable manners.'[1] This shows that intelligence is an innate character. While it may be stimulated by environment, it is not increased by it.

Intelligence tests were originally used to measure the ability of school children as a means of educational guidance, and they have fulfilled that object in no mean mea-

[1] Ross : *Groundwork of Educational Psychology*, p. 230.

sure. Today we are able to predict the possibility of individual children and thereby direct their mental growth accordingly. If parents know the intelligence of their children, they would not attempt to force them into careers for which they are not fit and much waste of time and money would be eliminated. Many adults are unhappy in their lot mostly because they have no ability for the work into which chance has thrown them. Intelligence tests would also reveal to parents and teachers more reliably whether their children are working to their full capacity. Many children develop bad habits because they are bright and quick and are not given enough work to keep them busy. And many lose interest in school work because they are too slow for it or cannot reach it intellectually. If the intelligence and ability of each child is known, the parent can plan for his carrer, and the teacher can adapt his teaching to the needs of each. Intelligence tests can be a good check on the teacher's work. If the àttainment of any class does not correspond to their scores in intelligence tests, the subject is not being properly studied. It may mean that teaching is inefficient or there is some other distracting circumstance. In either case it helps the teacher to discover the cause. Teacher's judgments about his work and pupils can be checked and corrected with the help of intelligence tests.

Intelligence tests serve to classify pupils into homogeneous groups. The I. Q. remains constant, but it cannot be the basis of classification. Grading should be done on the basis of mental age and special provision can be made for pupils of each group with a view to promoting their all-round growth and development. With special classes for gifted children as well as backward children, the teacher can be confident of reaching every pupil of his class and helping him to make the most of his opportunity in the classroom.

Many colleges use intelligence tests as a basis for selecting new admissions. In Indian universities all and sundry are admitted without any regard to their ability to profit by college education. The result is that a number of lives are wasted by failures and the academic standards tend to be lowered. The best course is to correlate the high school score with the score of intelligence tests and judge probable college success or failure on its basis.

Intelligence tests are also being used for the selection of personnel in several types of industry. Many progressive schools maintain vocational guidance departments which, on the basis of tests, advise pupils about suitable careers.

Besides, tests are being devised to measure personality traits like temperament, suggestibility, and the movement for mental measurement promises well.

12. Influence of Heredity and Environment on Intelligence

We have seen in Chapter 5 that the two aspects of life embraced under heredity and environment are interwoven from the time of birth, and cannot be separated and studied in pure form. The problem for education is not to decide a choice between the two aspects of life, but to know how the best possible environment can be provided for every child so that he or she gets from his or her entire inherited endowment all the value that is in it. Here we indicate briefly the nature of studies made in this direction and the conclusions suggested.

One study inquires if intelligence runs in families and collects large data of resemblance between parents and children to see if their scores can be correlated. It is found that in general parents of high intelligence tend to have children of higher intelligence than do parents of lower intelligence. This is only generally true, for there are many exceptions. And there is always the possibility that parents of higher intelligence tend to be better off economically and are able to provide a better environment, at home and in school, than parents of poorer intelligence. Heredity alone does not seem to be responsible for intelligence. Very superior intelligence is found in one or two members of a family of average intelligence and very inferior intelligence is found in one or two members of a family of average or even superior intelligence. Therefore the intelligence of a child cannot be predicted on the basis of our knowledge about his parents or his home environment. It has to be determined by some practical tests such as the intelligence tests.

Twins brought up apart have shown remarkable resemblance to each other in mental ability and twins brought up together in identical environment have shown marked divergence. Therefore it is not possible to lay down a general rule about the influence of nature and nurture on the intelligence of an individual. Several factors complicate the interpretation of the results of such studies.

Again, children have recorded a gain in I.Q. after being transferred from one environment to another, say from poorly equipped rural schools to well equipped urban ones. Those who have been sent to congenial nursery and kindergarten schools have gained in I.Q. but such gains have occurred mostly in children of average intelligence. But may be that the gain is due to re-testing, often children are not correctly appraised in the first test. Several studies have shown that a single test is not enough even if the test is given by a very shrewd examiner. Tests, therefore, should be repeated at intervals.

13. Cumulative Records

The main object of education is to foster the growth and development of individual gifts and responsibilities and for its realisation children must be daily observed under many conditions and the progress of each child as he passes through the school must be recorded. This record should help to interpret the individual child to many people, to the child himself and his parents, to his teacher, to his subsequent teachers and other people who are interested in his welfare. They will need information about his intellectual ability, his attainments, this social relations, his emotional development, in order to provide a basis for advice on important decisions at any period or to help him out of special difficulties which may arise. Such records are called *cumulative* because they are carried from year to year and are passed on from one teacher to another.

These records should be based on systematic observation of each individual child and should be continuously kept. As soon as the child joins the school, details about his physical, mental and social make-up should be entered together with details about his family, health and all there is to know pertaining to his growth. As the child matures, these records should be filled in. They should give a complete picture dealing with all the essential aspects of his growth. He will be constantly compared with what he was and with what his companions are. In fact this comparison is very important for proper emotional development. The child will learn to accept criticism as a means of growth.

A cumulative record should be a co-operative enterprise. It is not the responsibility of one single teacher but many teachers work together on it. Parents too can help and the child may write a sort of autobiography relating important facts about his personal life and history. Under proper guidance students of older classes can keep a fairly reliable record of their achievements, individual and classwise. Frequent conferences with parents, particularly where enrolment is small, are helpful in collecting very useful information about the environment in which children spend the rest of their time.

But records are not meant only to be kept and consulted on the day of writing a testimonial for a student. They should have a use and a function in the day to day programme of the school. If they contain significant data about children, they can be used as a means of understanding and guiding children. They can form the basis of parent-teacher conferences for vocational guidance and choice of career.

Now a question very naturally arises as to what should be included in these records. In general they should cover all aspects of the child's growth. The task of assessing intellectual ability is very simple, for besides traditional examinations there are several types of individual and group tests of intelligence. School attainments are also measured by achievement tests. The more difficult problem is to estimate emotional attitudes, social relations and personality traits. In England and America where vocational guidance has made considerable headway, fairly comprehensive record forms are in use and instead of merely describing each pupil's abilities, interests and personality they seek to interpret these facts in terms of the pupil's own peculiar needs and the ways in which they could be met. The record forms deal with the child's home circumstances, occupation of parents, material conditions, social status, the place of the child in the family ; his physical condition, the medical officer's report and recommendations ; bodily control, personal habits and speech ; outstanding good and bad qualities, and problems of personality.

But mere recording of observations is not enough. We

must interpret them, tracing causes of problems and difficulties of the child to such factors as nutrition, handicaps in the home and the like, and devising means of meeting his needs for an all-round development and growth. Such interpretations help the teacher as well in understanding the child more fully and on the basis of that understanding making better provision not only for individual children but also for the whole group, and revising his methods and approach.

In India cumulative records are not popular, and, where kept, are neither comprehensive nor functional. Generally speaking, programmes of counselling and vocational guidance have yet to enter our schools and it seems that the practice of keeping cumulative records will take some time before it is introduced in our schools as a part of our educational effort and provision.

14. Intelligence Testing in India

Adapting intelligence tests for use in India is not an easy task. Too many people think that it should only be a case of translating from English or any other language to one of the Indian languages. This is definitely not the case. Intelligence is indicated in a child when he begins to learn things from his environment by his own effort and on his own initiative without being taught by any one. Now what an Indian child will learn from his environment is quite different from what an American or an English child will learn from his environment. For one thing an English child begins to learn the use of a radio, telephone, electricity, mechanical transport, clock and the like much earlier than an Indian child and the tests used for him cannot be used for Indian children. It is not a question of differences in intelligence as some people assume but of the use they have made of their intelligence from their early age. Binet was right in insisting that his scale could be used for children living in a fairly homogeneous environment. Thus it is clear that tests for Indian children must be based on Indian subjects and must be standardised and validated with reference to Indian children. Comparison of tests or of scores by children from different countries on the same scale proves nothing for though intelligence is innate yet it can never be isolated from the effects of environment which varies from country to country and race to race and which starts working very early in life.

The first attempt at standardising mental tests in India was made by Dr. C. H. Rice of Lahore. It was an adpatation of the Binet scale and is described in his book *The Hindustani Binet-Performance Point Scale*. The tests were meant primarily for Punjabi children and were in Urdu and Panjabi but with slight changes could be used in Hindi. The next notable attempt was made by V. V. Kamat in 1939. He issued a revision of the Binet tests which could be used for Marathi and Kanarese speaking children. More than 1000 children were examined. He found that the range of I.Q.'s is much greater in India going as high as 165. In 1942 Dr. Sohan Lal of U. P. constructed and standardised a verbal group test of intelligence for 11 plus school-going children of the U.P. Since then Teachers' Training Colleges through their experimental psychology departments and psychological bureaus and institutes have undertaken the work of constructing and standardizing intelligence tests. Most of them are adaptations of the Stanford Revision. Pandit L. S. Jha, Dr. S. Jalota and Dr. S. M. Mohsin have done some useful work in this direction. Pandit Jha adapted the Simplex Mental Test by C. A. Richardson in Hindi, Dr. Jalota prepared a group verbal test for use among college students, and Dr. Mohsin has completed the standardisation of a verbal group test of intelligence in Hindi. A few test items from Dr. Mohsin's scale are given below.

I.

1. Cats are useful because
   a) they catch mice
   b) they are good
   c) they fight dogs
2. We buy watches because
   a) their sound is sweet
   b) they have hands in them
   c) they give time
3. We drink water because
   a) it is cold
   b) it freezes
   c) it quenches thirst

II.

1. Eating : Bread : Drinking :
   a) water *b*) iron *c*) brass *d*) stone
2. Cap : Head : Shoe :
   a) hand *b*) shirt *c*) feet *d*) finger
3. Eats : Hearing : Eyes :
   a) stool *b*) hand *c*) seeing *d*) playing

III.

1. If Sham is older than Basudeo and Basudeo is older than Hisan Chandi, how is Sham to Chandi ?
   a) younger *b*) elder *c*) better *d*) equal
2. Only bad people tell lies or steal, Savitri is a good girl. What will she do ?
   a) tell lies *b*) steal *c*) both *d*) nothing

3. My net is so small that long or fat fish will not be caught in it. I hear one fish has been caught. It must be

   a) long *b*) fat *c*) both *d*) neither

These tests are devised for all pupils of classes VI to XI but there is a table of norms for different ages and classes and by adding 100 to the difference between the score obtained by a person and the norm for the class or age-group I.B. (Index of Brightness) is obtained.

QUESTIONS

1. What do you understand by Intelligence Tests ? Discuss their value and limitations.
2. How do you obtain the Intelligence Quotient of a child ? Explain Mental Age and show how pupils may have different I.Q.'s with the same mental age or have different mental ages with the same I.Q.
3. How have Intelligence Tests helpled the teacher ?
4. What are the difficulties in defining intelligence ? Is it impossible to measure intelligence without defining it ? Discuss some of the definitions, and say which you accept and why.
5. Discuss the value and limitations of Binet's tests and show how they are supplemented by other types of tests.
6. What do you understand by Standardisation of Tests ? Discuss the characteristics of such a test. Does environment make any difference to intelligence ?

REFERENCES FOR FURTHER STUDY

1. Ballard : *Group Tests of Intelligence* (Univ. of Lond. Press).
2, Ballard : *Mental Tests* (Univ. of Lond. Press).
3. Ballard : *The new Examiner* (Univ. of Lond. Press).

4. Burt : *Mental and Scholastic Test* (Allen & Unwin).
5. Dumville : *Child Mind* (Univ. Tut. Press).
6. Freeman : *Mental Tests, Their History, Principles and Applications* (Houghton Mifflin).
7. Garret : *Great Experiment in Psychology* (The Century Co.).
8. Goodenough : *Mental Testing* (Rinehart).
9. Hughes and Hughes : *Learning and Teaching* (Longmans).
10. Kamat : *Measuring Intelligence of Indian Children* (Oxford Univ. Press).
11. Menzel : *The Use of New-Type Tests in India* (Oxford Univ. Press).
12. Mursell : *Psychological Testing* (Longmans).
13. Ross : *Groundwork of Educational Psychology* (Harrap).
14. Sherman : *Intelligence and its Deviations* (Ronald Press).
15. Spearman : *The Abilities of Man, Their Nature and Measure* (Univ. of Lond. Press).
16. Terman : *Measurement of Intelligence* (Harrap).
17. Woodworth : *Psychology* (Methuen).

CHAPTER TWENTYTHREE Attainments and their Measurement

1. THE NEED AND VALUE OF EXAMINATIONS

TESTING pupils' progress in studies is an indispensable part of the teacher's task and technique and to this end has been devised the system of examinations that is in vogue at present. Examinations are an ancient human institution. They help to determine the extent to which pupils have profited by their studies and to distinguish between those who have passed and those who have failed. Success in the examination acts as an impetus to young people for intense study, encourages fuller learning and promotes clear and definite understanding. Under their stress young people enter into a spirit of rivalry to achieve better and higher.

Examinations are necessary as a means of discovering the interests and abilities of children, and for scoring and grading the attainment of pupils in different subjects with a view to selecting suitable hands for different places in business and industry.

Examinations are also necessary as a test of the effectiveness of our methods of teaching. Education cannot improve unless we can determine the results produced by any educational policy, method or procedure. If the teacher wishes to know what the best method of teaching reading is, he must examine the results of the several alternative methods. Should he let children spend time in reading stories or should he teach word analysis ? Should he let them have ample free time in the library or put them on oral reading from a text ? The answer to these questions can be found by reviewing and examining the results of each method.

Examinations help to standardise instruction in schools or educational institutions subject to them. They have often been used as much as a test of teachers as of pupils, and the quality of a school has often been judged by the number of pupils who have successfully passed or distinguished themselves in examinations.

2. Their Failure

Of late the traditional system of examinations has been severely condemned and criticised. It tries to examine thousands of pupils at the same time and with the same yardstick. It assumes that the needs and abilities of all pupils at a certain age level are identical, that curricula and courses are adjusted to them, that the standards of assessment are unchanging and the opinions and judgments of examiners are invariably infallible. All these assumptions have been strongly questioned during recent years. Modern psychology has clearly shown that individuals vary in a large number of ways and the mere fact that a pupil has not been able to cope successfully with a certain type of examination should not be enough to condemn him as incapable of working with others who have passed. It may very often mean that the examination is not suitable either as a means of discovering the weakness of pupils or as a basis of remedying them. They serve neither diagnosis nor prognosis, that is, they can neither find out special aptitudes, talents or abilities, or special difficulties in various subjects, nor forecast or predict future possibilities of pupils. They treat them all as one uniform mass, the difference of a few marks may spell disaster and mar a promising career. In the name of fairness, detachment and impartiality, examiners prefer to know nothing more about the pupil except what is revealed in the written papers and very often that is not an adequate yardstick with which to measure the pupils' effort or achievement.

Such a system could have worked in an age when a selected few were needed to man the services, but today when we wish to educate everybody, to enable every boy and girl to develop all that is best in him or her, to extend to all of them the benefits of the highest education, and when opportunities of useful employment and social service are so large that every individual can turn to advantage his or her ability, the problem is not to pick and choose but to diagnose the type of ability each individual has and then provide opportunities for its maximum growth and development. To this end the present system of examination is not at all helpful.

In a number of countries systematic enquiries have been made into the examination system and the conclusions they have reached are most damaging. In the first place it is not a valid and reliable measurement of human capacities and their products. It has been very easy to demonstrate that no two examiners ever assign the same marks to a paper. and no examiner marking the same paper at different times ever succeeds in repeating his marks. And there is reason to suspect if an examination really tests what it professes to test. Too often the examiner does not know what has been taught in detail and how it has been taught. There are no fixed general standards of marking and the personal factor of the examiner plays all too important a part. Dr. Ballard says, 'Their weakness consists in their uncertainty—a capriciousness in the working and a lack of steadiness and accuracy in the results.' Secondly, these examinations have a very injurious effect on life and work in the school. The outlook of both teachers and pupils is vitiated by the dread and demands of examinations. Teaching work tends to be standardised to the general neglect of varying needs, interests and capacities, and 'the stress is laid on the external examinable aspects of subjects rather than on the deeper spiritual aspects. The scholars are subjected to periodic strains and anxieties which have adverse effects on the health of body and mind. Initiative and spontaneous work are discouraged in them as well as in their teachers, because they do not make for good examination results.'[1]

The most commonly used type of examination is the essay type. The pupils are asked to write their answers in the form of essays and the questions almost always begin with words : 'Describe', 'Discuss', 'Explain', 'Compare' and the like.

3. Attainment Tests

With the perfection of group tests of intelligence it was suggested that 'new-type' or 'objective-type' examinations should be devised and used in schools. These have been modelled on intelligence tests and because they are designed to measure attainment or achievement, that is, the degree of proficiency or progress made by pupils in the mastery of school subjects, they are called *attainment* or *achievement* tests. They seek to assess the results of organised training and instruction. If they are valid and correct they help to determine the change in pupils resulting from educational devices, methods, material or programmes. Such determination is of great value to teachers, headmasters, superintendents and instructors, in fact to everybody who is in some way connected with the education of children. They may have been emphasising some phase of the curriculum, using some new method of instruction, some special textbook or some plan of work or adding or removing some

[1] *The New Examiner*, p. 8.

activity from the school programme, and they need to know the outcomes of their effort. Tests of attainment reveal what items should be continued and what items should be modified or discarded. The games instructor will need them to find out if a particular activity or programme is serving the purpose for which it was introduced, and so will the librarian to determine if the concrete plan of library service is of any benefit to the young readers. No progress or improvement in school work and service is possible unless teachers are able to find out fairly reliably the results or effects of their methods and plans on the class as a whole and on each individual pupil.

Attainment tests may be teacher-made or standardized and both are of various types which we shall now discuss.

4. Teacher's Tests

Tests devised by teachers may be subjective or objective. Subjective tests are those in which a teacher's personal opinion, feeling or prejudice enters into the assessment of a pupil's achievement. Very often the general impression he has formed about the neatness, courtesy and smartness of a pupil weighs much more than any accurate and reliable evidence of his progress or ability. The mood and disposition of the moment is the main factor and there is no criterion by which the teacher's judgment can be verified or checked by others. Such judgements cannot be accepted as true and reliable for the very simple reason that the teacher himself is likely to change them and they are not supported or confirmed by other teachers of the same class. No doubt they are based on intimate knowledge obtained from personal contacts and go a long way towards indicating what a pupil can or cannot achieve, but too often teachers are unduly influenced by personal feeling and the classes are so large that it is not possible to give sufficient time to individual children.

Another type of teacher's test is the oral examination conducted by one or more teachers through oral questions and answers. In the past when classes were small this was a very common method of testing. In higher stages this method takes the form of interviews. But when the number is large it becomes impossible for a teacher to know every pupil's work well enough to be accurate in his judgment. Pupils who are nervous, shy, less talkative or smart are likely to be judged lower than they deserve to be. Again, teachers differ in their methods of assessment and their likes and dislikes may enter into their judgment. This method is extensively used in lower classes where children are too young to take written examinations.

A third type of teacher's test is the written examination. Its use is very widespread. Pupils are given written or printed questions and expected to answer them in writing within a prescribed time limit. The most common is the essay type and pupils are expected to recall and write the most important facts, principles or processes etc. The need, value and failure of such tests have already been discussed in the first two sections of this chapter. The factor of chance or luck plays too important a part in written examinations because questions cover only a limited range of subjects and it is possible for a pupil to know the rest of the course very well and yet fail.

With the success and popularity of group tests of intelligence teachers have begun to realise the need and value of what are usually called 'new type' *objective* tests. They are independent of the personal feeling, prejudice or attitude of the teacher and will yield the same score when given by different teachers or by the same teacher at different times. Subjective factors which enter into the traditional system of examinations are avoided. Here are a few examples.

Simple Recall Tests

The pupil gives a simple answer, usually a word or a phrase, to a simple direct question, as in the following:

Who discovered America? ....
Who invented the radio? ....
What is the chemical formula for water?.............
Of what State is Hyderabad the capital? ....
Through what States does the River Ganges flow? ......

Usually a large number of tests are printed on a piece of paper and the instructions to pupils are to fill in the blanks with correct answers. These questions may be given to the class orally and they may put down their answers against numbers denoting each question. Such tests emphasise definite knowledge and ready recall. The pupil has no time to guess. It is a fairly reliable test. But there is nothing new in it for such tests used to be given in the past as well. This type of test is for facts and bits of information without in any way emphasising relations between facts.

Completion Tests

This type of test consists of a sentence or paragraph from which one or more words or phrases have been omitted. The pupil is to fill in the blanks with suitable words or phrases so as to make sense. Here are a few examples.

The month of June is followed by............
Mahatma Gandhi died at........*in*.................
The Taj Mahal was built by...........*in*.........
Water is made of two elements..........*and*.........
Quinine cures................

The pupil has to recall the necessary word or phrase. In the construction of this type of test care should be taken that the blank, if filled in correctly, makes complete sense and there should be only one way of filling the blank. If the blank can be filled in several ways the test is unsatisfactory, as for example :—

The..........*of India is* ....

This test cannot be given orally and usually pupils are supplied types or printed copies of tests to fill in blanks. Like the previous test the completion test is reliable in assessing concrete knowledge.

The Multiple Choice Test

This type of test consists of test items which are to be answered by choosing a correct answer from among several answers. It is of two kinds, one in which there is only one correct answer and the other in which one answer is better than the rest. Here are a few examples of both.

1. Akbar was succeeded by

   Timur, Jehangir, Sher Shah, Mohammed Tughlak.

   The river Nile falls into

   The Bay of Bengal, the Red Sea, the Mediterranean, the Arabian Sea.

   Ram is married 1. to Sham's sister
   2. with
   3. by

   Hamlet was written by

   Shakespeare, Bacon, Goldsmith, Johnson.

2. Shoes are used for

   protection, comfort, show, pleasure.

   A good horse

   runs fast, is tail, looks grand, has long hair.

Tagore was a great
poet, philosopher, thinker, traveller.
Newspapers are used for
selling, printing, packing, reading, burning.

In the first type only one correct answer is to be selected and in ths second type the pupil has to give the *best* answer. In constructing this test care should be taken that alternative answers are not too obviously incorrect and the pupil is given sufficient exercise of discrimination. The correct or the best answer should not be given in the same order, and a very large number of questions should be given at a time. This number may go up to hundred. Pupils have only to underline the answer to questions printed on a sheet of paper. They should be told that they have to answer all questions. This test is a very reliable test of information though there is no provision for testing relationship among facts.

True and False Tests

This is a variation of the multiple choice test, the alternative answers being restricted to two, one true and the other false. There is an equal number of true and false statements concerning the material the pupil has studied, and all that he has to do is to study each statement carefully, deciding whether it is false or true and indicating his decision by writing 'true' or 'false' against it. This test is the best known. Here are a few examples.

Mark each statement True or False (T or F) or say Yes or No :

History is a record of battles.
History is a record of past events.
A plant differs from a star in that it is larger.

A planet, differs from a star in that it moves round an orbit.

Akbar abolished Sati.

Akbar founded the Din-e-Ilahi.

Syllogism is a silly remark.

Syllogism is a kind of reasoning.

This test, also known as the Alternative-Response test, looks simple but is not easy to construct. The alternative statements must deal with the essential part of the subject matter and only important facts should be included. The truth or falsity of statements should not be too obvious, half truths or falsehoods have to be avoided and a large number of statements should be included in the test. The score is equal to the number of correct answers minus the number of incorrect answers.

The Matching Test

The matching test consists of two separate groups of items which are related in some definite manner and the pupil has to match them. As for example.

(A) Lines are parallel	(1) If they have equal arcs
(B) Angles are equal	(2) If perpendicular to the same line
(C) Triangles are congruent	(3) If sides are proportional
(D) Triangles are similar	(4) If two sides are equal and proportional

Against 1, 2, 3 and 4 pupils may write A, B, C, or D. The matching test is also a useful teaching device and calls for accurate discrimination on the part of the pupil. It discourages memorising and promotes and tests knowledge and understanding. It is a difficult test to take if it is carefully constructed.

5. Standardised Tests

The tests described above have a limited range as they are devised by the teacher for use with his own pupils, but like intelligence tests, attainment tests may also be *standardised* and used for a large number of children. Quite a large number and variety of tests and scales have been designed by experts and are available to the educational public for use in the field of measurement. Let us study some of the principles on which tests are standardised.

In the first place a test must have a high degree of validity to be useful. A test is valid when it measures truly and accurately the acquired ability or quality one wants to measure and nothing else. For example, a test of reading should measure that and nothing else. Quite a number of pupils complain that they knew the answers to all the questions in the arithmetic examination but because the questions were too many or too lengthy they could not write out the solutions to all the questions. Such a test is not a valid arithmetic test. It is a test of speed of writing arithmetic symbols. Most of our present-day examinations turn out to be tests of writing speed and accuracy rather than tests of achievement in the several subjects studied. They are invalid for that reason. Again, we may use vague or ambiguous language in the test items and these may be interpreted in various ways. A very familiar type of question in history is the comparison between two kings or administrators. Such questions allow too large a margin for personal interpretation and have very little validity.

A valid test must include only those items which are important and essential, and which a pupil in a given subject should know. Several teachers may have to be consulted and several text-books may have to be studied to determine the material that is important enough to be included in a test. Secondly, a valid test should give results which compare favourably with other measures that assess the same type of achievement. For example, if we use a test to measure the skill of boys in typewriting, then suppose we are able to get and accept the employers' report on them two years later as a sound standard, the correlation between the tests and the reports would show the validity of the test.

A second characteristic of the standardised tests is indicated by the term *reliability*. To be reliable the test must give the same results when it is repeated. Often the test contains a large number of items and these are divided into two sets—odd and even—to measure that one set gives the same degree of accuracy as the other. It would be better to call it consistency rather than reliability, because the idea is that the test should give the same results on successive applications, particularly when the attainment it seeks to measure has remained unchanged. This is not easy to achieve except in standardised tests.

In making tests reliable we should make them long enough to include all the essential and important materials of a course. The test items may be more numerous but shorter so that pupils have no difficulty in dealing with them. The type of test items have already been described under objective tests devised by the teacher. In order to determine the self-consistency of the test a correlation between odd and even items may be obtained. If the correspondence between the two is high the test may be considered reliable. Or the same test and its equivalent form may be given on successive days and the results correlated. The correlations will indicate the degree of agreement or reliability.

A third characteristic of standardised attainment tests is that a score should have a definite meaning and value. The scores obtained from teacher-made tests can only be interpreted in terms of percentages, but scores from standardised tests are interpreted by reference to the performance in the same tests of many hundreds of unselected children of the same age as the particular child, as is done in intelligence tests. Certain standards have been made up of the average of pupils of different ages or grades and the scores are compared with them to determine whether the pupil's attainment is at, above or below a particular age or grade level. Suppose a ten-year-old child makes a score of 25 on a given test, the teacher refers to the standards made up and finds that this core is the average made by pupils of age 11, and he concludes that the particular pupil has educational age 11 though his chronological age is 10. His E.Q. (educational quotient) is obtained in the same manner as the I.Q., that is, by dividing the E.A. (educational age) by the C.A. (chronological age). This E.Q. means as much as the I.Q. except that it refers to the level of achievement rather than the level of intelligence. Like the scale of I.Q.s., an E.Q. of 100 is normal for a given age. 70 is below normal and 120 is above normal. The E.Q. indicates how well or ill a student is doing in his studies or in a particular subject. These E.Q.s, when compared with I.Q.s, will reveal whether the achievement of a pupil is the result of his mental ability. To make this easy, A.Q. (accomplishment quotient) is used. This is obtained by dividing the E.Q. by the I.Q. and shows if the pupil is making full use of his mental ability or has attained as much as his intelligence demands.

6. Types of Attainment Tests

Attainment tests have been constructed to measure almost every product of instruction and may be classified in a very large variety of ways. In the first place there are tests for every school subject or branch of a subject. There are reading tests, handwriting tests, arithmetic tests, language, geography, history and science tests. There are tests for several classes or grades, such as, pre-school, primary, high school or college tests. Again, there are tests measuring products of instruction such as motor skill, information, speed, quality, accuracy. There are some mixed tests which measure more than one product or aspect of instruction. Lastly, tests may be classified according to the purpose they serve. There may be tests for regulating admission to a course, for diagnosing difficulties in particular subjects, for measuring the range of information of new entrants to a class. Let us describe some of the tests.

Speed tests. A speed test usually measures either the amount of work of a uniform quality and difficulty which a pupil can do in a given time or the rate at which particular things are done. A definite time limit is an indispensable feature of this test. Speed tests are mainly emphasised in arithmetic, typewriting, reading. In arithmetic we may try to find out the number of problems a pupil can do in a given time or how much time he required in computing. In reading, the speed test will reveal the number of words a pupil can read in one minute. Speed tests in typing are well known. But speed tests can be constructed for only that product or aspect of achievement in which speed of performance is an important factor. For example, we may have tests of how quickly pupils can locate words in a dictionary.

Quality tests. A quality test measures how well pupils can do things regardless of time or difficulty. We may determine the quality of handwriting or signing, of composition or drawing. Obviously such tests are not easy to construct for these qualities are not quite tangible and there is greater likelihood of error. But what is usuall done is to compare the achievement of a pupil with samples or quality already accepted.

Accuracy tests. In reading, spelling, writing, typing, arithmetic and other subjects pupils do make mistakes and it is highly important to measure the accuracy of performance. This can be done by finding out the percentage of errors made in the test.

Athletic tests. Norms may be established with regard to the performance of a sample of pupils of a particular age or with the best records made by outstanding athletes. The activities most often tested are long jump, high jump, running, ball throwing and the like. In our drive to popularise athletics in schools and colleges we shall have to do much to standardize tests of athletic achievement. There will have to be different tests for boys and girls.

Diagnostic tests. These tests are constructed and given to discover special difficulties in various subjects. The subject is analysed into several parts requiring special types of abilities, interests, skills. This diagnostic examination of silent reading abilities may seek to test speed, comprehension, vocabulary, central thought, recognition of isolated words, recognition of phrases etc. Often pupils are efficient in one element and inefficient in another. Diagnostic tests reveal such inefficiencies so that they may be corrected.

Standardised tests are available in most school subjects appearing in the curriculum from the kindergarten to the high school but many more tests are available in 'tool' subjects such as reading, spelling, arithmetic and the like. Quite a number of 'batteries' of general achievement tests which measure achievement in the school subjects in a general way are available and are being used in Western countries. They reveal how well or ill a pupil has done in the school. But they are very general and do not provide any detailed evaluation of all aspects of the school subjects as taught in any one class. Therefore they have to be supplemented by other methods. Another criticism levelled against these tests is that most of them measure mere recall of isolated and unorganised facts and cannot test the ability to think critically or to use facts intelligently. Recently some attempts have been made to measure such abilities and we have tests for obtaining information, of applying principles, of interpretation and of 'fairmindedness'. The Wrightstone Tests of Critical Thinking in the Social Studies are designed for use in the elementary school.

7. Value of Standardised Tests

Standardized tests are widely used in progressive countries. They are convenient practical devices for classifying pupils according to their achievement and ability, for comparing groups and individuals with each other and for diagnosing difficulties of individual pupils. They reveal the reliability of the score and help research in psychology by collecting material for the benefit of educators. They are free from the defects and weaknesses of other methods of appraisal and are quite objective. Their contribution to our knowledge of human nature and ability is not inconsiderable and they have yielded much useful information about the value of educational methods and devices.

Standardized tests are not without their weaknesses. They often seem to be testing some very trivial aspect or element of learning but this is a fault of the test-maker rather than of the test itself. The movement of testing and educational measurement has not made much headway in our country, but if teachers make a start with 'home-made' tests similar to the standardised tests it may gather momentum.

8. Vocational Selection and Tests for Special Aptitudes

Making a living is a part of making a life and unless individuals are properly adjusted to work through which they earn their living they can neither be happy nor successful. Individual variations in ability, skill and understanding have already been emphasised and it implies that different men are suited to different jobs. If we place the right man in the right job, it benefits the employer, the employee and society. The employee benefits because if the job is after his heart, if he has ability and skill for it, he does it better and is happy about it. It gives him satisfaction, makes his work easy and keeps his spirit high. The employer benefits because satisfied workers who have aptitude for the job do it better. Efficiency and production rise. Society also benefits because it gets the best out of every worker.

The two World Wars underlined the need of selecting men for jobs which were highly specialised. Manpower is limited and to get the maximum out of it vocational guidance and selection had to be used. This movement grew out of psychological testing and tests were devised to select the right man for the right job.

The first requisite for such a programme is what has come to be known as job analysis. We must study what the workers do, how they do it, what are their duties, what tools they use, what are their working conditions and what qualities, abilities, aptitudes and skills are important for success and efficiency in the job. Obviously a salesman, a toolshop workman, a steno-typist, a manager, a taxi driver, a teacher, an engineer or a carpenter needs some distinctive ability and skill to succeed in his work. Such abilities are listed and occupations are classified according to the type of ability they need. If a person is employed in a job where dexterity of hands, arms or fingers is essential which he does not possess or possesses only in a small degree he cannot possibly do full justice to the job.

The second requisite is carefully standardised tests for some of the important abilities and skills. These special abilities have little relationship to I.Q. For example, an individual with superior general intelligence may be devoid of mechanical, musical or artistic aptitude. While a good many mechanics may be above average in intelligence, some of them are below average. It is impossible to predict general ability from special aptitude, and *vice versa*. Special abilities depend both on inheritance and training. Tests are now available which measure mechanical, musical or artistic ability as also aptitude for clerical work, teaching, law, nursing, engineering and science. Persons taking the tests are asked questions and given problems to solve that have an important relation to the occupation for which they are being tested.

For example, tests of mechanical aptitude seek to measure skill and speed in perceiving mechanical relations and in dealing with machines. J. L. Stenquist devised a test in which the subject was asked to assemble the parts of ten small devices, among them a bicycle bell, a push button and a mouse trap. He found a high relation between achievement score in the test and success in the workshop. This shows the validity of the test. D. G. Paterson and his associates constructed the well-known Minnesota mechanical ability tests. They set up four criteria for mechanical aptitude : 1) quality of work done, 2) quantity done well, 3) creativeness in construction, and 4) critical appreciation, evaluation and interest. The tests include assembling parts of gadgets, fitting cut-outs into matching holes in a board and analysing geometrical figures. These tests were later supplemented with ratings of interest and intelligence tests, with academic success and mechanical performance in the home. These mechanical tests have been found very useful. But it is not necessary that all who do well in mechanical tests will be happy doing mechanical or constructive work ; they might also be well up in other types of activity. Secondly, it is not essential that occupational interests should coincide with aptitudes. But one who does badly in these tests is not likely to succeed in this field.

Aptitude tests measure special ability apart from training but it is impossible for one's aptitude not to be affected by experience and training. They help to guide students towards suitable occupations, show applicant's fitness for a specific job and can be used for selecting persons capable of special work or responsibility. But as has been pointed out above they do not give reliable information about occupational interests or about personality traits like honesty or persistence.

9. Measurement of Interests and Values

The measurement of interests and values is of great importance to the teacher. They indicate the attitudes of pupils and in teaching many subjects like music, mathematics, art, literature and science, a major goal of the teacher frequently is to change and modify pupils' interests and values. With a knowledge of pupils' interests and values their reactions and adjustments to school programmes and to future vocational activities can be more reliably predicted. One non-verbal technique is to assess the time and money pupils spend on specific activities, but most measuring devices turn on individual pupil's responses to questions. A few well-known measuring devices are described here.

In one study *What I Like to Do* an attempt is made to

obtain an inventory of children's interests through 294 items some of which require affirmative and others negative answers. Allport's (G.W.) *Study of Values* contains 120 test items answers to which indicate the relative importance which the pupil attaches to six basic interests or motives in personality : theoretical, economic, social, aesthetic, political and religious. The revised version of 1951 is used primarily for college students. Besides these the teacher can make use of pupils' diary, free discussion, dream reports and self-evaluation reports to reach what students prize and cherish most in study and life.

Vocational interest tests are widely used for occupational guidance. The *Kuder Preference Record—Vocational* is widely used with high school students to indicate occupations with which the student may not be familiar but which are consistent with the type of things he ordinarily prefers to do. The manual classifies occupations according to areas of interest and the form gives eleven scores : mechanical, computational, scientific, persuasive, artistic, literary, musical, social service, clerical, outdoor, and verification. The conclusions of this test are used for guidance purposes.

Strong Vocational Interest Blank is another widely used interest inventory and is devised separately for men and women. The test indicates whether subjects mark the test the way successful people in various occupations mark it. There are fifty-seven scorable categories for men and twenty-eight for women.

These tests serve to provide only a picture of vocational interests and do not and cannot show into what occupation a particular individual should go.

QUESTIONS

1. What are the merits and demerits of the traditional system of examinations ?

2. Why should there be any examinations at all?
3. What do you understand by an 'objective test'? Give some examples of objective tests devised by teachers and show how you would proceed to standardise them.
4. What is an attainment test? What do you understand by its validity and reliability?
5. Discuss the value of oral tests and interviews. Are they reliable? If not, why not?
6. What do you understand by a 'standardised' test? Give some examples of standardised tests, and discuss their value.
7. What do you understand by vocational selection and guidance? Should the choice of career depend solely on aptitude tests?

References for Further Study

1. Ballard : *The New Examiner* (Univ. of Lond. Press).
2. Cattel : *Guide to Mental Testing* (Univ. of Lond. Press).
3. Douglas and Holland : *Fundamentals of Educational Psychology* (Macmillan).
4. Gates, Jersild, McConnel and Challman : *Educational Psychology* (Macmillan).
5. Good, Vari and Scates : *The Methodology of Educational Research* (Century Co.).
6. Greene, Jorgenson and Gesberich : *Measurement of Evaluation in the Elementary School* (Longmans).
7. Kandel : *Examinations and Their Substitutes in the United States.*
8. Symoners : *Measurement in Secondary Education* (Macmillan).
9. Valentine : *Psychology and its Bearing in Education* (Methuen).

Chapter Twentyfour — The Integration of Personality

1. The Meaning of Personality

Personality is not easy to define and a student of psychology has to be careful about the use of the term. In popular usage personality is understood to mean that in which one person differs from another. When we describe a person has having a personality, we mean that in some respect he stands out above the rank and file. It means that he has some character in an eminent degree or a combination of traits sufficiently striking to be noteworthy. Thus we describe persons as having ' a fine ', ' a strong', or ' a magnetic ' personality according as he has a fine appearance, is aggressive, or has pleasant manners. Religious and philosophical thought stresses the divine aspect or spirituality of man and uses personality as equivalent to self. Personality is often confused with character. But character is essentially a moral term referring to the standards of right and wrong and psychology cannot enter into the study of moral condemnation or approval of behaviour.

Psychologically, personality is all that a person is. It is the totality of his being, and includes his physical, mental, emotional and temperamental make-up. His experience, perception, memory, imagination, instincts, habits, thoughts and sentiments, constitute his personality. His tastes, style of life, beliefs, enthusiasms and the like colour his personality. His clothes, digestion or lameness are a part of his personality if they make a difference to his whole outlook on life and influence his total attitude towards society.

In our study of behaviour in the second chapter we pointed out the need of studying behaviour as one continuous whole or unity rather than piecemeal, in isolated acts. Now we may add that all behaviour is to be understood and interpreted as expressing and revealing a unique assortment of physical, mental and emotional qualities, a unity behind diversity of actions, a personality. If we are to understand an individual, we have not to study individual phases of his activity at any one moment but the fundamental integration of his entire experience and attitudes, that is, his personality.

Personality, thus, is made up of a number of elements. Personal appearance and physical constitution, knowledge and experience, intelligence and character, habits and temperament, attitudes and beliefs, all contribute to it.

2. Characteristics of Personality

The chief characteristic and indication of personality is self-consciousness. A person is a self-conscious being. It is precisely because the idea of self enters into his consciousness that a man is said to be a person or to have a personality. We do not attribute personality to a dog and even a child cannot be described as a personality because it has only a vague sense of personal identity. It is only a mature adult who through praise, blame, success, failure, begins to take an objective attitude towards himself, to see himself as others see him, that can be said to have a personality.

Secondly, personality is through and through social. Our consciousness of ourselves arises only in our interaction with other members of society. Not only do we pass judgments on personaliy from the social standpoint, but also its growth and development take place through our social experience. Personality implies the reactions of others to our own qualities and actions.

Thirdly, a personality is continually adjusting itself to its environment. All behaviour is adjustment to one's environment and one's own inner life. It is evoked by stimuli arising in the environment, and how an individual will act will depend upon his organic structure, his present condition, his attitude, goals and dispositions. When he has acted, he has attained a new balance between outer and inner forces. This means that both the environment and the individual have undergone a change. The behaviour of a thief, a postman, a wife, a salesman or a doctor is his or her way of adjusting to environment. This adjustment is not a passive submission to environmental conditions but a progressive modification of them to suit one's needs and purposes.

Fourthly, a personality is always striving for goals. Behaviour is better understood by reference to the end. All behaviour is purposive, it has a direction and our aims and goals direct it. Some of these goals are grounded in original nature and seek to satisfy man's deepest organic and psychological needs. They may also be acquired and learned from experience as man develops a number of wants not dictated by original nature but necessary in civilised society. These goals originating in instincts and acquired tendencies are the dynamic factors in personality.

To understand an individual or a personality we must consider what his goals are and how much conscious he is of them.

Lastly, a personality functions as a unified whole. Just as the parts of an organism never act in isolation but their activity is affected by the whole organism to which they belong, in the same way the several functions and activities, physical, mental, social or emotional, comprising a personality are affected by the total pattern. In early childhood the individual is a creature of impulses and fancy, but in course of growth it achieves restraint, and behaviour is unified into one whole which we call personality. Now there is greater consistency in the several acts of an individual and they can be understood as belonging to one personality. This achievement of unity or integration takes place largely through the exercise of internal control to which we give the name of *will* or the sentiment of self-regard. This has already been dealt with in detail in a previous chapter.

3. Types of Personality

The standards by which a personality is judged differ and hence there is little agreement about what constitutes a good or poor personality. Personalities have been classified in a number of ways and all that can be done here is to describe some famous classifications to enable the readers to understand people.

William James classified people into tender-minded and tough-minded. The former go by principles, are given to thinking, have an idealistic outlook and are religious and dogmatic. The latter go by facts, are materialistic, do not have any faith in religion and are inclined to be sceptical.

C. G. Jung, a German psychologist, has given us three types : the *extrovert*, the *introvert* and the *ambivert*. The *introvert* is too self-conscious, he is turned inward in his thinking and feeling. He is easily embarrassed and is timid and cautious. He is deliberate, thinks things out and has convictions. He is slow in making decisions. He is reserved and likes to be alone a great deal. He does not form friendships readily and keeps in the background on social occasions. He is a day-dreamer and prefers to read about things. He has a great perseverance and does not give up undertakings readily. The *extrovert* is self-composed, he is turned outward towards the world. He is seldom embarrassed and is plucky and bold. He is impulsive and often acts without thinking. He is hearty and social, and forms friends readily. He is fond of a crowd and enjoys being with people. He is easily swayed by the suggestions of others and turns from one activity to another in quick succession. He has little perseverance. He does not day-dream much. The *ambivert* is a mixture of both.

Kretschmer tried to relate mental types with certain physical characters. He recognised four types. The *pyknic* type is that of the jolly fat man, sociable, good-natured, friendly and genial. He is an extrovert, broad, sound in physique and of the John Bull type. The *leptosome* type is lean, sour-faced, unsociable, reserved, even shy and sensitive. The *athletic* type is hefty and forward and the *dysplastic* group is made up of various irregular types. Kretschmer tries to trace the prevailing types of insanity to each of these types.

Spranger classified people in terms of life values, that is, in terms of what things different people prize in life. He calls them ideal types as he is conscious that very few exemplify any pure type. The *cognitive* type is of the philosopher, scientist or explorer whose interest is knowledge and truth. The *aesthetic* type is interested in beauty and is found in artists. Then there are people interested in cutting down cost and effort, they are described as *economic*. Industrialists, businessmen and merchants may be placed in this type. The *political* type includes statesmen and politicians who are interested in wielding power. The *religious* type includes saints, mystics and priests seeking to relate the present with the next world. The *social* type is of reformers and social workers who are interested in the welfare of their fellows.

4. The Integration of Personality

Education should be of the whole personality. We cannot help the growth and development of any or some parts of the body without influencing the entire physical structure. Similarly, we cannot develop any mental power or trait without reference to the whole to which it belongs. It has been frequently emphasised in the course of this book that mental processes and activities are being separately analysed and studied only for a fuller understanding of the whole personality to which they belong or of which they are aspects. Personality functions as a whole, it is an organisation or integration of all the powers and qualities of an individual. Now the aim of education is that this organisation or integration should be a harmonious balance between one's desires and ambitions on the one hand and one's capacities and powers on the other. Only then can an individual be mentally healthy. When there is too much conflict between opposing desires or the individual seeks mutually exclusive goals, there is unhappiness, instability of mind, inefficiency, a mind divided against itself, and disorganization which may lead to insanity.

An integrated personality is balanced. The three aspects of mental life—knowledge, feeling and action—are equally developed in it. It should have scholarship and independence of thought, practical sense and skill, and generosity and kindliness of feeling. Could there be a more comprehensive ideal for education ?

An integrated personality should be harmoniously adjusted to environment, particularly the social environment. Social adjustment means the relationship between individuals. It is only when people know how to ' get on ' together that we will have a community of happily adjusted personalities. A number of people make themselves and others unhappy, spoil the work they have undertaken, go about spreading discontent and add to the lop-sided, unbalanced and chaotic state of our civilisation because they are over-emotional, too selfish, unimaginative, and domineering, or lack social experience. Many make a mess of their social relationships because they do not know what to say or do in social situations. An integrated personality is stable and balanced.

But this integration and balance is achieved only slowly by the child. In the beginning he is a creature of impulse which knows no law or direction. Blindly he reaches out into the environment for the means of satisfying his hunger, thirst and other basic drives and wants. He also seeks social approval and domination over his fellow beings. He submits to some and commands others. He forms purposes and designs and strives for goals. These bring order into his life of impulse and his life and behaviour reveal strivings, wants and satisfactions. When he is thwarted or obstructed he makes numerous and varied responses until by some action he overcomes obstacles and attains his goal. These obstacles may arise from the environment as when a child is prohibited by the teacher not to look outside, from the individual himself as when physical deformity or mental weakness stands in his way or from a conflict of desires as when the desire to be popular clashes with our hatred for the means we are compelled to adopt. These obstacles create tension and conflict which is followed by adjustment of some sort and learning. Such tensions arise in social relations, too, but if the two great institutions, the home and the school, provide for the progressive growth of the child's personality and the teachers and parents set a worthy model of social relationship, the child will acquire healthy ways of reacting to social experience.

Happily, the schools today are conscious of this urgent need. They have realized that mere instruction is not enough and are providing richer opportuinitis for social, competitive and co-operative work and experience. Scouting, games, social service, leagues, co-operative stores, school banks, art clubs, hobbies, trips and the like give opportunities to the young growing people to dominate over some and yield to others, to play the role of leaders and followers as the occasion demands. In Indian schools such activities are called extra-curricular, but the description is unhappy as it suggests something unimportant.

5. Maladjustments

We have seen how conflicts offer valuable opportunities for learning, for the invention of new and better ways of living. Life is such a struggle that a healthy personality should welcome and meet it. To have persistent motives, to be roused to stronger effort in the face of obstacles and distresses, to withstand failure, to breathe self-confidence and self-reliance and to lead a direct and persistent attack on obstacles and problems are the marks of a sane and healthy person. To evade and side-step them, to be satisfied with somthing else by way of compensation, to excuse oneself for failure or to find false reasons for it are some common ways of maladjustment. Let us consider some of them in detail.

Retreat. Many people instead of meeting reality in the face run away from it. It may be a physical escape and sometimes desirable, or it may be a mental withdrawal from a difficult task in favour of an easier one. The student may take up an easier subject, take to bed to avoid hard work or seek solitude. Many grown-up adults pretend to have heart trouble to avoid a hard game or climbing stairs or heights. Some seek complete retreat in suicide. Children run away from home to avoid rebuke from parents.

Retreat may be due to an extreme form of *introversion* which we have already discussed. The introvert tries to solve the problem of social inadequacy by withdrawing from all social contracts he can avoid. Marked introversion is a serious maladjustment and is to be found in 'shut in' personalities who are unable to find a satisfactory release for their emotions. An introvert broods over his failings and problems and worries about them. Such a pupil does not compel the teacher's attention as he is seldom haughty or mischievous. The remedy for such pupils is taking part in dramatics and appearing in public. A beginning may be made with classroom debates, recitations and dramatics, and later the child may be asked to appear before larger audiences.

Another maladjustment is that of *compensation*. An individual may have a feeling of inferiority because of a physical handicap, crippled limbs, poor dress or some other shortcoming. In extreme cases he may have an inferiority complex and may make heroic efforts to compensate for this inferiority. It may spur him to strive for superiority in other directions ; he may show excessive activity and become super-sensitive about his achievement. But there is a danger that he may seek compensation through futile and anti-social means. He may take to bullying, bragging, lying, stealing and other forms of undesirable behaviour. There are two ways of dealing with him One is to find out the pupil's view of life and try to convince him that it is mistaken. The second is to provide numerous and varied opportunities for physical, intellectual and social activity so that the pupil may compensate for his inferiority in one field by showing superiority in another.

Many people failing to solve their problems through successful adjustment seek satisfaction in phantasy or *day-dreams*. Instead of admitting failure and making up their mind to remove a weakness in order to succeed better next time, they day-dream of what they might have done and derive great satisfaction from this imaginary victory. This fulfilment of wishes in imagination is an escape from reality. As has already been pointed out, day-dreaming is normal and even healthy. Many great men have been day-dreamers weaving out great plans for social reform, political uplift or military strategy. Day-dreaming is a means of defining one's ambitions and goals. But it becomes a maladjustment when the individual instead of facing reality habitually substitutes day-dreaming for an active effort to solve difficulties. He withdraws from friends and functions, and builds up a world of make-believe of which he is the hero.

Frequently children inhibited in one sphere direct their interests in others. This has already been described as *sublimation*. Adolescents take part in dramatics, art clubs or music and it is a healthy outlet for their growing sex urge. A child who is unable to travel may read travel books. This is healthy and useful. But the substitute chosen by a child to work off his tension may be undesirable as when a child takes to stealing to attract attention or to express his urge for freedom. This is a maladjustment and the teacher should study individual children to direct their energies into healthy outlets.

Often when we have acted wrongly we search for reasons to justify our conduct and convince ourselves that we acted rightly. This is *rationalisation* or excuse-making. Having convinced ourselves that we acted rightly we encourage ourselves to make similar mistakes in future. The fox, unable to reach grapes, excused himself by thinking that they were sour. Many college students spending a great deal on seeing cinemas justify that extravagance by calling it a useful recreation after hard study, or a useful means of social education. Many children unable to spell console themselves that after all spelling is not so important as ready expression. It is easier to discover rationalization in other people's conduct and the teacher should help children to find out real reasons instead of faked ones.

Another maladjustment related to excuse-making is to throw the responsibility for our failure on others. A bad workman quarrels with his tools. Poor students blame the examiners ; disappointed clerks complain of favouritism or luck ; the tailor blames the texture of cloth ; the tennis player, the wind ; and so on. They may all be right, but they may all be overlooking the most important aspect of their failure, that is, themselves, their own lack of ability or perserverance. This is called *projection*.

It is difficult to prescribe a handy formula for overcoming these maladjustments. The teacher should guide children to face facts, develop tenacity of purpose and make intelligent adjustments to their environment.

6. Personality and the Home

The origins of personality can be traced to the early training of the child in the home. The inherited innate tendencies are present, but in what direction they are stimulated and developed depends upon the early influences of home life. There is a general agreement among serious students of child education that fundamental patterns of personality are formed during childhood. If parents provide a stimulating environment and a great degree of freedom, children will grow into strong, independent and self-reliant individuals. If on the other hand they are domineering and strict, order children about, and rebuke and punish them for small things, children will be timid, lacking in initiative and self-confidence.

Children tend to behave as their parents do. They belong to one family, share the economic and social status of their parents, submit to their discipline, take the parents' behaviour as their model and are influenced by their mutual relations. Over-affectionate parents make children too dependent, and over-strict ones make them too timid or too rebellious. Children are infected by the attitude of their parents towards the problems of life.

Recent studies have revealed that the position of the child in the family has much to do with the pattern of his personality. Thus the only child, the youngest child, the favourite child, the only son in a family of daughters or the only daughter in a family of sons, grows differently and develops emotional attitudes which make a difference to his or her personality. For example, the only child is likely to be pampered, parents are always hyper-anxious about his or her welfare, give him or her extra protection and regard, and unknowingly teach him or her to expect more from the social environment. The child grows self-centred, obstinate and less co-operative and may make a failure of marriage. These influences are not due to a child's position in the family but to parents' attitude towards the child.

The school should know the home influences on the growth and development of each child and many schools in the West employ 'visiting teachers' who inquire into the home conditions and influences of children. Their reports help the school to understand and guide children better, to correct and prevent serious maladjustments among their pupils.

7. Personality and the School

The share and responsibility of the school in forming the personality of a child is equally important, and quite a number of maladjustments are due mostly to the bad school environment. In many schools in India far too much emphasis is placed on marks and examination results, on distinctions, prizes and scholarship, and the entire process of education and learning is overshadowed by an unhealthy competitive spirit. Questions are asked and answered not to clear differences and help understanding, but to grade pupils. Every time pupils are given a task, they are anxious to know if it will be marked. There is hardly any feeling that learning is a social, co-operative process and the class is a unity. The stress on personal achievement breeds jealousies, conceits, defeatism and other maladjustments, and the joy of learning and living together is lost.

At present too much premium is placed on speed in answering questions, but the slow may not be dull. One who is not able to mug answers and deliver them in the examination hall may be an intelligent and thoughtful student. Again, too much emphasis is laid on knowledge and facts, and one who lacks it is naively judged to be a dunce and ridiculed. Conduct is judged in terms of examination results and mastery of subject-matter. This is unfair to a number of children whose interests lie in other directions and whose ability does not show to best advantage in an examination.

Teachers' attitude towards their pupils is not always desirable. They are impatient with pupils' errors and forget that they too are not omniscient and that children have a right to make mistakes. Some teachers ridicule, bully, tease and discourage their pupils. Their attitude is negative, prohibitive and cynical. All this makes the child develop a wrong view of life and work.

The school makes the man in more ways than one. It develops the child educationally and mentally. It gives him more knowledge, more opportunities to think and reason and a broader outlook on life. The school teachers habits of community living and is a great socialising influence. It helps the emotional development, cultivates tastes and attitudes, and offers material for building up ideals and aims for life. Most of the progressive schools have realised their great responsibility and are constantly revising their programmes to provide for the development of balanced personalities but in India tradition dies hard and a good many schools do no more than follow the time-honoured curricula.

8. Re-Education of Difficult Children

We have seen that maladjusted persons cannot play an effective role in life. The school has to forestall and prevent those faulty adjustments. But with the best of effort and attention the teacher has to face in every class pupils whose behaviour and attitude present difficulties and who are not profiting as much as they should by their stay in the school. Let us consider some of them.

1. The *obstinate*, disobedient, wilful and contrary-minded child is not uncommon. He is a nuisance both in and outside the classroom. It may be a case of simple self-assertion and the child may be just trying to find out the extent of his power. He may be rebelling against some arbitrary and unjust treatment at the hands of parents and teachers. Jealousy, favouritism, inferiority complex or conflicts in the nursery may lead to this negativism. Or it may be due to physical conditions such as malnutrition, eye-strain or fatigue. Some element of obstinacy is normal for all healthy children since they are very selfish in the beginning. Obedience, discipline, co-operation and consideration for others are the result of slow training and the teacher should treat such children with patience, understanding and sympathy.

2. Some children habitually play *truant*. They run away from home and school and it is considered a great offence. But the teacher is never able to get at the child's point of view. The child may be running away from the class be-

cause he feels he is not wanted by the teacher or his class-ellows. The teacher may have rebuked him badly or the class may have taunted him. Or he may have no interest in the school work. Often it is due to wander-lust among young people and they cannot bring themselves to sit still for hours on end in the classroom.

3. Some children are habitually *inattentive*. They do not attend to any lesson and are absent-minded. They either dream their school-time away or engage in reading a story while the teacher is busy teaching. In the former case the child is a definite introvert given to day-dreaming, and in the latter he may have no faith in the importance of the lesson or the ability of the teacher to do justice to the lesson.

4. Some children are habitual *liars*. They tell lies to escape punishment or because they are unable to distinguish between fact and fiction. But they may be telling lies to protect their friends or out of pique against the teacher. Children's lies are differently motivated and the teacher should treat each child individually.

It is easy to multiply this list of maladjustments and it is equally easy to enlarge the treatment of those that have been mentioned here as there is a fund of literature, both books and pamphlets, on child education and treatment. But space does not permit either course. The teacher for whom such difficulties arise in the course of his daily work expects that psychology should give him a rule of thumb by which he may be able to treat such children successfully. Many teachers who have had longer experience are too ready to pass on a formula for the guidance of the new teachers. Psychology can offer only general principles of guidance about behaviour, good and bad, and it is for the individual teacher to apply them to individual children. But perhaps one advice can bear repetition. Study each child with sympathy and patience, analyse your own attitude towards him, approach him with frankness and treat the offence rather than the offender. The objective attitude with a background of psychological knowledge will help the teacher to overcome many of the common maladjustments in his pupils' personalities.

9. Child Guidance Clinics

The most promising agency for the treatment of children with serious behaviour problems or problems of maladjustments is the child guidance clinic. A good clinic has competent psychologists, psychiatrists, pediatricians and social workers with sufficient clerical help to relieve the professional staff of routine work. It can, therefore, closely study the child's problems and suggest a plan for his correction.

When a child is referred to a clinic there are two lines of approach. The first is to obtain all available information about the child's past and the environment in which he has been brought up and in which he lives. The second is an intensive examination of the child himself. For the first, trained social workers interview parents, teachers, relatives and all those with whom the child comes in contact in one way or the other and collect facts about his failure to make adequate adjustments to his environment. This is the case history method we have studied in the earlier chapter. Facts of his home and family background and his school work come in handy to give clues regarding the possible cause of his difficulty. Secondly, the child is given a thorough physical examination by a competent physician to find out if he is suffering from any permanent or temporary physical handicap or defect. X-ray for tuberculosis or tests for infections and glandular weakness are given. Thirdly, there is the psycholgical examination consisting of intelligence tests, tests of attainment in different school subjects or diagnostic tests to find out any special disability. The psychologist is often able to secure evidence regarding personal and social traits. Fourthly, the psychiatrist interviews the child in an informal manner so as to elicit the child's own view of his conduct and his view of parents and relatives. He tries to win his confidence so that the child can talk to him freely without reserve and gives reliable clues to his motives. Then all four—the social workers, the physician, the psychologist and the psychiatrist—sit down to a conference, diagnose the child's difficulty and recommend treatment. This treatment is an individual matter and is bound to differ with individual children ranging from medicine to change of environment and play facilities, from a change in parental attitude to an allowance of money. Naturally, treatment has to be continued over a period of time and much follow-up work will be called for.

Available studies indicate that child guidance clinics have done some useful service in improving children's emotional health and personal adjustments. But these studies relate to clinics in the United States. In our country child guidance clinics are few and far between and no statistical data is available about their working.

10. Educational and Vocational Guidance

One of the most important functions of the secondary school is that of determining the abilities, interests, aptitudes and educational and vocational needs of the pupils and then guiding them to make the best use of those abilities and interests and become desirable members of the social order. It was in the early years of this century that vocational guidance was recognised as a form of social service which high schools should be called upon to render to help each pupil to find the vocation for which he is best suited. The idea, however, developed and the programme of guidance was conceived on a broader scale. Today guidance programmes seek to enable every pupil to know and understand his abilities and interests, to develop them as well as he can, to relate them to life goals and ultimately to guide themselves to a useful and desirable place in the social economy. In a way all education is guidance, every activity of the school aims at helping the pupil to find himself and the programme of schools helps to guide him in matters moral, social, personal and educational. His health, character, habits, sense of good citizenship and the like all come under the purview of education.

More specifically the programme of guidance aims at studying each pupil and maintaining cumulative records of his attainments, abilities and interests. The relation between the curriculum and the needs of groups and of individuals is closely studied to make suitable re-adjustments. All teachers are expected to co-operate in the programme not only to complete the individual records but also to understand the nature and value of each other's work and to make systematic use of achievement tests and other devices available in the school to appraise and evaluate the efforts of pupils. This broad approach is essential for the narrow objective of assisting the pupil to choose an occupation, prepare for it, enter it and prosper in it. To that end schools have to collect information about occupations and make it available to pupils and to counsel each individual with regard to his abilities and interests and with regard to the needs and requirements of various occupations in terms of abilities and skills. Finally, the school will help each individual pupil to select courses suitable for the vocation he has chosen.

11. The Education of Retarded Children

Those pupils who have not completed the work of the previous class in a normal amount of time are said to be retarded. They are failures and are not promoted. When children have to be taught in large groups retardation becomes a necessary evil. In India the large percentages of failures in public and internal annual examinations is a very common and acceptable feature and in fact quite a number of institutions are happy about the large number of failures in internal examinations so that results in public examinations bring prestige. From the point of view of the child retardation is a very serious step and every possible effort should be made to prevent it.

A retarded child is looked down upon and is punished for not having mastered a subject in a given period of time. Investigations have shown that most often such children differed from those that have never been retarded only in their mental level at the time of admission. When the school does not make any special provision for brighter pupils to skip classes by double promotion it seems very unfair to pull down others who are below average. The right course would be to conduct intelligence tests at the time of first admission and admit children on the basis of their mental age rather than their chronological age. The other alternative is to modify the course for the dull. Several children of sub-normal intelligence get admission into schools and mark time for two or three years in the same class. This waste could have been avoided if some tests had been used to find out if they make the same level of intelligence as the class or have a normal I.Q. The child is inferior in intelligence through no fault of his and it is the duty of the school to see if he is capable of benefiting by the course of instruction within the stipulated period of time.

At present the common criterion for admission to the first primary class is chronological age. Considerations of mental ability never come in and parents would never agree that their children be stamped dull, normal or superior even before they have had any schooling. Most of the retardation in primary classes is due to faulty admissions, undue emphasis on intellectual development at the cost of emotional and social development. To start a child by failing him is too cruel. It affects his whole personality. He may develop a sense of inferiority or of guilt, he may start hating the school and its inmates, violating all rules of discipline or bullying younger children with whom he is compelled to mark time. Most of the problem children in schools are those who have failed. Again failure compels him to learn what he has already been taught in the previous class, the school presumes that mere stay for another year will do, while what he needs is special help. In the first primary class too many boys fail because of the difficulty of learning reading.

Some teachers believe that the fear of failure will act as a successful incentive. Investigations prove the opposite. The ambition to pass works as a more powerful incentive. Experimental studies have also shown that if children are promoted on trial they make up and show better result.

On the other hand some plead for cent per cent promotion in Elementary and Secondary Schools to get rid of the problem of retardation. For one thing such a step will lead to such heterogeneity of pupils, ability and achievement in classes that teaching would become impossible. If pupils know that they are sure to be promoted any way, slovenly habits would be encouraged and the standards would fall. Both solutions, retardation and cent per cent promotion, are inadequate. The attempt to set up homogeneous groups on the basis of tests will prove abortive because parents will never agree that their child should be placed in a slow or inferior group. The remedy lies in adapting the curriculum to individual needs and to individualise teaching as far as possible. Remedial teaching wil prove effective if retarded children are made to feel that this is what they need most. The tasks given should be varied in nature and in difficulty according to the needs of children and the methods of teaching should also be different for different groups of the same class. The old custom of assigning uniform tasks to all pupils should be given up. The school organisation should also be made more flexible so that each pupil can pursue the programme he needs.

12. Testing and Judging Personality

Assessing and judging personality is an alluring job. It is also very necessary and important in certain life situations. Managers, factory superintendents, directors of departments, and heads of institutions are commonly called upon to judge people they are going to employ. Some claim an uncanny intuition for picking out suitable hands, others look into the past history, testimonials or associations of candidates and still others interview them. Popular thought judges persons by horoscopes, bumps on the head, facial expression and complexion, physique, shape and size of the hand or handwriting. But quite obviously these judgments cannot be reliable.

Following the elaboration of scientific methods of testing intelligence, attempts have been made to judge and measure personality accurately. The difficulty of the task is apparent. Human personality is complicated and every human being is a unique assortment of traits, habits and sentiments. Therefore accurate scales for measuring personality are not possible. But some promising efforts have been made and they are only briefly described here.

A common method of appraising personality is the *interview.* A relatively uniform situation is presented to various individuals and the differences in their responses enable us to infer underlying personality traits. A set of questions and their variables are presented and replies of subjects with accompanying behaviour responses are noted. When the interview is conducted by a psychologist the subject is allowed to tell his own story, to describe his difficulties and troubles and to interpret them freely. By encouraging him to talk freely the psychologist can know his inner feelings and intimate details of his personality. He can know what he wants to know as the subject is talking without reservation. Such interviews may be punctuated by questions which bear on the matter for which interviews are being held but such questions should be memorised by the interviewer and put as unobtrusively as possible. Psychoanalysts follow the technique of *free association* method in interviews. 'Say the very first thing that comes to your mind' and both the response and the time in which it is made are noted. The idea is to get behind the 'mask' or superficial facade of personality to deeper emotional complexes and organisational pattern, A highly skilled interviewer is able to interpret the responses of the subject far more deeply. How the subject speaks, what emotions he betrays, how he meets the eye of the interviewer and the like provide valuable clues. The interviewer has to be a good observer as well. But most often interviewers have different points of view and no training or experience. It is difficult to define the qualities of a good interviewer or fix upon desirable training or experience. Nor are skilful interviewers able to say what helps them most. The interview method, therefore, has serious limitations, and cannot be considered reliable. Its limitations are sought to be overcome by making it longer or by having several interviews. But they cannot be made objective. The interviewer may have faulty observation and memory, he may be victim of the 'halo' effect overestimating character, intelligence and the like simply because the subject presents a neat dress or smart appearance. But the interview method is still our only method for much of the personality assessment work as it affords opportunities for obtaining a large measure of understanding of the person.

A variation of this method called the *stress interview* was used during the war to test the capacity of the candidate to stand emotional and intellectual strain. He was allowed to invent a cover story and then face a group of interviewers. The interview consisted of merciless cross-questioning under very disagreeable conditions such as very strong light, insulting questions asked in a tense, threatening atmosphere. The idea was to see how long he can last under strain and duress.

Personality questionnaire method presents a list of questions to the subject who will answer them independently. This saves a lot of time and helps people to answer questions frankly. But the valuable clues picked up during the course of the interview are not available. The first test of this type is R. S. Woodworth's 'Personal Data Sheet' devised in 1918 to test emotional stability or neurotic tendency among soldiers. It had 116 questions each answered by yes or no. The items he chose related to various physical symptoms, fears, worries and all those attitudes which indicate mental and nervous disorder. Some of the questions are : Do you usually sleep well ? Do you have nightmares ? Do you often faint ? Do you feel tired most of the time ? This type of questionnaire gives a rough measure of personality traits. Many recent questionnaires confine themselves to specific personality traits, for example, Allport Ascendance-Submission test in which the subject is asked how he feels in a number of social situations and how he has reacted towards them. In testing leadership, for example, it is asked : Do you seek to meet the important person present at a reception ?, and the scoring is to be: usually, occasionally or never; or Do you feel reluctant to meet him ?, and the scoring is to be: yes, sometimes or no.

Another method of personality questionnaire is to have a large number of questions and then to determine what questions in the list will be answered in the affirmative and negative by normal persons and then to infer that abnormal persons will answer them in the opposite manner. The Minnesota Multiphasic Personality Inventory consists of 550 statements of which the subject has to say whether they are true or false. The answers of normal people are compared with those of abnormal people and thus tests are marked out for testing a specific kind of abnormality. This type of questionnaire has helped in the diagnosis of abnormal traits.

But persons answering questions may lie, evade or give dishonest replies to questions. To avoid that *performance tests* are used. The earliest performance tests of personality were J. E. Downey's tests based on handwriting. For example, the subject is asked to write as he usually does and then to write it as fast as he can. The difference between the two indicates freedom from inhibition. Allport and Vernon test shows that handwriting, walking and reading speed, or ability to estimate areas and distances, give evidence of consistent personality patterns. But the best performance study of personality is an honesty test devised by H. Hartshorne and M. A. May. Children were placed in many natural situations wherein they could easily cheat. They could copy or exchange answers, lie or steal, and it was found that there is no general trait of honesty or dishonesty. Almost all children were dishonest in one situation or the other and many habitual liars did not steal.

Recently the interest of psychologists has swung round to what are known as *projective techniques*. A person is called upon to say what a cloud looks like to him or to interpret a picture containing people and if he interprets such indefinite items in the same general way, it may reveal important trends of thinking, attitude, interest and emotion. The situation has no structure or plan and all that he sees is what he 'projects' from his own personality. The best known projective technique is the 'inkblot test' prepared by H. Rorschach, a Swiss psychiatrist. It consists of ten cards, each containing a rather elaborate inkblot. Some blots are in shades of gray and black, others are in colour. The subject studies each blot and tells what he sees in it. He can spend as much time over each card as he likes. His responses are recorded to see 1) whether he responds to the whole blot or to a portion of it, 2) to what part or aspect of the blot he has reacted, such as shade, colour, form, perspective or motion, 3) with what object has the subject identified the blot, an animal, plant, person or an inanimate object, 4) whether his response is entirely original. Seeing whole figures indicates high intelligence and ability to see wholes and take a whole view of things. Seeing forms in motion, specially human forms, means vivid imagination. Ready response to colour means impulsiveness. Seeing mostly animals suggest lower forms of intelligence.

It is claimed that projective techniques give a person a chance to express his private world of personal feelings, meanings and values. But psychological opinion is divided. While G. Allport and H. E. Garret question if these tests reveal much, R. S. Woodworth thinks that supplemented with other methods of study these tests can help in sizing up personality difficulties of abnormal and subnormal persons.

Another widely used projective technique is the *Thematic Apperception Test*. It consists of three sets of ten pictures, one set is meant for use with both men and women, another for men and a third for women. The pictures are shown in a definite sequence and the subject is asked to make up a story on the basis of what he sees in those pictures. It is believed that he will project his own experience, biographical data, major conflicts, interests and problems into his description of the pictures. It is claimed that findings of this test are borne out by reference to the case history. While the 'inkblot tests' present a situation which has no structure or plan, the T.A.T. has a structure but it has no quantitative scoring. It only helps the individual to verbalise his thoughts, his frustrations and his urgent needs and gives a picture of the pressures on his life and personality.

Questions

1. What do you understand by personality? Is there any relation between personality and physique? How would you seek to develop a healthy personality among children?
2. What is the meaning and value of an integrated personality?
3. What do you understand by adjustment? Describe some of the common maladjustments among children.
4. How would you deal with a child who is shy, with a child who is obstinate, and a child who is nervous?
5. What are the common conditions among Indian schools

that hamper the development of a wholesome personality and how would you change them?

6. Discuss the role of the home and the school in building the personality of a child.
7. Discuss the place and value of educational and vocational guidance in secondary schools.
8. How will you deal with the question of very large failures in schools?
9. Describe some of the methods of testing and judging personality.

REFERENCES FOR FURTHER STUDY

1. Adler : *Understanding Human Nature* (Greenberg).
2. Allport : *Personality : A Psychological Interpretation* (Harper).
3. Freud : *Beyond the Pleasure Principle* (International Psycho-analytic Press).
4. Gilliland, Morgan and Stevens : *General Psychology* (Harrap).
5. Haggard : *The Anatomy of Personality* (Harper).
6. Jung : *Psychological Types* (Kegan Paul).
7. Kretschmer : *Physique and Character* (Harcourt Brace).
8. Lewin : *Dynamic Theory of Personality* (McGraw Hill).
9. Morgan: *The Psychology of the Unadjusted School Child* (Macmillan).
10. Powers : *Psychology in Everyday Living* (D. C. Heath).
11. Scharlieb : *The Psychology of Childhood* (Constable).
12. Sprott : *General Psychology* (Methuen).
13. Stagner : *Psychology of Personality* (McGraw Hill).
14. Woodworth : *Psychology* (Methuen).

CHAPTER TWENTYFIVE

Guiding the Individual Child

AN attempt has been made in this book to provide the teacher with an insight into the nature of the child and the processes through which he grows, learns and develops so that he may plan his teaching procedures and programmes to his pupils' best advantage. It has been emphasised throughout this book that the teacher should so manipulate the classroom situation and the atmosphere of the school that he gives his pupils the fullest scope for self-expression and creates the conditions for maximum growth. This means that the teacher should put psychology to use in his day-to-day work but he can do this effectively if he is ready to adopt new ways and function as a learner.

Ultimately, however, every teacher will have to translate his ideas and ideals in terms of actual children just as a doctor learns general principles of diagnosis and treatment but has to use his general knowledge with individual patients. Every teacher has not only to study growth and development but also direct and guide the processes of growth. Guidance is the basic function of all education, and in this chapter we will study in detail what guidance means, what goals and procedures are implied by the concept of guidance, how individual children should be studied, and what tools and techniques should be employed by the teacher for effective and useful guidance. We will also indicate the principal areas of guidance and the opportunities which every programme of guidance should provide for moulding the life and personality of every child and for changing and reconstructing society. We have already dealt with the guidance of difficult, maladjusted and retarded children and the reader must have formed fairly clear ideas about the guidance responsibilities of the teacher.

1. The Meaning of Guidance

The term *guidance* suggests at least two individuals; one with a goal or purpose to be achieved and the other with some special knowledge and experience necessary for helping the former to reach that goal. The child's task is to learn, to acquire knowledge of the world in which he is going to live as an adult and skills which will help, to learn adjustments which will help him to enjoy working with his fellows, and to prepare himself for some occupation which will suitably employ his abilities and help him earn his living. The teacher's task is to guide and help these acquisitions and learnings. Obviously this means that education is synonymous with guidance, the guidance of learning and development.

The work of guidance is anything but easy. He who guides has to work with living organisms, pulsating with needs, motives and interests, for ever trying to do and achieve things and growing and developing into a balanced personality. The teacher, in the first place, must encourage, stimulate and energise his pupils, he must arouse their interests, enthusiasms and ambitions, and he must open new areas of work, achievement and fulfilment by creating an attitude of courage and confidence. Secondly, he must help young people to stand on their own legs, manage their own affairs and build habits of self-discipline, self-direction and self-criticism. Teaching discipline is not a simple and easy task but it becomes so when it is not imposed from without by some superior authority in power but comes from within through an understanding and realization of social purposes and goals. Thirdly, the teacher must impart knowledge and understanding of the universe, the world of things, places and persons in which every one of us has to live and move. The young person must be helped to reach and enjoy our great social heritage in literature, music and art so as to know and understand the great secrets of nature stored in different sciences. Knowledge should develop thinking and problem-solving and the young people should cultivate the habit of drawing their own conclusions on the basis of knowledge and facts. Fourthly, the teacher must visualise some type of social and economic order which he wishes to bring about and then see how the individual child can be helped to make adjustments to that order for the benefit of both the individual and society. Since he would like that such adjustments continue even after the child has left school, teaching and learning should aim at building more or less permanent habits and attitudes in the child. Lastly, for success and happiness in life, the child should be guided to develop a healthy style of life. Looking around the teacher will find that in his class some pupils are unduly domineering, shy, submissive, accepting inferior position and the like, and he will have to dig deeper to discover their hidden drives, unexpressed needs, tensions and conflicts and to see what he can do about them.

There can be no doubt that guidance makes the pathways of learning straight and clear but it is possible that too much guidance may defeat the very purposes for which it is given. When the tutor at home solves problems of arithmetic for the child there is no assurance that the child has really learned to solve problems. Effective learning is possible only through self-initiated and self-directed activity and guidance should only supplement the pupil's own efforts at learning. That is why the main emphasis in modern concepts of guidance is on self-direction, self-development, and self-realisation on the part of students with the help of the school. Guidance is not merely giving *ad hoc* advice or directions, it is not the imposition of the views of the guide on those who are being guided. One who guides does not try to make decisions for those whom he guides nor does he carry their burdens for them. It is a programme centred essentially round individual children, helps them to understand themselves and the world in which they live, and to promote harmonious and productive adjustments between the two.

2. What Guidance Assumes

Modern education aims at the balanced development of all aspects of personality, and guidance seeks to individualise all education, to bring to bear on the individual those influences which stimulate and help him, through his own efforts, to develop his abilities to the best. He is encouraged to make the most of his abilities and opportunities. Ultimately the school community is made up of individuals, and the merit and effectiveness of the community, class or group will rest on the merit and effectiveness of individual students. If the individual is not pulling his full weight and making the most of his abilities and opportunities, the progress of the group will suffer. We know too well how a slow worker or a shirker pulls back the whole class. He has to be given special attention so that the progress of the entire class is not hampered. Guidance is exactly what such students need. The teacher has to know and understand each student and to help them to make suitable adjustments to problems and difficulties of learning.

Let us enumerate some of the basic assumptions of guidance.

1. Each student is unique ; no two individuals are alike. They differ in physical, mental and emo-

tional characteristics, and these differences must be considered in all educational programmes.

2. The student is an independent personality and has a right to develop as an individual to his fullest potentiality.
3. The student is more important than the school and therefore the school regulations and the school environments should be changed or re-arranged to suit the requirements of individual students.
4. The individual grows and learns best through and by his own effort and direction. Guidance does not improve students, it only helps them to improve themselves.
5. Rapid social changes have multiplied conflicts and tensions and call for more complex adjustments on the part of every individual. He has to grasp new ideas and adjust himself to the pressures they impose. He has to learn new methods of work, develop new attitudes and make numerous contacts with people.
6. Every individual must be rightly placed in employment. He should choose, secure and succeed in a job he likes and doing which he feels happy. Only then does he gain in respect and confidence, and can contribute to the stability and progress of society. Work situations in our times require specialisation and therefore individual aptitudes and job requirements must be carefully co-ordinated through an effective programme of guidance.

3. Types of Guidance

Too often guidance has been understood to mean advising and helping children to choose subjects of study and adopt improved methods of working for better results in examinations. But the schools of our times are assuming greater responsibilities on behalf of their students and there is hardly any area of life and work for which the teacher is not called upon to offer help and guidance to his students. Modern life is so highly complicated by man-made institutions, rules and traditions that it is considered necessary to make special provision in schools for helping young people to understand and to adjust themselves to the demands of a rapidly changing environment. It may be argued, not without reason, that the teacher may find it almost impossible to be able to render adequate guidance in every area of life and work but it is hoped that if the school staff works in close cooperation distributing responsibilities among themselves the difficult and subtle task of guidance may become less difficult.

Often children join a school without learning the habits which they should have learned at home. They do not know how to eat in company, they do not know how to keep their hands, teeth, clothes or face clean. Some of them have no manners, others are suffering from common ailments like mild cough, weak sight, and still others have no laces in their shoes or buttons to their shirt. When parents fail to do their duty the school has to step in. Thus the modern school is doing much that should have been done elsewhere.

The first area of guidance is that of adjustments to social conditions, to things and persons around an individual. This is *personal* guidance. It seeks to study the psychological needs of young people and problems of adjustment and getting along with people. We have already seen maladjustments develop and what should be done about them for the re-education of children. Our schools have programmes of study and games, of debates and dramatics but the personal and emotional needs of pupils are entirely neglected. Some pupils in each class have really acute problems and serious difficulties, and are emotionally disturbed Some of them hate study, others are at war with the world and hate everybody. Some lack confidence, others are too aggressive and domineering. They need special treatment. In a rapidly changing social scene and with equally rapidly changing needs young people are bound to suffer from anxiety. A new teacher, a sick mother, an unemployed father, a new sister born at home, shifting the house to a new locality and scores of other things engage the mind and attention of children, and if they are less attentive, and less enthusiastic about games, and wish to keep away from all work and play it is not surprising. The teacher should be able to see such changes, dig deep into the psychological needs and worries of young people and then help them to overcome their difficulties. Personal guidance will make for effectiveness, efficiency and happiness of pupils.

One area of personal guidance is health. Each pupil should be helped to build and maintain the best type of physical and mental health he can achieve. Advice concerning exercise, diet, work and the like should be given to each student so that he or she keep alert, active, free from disease and in good physical form. Many students keep long hours of study near the examination and the strain tells on their diet and health. Teacher's advice will be very welcome just as physical instructor's guidance about diet, rest and sleep during training for games and tournaments proves very useful.

Another area of personal guidance is the right use of leisure. Monotony and boredom are powerful enemies of health and efficiency. If young people are encouraged to cultivate healthy interests and acquire hobbies it will help them in later years to offset the tedium of leisure hours.

In view of the growing reduction in working hours this type of guidance is very important. A wise use of leisure wards off weariness and may sometimes lead to fruitful hobbies.

Another area of personal guidance is morality. Moral guidance seeks to cultivate among young people a strong moral consciousness, a knowledge of what is right and the will to pursue it. In a world in which moral distinctions are for ever eluding us and the moral fibre of society is fast weakening people have begun to accept and live with corruption and dishonesty, with adulteration of things and deceit. Ethical and character guidance is of crucial importance for the moral health of society and administration.

Civic guidance seeks to develop among young people a civic sense so that he grows into an effective and efficient citizen with a sensitive regard for cleanliness in public places, for the laws of the government and for the welfare of the community and the nation.

Another area of guidance is education. *Educational* guidance is concerned with the development of pupils as persons, with their success and failure in learning, the selection of courses and programmes of study, meeting difficulties in their present courses and choosing courses and institutions for higher training. Problems and difficulties which pupils experience in learning situations overshadow their adjustments to life situations, and therefore it is extremely important that educational guidance should be systematic and effective. That is why it is insisted that all good teaching should include educational guidance.

Educational guidance seeks to help pupils to make their educational plans consistent with their abilities, interests and goals and to select appropriate curricula and courses, that is, to adjust their academic load accordingly, to arrange their study time fruitfully, to accept full responsibility for learning, and to make the most of opportunities for better study and learning offered by the teacher, the school and the home environments. Educational guidance helps pupils to explore educational possibilities beyond the school level and select institutions for higher training after the school. An effective programme of educational guidance should be able to suggest what changes in the curricula, teaching methods and administrative work are called for to meet more fully the needs of students.

Vocational guidance helps the pupil in choosing an occupation, in preparing for it, in securing a job and in making progress in it. Vocational guidance is closely related to educational guidance at the high school stage. The choice of elective or optional subjects at the beginning of the high school course is to a very large extent determined by considerations of what occupation or way of making a living the student is going to adopt after finishing his education. He may have to study further in professional colleges or training institutions but the die is cast in his choice of subjects on entering the high school. His range of interests and abilities is as important as the trends in employment opportunities.

It must not be presumed that these types of guidance are separate from each other or they are to be given by different people. Life is one, the individual is being educated as a whole person, not piecemeal in several spheres, and like life and education guidance is also a whole unified effort to help the individual student in different phases and aspects of life and work. In a broad way guidance is implied in every activity of the school and it is as it should be, for the aims of education and guidance are identical as enabling young people to understand their abilities and interests, to develop them to the maximum, to relate them to aims and purposes of life and to reach self-direction and self-realization as efficient as effective members of society.

4. Studying the Child

All guidance service, it must have already been realised by readers, must begin with a knowledge and understanding of the individual child. We must study very carefully what patterns of interests and abilities he has and how he is generally motivated in his day-to-day behaviour. Let us enumerate some of the ways in which the individual pupil is to be studied. Some of these methods have already been discussed in earlier parts of the book but their recapitulation here will be very relevant and useful.

Direct *observation* of a child under a number of varying circumstances often offers more valuable information for the time spent than any other method. By observing and studying him in the classroom, playground or library or while he is participating in extra-curricular activities useful information can be collected about him. But this observation should not be casual or confined to one teacher. It should be done methodically and with skill by a number of teachers who have had adequate training and sufficient experience in assessing behaviour and interpreting motivation. On the other hand, when observations are biased or incomplete they may be worse than useless for it may either lead to wrong action on the part of the teacher or give distorted view to other teachers when reports are compiled. It is a common experience in any school that the same behaviour in the same child is differently interpreted by different teachers. The teacher should observe accurately and enter into the feelings of the child before his observation can be used with advantage for guidance.

1. To be effective observation should be planned. The teacher should make up his mind beforehand as to what

activities he is going to observe and for what purpose he is going to observe them. He should interpret children's behaviour only after he has had opportunities to observe it under varying circumstances. A written record should be made directly after an observation. With the lapse of time details are sure to be lost or coloured. And every time the teacher makes an observation he should try to put himself in the place of the child; this will help him to understand the attitudes of children more accurately. It is a pity that during training teachers are not given practice in the observation of children and interpretation of their behaviour.

2. Medical check-up should reveal not only height, weight or chest expansion but also any pathological disturbance which may be hindering physical, mental or social growth, and preventing participation in games, concentration of attention or mixing with other children. Many cases of problem behaviour in the class, negligence in study, retardation or failure are due to some physical defect or ailment. For example, how can a boy attend to what the teacher is writing on the blackboard when due to short sight he is not able to read from the blackboard ? What havoc bad liver, hastily eaten meal or a badly pinching shoe can do to the mental outlook of a child should not be overlooked by any teacher.

3. *Interview* is a special kind of observation. Here the teacher tries to observe the child's behaviour in a face-to-face relationship. Some interviews may be directed toward the treatment of maladjustments among children but they can also be used to secure information which will help in planning the work of teaching and learning. What information the child gives to the teacher during the course of an interview will depend on what confidence of the child the teacher enjoys and how much rapport or good relationship the teacher has been able to establish between the child

and himself. Such interviews may shed very useful light on the learning difficulties of the child or on his adjustment problems or personality disorders.

The teacher should be very careful that he does not play the boss during the interview but tries to win the confidence of the child. The interview should be as informal as possible and should not be different from the day-to-day meetings which the teacher may be having with his pupils. The child should never be made to feel that he is in the dock and has to explain some part or aspect of his behaviour. The teacher should listen and encourage the child to talk freely and frankly. Very cool and sympathetic approach is far more helpful in securing information from the child than threatening and tearing attitude. The child should be made to feel that this interview is going to help him and not to accuse and punish him.

Parents too may be interviewed to seek information about the child to provide him with the most suitable educational experience and to obtain additional insight into the causes of the behaviour of the child who already has difficulties in adjustment. Such interviews should be held when the child first joins the elementary school and the teacher's approach during interview should be such that parents are not allowed to feel guilty for what they have or have not done for their children. Their pride in their children should not be injured because too many parents have so identified their own self-respect with their children that anything said or done against their children is not swallowed by them. Parent-teacher associations are good but it is not possible to deal with individual cases in such meetings.

In conducting interviews with children and parents the teacher should not lose sight of the cultural and caste-differences in their background and should try to understand parental attitudes to children. In some communities children are very tenderly treated and parents resent the harsh discipline of the school, in other communities parents take an objective attitude and do not like soft methods. While the teacher should take both attitudes into account he should follow his own view of the situation and use this background as a help in further understanding of the child.

4. Much information about children can be gained through a close study of their *creative activities*. The teacher should study the essays, stories, drawings etc. of children very closely for these are outlets for the release of tensions and frustrations and for the expression of their hidden needs and motives. Such revelations are made by children unwittingly and without conscious knowledge and therefore are all the more real and true. Such themes as 'What I would like to be', 'Last night's dream', if done with sincerity, reveal very valuable information about the hidden urges of the child.

5. *Cumulative records* which have been described in detail in the chapter on *Intelligence and Its Measurement* also provide very useful information if they are comprehensive and prepared by a number of teachers in co-operation. They will reveal not only scholastic progress of the pupil but also his interest in extra-curricular activities, his relations with his classmates, judgments of previous teachers, family history and the like.

6. *Case histories* are the most useful and comprehensive of all methods of special inquiry. They are most suited to the study of maladjusted children or those who show unusual but underdeveloped abilities. Their preparation needs special training and the help of parents, doctors, social workers and others who know the child intimately is called for in completing them. Often a psychiatrist's help is also needed. Taken seriously and studied carefully case

histories shed considerable light on some of the knotty problems and difficulties of students in and outside the class-room.

7. Then there are numerous *tests* which have been described in detail in a previous chapter. Intelligence tests, attainment tests, personality tests, tests of interests and aptitudes and the like all reveal some important aspects of the child and taken together their scores if rightly interpreted will contribute to build a fairly full picture of the child.

Group and individual tests of intelligence will yield I. Q. which, if compared with A. Q. (attainment quotient), will reveal if the pupil is pulling his full weight. A school should administer certain tests to all students at least once a year and supplement it with special tests to be taken by certain selected students.

A good testing programme should include scholastic aptitude tests to measure the aptitude required to succeed in school work, tests of achievement in several school subjects and tests of interests.

Usually group tests should be given first to be followed by individual tests for more specialised appraisal. Sociometric tests will reveal adjustment needs of pupils.

8. Finally the most important thing for the teacher to study and know about a child is the degree of adjustment or maladjustment, and to this end he may employ *adjustment schedules* which are also called self-report blanks, adjustment questionnaires or inventories. These are designed to study such aspects of personality as self-confidence, introversion, dominance. They consist of a series of questions answers to which will reveal attitudes, feelings and patterns of behaviour indicating maladjustments.

These schedules are difficult to make up, for formulating questions which are understood by all and have the same meaning for all is not an easy task. When they require only 'yes' or 'no' to answer they are unable to show the intensity or acuteness of the symptoms of maladjustments. Nor is their validity or reliability very clear. Yet they are widely used in America and have been formulated for all stages of the school course. They may not be very revealing by themselves but taken along with other sources and methods of studying children they can be very useful.

Representative schedules are *Character Sketches* devised by J. B. Mallar and *California Tests of Personality* for elementary school pupils, and the *Bell Adjustment Inventory* is for high school students. The latter provides measures of adjustment in four areas: home, health, social and emotional. At the college level *Bernreuter Personality Inventory* is used and for adults *Minnesota Multiple Personality Inventory* (MMPI) seeks to assess traits or areas of maladjustment. But the interpretation of scores from these schedules is very difficult for the teacher and should be left to a clinical psychologist or psychiatrist.

5. Studying Occupations

Vocational guidance is a broad field and one who is responsible for guiding students to choose a suitable occupation must know the history, attainments, interests and personality of the student and must be familiar with work areas, occupations and professions and the requirements and conditions of admission to training institutions preparing entrants to the different professions. We have already dealt with the first in the previous section and we must now discuss how much a teacher should know about work area to render vocational guidance.

At present many bright students in schools opt for biology to join a medical college or for mathematics to join an engineering institution. Others have vague notions as to what they are going to do after leaving school, and a large majority just drift seeking what degrees or diplomas come their way in the hope of landing a job in which such qualifications may be found useful. When they find themselves unable to carry on in professional colleges or find the work unpalatable, they yield to frustration and develop a sense of grievance against society. For effective vocational guidance the teacher must know :

1. What general education is necessary in any work area ? What special course should be studied to qualify and what subjects should be intensively studied for achieving proficiency in that line ? What percentage of marks is necessary to ensure admission to the training or professional college ? What is the cost and duration of the professional course ?
2. What abilities and interests are specially required for success in any course or profession and if the individual student possesses them ? Most of the professional courses like medicine and engineering expect the students to keep long hours, and it is necessary that they should have physical stamina, good sight and strong interest.
3. What are the satisfactions one gets from a particular vocation ? How much is he able to earn? What are the chances of promotion and advancement ? What social advantages and opportunities for gaining popularity one gets ? The social advantages of a doctor are different from those of an advocate or an engineer.
4. How safe and secure one's future is in different vocations ? For example a doctor or an advocate can work as long as he can but an engineer or a professor has to retire at a certain age.

The school can collect information about different

courses and professions and display it in the library. Tests of interests and aptitudes may indicate for what particular group of occupations a particular student is best fitted, but the choice has to be made by the individual student himself after considering his family resources and the like.

6. Guidance and the School

One of the most important functions of the secondary school is that of determining the abilities, interests, aptitudes, and educational and vocational needs of pupils and then guiding them to make the best use of those abilities and interests and become desirable members of a social order. It was in the early years of this century that vocational guidance was regarded as a social service which high schools should be called upon to render to help each pupil to find his vocation for which he is best suited. The idea, however, developed and the programme of guidance was conceived on a broader scale. Today guidance programmes seek to enable every pupil to know and understand his abilities and interests, to develop them as well as he can, to relate them to life goals and ultimately to guide themselves to a useful and desirable place in the social economy. In a way all education is guidance, every activity of the school aims at helping the pupil to find himself and the programme of the school helps to guide him in matters moral, social, personal and educational. His health, character, habits, sense of good citizenship and the like, all come under the purview of education.

More specifically the programmes of guidance aim at studying each pupil and maintaining cumulative records of his attainments, abilities and interests. The relation between the curriculum and the needs of groups and individuals is closely studied to make suitable re-adjustments. All teachers are expected to co-operate in the programme not only to complete the individual records but also to understand the nature and value of each other's work and to make systematic use of achievement tests and other devices available in the school to appraise and evaluate the efforts of pupils. This broad approach is essential for the narrow objective of assisting the pupil to choose an occupation, prepare for it, enter it and prosper in it. To that end schools have to collect information about occupations and make it available to students and to counsel each individual with regard to his abilities and interests and with regard to the needs and requirements of various occupations in terms of abilities and skills. Finally, the school will help each individual pupil to select courses suitable for the vocation he has chosen.

The next question is who should give this guidance. Obviously the school is the most logical institution to undertake the task of guidance. Parents cannot do it as most of them have their own personal interest and ambition in directing the lives of their children. It would be better if parents and teachers co-operate. In the past the responsibility for administering the programme of guidance was left to one single teacher called the counsellor. Even under the scheme of training for what are called Career Masters, one of the teachers cannot undertake the responsibility for guidance. Left to one counsellor or career master a pupil will be guided once for all time and guidance programmes will get only occasional emphasis and sporadic effort. The best plan is to distribute pupils among a number of senior teachers and make each one of them responsible for a group of pupils about whom he should collect all relevant information, keep necessary records and give individual guidance. Guidance is not the work of one teacher, all must take part in it. The author had appointed a wholetime psychologist in his institution, and he tested pupils, kept individual records with the full co-operation of all teachers and there was a career master who was supposed to collect all information about different occupations. But so long as tests of special aptitudes standardised in India are not available, as they are not at present, such programmes will lack in effectiveness.

7. Who Should Guide?

What are the qualifications of a counsellor? The counsellor should be a person of deep insight, sensitivity of intellect, and conscience, and must have a wide range and depth of personal qualifications to understand and deal with young people of a wide variety of interests and abilities. His main task is not to give unchallengeable advice or indicate a definite course of action as the only suitable solution of the pupil's problems but to help him to achieve self-direction and self-adjustment. The initiative and effort in choosing and achieving goals are to be entirely of the pupil and the counsellor is to assist him to stand on his own two feet. No doubt he is better informed and can think much more clearly but nevertheless he should not lose sight of the main objective of assisting the pupil to manage his own affairs, direct his own effort and make his own choice.

The counsellor should be an optimist who believes that there is hope for everybody and that things can be done better.

The counsellor should be a person who understands himself and his objectives, and realises his definite attitudes and prejudices. Capacity for a realistic self-appraisal of one's own personality is a very important qualification of a counsellor.

8. Advantages of Guidance

A programme of guidance has many and varied advantages. In the first place it conserves and develops human resources. The number of problem children who could be helped to live at peace with themselves and their fellows, of juvenile delinquents who could be helped to become useful citizens and of frustrated people who could be helped to find the square hole and achieve vocational success, self-confidence and happiness is easily very large and is a loss to the nation. Guidance could reduce the loss.

Secondly, large expenditure on education is being wasted today because students are not helped to know and assess their own interests and abilities, to make wise choice from among a wide variety of courses and vocational opportunities and to achieve wholesome personal and social adjustments. A comparatively small expenditure on guidance would be a financial saving as it would help us to get the best out of our present budgets.

Thirdly, when a pupil makes a wrong choice of courses, he loses interest, becomes irregular in work and attendance, and may leave the school. Such pupils cause all-round frustration to themselves, to teachers and to parents. Guidance may help to reduce such frustrations.

Fourthly, it is obvious that guidance saves time and energy of teachers and pupils by reducing problems in and outside the class-room.

Lastly, schools providing programmes of personal, educational and vocational guidance will have a healthy and improved emotional climate with students earnestly engaged in the pursuit of educational goals, intent on making their careers and maintaining happy and cordial relations with their fellow students and teachers.

QUESTIONS

1. What is the value of studying children and how would you proceed to study a particular child ?
2. What do you understand by 'guidance'? Describe some of the areas of guidance.
3. What are the dangers of joining a wrong job in life ?
4. What programme of guidance would you suggest for a common high school in India ?
5. What are the advantages of guidance to the school ?
6. What are the assumptions of guidance ? What do you understand by 'child-centred' education ?
7. What qualities are needed in a teacher who wishes to guide students ?
8. Describe in detail some of the important methods of studying individual children.
9. Of what use has psychology been to a teacher ?

REFERENCES FOR FURTHER STUDY

1. Blair, Jones and Simpson : *Educational Psychology*, The Macmillan Company, N.Y.
2. Bhatia : *A New Deal in Secondary Education*, Orient Longmans, Calcutta.
3. Gates, Jersil, McConnel and Challman: *Educational Psychology*, Macmillan.
4. Griffith : *An Introduction to Educational Psychology*, Rinehart.
5. Skinner : *Educational Psychology*, Prentice-Hall.
6. Sorenson : *Psychology in Education*, McGraw Hill.
7. Trow : *Introduction to Educational Psychology*, Houghton Mifflin.
8. White : *Studying the Individual Pupil*. Harper and Brothers.

Index